MW00366752

WHO WROTE THE BOOK OF LOVE?

Who Wrote the Book of Love?

Lee Siegel

THE UNIVERSITY OF CHICAGO PRESS
CHICAGO AND LONDON

Lee Siegel is the author of numerous books, including *Love in a Dead Language* and *Love and Other Games of Chance.*

The University of Chicago Press, Chicago 60637
The University of Chicago Press, Ltd., London
© 2005 by The University of Chicago
All rights reserved. Published 2005
Printed in the United States of America

14 13 12 11 10 09 08 07 06 05   1 2 3 4 5

ISBN: 0-226-75700-5 (cloth)

Library of Congress Cataloging-in-Publication Data

Siegel, Lee, 1945–
Who wrote the book of love? / Lee Siegel.
p. cm.
ISBN 0-226-75700-5 (alk. paper)
1. Boys—Fiction. 2. Teenage boys—Fiction. 3. Beverly Hills (Calif.)—Fiction.
I. Title
PS3569.I377W48 2005
813′.54—dc22
2005000539

♾ The paper used in this publication meets the minimum requirements of the American National Standard for Information Sciences—Permanence of Paper for Printed Library Materials, ANSI Z39.48-1992.

To my brother, Robert—
for so much fun
since the very beginning

Book of Love
(The Monotones, 1958)

I wonder, wonder who, who-oo-ooh WHO
[*drum beat*] Who wrote the Book of Love?

Tell me, tell me, tell me
Oh, who wrote the Book of Love?
I've got to know the answer
Was it someone from above?

Oh, I wonder, wonder who, mmbadoo-ooh, WHO
[*drum beat*] Who wrote the Book of Love?

I love you darlin'
Baby, you know I do
But I've got to see this Book of Love
To find out why it's true

Oh, I wonder, wonder who, mmbadoo-ooh, WHO
[*drum beat*] Who wrote the Book of Love?

Chapter One says to love her
You love her with all your heart
Chapter Two: you tell her
You're never, never, never, never, never gonna part
In Chapter Three remember
The meaning of romance
In Chapter Four you break up
But you give her just one more chance
By Chapter Five she loves you
And all your dreams come true

Oh, I wonder, wonder who, mmbadoo-ooh, WHO
[*drum beat*] Who wrote the Book of Love?

Baby, baby, baby
I love you, yes I do
Well it says so in this Book of Love
Ours is the one that's true

Oh, I wonder, wonder who, mmbadoo-ooh, WHO
[*drum beat*] Who wrote the Book of Love?

AUTHOR'S NOTE

Despite the fact that so many of our experiences are, coincidentally, identical, Lee Siegel, the boy portrayed in this chronicle, should not be confused with Lee Siegel, the adult author of this book. This character, who has shown up in my other books, including *Love in a Dead Language* and *Love and Other Games of Chance,* has consistently tried to pass himself off as me. And, from time to time, I have, I must confess, identified with him. The similarities between us are, however, less relevant than the differences, and, of these differences, the most pertinent one is that while his obsession is with love, mine is merely with trying to write about it.

CONTENTS

1 Chapter One Says to Love Her,
You Love Her with All Your Heart
1950 ♥ 1951

49 Chapter Two: You Tell Her
You're Never, Never, Never, Never,
Never Gonna Part
1952 ♥ 1953

91 In Chapter Three, Remember
The Meaning of Romance
1954 ♥ 1955

131 In Chapter Four, You Break Up,
But You Give Her Just One More Chance
1956 ♥ 1957

171 By Chapter Five, She Loves You,
And All Your Dreams Come True
1958 ♥ 1959

Chapter One Says to Love Her, You Love Her with All Your Heart

1950♥1951

Part of my plan has been to try to pleasantly remind adults of what they once were themselves, and of how they felt and thought and talked, and what queer enterprises they sometimes engaged in.

Mark Twain, *The Adventures of Tom Sawyer*

From the very beginning the child has a sexual life rich in content, though it differs in many points from that which later is regarded as normal.

Sigmund Freud, *A General Introduction to Psychoanalysis*

1950

Premier Joseph Stalin announces that the Soviet Union has an atomic bomb, and President Harry Truman orders the United States Atomic Energy Commission to develop a hydrogen bomb; the Korean War begins, and Senator Joseph McCarthy discloses that he has a list of 205 Communists in the United States State Department; on national television, Bill Boyd stars as Hopalong Cassidy, "America's favorite cowboy," and Ethel Waters stars as Beulah, America's favorite Negro maid; Kraft Foods introduces the world's first commercially packaged individual cheese slices, and a plastic developed under military contract during World War II finds a market throughout the free world as Silly Putty; Walt Disney's *Cinderella* premieres in movie theaters, and Hank Ketcham's *Dennis the Menace* appears in newspaper comic strips; *In the Beginning: A Children's Book about Grown-up Love,* by Dr. Isaiah Miller, is banned in thirteen American states, and Henry Miller's *Tropic of Cancer* is still banned in all forty-eight; my father is hired as the medical director at Twentieth Century-Fox Studios, and my mother takes a break from her acting career to write a romance novel and give birth to my brother, Robert.

In the beginning sex created heaven and earth. The earth was formless and void, and darkness was on the face of the deep. The spirit of sex swept over the waters. And then there was light.

I am four years old, maybe just five, and the light penetrates the snug passageway of draped blankets into a cozy cave behind the red velvet couch in the room where my mother is typing.

Reaching out for the bright beam, I am entranced by what seems to be the light touch of light on my palm. Slowly I close my fingers around the glow. As the fingertips of my other hand begin to move in a slow circle against the dark back of the soft sofa, a warmth radiates up my arms, through my shoulders and neck, and down into my chest and stomach. My face is flush.

Breathing deeply, slightly trembling, at once soothed and aching, I am a little afraid and yet very eager for more of the ineffable sensation. When I close my eyes, I can see myself. I say my name, hear it, and repeat it. Raising to my mouth the hand that holds the light, I feel my lips feeling my skin. I smell my fingers, and my tongue tastes the taste of my mouth. For the first time in my life, I am aware of my body as my body, and aware of that awareness as my awareness, feeling all parts of my body, inside and out, consolidated and structured into me, myself, and I, an animate form distinct from all other bodies and things. My body's pleasure is my pleasure, generating the idea of the first person singular as it predicates a range of future pleasures, desires, and secrets.

It's my first memory of myself. This is not to say that I do not have earlier recollections of other people, of my mother and father, an uncle, grandmother, neighbor, and strangers too, and of other things. There are memories of memories: a gray elephant small enough to fit into my hand; the smell, sound, and sight of the peeling bark of a eucalyptus tree in the backyard; the scent of leather seats in my father's new Cadillac; the feel of a blue paisley silk bathrobe; the taste of a piece of black licorice snatched from a cracked crystal bowl; showering rain on a green canvas awning; the squeak of wooden stairs in a dark stairwell; a ring of toadstools on the front lawn; white sheets on a clothesline ruffled by a warm breeze; the steady sway of the pendulum of an ornate antique clock high on the mantle and its sudden, delicate, and deliberate ding-ding-ding; and the tap-tap-tap of my mother's typewriter. . . .

But this recollection of myself crouched down behind the sofa, stroking the velvet and holding sunlight in my hand, is my first memory of myself as me. And it is my first memory of what I would gradually come to anticipate, recognize, beckon, and welcome as sex. In the beginning was the flesh. And the flesh becomes words.

"Lee, darling," my mother would call out, "are you there?" I might then crawl from my makeshift cave to approach the desk at which she was typing. She'd be sure to kiss my cheek, stroke my hair, say something sweet, or smile to say the very least. She was writing a book. "A love story," she said, if I remember rightly.

There was an empty crib in the room, and my mother was pregnant. Once my brother was born, the room became his and, when it was refurnished as his nursery, the red velvet couch was moved into my room. It was on that divan that I learned about sex.

Sitting next to me there, my mother read from a book that was meant to ready me for the birth of a sibling by revealing what it was that my father had done so that my mother would become pregnant, not only with my brother, but with me as well. I learned that I would never have been born if my father had not used his reproductive system to put things called *sperms* into my mother's reproductive system, where a little egg lay in waiting for the boldest, swiftest, and strongest one among them. The fantastic procedure, what the book called "*coitus* or *sexual intercourse* or sometimes, less formally, just *making love,"* amazed me from the very beginning.

Several years ago, while visiting my mother at the house that is the setting for this reminiscence, I happened to discover, in a dusty basement that in the 1950s was supposed to be a bomb shelter, the long lost book of love in a carton of old children's books that was stacked together with other storage boxes of a childhood's jetsam, all ready to be picked up by the Salvation Army.

I recognized it immediately. On the tattered cover, in bold print superimposed over a washed-out black-and-white photograph of a statue of Cupid and Psyche, is the title: *In the Beginning: A Children's Book about Grown-up Love.* And below the white marble adolescent lovers is the author's name: Dr. Isaiah Miller, MD.

Dr. Miller had inscribed the book for my parents: "For the beautiful Noreen and Doctor Lee, in hopes that Little Lee, in coming to understand the wonder that is sex, will better appreciate the miracle that is love. Your friend as always, Izzie, April 1, 1950." Published in a limited edition by the Livingstone Press with a note of acknowledgment "to Sigmund Freud, Wilhelm Reich, Alfred Kinsey, and Ernest Grafenberg, comrades in the battle against sexual ignorance, repression, and hypocrisy," the children's book had been censured by church leaders, ladies' groups, and Republicans.

Dr. Miller, my mother's obstetrician and gynecologist, would deliver my brother into the world in 1950, just as he had me in 1945. His book begins with a creation myth:

> In the beginning there was a tiny cell called a *sperm.* One night he met another cell, known as an *ovum.* He entered into her and, all at once, they became one—a *fertilized cell!* The one divided into two, and they divided again, and again, and again, remaining one while continuing to divide, to become a little *embryo* who began to grow into a *fetus.* And that fetus became *you!* This book is about you. It is about where you came from, how you were made, and why you are here.

Like this book, *In the Beginning* has five chapters: What Is Love?; The Birds and the Bees, Elephants and Fleas; Snaps and Snails and Puppy-dogs' Tails; Sugar and Spice and All That's Nice; Love, Marriage, and the Baby Carriage. Chapter 1 responded to its titular question by trying to convince me that I already knew the answer:

> Everybody knows what love is! It can describe how you feel about your puppy or a kitten if you have one, or even a favorite doll if you are a little girl.

It's how you feel about your Mommy and Daddy, and how they feel about you. Religions teach us that God is love. We can love so many things! We are born from love, to love and be loved. Love makes the world go round, as the poets say, and it is love that makes life worth living. There's a special kind of love that you will feel when you grow up and become an adult. This kind of love makes two people want to get married, have a baby, and be together forever. When you feel this kind of love, you will want to engage in something known as *coitus* or *sexual intercourse* or sometimes, less formally, just *making love*. That's what you'll have to do in order to have a baby! But it's also what you'll want to do just to be close to the one you love. We'll be learning all about that in Chapter Five.

One down, four to go, and, although I could hardly wait to get there, I had to be patient because, in order to understand the fifth chapter, a child supposedly had to master the basic ideas and fundamental vocabulary presented in the sections preceding it.

Some of the things in chapter 2, "The Birds and the Bees, Elephants and Fleas," were interesting in an academic sort of way—like the fact that although opossums are pregnant for only a little more than a week, elephants remain so for almost two years. I also learned that "the male Bonellia sea worm is so little that he must crawl up inside of the female's reproductive system to fertilize her eggs."

Things picked up in the third chapter, "Snaps and Snails and Puppydogs' Tails" (interrogatively subtitled "What Are Little Boys Made Of?"). When it came to elucidating the penis, I thought that Dr. Miller had hit the nail on the head:

The *penis* is what some boys sometimes call their weenie or wiener, weewee, peepee, peanut, pecker, willie, dickie, peter, and many other pet names. It's what they use to go number one, what is technically known as *urination*. Usually the penis is lazy and lax, hanging down soft and limp. Sometimes, however, when a boy wakes up in the morning, he will discover that his penis has become hard and stiff like a finger, but much bigger. This is called an *erection*. Some boys sometimes call it a "boner." But, don't worry, there isn't any bone in it! We'll be learning all about why boys have erections in Chapter Five.

There was a schematic line drawing that was labeled "Map of the Passages and Places in the Male Reproductive System." I discovered that, by turning the book upside-down, I could change the indolently pendulous penis into the most exuberant of boners. Although the illustration located the testicles on either side of the penis, the text put them back in their proper place:

Hanging beneath the *penis,* boys have a small sac in which there are two little ball-shaped organs known as *testes.* When a boy is young and still growing, his testes are very sleepy and so don't want to do very much. But when he's about thirteen or fourteen, his testes will wake up, ready to do an important job. At this time, the boy will notice that hair has begun to grow on the pubic region. Since the testes will then remain awake even while the boy is sleeping, the boy may begin to find a strange substance on his pajamas or sheets in the morning. This substance is called a *seminal emission.* The boy should not be disturbed, afraid, or ashamed of this. No, he should be proud of it! It means that he is becoming a healthy and virile man, capable of *sexual reproduction.* Some boys, discovering that seminal emissions are accompanied by a feeling of pleasure, will begin to purposefully try to cause those emissions by manipulating the penis with their hands. This is called *masturbation.* Boys who feel the desire to masturbate should not be ashamed or feel guilty. It is a natural urge, another healthy sign that a boy is growing up.

It is surprising to me now, given passages like that one, counseling boys as it does to take their penises in their own hands and to take pride in wet dreams, that Dr. Miller's book was not banned in more than thirteen of the states of the puritanical America of 1950.

Although I was too young at the time to have seminal emissions to be proud of (no matter how much or what manner of manipulation I might have tried), I was at least able to take pride in something I learned from *In the Beginning* about my somnolent testes. They were made of tiny tubes, which, if unraveled and stretched out in a straight line, would, according to Dr. Miller, be over a third of a mile long. This meant, I reflected, that one of my testes could reach from my house all the way down Maple Drive to the house near the corner where, I had noticed during a walk with my mother, a girl about my own age lived.

I thought about her as my mother read chapter 4, "Sugar and Spice and All That's Nice (What Are Little Girls Made Of?)," to me:

Girls have something called a *vagina.* It is what some girls sometimes call their peepee, weewee, or private. Girls don't have as many names for their sex organ as boys seem to have for theirs. Maybe that's because boys like to talk about theirs more. Or maybe it's because, at first glance, it doesn't look like very much is there. But there is, in fact, a lot more to a girl's reproductive system than meets the eye. While technically the term *vagina* refers only to the birth canal, less formally the word is often used to refer to the female sexual apparatus as a whole.

It was natural for me to hear the homonym when my mother said "whole."

Finally we got to chapter 5. At last it was elucidated—"*coitus* or *sexual intercourse* or sometimes, less formally, just *making love*"—the whole shebang, the nitty-gritty, the when, where, how, and why of who puts what in what. I learned that "Mother Nature sends blood to the penis to make it big and strong not only when there is a desire to have a baby but also when two people just want to be close to each other and show how much they love one another in a special way."

My mother was eager to proceed to the explanation of what was going on in her "workshop," of how the tiny embryo that, as illustrated in the book, looked no different than the embryo of a fish, turtle, chick, rabbit, pig, or calf, had developed into a human being inside what the book called her *uterus* or *womb*. But, as far as I was concerned, the climax of the book had already come: "Mother and Father will lie close together, arms about each other, feeling pleasure and happiness, while the erect penis moves in and out of the vagina with rapid motions until sperm-bearing fluid comes out of it."

In the Beginning had been given to me for Chanukah along with another book, *Shalom, Shalom: A Child's Guide to Jewish Life,* from which my father, seated in his customary spot at the bar in our library, had read aloud to me. The olive, with its red pimento stuffing, in his martini reminded me of the drawing of the ovum with its nucleus in *In the Beginning*. "God," according to the Judaic primer, "commanded our forefathers not to eat certain foods. These include ham, bacon, and pork." And this same God, I learned, also had an interest in my penis: "God commanded our forefathers to remove the foreskin from the penis of a newborn child. This is called *circumcision*." My father proudly informed me that, because I had been circumcised, my penis would look just like his, and like that of his father, and his father's before him, all the way back to Abraham, Isaac, and Jacob. Having been circumcised, my penis would, furthermore, be easier to keep clean than a non-Jewish penis. The book on religion, however, never got around to the good stuff about penises—erections, seminal emissions, or how they move in and out of vaginas with rapid motions.

I recall several of the other gifts I received that Chanukah: an unbreakable plastic miniature replica of a US Army "Big Shot" M551 Howitzer from my uncle Joe, Eskimo mukluks from my grandmother in Wenatchee, and, from my mother, a model of Noah's ark with lots of little plastic animals, two of each kind (oddly, in retrospect, including two cows and two bulls). Neezer, the man who came three times a week to clean our house and wash my father's Cadillac, gave me a gift-wrapped yellow plastic egg containing a blob of Silly Putty. When my father explained that Neezer had referred to the gift as a "Christmas present" because he wasn't Jewish, it occurred to me that it was a good thing that Neezer, since he had a non-Jewish penis, was so good at cleaning.

Unless I counted members of my family or imaginary pals (like Johnny Cassidy, the five-year-old cowboy who rode bucking broncos with me, or Little Beaver, the five-year-old Indian who helped me arrange the blankets over the red velvet couch in my room into a tepee), Neezer was my best friend in the world. He showed me a few of the things Silly Putty could do, including bounce when rolled into a ball and, when pressed against Dennis the Menace in the comics section of the newspaper, capture a perfect image of little Dennis. I discovered that by pressing Silly Putty against the "Map of the Passages and Places in the Male Reproductive System" in *In the Beginning,* I could get a pretty good reproduction of the illustration. Even though the schematic penis was not as vivid as Dennis the Menace, it was clear enough to entertain me as, after elongating it with a good stretch of the flesh-colored Silly Putty, I'd wiggle it about.

Sitting next to me on the red sofa, my mother read not only *In the Beginning: A Children's Book about Grown-up Love* to me but also another book, *Once upon a Time: Children's Best Loved Tales.* Like someone long deceased, the physical form of the book has vanished, but its stories still haunt me. These tales may have been loved *for* children, but it's hard to imagine that they were ever loved *by* children because childhood, as depicted in them, was intractably fraught with giants, ogres, witches, ravening wolves, malevolent stepparents, tenebrous forests, grim castles, and boiling cauldrons. I was particularly unnerved by "Hansel and Gretel" as my mother read aloud the words that the boy and girl had overheard their mother secretly say to their father, the woodcutter, when she thought the children were asleep: "Early tomorrow morning we will take the children into the forest. There we will light a fire for them, give each of them a piece of bread, and tell them to wait for us while we go to do our work cutting wood. We will leave them there, and they will not find the way home again. And then, at last, we shall be rid of them."

The fairy tale was so disturbing that I hid the book so that my mother would never be able to read it to me again. Loosening one of the upholstery nails that secured the burlap lining under the wooden frame supporting the springs of the red velvet couch, I slipped *Once upon a Time* into the space there and pushed the nail back in to close the gap between the cloth and the wood.

"Where is *Once upon a Time?*" my mother, having come to read to me before I went to sleep, asked as she looked around the room for it. I held up *In the Beginning* for her.

"No, darling, not that one. We must have read it a hundred times by now," she remarked as she searched my shelves and drawers. "The other one, you know, the story book. Your grandmother read it to me when I was your age. I can remember her reading 'Cinderella' as if it were yesterday. Where could it have gone?"

"I don't know," I answered nervously, fearful that my mother would know that I knew precisely where it was. I was as astounded as I was relieved to discover that she did not. It was, as far as I can remember, my first lie. It gave me my first intimation of the inimitable pleasure of successfully lying to a woman.

Before that moment, I had unquestioningly assumed that my mother would innately know all that I thought or felt, or had or had not done. It was a fine feeling to deduce that she was not necessarily aware of these things unless I told her. Just as I had hidden *Once upon a Time* inside the red velvet couch, I could, I realized, conceal things inside myself.

Because of the soon-expected baby, it was with some difficulty that my mother got down on her knees to look for the missing book under the bed upon which I was lying.

"Maybe someone stole it," I remarked with the most authentic nonchalance that I, as a beginner at lying, could simulate. And then, to make sure that Miss Crim, my babysitter, and not my friend Neezer, would be the prime suspect in the robbery, I added that the last time I had seen it was the previous night when the babysitter had read the story of Cinderella to me.

Finally giving up the search for *Once upon a Time,* my mother diffidently agreed to read *In the Beginning* once more. I opened it to chapter 5.

The success of my inaugural prevarication, providing me a glimmer of feelings of independence and an inkling of the potential power of lies, made me eager to fabricate again. Experimenting with untruth, by trial and error, it was soon clear that, not only did I have the capacity to use speech to conceal truths, I could also, with false words, create realities. In a test of this hypothesis, I informed my mother that, from my bedroom window, I had seen a strange man in our backyard, "He crawled over the back gate and was snooping around." I knew that she had believed me as soon as she telephoned the Beverly Hills Police Department.

Never having lied to a man before, let alone a policeman, I became worried that perhaps people could be sent to jail (and kids to reform school or a foster home) for lying to the police. In being questioned ("What did he look like?" "Tall or short?" "Thin or fat?" "Old or young?" "Was he colored?" "What was he wearing?" "Anything else you can remember about him?"), I intuited that it's the particulars that make a canard credible. And so, in realistic detail, I described the tall, thin, old white man dressed in the dirty brown overcoat, wearing a beat-up gray hat, black gloves, and sunglasses who, I suddenly remembered, walked with a limp.

When the policeman assured us that patrolmen in Beverly Hills would keep an eye out for the man and, if they spotted him, take him in for questioning, I knew that, if they did capture and interrogate him, they'd never believe a thing a shady character like that might say to defend himself, even if it was the truth. It would be his word against mine.

Mindful that a mastery of the art of mendacity required some determination of the boundaries between the believable and the unbelievable, I surveyed the limits of credibility and credulity. Just to see how far I could go, I swore to my mother that I had seen an elephant in our backyard that day: "I think he must have escaped from the zoo."

That my mother laughed, tousled my hair affectionately, and said she'd telephone the zoo to ask if any elephants were missing made me think about it: either my mother was incredibly stupid or she was just pretending to believe me and, in so doing, was lying to me. Countering her move in the new game by pretending to believe that she believed me, I did my best to out-lie her. Her subsequent affectionate smile attested to a truth about falsehood: in some circumstances, there are people who are so charmed by the lies of certain other people that they would like, and so sometimes even try, to believe things they know are completely untrue. I wanted to believe that my mother believed the story about the elephant in our backyard.

One day, as I was telling Neezer about the horses that I had ridden with my pals, Johnny Cassidy and Little Beaver, I became so encouraged by what seemed to be the limitlessness of his gullibility, that I dared to claim that, best of all, I liked riding "bucking broncos."

"That's really something," said the generously smiling man, scrubbing the blue tile in my parents' shower with a sponge full of foaming cleanser. "I've got a friend with a bucking bronco. He lives nearby. When I'm finished with my work, we can go over there, and you can have a ride."

As I fabricated excuses, Neezer countered with ways around them: when I claimed that "I have to go to the store with my mother today," he said, "That's okay, we can go tomorrow"; when I explained that my cowboy boots were at the shoe repair shop and that I couldn't ride without them, he offered to buy me a new pair. Thanking him, and insisting that I'd really like to ride that bronc someday, I divulged that my parents wouldn't allow it. They were punishing me by not allowing me to ride any more bucking broncos for a year. When he asked what I had done to deserve such a severe punishment, I confessed: "They caught me lying to them."

"Well," Neezer nodded as he washed the dirt right down the drain, "they're right. A boy shouldn't lie to his parents. I guess I'll just have to wait till next year to see you ride that horse."

I wondered whether Neezer really did believe me. Although I didn't have the nerve to test it by taking up his offer, I suspected that Neezer didn't really have a friend with a bucking bronco. Although it seemed fair to me for kids to lie to adults, there was something wrong about adults lying to children. That Hansel and Gretel's mother and father tried to deceive them was what made the fairy tale so harrowing. The witch in the story lied too: "Dear children," my mother read out loud, "do come in and stay with me. You will have milk and pancakes with sugar and apples to eat, and pretty little beds to sleep in. No harm shall come to you here." On the other hand, it was in knowing how to lie that Gretel saved Hansel from being cooked and eaten by the witch. The little girl had out-lied the old woman. Lies could be a matter of life and death.

That my mother seemed to believe all my fibs and fabrications led me to conclude that it's easier to successfully lie to someone who loves you than to someone who does not. And, just as love tempts that person to want to believe you, so love makes you want to lie to the people you love, to lie because you love them (and so don't want them to be hurt or saddened by some unfortunate truth), and to lie because you want them to love you in return (and so don't want them to be disappointed or angered by some other unpleasant truth). In order to love, I came to understand, you must learn to tell lies, and even more difficult than that, you must learn to believe them.

I was to learn in the ten years that are chronicled in this book that sex, no less than love, as both a source and expression of love, likewise makes liars of us at the same time that it makes dupes of us. It's practically impossible not to lie about sexual desires, hopes, fantasies, reveries, and exploits: all of the boys remembered on these pages lied about sex, swearing that they had done what they hadn't; and girls lied about it too, saying they hadn't done what they had. Children have no choice but to lie about sex to their parents, and parents, I came to understand, must lie to children about it too. There's just something about sex that makes you want to lie. You must, if you have any decency or dignity at all, lie about sex.

At the age of five, my favorite lie was already an erotic one, a simple fiction that generated a series of little episodes in a thrilling romance in the making. I told my mother, my father, Uncle Joe, Neezer, Harry Nishida our gardener, Chico the pool man, my next-door neighbor "Little Mike" Shulman, and everyone else whose circumstance allowed or constrained them to listen, that I had a girlfriend. In meticulous detail, I'd describe the small, thin, young girl with pretty white skin, dressed in a clean gingham smock, who, as unbelievable as it was, wore sunglasses just like the ones that the tall, thin, old white man in the dirty brown overcoat had been wearing when he climbed over the gate into our backyard. A name brought her to life: "Gretel. Yes, Gretel. Gretel Woodcutter." She'd follow me on hands and knees into the snug cave that I'd make for us by draping blankets over the back of the red velvet couch in my room. I did, really and truly, love Gretel. And I believed with all my heart that, since she loved me as well, we would someday get married and then, in order to have children and show one another how much we loved each other, do the amazing thing described in chapter 5 of *In the Beginning*.

One night I recounted my first encounter with Gretel to Miss Crim, the gaunt and pale babysitter who was called to our house whenever my parents went out for the evening: I had gone to the Santa Monica pier with my mother to buy fish. The moment I saw the hapless little girl fall off the pier, I bolted from the fish store and ran to dive into the ocean after her. Despite the powerful waves that were trying to pull us out to sea, I somehow found the strength to swim in to shore, paddling with one arm while holding on to Gretel with the other.

"You know that's not true," Miss Crim gallingly glowered, her coppery hair tied so tightly into a netted bun that the corners of her eyes were stretched back.

"It is true," I lied with a conviction that a deft dissembler never backs down from his prevarications.

"God punishes liars," Miss Crim warned. "'Thou shalt not lie!' That's what God commanded, and God always means what he says. If you lie, you'll go to Hell."

Because she refused to ever either believe my lies or even play along that she did, I didn't like her or believe, despite what she would say about me to my parents in my presence, that she liked me. And I was, furthermore, frightened by the things that, once my parents had left for Don the Beachcomber, Chasen's, or the Mocambo, the babysitter was sure to talk about: God, Communism, and Adolf Hitler.

I tried to tell my parents that the woman was strange, but they didn't seem to take me seriously. That Miss Crim had worked at the Peter Pan Nursery School in Santa Monica during World War II, that she was registered with the West Los Angeles Board of Professional Babysitters and Geriatric Companions, and that she wore a large brooch attesting to her having once, in 1948, been declared an "American Christian Woman of the Week," gave her credibility. She had, furthermore, come highly recommended by our next-door neighbors, the Shulmans, whose sons, "Little Mike" and "Big Doug," were, according to their parents, "crazy about Miss Crim."

Adolf Hitler, the babysitter divulged in whispers as if someone might be eavesdropping, was still alive and working as a salesman at a shoe store in Santa Monica. After faking his death in Germany, he had shaved off his mustache, dyed his hair red, changed his name to Adolf Shultz, come to the United States, and become a citizen by marrying an American woman of German descent. Miss Crim had realized this while babysitting Adolf Junior, upon unearthing certain incriminating documents hidden in a shoe box under Mr. and Mrs. Hitler-Shultz's bed.

Although I wasn't quite sure who Hitler was, I knew he had done terrible things to Jews; and I was aware that I was a Jew (although I wasn't quite sure what that was, other than that it meant that I wasn't supposed to eat ham, bacon, or pork and that I had a penis that was, like my father's, easy to keep clean). And thus I became afraid to go to Santa Monica with my mother, worried that, once we were there, she might decide to shop for shoes.

By her own account, Miss Crim had babysat for other nefarious characters as well, including both gangster Mickey Cohen and Communist Myron Spellman. Although Mickey Cohen didn't have any children, she reported, "he hires a babysitter for Longy and Lucky whenever he goes out. Mr. Cohen loves those dogs." Myron Spellman, on the other hand, did have children, two sons, and "because he had tried to brainwash them with Communism," his wife was divorcing him and taking the boys away with her to San Diego. The terrifying news was that Mr. Spellman lived across the alley behind my house. I was afraid to go near the place.

Although I don't remember exactly what Miss Crim told me about Communism, the gist of it, as reconstructed in retrospect, was that the Kremlin was doing everything in its power to make faceless slaves and soulless automatons of the entire human race. For some strange reason, the Communists wanted to eradicate happiness, peace, freedom, and even love from the face of the earth. Even more egregious, they were liars: they claimed that God did not exist. Establishing his headquarters in Moscow, Satan had turned the churches in Russia into juvenile detention halls, where children my age were sent for brainwashing. All of this, I was informed, had been foretold in the Bible, a book from which Miss Crim read to me a story about a monstrous red dragon with seven heads and ten horns. The Bible was as scary as *Once upon a Time: Children's Best Loved Tales.*

Miss Crim's champion of hope in the battle against the red dragon of Communism was someone named J. Edgar Hoover. And although I did not, at the time, have the faintest idea as to who he was, I can still remember exactly what my babysitter had to say about him. J. Edgar Hoover, she reported, had been anticipated and extolled in the Bible: "J. E. Hoover," she murmured meaningfully: "Je hoover, Jehoover, you know—Jehovah!" In retrospect, it must be admitted that, except for the rumors about cross-dressing, the director of the FBI and the Lord of Creation, did, in terms of their attitudes toward surveillance and judgment, law and order, and crime and punishment, have a lot in common.

Miss Crim had evidence that Communist women from the Soviet Union had snuck into the United States and that they were using sex to lure unsuspecting American men into their iniquitous army of spies, saboteurs, and disruptionists. The word *sex,* in her articulation of it, started and ended with an ominously sibilant hiss. According to my babysitter, these female predators hunted for their prey in bars and nightclubs; that caused me to worry that some of them might be frequenting Don the Beachcomber, Chasen's, or the Mocambo.

Seated on the same red velvet couch where my mother, by reading *In the Beginning* to me, had tried to assure me that sex was good because it had to do with love, Miss Crim tried to convince me that it was evil. Her homilies on the sinfulness of sexuality were delivered in reaction to my *Children's Book about Grown-up Love.* On her first night as my babysitter, I had asked her to read chapter 5. Taking the book in her hands, she had smiled, no doubt assuming from the title that it might provide religious instruction suitable for a youngster. No sooner had she opened it, however, than her smile turned into a ghastly grimace and she cast the text aside as something unclean. And then she drew a Bible from her bag.

Just as I have had to imagine the rhetoric that Miss Crim probably invoked to explain Communism, likewise, unable to recall the exact vocabulary with which she vilified what *In the Beginning* called "*coitus* or *sexual intercourse* or sometimes, less formally, just *making love,*" I must try to guess at the terms she might have used: certainly *adultery, prostitution, masturbation,* and *homosexuality;* probably *orgies, fellatio, cunnilingus,* and *sodomy;* possibly *sadomasochism, bestiality,* and *pedophilia;* and maybe even—although I know it's a long shot—*necrophilia, coprophilia,* and *coitus inter mammillas.*

I do, however, remember the general drift of the sermons on sex, delivered while rubbing the textured black leather cover of her Bible with white fingertips, well enough to loosely paraphrase her exegesis of Genesis 3. If, as *In the Beginning* alleged, sexual intercourse was necessary to create a human being, how, she asked, were the first human beings created? She had me there and took it upon herself to unravel the conundrum: Adam and Eve, the first human beings, were created not by sex, but by God. God didn't need sex to make them. God made Adam out of clay and Eve out of one of Adam's ribs. They could have lived happily ever after in the Garden of Eden. But sex ruined everything. God warned them that they could eat anything growing in the garden except one particular fruit. "Ye shall not eat of it, neither shall ye touch it, lest ye die." I suspected that Miss Crim had that part wrong, deducing, from what I had learned about religion from *Shalom, Shalom: A Child's Guide to Jewish Life,* that it was no fruit that God would have forbidden them to eat. No, surely it was ham, bacon, or pork.

Just as the Kremlin brainwashed women into joining the Communist party, so had Satan, according to Miss Crim, convinced Eve to eat the forbidden fruit (or forbidden meat, if my father did, in fact, know more about God than my babysitter did). And just as the Soviet women who have infiltrated the United States use their feminine wiles in nightspots to tempt American men into betraying their county, so Eve in the Garden of Eden beguiled Adam into betraying God by eating the fruit (or ham) that she had tasted. Sexual desire in a woman is a sign that she is being tempted by Satan; and a man's sexual arousal is symptomatic of his being tempted by a woman to disobey God. "And then, after they had sinned," Miss Crim whispered, "they tried to hide from God."

If only Adam and Eve had obeyed God, Miss Crim elaborated, there would never have been any sexual desire nor any need for sexual intercourse. But the addicting taste of the forbidden fruit had instilled that desire in them. They had to put on clothes to hide those parts of their bodies which, when seen, tempted them to defy God again. To punish man and woman for their disobedience, God expelled them from the garden and took away the gift of eternal life that he had given them in the beginning.

The climax of this revelatory prelection on sex was, given its dire implications for my pregnant mother, very upsetting: because a woman had brought sin into the world, all future women would, as a punishment, be constrained to undergo excruciating pain in giving birth. The only way out of that suffering was abstention from the act that caused pregnancy. All of this explained why Miss Crim, like (as she pointed out) Jesus Christ and J. Edgar Hoover, had never been married nor had any children.

Wondering whether or not Miss Crim might be either wrong or lying, since *In the Beginning* had said nothing about the torment of giving birth, I asked my mother about it. Naturally I became distraught and afraid for my mother upon hearing from her own mouth that, yes, having a baby was painful. But, my mother tried to assure me, the enormous joy of having me as her son made any pain she might have felt during my delivery insignificant. "It's just a very little part of the most wonderfully pleasurable of all experiences," she tried to reassure me, going so far as to add that she was looking forward to the impending birth of my sibling. My mother was, I figured, probably lying, just saying all that to protect me from an awful truth.

After kneeling by my bed to lead me in a prayer petitioning God to protect the United States from the red monster of Communism, Miss Crim would, as she turned off the bedside lamp and wall lights, always say, "Goodnight, sleep tight, and don't let the bed bugs bite." I'd then have to remind her to turn on the Mickey Mouse nightlight that was plugged into a wall socket near my bed, insisting on the faint light because of all the fears that the woman had instilled in me—fears of bugs in my bed, the horned red dragon in the Bible, a shoe salesmen in Santa Monica, Mr. Spellman just across the alley, and a God in heaven who was so strict and mean that he'd punish you with pain and death just for eating either a piece of fruit or a slice of ham (whichever it was). Once Miss Crim had left my room, I'd wrap an arm around one of the pillows on my bed, whispering, "Goodnight, Gretel," as I pulled the blankets up around our necks to keep us warm in the frosty forest night. "Don't be afraid, Gretel. No, let's not be afraid."

I was still awake one evening when the babysitter tiptoed back into my room. By shutting my eyes and breathing audibly, I feigned sleep. Apparently falling for my subterfuge, Miss Crim then began to dance slowly around my bed, taking care as she did not to make any noise that might awaken me. By opening my eyes just slightly into a narrow squint, I could see her, faintly but clearly enough by the light of my Mickey Mouse nightlight, as she, much to my astonishment, wiggled her pelvis about. Then suddenly, as unbelievable as it may seem, she hoisted her skirt up above her waist, revealing that she wasn't wearing any underwear. That's when I saw the big patch of tawny fluff that, because of its location, I was able, by the grace of chapter 4 of *In the Beginning* ("Sugar and Spice and All That's Nice"), to identify as the visible part of the notorious vagina, Miss Crim's forbidden fruit.

The next morning, I disclosed to my parents that, the night before, when they had gone to Don the Beachcomber for dinner and then dancing at the Mocambo, Miss Crim had shown me her vagina. That my father laughed and my mother continued to call Miss Crim to babysit insinuated that they imagined that I was imagining it—not so much lying, but just imagining it because children imagine lots of things, especially when it comes to sex. Just as nowadays parents always believe it when their kids say things like that, in those days they hardly ever did.

I've wondered about it for years. Why did she do it? Or did she really? Perhaps I had, on the night in question, actually fallen asleep and merely dreamed that she had done it. Or perhaps memory has, to beguile, intrigue, or amuse me, lied. No, I believe that I am telling the truth when I testify that Miss Crim exposed herself to a little boy whom she believed was fast asleep. Sex, I learned during the years covered in this book, makes us do funny things no less than it makes us imagine, remember, and believe funny things.

Right after my brother was born, my parents hired Sally May Carter as a full-time live-in maid to do the house chores and take care of me, so I never had to see Miss Crim again. Although I was happy about that, I was sad that I was not going to be seeing my friend Neezer anymore either. There was some consolation, however, in the thought that at least I wouldn't have to ride a bucking bronco the following year.

It was Neezer who had found Sally for us at his church, where, he testified, the woman sang "with the honeyest voice you ever heard. If her singing don't make the Lord happy, nothing does."

If I claimed that I couldn't fall asleep without a song, Sally would sing "Go down, Moses" as mellifluously at my bedside as she could have possibly done by any pulpit: "Way down in Egypt's land. Tell old Pharaoh to let my people go!" And then "Shit, boy," she'd say, "you go to sleep now or Mama Sally's gonna have to whup ya." Despite the threat, I never feared her spankings any more than Brer Rabbit feared the briar patch. They were the gentlest of taps on my bottom, always accompanied by a smile that allowed for a glimmer of light on her gold front teeth to glitter through it with as much sparkle as any twinkle on any star in any Walt Disney cartoon. "That'll teach you, boy," she'd say. Throughout the ten years during which she lived with us, Sally May Carter always addressed me as "boy," never as "Lee."

Sally was strong enough to lift our full icebox with one arm as she swept under it with the other. Although I know this cannot be true, memory swears to it. Sally May Carter was, I believed, the strongest woman in the world. I was confident that if the tall, thin, old white man dressed in the dirty brown overcoat who had once crawled over the back gate into our yard came around again, Sally would protect me. She could take care of him, not to mention Hitler or the Communists, even if an entire gang of them showed up to try to take me to a juvenile detention camp for brainwashing.

Like my mother, Sally seemed to believe my lies. "That's wonderful, boy," she said when I told her how I had saved Gretel from drowning and when I recounted my perilous rides on bucking broncos. One day, as I watched her ironing, I boasted that my father, the Hollywood doctor, had saved the lives of Hopalong Cassidy, the Lone Ranger, Tonto, Red Rider, Little Beaver, and Dennis the Menace.

"He's cured just about everyone," the maid said with a credulous smile. "That's nice. So, boy, you must wanna be a doctor like your daddy when you grow up. Then you can cure everyone too."

Under the sway of my affection for Sally, I heard myself say, "No, I want to be a Negro like you and Neezer when I grow up."

"Shit, boy," Mama Sally muttered, her head shaking a "no, no, no," as her vast bosom jiggled with whole-hearted laughter, "no, you don't."

When I swore I did, she stated that it would take a miracle to make a Negro out of me and that, if I really did want that, I'd have to pray to the Lord for it. So each night after that, when Sally May came to my room to tuck me in, I'd kneel down by the bed and put my hands together in solemn prayer: "Dear God, please help me to become a Negro."

"You be careful," she warned with a laugh, "God's gonna believe you." And then she sang "Go down, Moses" for me.

Sally's God was much nicer than Miss Crim's: he enjoyed sweet singing; lies didn't bother him; and he didn't care what kind of fruit or meat products people ate. Sweet Jesus loved everybody (maybe even Communists and Adolf Hitler), and that, I figured, was either because he was God or why he was God, or at least it was because and why he was Sally May Carter's God. Sally's Lord seemed, furthermore, to approve when a man and woman did what so annoyed Miss Crim's Jehovah. "Sweet Jesus," Sally would say again and again on Saturdays, the day Shorty came to spend the night and then take her to their church early on Sunday morning before I woke up: "Sweet Jesus, Shorty's coming! Yeah, that little old man's comin' to give Mama Sally some sugar." Laughter divulged the abundance of her delight in love.

On Saturday nights, after Sally would have said goodnight to me and gone to join Shorty in her room, I couldn't help but think—since Shorty was as small as Sally was big—of the Bonellia sea worm, "so little that he must crawl up inside of the female's reproductive system in order to fertilize her eggs."

One night, after petitioning God to turn me into a Negro, I asked Sally to read chapter 5 of *In the Beginning* to me as a bedtime story. Assuring her that it was really good, I noted that it was about "*coitus* or *sexual intercourse* or sometimes, less formally, just *making love.*"

"You don't need no book to know about that," Sally insisted. "The Lord gives everybody that know-how. Sweet Jesus! When the time comes, you'll know just how to give your little Gretel all the sweet lovin' she wants. That little thing of yours will tell you what to do."

"It's called a penis," I said, flaunting my mastery of the technical terminology.

"No matter what you call it," Mama Sally beamed, "it'll tell you just what to do, boy, and it won't be askin' you about what you been readin'."

When my mother came home from the hospital, I asked her if it had been painful. "No," she lied, "not at all. It was beautiful."

After being coerced into cradling my new brother in my arms, I was informed by my proud father that Robert was circumcised, just like us. He showed me the bandaged penis and the dried remains of the umbilical cord. Handing the baby back to my mother, I decided to go out West, where seldom was heard a discouraging word. I had discovered that, by rearranging the pillows and bolsters on the red velvet couch in my room and draping a blanket over the top of it, I could turn the sofa into a wagon in a wagon train. Joining me in there, the bed pillow that was Gretel Woodcutter became frightened as we ventured into Indian country. Doing my best to protect her, I fired an entire potato of bullets from my Potato Pop Pistol at the wild redskins hollering in my room.

"Shit, boy. You stop that," Sally May Carter commanded as she appeared on the battlefield, "or Mama Sally's gonna have to whup ya." Demanding that I hand over the spud gun and what was left of my ammunition, she enjoined me to help her pick up all the little white bits of potato from my carpet. "Tonight, boy," she threatened, "you're gonna eat deep-fried bullets for dinner."

If my parents went out on a Wednesday night, which I always hoped they would, Sally May Carter would let me stay up late to watch wrestling with her on our ten-channel Spartan television receiver with a mirror in it to project the images up onto a plastic screen, all encased in an antique mahogany cabinet with brass fittings.

Sitting on Sally's lap, my head comfortingly cushioned between a grand pair of mammary pillows, I'd be soothed by the scent, a heady blend of Murray's Superior Hair Dressing Pomade, Nadinola Greaseless Bleach Cream, Johnson's Baby Powder, Triple-X Dipping Snuff, Ajax, Crisco, something sugary (molasses, or maple or Karo syrup), and something else, an indescribable aroma that I have not smelled in almost half a century but would recognize immediately—Sally May Carter's own natural scent, constant under the flux of the other aromas. On Saturdays, in anticipation of Shorty's arrival, the flowery odor of her De-Luxe Royal Rose Imported Eau-De-Cologne for Ladies added oomph to the bouquet.

Mama Sally often held me in her arms, but never, in ten years, did she, as far as I can remember, ever kiss me. And, for some reason, although I'd lay my head against the clean white cloth of uniform over her expansive bosom and hug her, I never kissed her either.

Sally May Carter called Wednesday-night Wrestling from the Olympic Auditorium "Mama Sally's show," and Bobo Brazil, the Brown Bombshell, "Mama Sally's man." She would shout to the wrestler from her seat in our living room with all the urgency of someone at ringside: "Shit, Bobo, get up! Don't let that white man bump your head." She had taken it upon herself to coach the wrestler, advising him when to do a drop kick or use a half nelson, bear hug, hammer lock, or claw hold.

Once *Amos 'n Andy* began to be broadcast on television, it became Sally's duty to counsel Sapphire. "Get out that house now, lady," she advised after spitting her lower lip full of dipping snuff into a Yuban coffee can. She laughed so uproariously that tears streamed down her cheek when Sapphire, having done just what Sally had told her to do, caused Kingfish to fret, "Holy Mack'el, Andy, I can't find Sapphire. She done disappeared! And I knows it's serious this time. She done left me before, but she's always left an insultin' letter."

As we watched *Beulah* together, however, Sally never talked to the lovably hefty housekeeper who took care of the little Henderson boy. Perhaps she watched the program not so much for entertainment as in order to pick up tricks of the trade, which consisted not merely of cleaning a house and looking after a child but of doing so according to a set of conventions established for playing the part of a Negro domestic servant in a prosperous white American home. Sally wore the very starch-sheened white mercerized broadcloth uniform that was the costume of the actress who played Beulah on television. She also always left the box of batter mix out on the table when she made pancakes for our breakfast—it was perhaps so that the portrait of Aunt Jemima would assure us that Sally May Carter was, with a yellow-checkered bandana around her head, the real thing. Sally had perfected Aunt Jemima's radiantly carefree smile.

"What would we do without Sally?" my mother said as, sitting with Robert in her lap, she directed the maid where to move the furniture and set the cases of champagne that had been delivered in preparation for the New Year's Eve party. Even though there were still quite a few hours until 1951, I was allowed to put on one of the party hats. I was not, however, permitted to blow the horns that would herald in the new year because, when I did so, it made my baby brother cry.

An actress who was coming to the party with the director of the movie she was currently shooting at Twentieth Century-Fox, the studio where my father worked, had no choice, my mother explained, but to bring her young daughter. The film star hadn't been able to find a single babysitter available on New Year's Eve. Even Miss Crim, whom my mother had recommended to the actress, was busy. It occurred to me that my former babysitter might be ringing in the new year by showing her vagina to the Hitler boy.

"Her name is Eve," my mother mentioned when informing me that the little girl was going to sleep on the red velvet couch in my room. "When Sally tells you to go to bed, I want you and Eve to mind her."

Eve, I learned, would soon be appearing as the daughter of frontier settlers kidnapped by Indians in the opening scene of the movie *Apache Princess,* in which her mother starred as that little girl grown up. Raised by the Indians, she considered herself one of them until she fell in love with an officer in the United States cavalry. Love transformed her back into her real self. Although Eve didn't have any lines in the movie, she did have to cry convincingly.

I was dressed for the evening in my red flannel fireman's pajamas, blue paisley silk robe, Eskimo mukluks, and a gold glitter-gilded cardboard New Year's Eve party hat when the little girl arrived, likewise ready for bedtime lounging in an ankle-length pink flannel night dress and a white silk robe, trimmed around the collar and cuffs with white fluff. Her bedroom slippers were twin white fur bunnies, each with a black-bead nose and pink-bead eyes. As my mother put a silver glitter-gilded party hat on the girl's head, I was immediately struck by how very cute she was. Her large brown eyes were reminiscent of the eyes of a fawn with whom young Bambi played in the Walt Disney cartoon that had given me nightmares.

"They're adorable together," her mother beamed as she handed her mink stole to Sally. The man with her winked at me as, taking the cigarette out of his mouth, he leaned over to whisper in my ear: "Careful kid, she's a vamp, just like her mother." I wondered whether that was good or bad.

While the front door was still open to greet the actress, none other than Dr. Isaiah Miller and his wife arrived. "Darling," my mother said, "this is Dr. Miller. He's my doctor. He delivered Robert. And you too. He wrote *In the Beginning: A Children's Book about Grown-up Love.*" And then, turning to the writer-physician, she announced with a jokey laugh that he was my favorite author: "Because of your book, Lee wants to be a gynecologist when he grows up."

After shaking my hand, the bald doctor, his generous lips locked in a grin that forcibly closed his eyes into a squint, introduced his wife with a confession that he could never have written the book without her. I figured that meant that they had performed coitus a lot. Although she wasn't at all pretty, I suspected that what Dr. Miller had written about the vagina in chapter 4 of *In the Beginning* might also be true of Mrs. Miller: "At first glance, it doesn't look like very much is there. But there is, in fact, a lot more than meets the eye."

With the actress's mink, the director's white silk scarf, and the Millers' overcoats thrown over her shoulder, Sally, taking the little girl in one hand and me in the other, pulled us to her room, where she dumped the guests' garments on top of the ever-growing pile of coats on the bed. Then she led us to the adjoining kitchen, where we were installed at the table. "Shit boy," Sally muttered, "you lied to Mama Sally! I heard what your Mama said. You told me you wanna be a Negro when you grow up. You know you're not supposed to lie."

"I wasn't lying," I answered in self-defense, "I do want to be a Negro. I want to be a Negro gynecologist."

After telling me and a silent Eve that we could help ourselves to the hors d'oeuvres from the silver platters on the table, Sally warned us that we were not to touch the rum babas in the bowl in the middle of the table. They would be served to the adults with champagne at midnight. "Ye shall not eat of it, neither shall ye touch it," I remembered, "lest ye die."

Sally left with a full tray of fried cheese-and-nut balls balanced on one hand and, on the other, a platter of pink boiled shrimp skewered on toothpicks for dipping in the bright red cocktail sauce. Shorty, uncomfortably costumed in a formal butler's uniform that my father had rented for him, was opening champagne bottles and filling glasses. Whenever he saw that there was no one in the kitchen except for Eve and me, he'd take a quick swig of the wine straight from the bottle and then wink at us.

While I was filling up on cucumber slices topped with crab dip, washed down with White Rock ginger ale from a champagne glass, Eve neither ate nor spoke. Her large deer-eyes were fixed on the rum babas in the center of the table.

"It's okay, little girl," Shorty whispered to Eve with a sly smile. "Go ahead if you want. They taste good. Sally won't notice if one of them disappears." Looking around just as Shorty did prior to each surreptitious swill of champagne, Eve grabbed a rum baba and popped the whole thing into her mouth. Her eyes so sparkled with delight that I could not restrain myself from following suit. No sooner had I closed my lips down around the forbidden dessert than I heard Mama Sally exclaiming, "Sweet Jesus, Dr. Siegel's gettin' higher than a Georgia pine," as she returned to the kitchen.

I slid out of my chair to hide under the table. As Eve joined me there, I noticed again how cute she was, cuter even, I mused, than Gretel Woodcutter.

"Shit, boy," Mama Sally commanded, "get out from under there."

Banished from the kitchen for the rest of the evening, we were ordered to go upstairs to my room, where Sally had made up the red velvet sofa into a bed for Eve. Setting her carrying case upon it, the little girl began to unpack: a Cinderella doll, a Cinderella coloring book, a box of forty-eight Crayola Crayons, a tube of Ipana tooth paste and a Bucky Beaver toothbrush, a hair brush, a box of Brach's chocolate-covered cherries, and a small framed photograph of a man who I guessed might be her father. It was my first glimmer of the delight of watching a woman unpack an overnight bag.

My mother, carrying my brother, whom she had been proudly showing off to party guests, entered my room, and after handing the baby to Sally with a request that she change his diaper, she kissed me on the cheek and told us, Eve and me, to have fun but to mind Sally. "Happy New Year, children," she said, then kissed my other cheek and returned to the party.

Eve, who still hadn't said one word or eaten anything but the rum baba, seated herself at my desk and opened the boxes of both her Brach's chocolate-covered cherries and her Crayola Crayons. Without offering me a candy, she ate one herself, and then, after thoughtfully selecting several crayons, she began to color the four horses hitched to a pumpkin-shaped carriage. Her Cinderella doll, seated on the desk, and I watched as she colored one horse green, one blue, one purple, and one pink. Although I was not very impressed by her sense of color, I admired the way she kept those colors within the black lines.

I didn't mind Eve's silence because I had lots to say. I told her about the bucking broncos I had ridden and about the little girl who had fallen off the Santa Monica pier: "I'm glad I was able to save her life. But now I've got a problem. She wants to be my girlfriend, and so she keeps coming over. I don't know how to get rid of her. She's really cute, but she's not my type. Whenever she colors, she can't even keep the colors inside the lines. I hate that."

Still, Eve said nothing. And so I kept talking, recounting how I had chased some Communists out of our backyard by shooting at them with my Potato Pistol. To substantiate the story, I showed her the spud gun in question as well as other weapons from the arsenal in my closet—a K-Pop Popper range rifle that fired ping pong balls, a pink plastic Little Squirt water pistol, and my US Army "Big Shot" M551 Howitzer.

Eve had finished the entire box of chocolate-covered cherries without offering a single one to me, and still not having said a word, she turned the page in her coloring book. With a pink crayon, she began to gingerly color in the gown of the dancing Cinderella. If I had known how to read, I might have retrieved *Once upon a Time: Children's Best Loved Tales* from within the red velvet couch and read to her the Cinderella story from it. Instead I set my copy of *In the Beginning* on the desk and, since she had put aside the pink crayon for a blue one with which she was coloring the face of the prince who danced with Cinderella, I took the liberty of picking up her pink Crayola to color in the illustrated row of embryos in my book. "A fish, a turtle, a chick, a rabbit, a pig, a calf, a human," I noted. "You can hardly tell them apart." Discovering that, because the embryos were so small, it was very difficult to stay within their outlines, I quickly flipped the pages until, coming upon the schematic drawing of the male reproductive system in chapter 3, I started coloring again. Fortunately the penis was big enough for me to keep the pink of the crayon within the lines around it.

"This thing's called a 'penis,'" I said in an adultishly lackadaisical tone. Disappointed, but hardly surprised, that Eve didn't even look at the penis, I closed the book on it. Giving up all hope that she would ever speak to me, feeling awkward and, in my self-consciousness, not quite knowing what to do with myself, I decided to make a cave behind the velvet couch on which Eve would be sleeping. After draping the bedspread from my bed over the back of it, I crawled into the refuge and, sitting there, wondered if her obdurate silence indicated an indifference to me or if, on the contrary, it might by any chance be a sign of an attraction that made her too shy to speak.

Suddenly the curtain of blanket over the entrance to my cave moved, letting in a light that made a silhouette of the little girl peering in at me. "This is my hideout," I said. And without uttering a word, she crawled in and arranged herself so that the bunnies that were her slippers were facing me. "This is where I'm going to hide when the Russians try to take over America," I told her, and then, as I was explaining the Communist plot to put an end to happiness and freedom, I saw that her fingertips had began to move in a slow circle against the dark back of the sofa. Joining Eve in her silence, I too let my fingers reach out to touch the velvet, and then, as they stroked it, I felt that I could feel her pleasure and sensed that, as I did so, she could feel mine. I was, I realized, in love.

"Come out of there right now," I heard Sally demand. "It's time for you children to go to sleep."

Pulling apart my cave to remake my bed, Sally dispatched Eve to the bathroom. "Shit, boy, what were you doing in there with that little girl?" She didn't wait for answer. "Sweet Jesus, little boys ain't no different than grown men."

By the time I had taken my turn in the bathroom, Eve had removed her party hat, slippers, and robe, and Sally had tucked her into the bedding on the couch. Crawling into my own bed, I pushed the pillow that was occasionally Gretel aside. Having fallen in love with Eve, I was determined to break up with the woodcutter's daughter. Eve's empirical existence in the phenomenal world gave her an edge on Gretel as a candidate for the object of my longings and subject of my reveries.

After turning off the lamps and on the Mickey Mouse nightlight, Sally left the room with warnings of what she'd do to me if she heard a peep from either of us. Listening to the sound of the party, I heard unintelligibly mingled boisterous conversations, the popping of champagne corks, the clinking and clattering of glasses, silverware, and plates, and rolls of jubilant laughter, out of which I could, now and then, discern the inimitably exuberant guffaw of my father. A record was playing on the Victrola: "Salagadoola mechicka boola bibbidi-bobbidi-boo," Perry Como and the Fontane Sisters sang. "Put 'em together and what have you got? Bibbidi-bobbidi, bibbidi-bobbidi-boo!"

Eve's mother, made faintly visible by the nightlight and the glow that seemed to follow her in from the hall when she opened the door and entered my room, glided to the couch, sat down next to her daughter, and whispered things I could not hear. The actress's perfume fraganced my room deliciously. It was the odor of adult women who were loved by grown men and loved them in return. I heard a kiss, a "Goodnight, sweet Eve," and a "Happy New Year, my beautiful little girl." And then, for the first time since she had arrived at my house, I finally heard Eve's voice. "I love you," she said as her mother rose and walked out of the room, leaving the door just slightly ajar.

I wished I were an adult at the party downstairs. I wanted to be drinking champagne, eating rum babas, smoking cigarettes, telling stories that made perfumed women laugh so hard that tears rolled down their cheeks. If my wish had come true, I would have taken Eve in my arms and circled the room with her to the music that I could hear:

My heart has wings, and I can fly;
I'll touch ev'ry star in the sky!
So this is the miracle that I've been dreaming of,
Mmmm, mmmmm. So this is love!

"Pssst," I whispered, making a forbidden peep. "Are you awake?" There was no answer, but, since Eve hadn't said anything to me all evening, I couldn't take the silence as evidence either that she was awake or that she was asleep. I can't imagine what I might have dared to say or ask had I known which one it was.

When I woke up in the morning, Eve was gone. But I could still smell her mother's perfume.

After putting on my New Year's Eve party hat and Eskimo mukluks, I went to see what was going on in the house. My father was snoring in his bed, my mother was feeding Robert in the nursery, and Sally May Carter was cleaning up the festive mess in the living room.

"Happy New Year," I said, and Sally laughed. "I know you're gonna have a happy new year, boy," she promised, "because later this year you'll be startin' school. You'll learn readin' and writin'. And you'll make some friends. There's gonna be some fine little girls at the school." Sally May Carter laughed again. "Sweet Jesus, after last night, Mama Sally knows her boy is crazy about the girls."

I didn't care about making new friends, and Eve was the only girl I was crazy about. But I was happy with the thought that I would soon learn to read. Once I did so, I'd be able to study *In the Beginning,* and other books on the same subject, on my own. And once I learned to write, I decided, I'd write a letter to Eve. I'd write the very three words that were the only words I had ever heard her say:

I LOVE YOU

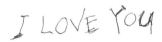

1951

The Roy Rogers Show, The Adventures of Kit Carson, and *Adventures of Wild Bill Hickok* premiere on television, and Eddie Cantor plays a Jewish cowboy on *The Colgate Comedy Hour; Deputy Dick's Kiddie Korral* is broadcast on television on weekday afternoons in the Los Angeles area until Richard "Deputy Dick" Pearson is arrested for indecent exposure outside the Samuel Clemens Elementary School in Santa Monica, and, also in Santa Monica, Leon Grimes, one of seven Little Oscars appearing at supermarkets across America in an Oscar Mayer Wienermobile, is arrested for drunk driving; Scott, Foresman, and Company revises the *Dick and Jane* readers, and the House Un-American Activities Committee subpoenas Myron Spellman for hearings after the filming of his screenplay *See Dick Run* is canceled because producers consider it sympathetic to the ideals of the Communist party; my mother stars in *Storm over Wyoming,* and Eve W—— appears as her mother as a young girl in *Apache Princess;* Florence Chadwick swims the English Channel in sixteen hours, and Clover Wiener takes swimming lessons in the pool at my house for one hour each Tuesday after school for sixteen weeks.

Unless I count Gretel Woodcutter or Eve W——, Clover Wiener was my first girlfriend. If existing in reality wasn't an issue, Gretel would certainly qualify, as would Eve if my feelings were all that mattered. But in order to consider Eve truly a girlfriend, I would have had to imagine that she counted me as a boyfriend, that affections, though unarticulated, were reciprocal, and that fantasies, though different in content for a boy than for a girl, were correspondingly compelling. Since I had only seen Eve once and she had never spoken to me, it was difficult to know how she felt about me. But I was confident that Clover liked me as much as I liked her, that she knew I liked her as much as she liked me, and that the more I liked her, the more she liked me, and vice versa. And that, I believed, was true love.

Although we were both in Mrs. Lovell's first-grade class at Ponce de Leon Elementary School, we didn't actually speak to each other in the classroom, the cafeteria, or on the playground, and we only looked at each other by accident. Our amorous complicity was a secret, and our interactions were extracurricular. We knew that if word got out, our classmates would be sure to make fun of the romance: "Lee and

Clover sitting in a tree, k-i-s-s-i-n-g. First comes love, then comes marriage, then comes Lee with a baby carriage."

I didn't learn the name of the little girl who, I had noticed, lived down the block from me on Maple Drive until the first day of school. After leading us in our first salute to the flag, slowly enunciating each word and pausing for us to repeat after her ("I pledge . . . allegiance . . . to the flag . . . of the United States of America"), a patriotically red-white-and-blue-spirited Mrs. Lovell (ruddy red-haired, powdery white-skinned, and bulging blue-eyed) instructed us to be seated. And then, in what we would soon learn was alphabetical order, the teacher called out each student's name, at which point we were to stand, repeat that name, and, "with a great big, happy smile," say "a great big hello" to our "new friends." When Mrs. Lovell called "Clover Wiener," several of her "new friends" snickered. The little girl in the pastel-blue jumper dress, her fair hair in braids, stood to adamantly and unsmilingly insist (with a slight lisp due to a missing front tooth) that Wiener was pronounced "Veener."

Despite the pronunciational pronouncement, Clover was subsequently and mercilessly teased on the playground: "Clover Wiener is a wiener," "Clover Wiener's got a wiener," "Clover Wiener doesn't have a wiener," and other variations on that theme. Although it was the boys who verbally demonstrated a developing mastery of the wit and rhetoric of ridicule, the girls enthusiastically participated in the joys of mockery by giggling.

"Vee, vee, vee," Clover stammered as she broke into tears. "It's pronounced Veeeener." Having been teased on the first day of school for my name as well ("Siegel's a bird! Sea gull, sea gull!"), I was sympathetic. But being called a bird was substantially less humiliating than being characterized as a hot dog and, at the same time, through the magic power of language, a penis. A Wiener by any other name was still a wiener. And "wiener," if you knew the cryptic semantic code, was a dirty word, naughty and hilarious. Poor Clover would have to live with that until she could get a new name by getting married.

Before ever speaking to one another, we had held hands when, arranging us in a ring, boy-girl-boy-girl, Mrs. Lovell serendipitously posted me next to Clover. "Ring around the rosie, pocket full of posies," we sang, skipping hand-in-hand around the circle until, "ashes, ashes," we all fell down. As we tumbled to the grassy ground, her shoulder bumped my side, and then, as, rolling over, we let go of each other, teacher, teacher, I declare, I saw Clover's underwear.

It was on the threshold of my home a few weeks later that we spoke for the first time. As she stood there, looking shyly down, her finger nervously massaged her gum at the site of the missing tooth. Her other hand clutched a fold in the dress of the woman who introduced herself to my mother as Mrs. Jane Wiener (unabashedly pronounced with a *W*), the wife of Dr. Richard Wiener (also pronounced with a *W*), who, she added, "knows Dr. Siegel from the studio. And this is our daughter Clover. She tells me that she's in the same grade as Lee at Ponce de Leon. We live just down and across the street, at 702. I hope Lee will come to play with Clover." Mrs. Wiener wanted something.

Although the Wieners did have a tennis court, they did not (sad as it seemed at the time) have a swimming pool. Since, with so many pools in Beverly Hills, it was dangerous not to know how to swim, the Wieners were eager for their daughter to take swimming lessons. Mrs. Wiener asked if they could use our pool on Tuesday afternoons. They had hired former Olympic swimmer Fitta Knullaman to teach Clover, and, in return for letting them use our pool, Mrs. Wiener offered free access to their tennis court if I wanted to take tennis lessons. To sweeten the pot, she added that I could join Clover for the swimming lessons that would be fully paid for by the Wieners. As a matter of pride, I hastened to boast that I was already a good swimmer. I had, after all, once swum out into a turbulent sea to rescue little Gretel Woodcutter from drowning.

"I'm sure you are a fine swimmer," Mrs. Wiener responded with an indulgent smile, "but Fitta will teach you new strokes, how to float on your back, do an underwater somersault, and other secrets of professional aquatics." That's when Clover spoke to me for the first time. Looking up, she removed her finger from her mouth to say, "I'm going to swim in the Olympics someday."

After competing on the Swedish team in the 1948 Olympic games in London (and finishing second only to Flamoes Van Neuken of the Netherlands in the 200 meter breaststroke competition), Fitta Knullaman had come to Hollywood in the hope of following in the wake of Johnny Weissmuller by becoming a movie star. It was in fact that very Tarzan who had introduced her to the producer who hired her to do the strenuous stunt swimming in a rubber mermaid suit for Ann Blyth in *Mr. Peabody and the Mermaid.* She had also been the underwater double for both Debra Paget in *Bird of Paradise* and Eve W——'s mother in *Lagoon of Love.*

Clover's father, a veterinarian specializing in the ailments of animals in the movies, had met Fitta on the set of *Lagoon of Love,* where he had been called to cure Eve's mother's costar, Dickie the Dolphin, of (so Clover later divulged in strict confidentiality) diarrhea. "Imagine what it would have been like for Fitta underwater with Dickie if my Dad hadn't come to the rescue."

We discovered that we had things in common: my father's patient, Rory Calhoun, had ridden her father's patient, Buster, in *Massacre River*. Dr. Wiener, his daughter boasted, had also treated Francis the Talking Mule, Bullet the Wonder Dog, Pierre (the chimpanzee in *My Friend Irma Goes West*), and, most impressive of all, none other than Silver, the Lone Ranger's "fiery horse with the speed of light and thundering hooves."

I was disillusioned to learn from Clover that there were actually four different white horses that played the part of Silver: one to gallop fast, one to rear, one to stand still when the Lone Ranger leaped into the saddle, and one to whinny and shake its head up and down. Her father had treated the one that reared: "His name isn't really Silver. It's Whitey." Whitey, Clover further confided, had also been hired to play the part of Topper, Hopalong Cassidy's horse, for rearing scenes when the regularly rearing Topper (a horse named Bill) was sick. Dr. Wiener had treated Bill on that occasion and, on other occasions, he had taken care of Buck, Barney, and Beau, the three other white horses who played Topper. Whenever I'd ask Clover what sickness a particular patient of her father had, the answer was always "diarrhea"; the only thing to conclude was that either a gastrointestinal epidemic was devastating Hollywood's animal kingdom or Clover was making it up. I figured the little girl was probably, like me, a liar.

I hadn't initially wanted to take swimming lessons with Clover Wiener from Fitta Knullaman (who had done for Debra Paget and Ann Blyth what Whitey had done for Silver and Topper), but as I came to realize how impressed Clover was with my swimming, I began to look forward to Tuesday afternoons with Clover and Fitta. I discovered then how very much it pleases me to impress girls. Other sources of delight also came to be realized during those afternoons in the water.

Looking at the two of them, both in Catalina bathing suits, I imagined that by the time Clover was on the US Olympic swim team, her body would have ripened into something like Fitta's. Like Fitta's arms and legs, Clover's limbs would become leanly muscular, almost masculine in a mysteriously fetching feminine way. Her breasts would be not too large, not too small, but, in the words of Baby Bear in the story of Goldilocks, "just right." Clover's future body was especially breathtaking when the white bathing suit was wet: that's when Fitta's coy nipples brazenly announced their presence; that's when the nylon's mandate to conceal was subtly challenged at the crotch by a vaguely raised, heart-shaped patch of slight darkness that, thanks to Miss Crim, I knew was hair.

For the time being, however, no matter how soaked Clover's pink swimsuit became, it had nothing to reveal. Her white rubber bathing cap was lavishly festooned with fleshy red rubber roses and limp green rubber leaves. A pink nose clip, blue goggles, and white earplugs prevented water from getting into any of the openings into her head except her mouth. On her feet she wore green rubber fins, and inflatable red water wings were strapped to her back.

One afternoon, noticing Clover, harnessed in those water wings, kneeling at the edge of the pool, looking down into the water for the nose clip she had dropped, I was reminded of the enchanting girl, so unabashedly naked under the diaphanous veil wrapped around her loins, gazing from a rock into rippling water, on White Rock soft drink labels. Except for the White Rock Girl's nymphal coiffure, rouged lips, and pert breasts, and except for the fact that her wings were delicate, gauzy, and almost transparent while Clover's were big, floppy, and bright red, the two girls looked a lot alike. I did not know at the time that the White Rock Girl was Psyche, the same girl who, in the embrace of a young boy, none other than Cupid, appeared on the dust jacket of *In the Beginning: A Children's Book about Grown-up Love.*

Clover, it must be told, had a long way to go before she would qualify for the Olympics. While I was mastering the breaststroke and frog kick, she was still struggling with the dog paddle. Every time her face went underwater, she'd frantically raise it back up to gasp for breath. That she flailed rather than swam caused her to frequently kick, bump into, or grab on to me in the water. I discovered that her touch (whether violent, awkward, or desperate, accidental or on purpose) pleased me as much as her admiration, and all the more so in conjunction with it.

Fitta tried to teach us to float on our backs so that we would be able to take rests in the unlikely event that we ever had to swim a very long distance in a very large body of water. "Reach out with your arms, let your feet float up," she coached, and I relished the feel of her stalwart hand in the small of my arched back as she gently held me up and horizontal. "Relax, Lee. Yes, yes, that's good. Hold a deep breath. Clover, keep your chest high. And raise up that pelvis. Let your head fall back until your ears are under the water."

For the sake of mastering that particular natatorial feat, Clover insisted on wearing her water wings in front rather than on her back. In that position they looked like huge breasts, rivaling in prodigiousness even those of Sally May Carter. I couldn't help but think of the plastic inflation valves, one on each water wing, as nipples, those succulent nodules that were always sure to make an immodest appearance through the wet white nylon of Fitta's swimsuit. I offered to inflate the wings for Clover. With my lips around the protuberant valve of first one and then the other float, I closed my eyes and felt each wing in turn filling with my breath, swelling up to become firm in my hands. Clover thanked me as she strapped them on her chest.

When, at the end of our lesson, Clover climbed out of the pool, shivering and slippery, with glistening rivulets of water trickling down goose-bumped legs to form a pool around her frog-foot swim fins, her teeth would always chatter. Once she removed her water wings, swim cap, nose clip, goggles, ear plugs, and fins, Fitta would wrap a large white terry towel around her. Then, curled up on the blue canvas chaise longue, the warm soft towel covering everything but her face, she looked, I thought, cuter than ever. More than cute, even more than very, very, very cute. Clover Wiener, I descried, was beautiful. I began to think about her more than I thought about Eve. I was once again, I realized, falling in love.

Wrapping a small beige towel around my waist, over my bathing briefs, to parade around the pool, I'd imagine, as I strutted past her, that I probably reminded her of the son of Tarzan. He was a good swimmer too. "Me Boy, you Clover."

If, as was most often the case, Mrs. Wiener was late in picking her daughter up, Sally May Carter, after commanding us (the girl first and then me) to change into dry clothes in the pool house, would serve us a snack by the pool. I was partial to White Rock cola to drink and Wilno kosher hot dogs (the only brand my father would allow in the house) with Kraft DeLuxe cheese slices melted on them to eat. Of course, I always took care not to refer to the hot dogs as "wieners."

If Mrs. Wiener still hadn't arrived by the time we had eaten, Clover would be sure to ask to see my baby brother. "He's so cute," she'd say. "I wish I had a baby at home." After our first swimming lesson, Clover had convinced Sally May Carter to give her diaper changing lessons, something, they agreed, that every girl should learn in preparation for becoming a mother, if not a Negro maid. During those tutorials, I'd stare at Clover staring, always with considerable fascination, at Robert's penis, appearing so enormous in contrast to his little body. She seemed to think it too was pretty cute.

When Clover's mother finally did arrive, she would, after perfunctorily apologizing for being late, usually invite me to come to their house to play after school the next day or, if I couldn't make it then, on Thursday, or both, or any day for that matter.

No sooner would I have arrived at the house, than Mrs. Wiener would be sure to announce that she had to go out but she'd be back soon. And then, after telling us to be good and to help ourselves to the pitcher of cherry Kool-Aid in the icebox and the graham crackers in the cupboard in the butler's pantry, she would hurry off on foot, never taking the car to wherever it was she went.

Clover always insisted that I follow her up to her room to say hello to her dolls: Posie, Toodles, Tiny Terry, Muffie, Sweet Sue, Baby Baby, Pretty Pinky, and Little Mermaid. Just as she knew I didn't want to do that but did so only because I liked her, so she, even though she didn't want to but because she liked me as much as I liked her, would consent to turn on the television and watch *Deputy Dick's Kiddie Korral.* I surmised that the reason Clover didn't like the show was that, because the program was sponsored by the Oscar Mayer Company, the dreaded word "wiener" was frequently used on it. Whenever it was, I would, in order not to embarrass her, politely pretend not to be making any association between a hot dog, Clover's surname, and a penis.

Every afternoon, in addition to showing old cartoons and sundry episodes of *The Little Rascals,* Deputy Dick invited children from a different elementary school in the Los Angeles area to appear on the program and play a game with him. One day the students in the first-grade class of the Samuel Clemens Elementary School in North Hollywood played "Guess What?" Each kid had a glass of chocolate milk from which they were allowed to take one gulp each time he or she guessed what one of the members of Deputy Dick's Posse was dressed up as. The first contestant to drink the whole glass of chocolate milk would win a package of one dozen Oscar Mayer wieners, a Wiener Whistle, and a toy model of the Wienermobile.

It was fairly easy for the Samuel Clemens students to identify the circus clown, cowboy, ballerina, hula girl, nurse, and Indian chief. It was a little harder to guess that the man in the top hat, holding a whip and a chair, was a lion tamer; and several children mistook the magician for Dracula and the deep-sea diver for a visitor from outer space. One of the girl contestants thought, presumably because of the mushroom shape of his oversized white toque, that the man dressed as a chef was supposed to be an atomic bomb.

The game inspired Clover: "When you come over next week, I'm going to dress up as something. And you try to 'Guess What.' And you too—you dress up, and I'll guess." The proposal gave me an opportunity to show off the cowboy outfit that my parents had given me for Chanukah.

"*Baruch atah Adonai, Elohenu melech ha-olam,*" my father, seated in his customary swivel chair in our library-bar, solemnly recited, "*ve-tzivanu le-hadlik ner shel Chanukah.*" Wearing as always the customary white uniform of black maids, Sally May Carter, no doubt mystified by the weird way in which Beverly Hills Jews were celebrating Christmas, was holding Robert in her lap. My mother helped me light the first candle on the menorah.

After opening a bottle of champagne for my father and herself and a bottle of White Rock ginger ale for Sally, Robert, and me to drink from champagne glasses, my mother fetched a gift for me from under our Chanukah tree, a white-flocked pine decorated with blue Christmas lights, blue Christmas bulbs, and a silver Star of David on top. Eagerly ripping the green ribbon and red wrapping from the box, I was delighted to discover a cowboy outfit from FAO Schwarz in New York—a plaid shirt, a brown vest with a sheriff's badge permanently affixed to it, a blue bandana, a western belt with a lucky horseshoe buckle, a cowboy hat, and, best of all, mock-leather fringed chaps. I loved the fringe.

The accessories came on the successive nights of Chanukah: black and white Hopalong Cassidy cowboy boots (second night); a Roy Rogers holster with twin Roy Rogers six-shooters that fired real caps (third night); a Range Rider cowboy canteen and Kit Carson saddle bags (fourth night); *The Illustrated Golden Book of the American Cowboy* (fifth night); a Gene Autry lunch box and thermos (sixth night); and a Howdy Doody ventriloquy dummy (seventh night).

On the eighth night, before opening my last gift (plaid flannel cowboy pajamas and ranch house bedroom slippers), as my father recited the Jewish blessing, I, with Howdy Doody sitting in my lap, tugged on the ring at the end of the string on the wooden dowel hidden inside his torso. Through the magic of ventriloquy, it really did look like Howdy Doody was saying the words: "Blessed art Thou, O Lord Our God, who has commanded us to kindle the Chanukah lights."

All decked out in my Wild West duds, I looked at myself in the large mirrors on the closet doors of my mother's dressing room. If the doors were opened at just the right angles to each other, I could see myself from all sides, and, when the mirrors faced each other just so and I squeezed in between them, millions of cowboys lined up behind me, and another million faced me. And all of them were me.

Reckoning that I looked a bit like young Dick West, the cowboy boy who was lucky enough to be Range Rider's sidekick, I pretended to be him, drawing my six-guns and firing a round of caps at Jack Black, a really bad, bad guy, a Mississippi gambler turned rustler, who, in one episode of the show, had tried to ambush Range Rider. I loved both the smell of the caps and the way the sound of them made my baby brother cry.

Dressed to kill in cowboy clothes, I decided to ride my horse, Lucky, a bucking bronco that I had broken, over to the Wiener spread to play "Guess What?" as promised. After throwing a saddle (the bed pillow that had previously been Gretel Woodcutter) over Lucky's back (one of the two arms of the red velvet couch in my room), I mounted up, gave Lucky a gentle kick, and said, "Giddyup." He reared like Whitey, shook his head up and down, and then, with fiery hooves, galloped away as fast as the horse who played Silver for the running scenes in *Adventures of the Lone Ranger.*

Figuring that Lucky was tired and hungry after running so far at the speed of light, I dismounted in a pasture and, patting his neck affectionately, instructed him to stay put until I returned. Leaving my horse there to graze on my grass-green wool carpet, I started out on foot to the Wiener's.

Coming down the stairs into the kitchen, I saw Sally May Carter mopping the linoleum. Sneaking up behind her, I drew both my six-shooters and ordered her "to stick 'em up." "Shit, boy," she laughed as, turning around, she set down her mop to raise her hands above her head. "Please don't shoot Mama Sally," she pleaded.

I was hardly halfway to Clover's house when Frank Hardy, a fifth-grader at Ponce de Leon who had red hair and freckles like Howdy Doody's, appeared outside his house. It was just like when Jack Black had come out of the saloon to shoot Range Rider. "Hey you! Little cowboy!" he shouted. "Where's your horse? Hey cowboy, I'm talking to you! Come here, I want to see your guns." Crossing the street to avoid passing close to him, I kept walking, hoping that if I ignored him, he'd leave me alone.

"Only babies dress up like cowboys," he razzed. "You're a baby." I knew he was wrong about that: first of all, Range Rider, Red Rider, Roy Rogers, Hopalong Cassidy, Kit Carson, and Gene Autry all dressed up as cowboys, and they weren't babies; second of all, my brother Robert was a baby, and he didn't dress up as a cowboy. But I didn't want to argue with the formidable Hardy as he continued to mock me: "Cowbaby, cowbaby! Come here, you little wienie! Come here!"

I prayed to the God who had commanded my family to kindle the Chanukah lights in memory of the time he had protected my forefathers from the wicked tyrant, Antiochus, not to let Frank Hardy beat me up. Like Antiochus, Hardy wasn't Jewish. And that meant his penis was dirty.

Once I was past the jeering villain, only a few doors from Clover's house, I broke into a run for dear life, something not very easy to do, I discovered, in Hopalong Cassidy cowboy boots. It occurred to me that this was why the cowboy wasn't named Runalong Cassidy.

Opening the front door, Mrs. Wiener greeted me impatiently: "Lee, you're late. Clover's waiting for you in the rumpus room. I have to run out. I'll be back soon. Don't leave her alone."

Before I could begin to try to "Guess What" Clover was, she yelled out, "You're a cowboy. That's easy." After downing a glass of chocolate milk, she said, "Now it's your turn. What am I?"

"Well, you're wearing swim fins and a bathing suit, so you must be some kind of swimmer. Are you an Olympic swimmer?"

"No," she answered, "but you're on the right track. It has something to do with water."

"You're wearing a blonde wig and bright red lipstick," I observed, "so maybe you're a movie star."

"No. But because of what I am, I would probably be asked to be in the movies," Clover hinted, and then, as a bonus clue, she began to make bubbling sounds, puffing out her cheeks and holding her breath.

Because there was a necklace of seashells around her neck and two scallop shells were secured to her bathing suit, each in one of the two places where a pretty breast would someday be, I guessed that she might be a Hawaiian hula girl or a Polynesian princess like Debra Paget in *Bird of Paradise.*

"No," she groaned impatiently, pointing to her legs, around which she had wrapped what appeared to be a green vinyl outdoor picnic tablecloth. I didn't know what to say. A full glass of chocolate milk on the coffee table was waiting for me to answer correctly.

Exasperated with my intractable nescience, she finally revealed her identity: "That's my tail. I'm a mermaid. Haven't you ever seen a mermaid?" She held up a book with a portrait of a mermaid on the cover and, since she couldn't walk toward me with the tablecloth wrapped so tightly around her legs, she signaled for me to join her on the couch to inspect it. She gave me permission to drink the chocolate milk even though I had lost the game.

"This is my favorite story—*The Little Mermaid,*" she announced with a wistful sigh as she thumbed through the pages, stopping to open the book wide and turn it toward me every time she found an illustration of a mermaid.

"I'll read it to you," she insisted, and even though I would rather have been watching *Deputy Dick's Kiddie Korral,* I agreed to listen. Clover was vastly more talented at reading than she was at swimming.

The first time I had heard Clover read was earlier that year in school. Mrs. Lovell had called on her to read aloud from *Fun with Dick and Jane*: "'No, Sally, no,' said Jane. 'You cannot play with Dick. You are too little. You are a baby. Dick is big. I am big too. I can play with Dick.'" I did not yet know that "dick," like "wiener," was a dirty word. I didn't learn that until the second grade, when Big Doug Shulman, my friend Little Mike's older brother, told us the joke "Tom, Dick, or Harry—who shall I marry? Tom, because his dick is hairy!" I didn't learn that "Come Spot" was dirty until the seventh grade.

After Clover had been commended for her reading skills, it was my turn: "'Oh Jane, you are funny,' Dick said. 'You are in this family. Our family is funny.'" I did not think the family was funny. They did, however, talk funny, and there was something funny about them. All the white space on the pages of *Fun with Dick and Jane* gave me a disconcertingly empty feeling. In every story, both Dick and Jane were sure to declare, "This is fun!" even when they were doing things like setting the table for Mother, going for a ride in Father's car, pretending that a laundry basket was a boat, or jumping over blocks. But I was never convinced that they were ever really having any fun. I sensed something funny going on behind the facades of fun as rendered in unnatural primary colors.

Whenever nameless Father came home from his undisclosed work, Dick and Jane ran to greet him at the gate as nameless Mother, in her pastel housedress and white apron, stood woodenly at the door with a weirdly smiling Baby Sally. They never welcomed the man in the dark suit with a hug. Never in the book were there any physical expressions of affection, nothing intimate, no tender touch, not a single kiss. There were never any verbal declarations of love, just "You are funny."

The family may have appeared happy to some beginning readers, but I for one suspected that they were just pretending, constrained (for some terrible, undisclosed reason) to act happy and reiterate, again and again, that they were having fun.

Dick and Jane reminded me of Hansel and Gretel. Just as the woodcutter's children, after overhearing their nameless Father and nameless Mother discussing their plan to abandon the children in the forest, where they would be eaten by wild animals, pretended that nothing was wrong, so Dick and Jane faked their hollow cheer. Their smiles looked forced. They knew, I supposed, that their parents were not to be trusted. Maybe they were Communists. In the very beginning of the book, the children had practiced their escape: Jane said, "Run, run. Run, Dick, run." Dick said, "Come, Jane. You come too. Run, Jane, run. Run, run."

Just as the parents of Hansel and Gretel feigned affection for their children so that the kids wouldn't suspect that they were going to be forsaken, so Father and Mother, I imagined, were concealing sinister impulses and dark designs. Mother said a visit to Grandmother's farm would be fun. Just as an old woman in the forest had given gingerbread to Hansel and Gretel, so Grandmother on the farm plied Dick and Jane with cookies. "Animal cookies," said Jane. "And some little girl cookies too. This is a big surprise. This is fun."

As Clover read that passage aloud in class, the words of the fairy tale came back to me: "The old woman had only pretended to be kind. She was really a wicked witch who lay in wait for children, enticing them with gingerbread and then surprising them by locking them up in a stable, where she fattened them up in order to kill, cook, and eat them."

Maybe it was because I did not have a sister that I did not think of either Hansel and Gretel or Dick and Jane as brother and sister but, rather, as boyfriend and girlfriend. By draping a large sheet over a clothesline, in a story called "The Funny House," Dick and Jane had made a tent where they could hide from their parents. "'See our house,' said Jane. 'I am the mother. Dick is the father.'" Clover said she'd like to make a house like that: "Yes. A funny house."

While learning how to write that year, I discovered that the word "love" was embedded in Clover's name. For the first time I sensed the magic power of written words.

"*The Little Mermaid,*" Clover assured me, adjusting the position of her piscatorial tail on the couch as she opened the book to the first page, "is much better than *Fun with Dick and Jane.*" She ran her finger over the words as she read: "Once upon a time, far out in the ocean, where the water is very, very, very, very deep, and as blue as the prettiest cornflower and as clear as crystal, there lived the Sea King. The walls of his palace were made of coral and the roof was formed of seashells that opened and closed as the water flowed over them. In each shell there was a glittering pearl, and each pearl was fit for the diadem of a queen." I knew that Clover was not really reading, but faking it by reciting words that had been read to her. We had not yet learned to read that well. I did not, at that time, know what "diadem" meant any more than I knew the secret meaning of "dick," and I doubted that Clover did either. She stopped the simulated reading to show me the illustration of the Sea King's daughter, the little mermaid, and inform me that she was "very, very, very, very beautiful."

After the first few pages, Clover must have forgotten the words that had been read to her; she was obviously making up the story. The little mermaid had swum up to the surface of the ocean to rest: "She floated on her back. She let her head fall back until her ears were under the water. She kept her chest high and raised up her pelvis. After a while a boat came by. There was a cowboy in the boat. He waved to the little mermaid."

Interrupting her, I pointed to the illustration of the boy in the book. "That's not a cowboy. I'm a cowboy. He's not wearing a cowboy hat. He's wearing a crown. He's a prince."

"That's right," an undaunted Clover answered. "He's the Prince of the Cowboys. You know, like Roy Rogers is King of the Cowboys and Dale Evans is Queen of the West." The Little Mermaid gave the Prince of the Cowboys swimming lessons so that he could visit her underwater. She visited him on his ranch, where she learned to ride bucking broncos sidesaddle. "And so," Clover concluded, "the mermaid and the cowboy got married. They spent half their time underwater and the other half on the range. And they had lots and lots of children."

"How could they have kids?" I asked.

"What do you mean?"

"Well, you know—her fish tail," I answered. From the quizzical expression on the mermaid's face, I surmised that she did not know about what *In the Beginning: A Children's Book about Grown-up Love* called "*coitus* or *sexual intercourse* or sometimes, less formally, just *making love*." I felt I ought to teach her. It was the least I could do for my girlfriend.

So, on the following Wednesday, packing up my copy of *In the Beginning* in my Kit Carson saddle bags and dressing up in my cowboy outfit, I once again set out for the Wiener spread and was greatly relieved that bad guy Frank Hardy did not catch me sneaking past his house. The little mermaid was waiting for me and, as soon as her mother left, I got started, using the same method to read *In the Beginning* that Clover had used to read *The Little Mermaid.*

"When girls grow up," I began from the "Sugar and Spice and All That's Nice" chapter, "they will have something known as an *ovum* inside of them. It means egg. Boys will have something inside of them called *sperms.* It means seeds. When a seed gets planted in an egg, a baby will grow." I showed her the illustrations of both the round egg (that still looked to me like a martini olive with a pimento in it) and the squiggly sperm (that resembled a tadpole with a big head and a very, very long tail). And then I turned to "The Birds and the Bees, Elephants and Fleas," where it was explained how fish (and, inferentially, other creatures with fish tails) make babies: "Human girls have only one ovum.

But millions of ovums come out of fish girls. The boy fish then puts his sperms in the water. Because those sperms are really good swimmers, they find the eggs and bury themselves in them."

Flipping forward to "Love, Marriage, and the Baby Carriage," I continued the feigned reading. I based my narrative loosely on the actual text and drew some of my rhetoric directly from it, but in order to make my point and, at the same time, to keep from embarrassing either of us too much, it was necessary to edit: "Animals and people who don't live underwater need to do something special so that the sperms can swim to the egg when there's no water to swim in. This special something is called *coitus* or *sexual intercourse* or sometimes, less formally, just *making love*. In order to do this, a boy needs a special thing to put his sperms inside a girl. And the girl needs a special opening for the boy to put his special thing into. The boy's special thing is called a *penis*. Penis. P-e-n-i-s. The girl's special opening is called a *vagina*." As I did not remember how to spell that word, I turned to the schematic "Map of the Passages and Places in the Female Reproductive System" to find the word and point it out to her. It began with a *V*, like Viener. And then I pointed out the penis to Clover on the corresponding map in "Snaps and Snails and Puppy-dogs' Tails."

All of this was foreplay, taking us closer and closer to the act in question: "When a boy is little, he uses his penis to go number one. But when he becomes a man, he uses it to put sperms in a woman. When a girl is little, she uses her special opening to go number one too. But when she grows up, she puts a penis in it." Finally ready to recite my favorite passage as memorized by heart, I decided to emend the beginning of it because "Mother" and "Father," the words used in the original, would be, I figured, as unpleasantly associated with the robotic parents in *Fun with Dick and Jane* in Clover's mind as they were in mine. "The man and woman lie close together," I pretended to read, "feeling very happy while the penis moves in and out of the vagina with rapid motions until sperm-bearing fluid comes out of it."

"Oh, I knew that," Clover insisted with a snicker. "I know all about sex."

"Well," I said to make my point, "that's why a cowboy and the fish-girl can't have a baby."

Despite her claim to know about sex, she still didn't seem to understand. Again she asked, "Why?" Worried that direct explanation would sound too dirty, I considered other ways of clarifying the sexual problems that would necessarily arise for a cowboy and a mermaid in love.

When I went to Clover's the next week, I brought along my Howdy

Doody ventriloquy doll. Once again I was costumed as a cowboy, and again she was a mermaid.

As soon as Mrs. Wiener left the house, after declaring, as usual, that she'd be back soon, I told Clover that Howdy wanted to meet her dolls. After unwrapping her fish tail and taking off her flippers so that she could climb the stairs, she led the way to her room. Once there, she put her tail and caudal fins back on and then sat on the bed to speak to the dolls who were cuddled up against her pillows. "Girls, you have a special visitor today. His name is Howdy Doody. He's a famous television star. Mr. Doody, these are my best friends: Posie, Toodles, Tiny Terry, Muffie, Sweet Sue, Baby Baby, Pretty Pinky, and Little Mermaid."

With my hand buried inside Howdy's torso and my forefinger tugging on the ring on the string that made his mouth open and close, I tried my best to simulate Howdy's squeaky voice. Straining not to move my lips, I said, "Hello, girls. I'm here to show you how to make a baby. I'll be the daddy, but I'll need a mommy. How about you, Muffie? Come on over here."

Clover helped Muffie move across the bed to recline in front of Howdy. Clover, Posie, Toodles, Tiny Terry, Sweet Sue, Baby Baby, Pretty Pinky, and Little Mermaid, all of them utterly fascinated, watched as Howdy (after I had helped him raise the doll's little lace-trimmed pink velveteen party dress up above her waist) took his position in between Muffie's legs and bounced up and down on her a few times. Then, as the cowboy dummy stood up, his mouth began to open and close: "Okay, Muffie. I have put my sperms in your vagina so that we can have a baby."

Even though Toodles was not a ventriloquy doll, she seemed to speak as Clover, her lips only barely moving, walked her across the bed to lay her down next to Muffie: "I want to have a baby too. Please, put some sperms in my vagina." While Toodles did not have a maneuverable jaw, she did have movable weighted eyelids, and so, as she and Howdy did that special thing called "*coitus* or *sexual intercourse* or sometimes, less formally, just *making love*," her eyes opened and closed in a rhythmic blinking that intimated a delirious rapture.

"Look, look," said Clover. "See Howdy. Look. See Toodles. See them go up and down. Up and down. Oh, look. Howdy and Toodles are funny. This is fun."

Since Posie was wearing a one-piece playsuit rather than a more conveniently lift-up-able dress, Clover had to completely undress her for her turn to join in the fun. As she did so, she asked Howdy to take off his clothes too. While he was willing to remove his cowboy boots and jeans, he insisted on keeping on his plaid shirt, blue bandana, and the brown leather gloves that were painted onto his hands. That he had lumpy white cotton legs with no knees would have been embarrassing enough for Howdy if he were alive, but Clover noticed something even more humiliating: "He doesn't have the special thing!"

"Well," I answered in defense of my dummy, "Posie doesn't have the special opening either. We'll just have to pretend." And pretend we did as Howdy and Posie gave themselves over to the voluptuous transport of carnal passion. Clover led the chorus of girls in the peanut gallery in hymeneal song:

It's Howdy Doody time!
It's Howdy Doody time!
Let's give a rousing cheer,
'Cause Howdy Doody's here.

After Tiny Terry, Sweet Sue, and Pretty Pinky had, each in their turn, taken in their fair share of the sperm-bearing fluid from the thrusting, cotton-stuffed loins of the famous television personality from Buffalo, New York, Clover spoke to Baby Baby: "You cannot play with Howdy Doody. You are too little. You are a baby."

Only Little Mermaid was left. Clover looked at her, then at Howdy, then at me, then back at the doll. I interpreted her frown as a sign that I had successfully demonstrated to Clover that, no matter how much they loved each other, the cowboy and the mermaid could not have a baby. It was physically impossible for him to put his sperms in her.

The frown suddenly transformed into a smile as Clover began to unwrap her tail: "I'm going to fill my bathtub. Little Mermaid can put some eggs in the water. And then Howdy can release his sperms into the tub so that they can swim to her eggs."

I had to apologize for Howdy: "He doesn't know how to swim."

"We can teach him," Clover insisted. "We can even ask Fitta to give him lessons!"

"No," I explained on the dummy's behalf, "if he goes in swimming, his legs will swell up and get waterlogged. The water will fill up the inside of his body. He's not waterproof."

Silently picking the little mermaid up and tenderly cradling the doll in her arms, Clover frowned again. Motionless and mum, Muffie, Toodles, Tiny Terry, Sweet Sue, Pretty Pinky, and Posie were in a pile on the bed. The bodies were contorted, the limbs all akimbo. And next to the heap of lifeless girls lay an exhausted and depleted Howdy Doody. His pants were still off, exposing his ghostly white and weirdly crackless butt. Although he was lying on his stomach, his head faced backward, his neck wrenched so far out of its socket that the wooden dowel that was his spine showed above his blue bandana. Inert, unfocused eyes gazed blankly into space. The red spots on the television cowboy's face looked more like chicken pox than freckles. That his jaw hung limply down, leaving his huge lower lip well away from his buck teeth, revealed that his tongue was missing. Making love to all those girls had, it seemed, been too much for Howdy Doody. He looked dead.

Clover never dressed as a mermaid again and I never took Howdy Doody back to the Wieners'.

"Help yourself to the cherry Kool-Aid in the icebox. I made a fresh pitcher of it for you," Mrs. Wiener announced. "Be good, children. I have to run out for a little while."

We were watching an episode of the *Little Rascals* in which Alfalfa was singing "I'm in the Mood for Love" for Darla on the *Deputy Dick Kiddie Korral* show, when Clover suddenly announced that she had to "go number one." She shyly confessed that she was afraid to sit on the toilet alone because she sometimes had a dream in which there was a snake living in her toilet. When, in that nightmare, she tried to go to the bathroom, the dreaded serpent would come up and "bite my tushy or burrow into my private."

Clover implored me to accompany her into the bathroom, where I then protectively watched over her as she raised up her pink cotton skirt, pulled down her white cotton panties, and cheerfully took a seat.

Over a trickling sound, words were whispered with a touching bashfulness: "I've never done this with any other boy before." For reasons that neither of us quite understood, we both knew that this intimacy was naughty. It was bad, and that was what made it so good. Clover beseeched me to promise never to tell anyone about it, "Never. Never ever." As I was no cad, I solemnly vowed that, no, I would never tell anyone, never ever, not even my parents, no one (well, except, maybe, my friend and next-door neighbor Little Mike Shulman).

After demurely blotting herself with a dainty square of toilet tissue, Clover raised the seat and, without flushing the toilet, asked if I also needed to go number one. After taking off my fringed chaps and Roy Rogers twin six-shooter holster, unfastening the lucky horseshoe buckle on my western belt, and then, nervously, unzipping my cowboy jeans to drop them around my Hopalong Cassidy cowboy boots, I pulled down my Jockey briefs, took careful aim, and did it. It was the first time for me too.

The illicit pleasure that Clover and I had discovered in her bathroom was too sumptuously luscious to go unrepeated. I started going over to the Wiener house not just once a week but as often as I could, always taking along an extra supply of Kool-Aid in my Range Rider cowboy canteen for us to drink once we had finished off the pitcher that her mother would have made for us before going out.

I couldn't help but think about Clover on those mornings when I woke having to pee so badly that my penis was stiff. I had learned from *In the Beginning* that the scientific name for a penis in that state was "an erection," and I was considerably intrigued by what the book had to say about it: "When a boy grows up and gets married, he will sometimes have an erection even when he does not need to go to the toilet. He will have an erection when he and his wife decide to have a baby or even sometimes when they just want to be close and show each other that they love one another in a special way." I assumed that I would marry Clover one day. In her bathroom, several times a week, we were already and inveterately showing one another that we loved each other in a very special way.

One day after our swimming lesson, while we were having our poolside snack, Clover rather timidly announced that she had something to tell me. "It's a big secret. I hope you won't be angry with me. Please don't get mad."

I was afraid that she was going to tell me that she had urinated with another boy. I was well aware that, on several occasions, Leo Roth had gone over to the Wieners' house with his father who sometimes played tennis with Dr. Wiener. Ever since I had first seen him, on our first day in the first grade, there was always something about Leo Roth I didn't trust.

I was so relieved not to be hearing a confession of infidelity that I was not even slightly perturbed when my girlfriend divulged that, during our swimming lessons, she would often pee in my pool: "I like the way it warms my legs. But, as soon as the warm feeling goes away, I always swim away from it as fast as I can." No, I was not angry. On the contrary, once I knew about it, if, when swimming behind her, I felt an underwater wave of warmth, I would release my own urine into the swimming pool just as a male fish instinctually releases sperms when he enters into waters that are ovum rich.

One day, right after flushing the toilet in her bathroom, as we stood together, side by side, watching our commingled urine disappear, a spectacle that inevitably made me slightly wistful, Clover suddenly announced that she wanted a pet fish: "I asked my mom to buy one for me. But she says that, because my father is a veterinarian and works with animals all day long, he doesn't want to come home to any. But I want a fish anyway. Actually I want two fish, a boy and a girl. And they could have baby fish. I'm sure that if I brought two fish home, my mom would let me keep them. She's pretty nice."

I had my heart set on getting those fish for my girlfriend. And I knew exactly where to find them. There was a large fish pond in the backyard of the Spellman house. Little Mike Shulman, my next-door neighbor, always right before me in alphabetical order for school activities, and I had discovered it on one of our explorations of the alley between Maple Drive and Elm. We had surreptitiously peered into the yard of every house that backed onto the alley.

On those adventures up and down the alley, Little Mike would always insist that we go first to the backyard of Debra Paget. He hoped to see again what he swore he had seen once before. Standing on the movie star's garbage can to look over the wall and into her yard, he had, in an excited whisper, said, "I see her. She's getting out of her swimming pool. She's naked!"

Ignoring my plea to come down from the only perch so that I could have a turn, he wouldn't budge. "She's completely naked. I see her boobies. And her hairy weewee. Oh, God, she's beautiful!"

"Come on, climb down," I begged. "Let me see."

After he had finally, and not at all willingly, given up his one-man grandstand, I crawled up and slowly raised my eyes above the top of the wall. There was no one in sight—no one in the yard, no one in the pool, no one on the back porch. No ripples in the pool, not even wet footprints around it. "No one," I said.

"She must have gone into the house," Little Mike insisted, "I swear on my mother's life, I saw her. She was naked." Even though I didn't really believe him, it was thrilling to imagine that it might be true and that, on future expeditions in the alley, we might be lucky enough to see other naked bodies or even bear witness to some illicit act.

Three doors down from Debra Paget's home was the scariest place on the alley, even more fearsome than the Hardy house, which was patrolled by a ferocious Doberman pinscher. Little Mike and I were afraid of the Elm Street house because Mr. Spellman, the man who lived in it all by himself (ever since his wife had left him earlier that year and taken the children with her), was, we had been informed by Miss Crim—a Communist! Miss Crim had been Little Mike's babysitter too.

Because we feared even going near the place, looking into the yard was a genuine act of courage. It would take a hero as daring as Range Rider to actually go over the rear wall and steal fish from the pond there. Emboldened by love, I was determined to do just that for Clover. She insisted on coming along with me on the perilous mission.

And I was as impressed by her adventurousness as she was by my gallantry.

By that time, we were no longer taking swimming lessons: Fitta Knullaman had quit after being cast to costar with Pepe Pelotas in a movie called *Atlantis;* and Clover imagined that, after sixteen weeks of instruction, she swam well enough to continue without a coach. Clover's mother was more than happy to continue bringing her daughter to our house on Tuesdays after school, provided that we promised not to go in the pool without adult supervision. And since she did not know how to swim, Sally May Carter did not count as an adult. "Shit," Sally had muttered, "if the Lord wanted us to swim, he would have given us fins."

Anxiously waiting for her on the Tuesday chosen for the exploit, I was ready for action: I had already procured the wire mesh strainer to catch the fish with, and the large empty mayonnaise jar to put them in, from Sally.

"Come on, Clover," I commanded as soon as Mrs. Wiener had left, and we were off, out my back gate and down the alley, straight to the rear garden wall of the house of the Communist. "This is fun," said Clover.

With my heart pounding frantically, hands trembling, knees shaking, and mouth dry, I did my best to conceal my fright from the seemingly intrepid Clover as I went over the wall. After passing the strainer and mayonnaise jar to me, she nimbly scaled the barrier. Then, dropping to our knees, we crawled silently and stealthily toward the fishpond, trying all the while to keep the shrubbery as cover between us and the house. Next, lying down on our stomachs, we cautiously inched our way out of the bushes to conceal ourselves behind a large rock by the side of the pond. Peeking out from behind that rock, I made sure the coast was clear before submerging the mayonnaise jar in the water to fill it for the fish I'd catch. Handing the jar back to Clover and taking up the strainer, after once more checking to see that it was safe, I quickly scooped and, much to my own amazement, discovered that I had caught a goldfish. I flopped the flip-flapping little creature into the jar and then leaned back against the rock to catch my breath and calm my heart. Encouraged by the smile appearing on Clover's lips as she looked at her new pet, I again dipped the strainer in the pond. No luck that time. But one, two, three more tries (hiding momentarily behind the rock between each one) and I finally had the second fish.

Our mission accomplished, I wanted to get out of there as quickly as possible. But Clover stopped me: "Get some algae out of the pond. The fish won't be happy living in a mayonnaise jar if there isn't any algae in it. Fish love algae."

Unable to refuse my girlfriend anything, I again cautiously emerged from behind the rock, and then, as I dipped the strainer into the water for the algae, I looked up and toward the house. What I suddenly saw so startled me that I dropped the strainer into the pond as I lunged back to cover in shock. I was afraid that the person I had seen in the open window on the second floor of the house, smoking a cigarette and staring blankly out into the garden, might have spotted me as well. I was stunned, rattled, and confused by the horrible discovery that I had made. It was Mrs. Wiener! It was terrible but true—Clover Wiener's mother was a Communist! All those afternoons when she had gone out, leaving Clover and me alone, it was, I deduced, so that she, unbeknownst to her husband and daughter, could sneak off to what Miss Crim had called a "Communist party" at the Spellman house. There was no other explanation for her being there.

"What's wrong?" Clover asked. "Where's the algae? Where's the strainer? What's wrong?"

I feared for Clover, worried that her mother would take her to the Soviet Union, dress her in a drab gray uniform, and send her to a juvenile detention hall, where they would wash her brain. Despite my concern for her safety, I didn't dare tell Clover the ghastly truth about her mother. I vowed to myself never to tell her, not to ever tell anyone, not even the FBI, no one, not even my parents, no one (well, except maybe Little Mike Shulman).

"We've got to get out of here as fast as we can," I frantically whispered. "Keep your head down. Whatever you do, don't look up. Come on, let's go."

As we waited outside the front door of my house for her mother to pick her up, Clover held the mayonnaise jar in her lap, smiling happily as she gazed at the two fish in the algae-less water. "I love my fish," she said. "But now I've got to figure out what to name them. What do you think? Dick and Jane, Roy and Dale, Alfalfa and Darla, Howdy and Muffie, Spot and Puff, Goldieboy and Goldiegirl? I don't know. What do you think?" I was too upset to think.

Before she could decide on the names, her mother arrived. Just like the evil mother in "Hansel and Gretel," Mrs. Wiener pretended to be normal. Not knowing where the fish had come from, she said that, yes, Clover could keep the pets and that it was sweet of me to have given them to her.

I watched them walk down the street. Clover so innocently trusted her mother that she allowed the Communist secret agent to carry the mayonnaise jar.

I was too afraid to ever go to the Wiener house again, and if Mrs. Wiener telephoned to ask if she could bring Clover to my house, I'd always make up some excuse so that she couldn't. As always, Clover and I avoided speaking to each other at school. One day, however, I found myself in line behind her at the water fountain.

After taking a long drink and then wiping her mouth with the back of her hand, she turned to me and spoke: "The fish died."

"Oh," I answered, "that's too bad." And then I stepped forward, leaned my head into the ceramic fountain, turned the metal knob, and drank. By the time I had finished, Clover was gone.

And that, so far as I can remember, was the last time I spoke to Clover Wiener until 1958, when, in the eighth grade, I asked her to be my date for Chip Zuckerman's bar mitzvah party.

Chapter Two: You Tell Her You're Never, Never, Never, Never, Never Gonna Part

1952♥1953

Becky put her small hand upon his and a little scuffle ensued, Tom pretending to resist in earnest but letting his hand slip by degrees until these words were revealed: "I love you."

Mark Twain, *The Adventures of Tom Sawyer*

The child is capable long before puberty of most of the psychical manifestations of love—tenderness, for example, devotion, and jealousy. Often enough, too, an irruption of these mental states is associated with the physical sensations of sexual excitation, so that the child cannot remain in doubt as to the connection between the two. In short, except for his reproductive power, a child has a fully developed capacity for love long before puberty.

Sigmund Freud, "The Sexual Enlightenment of Children"

1952

Amateur American hypnotist Morey Bernstein contacts nineteenth-century Irish colleen Bridey Murphy in the body of Colorado housewife Ruth Simmons, and Danish physician Christian Hamburger surgically transforms ex-GI Mr. George Jorgensen into Miss Christine Jorgensen; in a successful test of a hydrogen bomb, the United States obliterates three islands of the Bikini atoll, and the bikini bathing suit is banned from beauty pageants for giving an unfair advantage to wearers; first issues of both *Confidential* and *Mad* magazine are published; the Palmer Paint Company introduces Paint by Number kits, and the Hasbro toy company puts Mr. Potato Head on the market; Angelo Portinari appears on television for questioning by Estes Kefauver's Special Committee on Organized Crime in Interstate Commerce, and my mother appears with Marilyn Monroe and Zsa Zsa Gabor in *We're Not Married;* Dwight D. Eisenhower is elected president of the United States, and Herbert H. Gordon is appointed cubmaster of Beverly Hills Cub Scout pack 48; a human being, Judy Tyler, replaces a marionette as Princess Summerfall Winterspring on the *Howdy Doody Show,* and Donna Young replaces Babs Cohen as Laughing Flower, the Indian maiden, in the Ponce de Leon Elementary School production of *Fountain of Youth!*

"By the shores of Gitche Gumee, by the shining Big-Sea-Water, stood the wigwam of Nokomis, Daughter of the Moon, Nokomis. Dark behind it rose the forest, rose the black and gloomy pine-trees, rose the firs with cones upon them." With closed eyes, I could see a darkness, and in that darkness rose a forest of enchantment, rose the dream of Hiawatha. As a bosomy Mrs. Murphy read to us, my head was cradled in arms folded over one another on the little wooden desk top in the class room of Ponce de Leon Elementary School in Beverly Hills. The stream of words was a forest brook and, floating on its balmy currents, drifting in its restful rippling, I "heard the whispering of the pine-trees, heard the lapping of the waters, sounds of music, words of wonder."

When reading to her second-graders each day after lunch, Mrs. Murphy was Nokomis, fallen from the moon, Nokomis, fallen "downward through the evening twilight, on the prairie full of blossoms," roses fallen into our classroom, old Nokomis, Mrs. Murphy.

We were calmed and comforted with timbre, tone, and tempo and lullabied by Mrs. Murphy as Nokomis "lulled him, Hiawatha, into slumber."

You didn't need to know the meaning of the words to be transported by the rosy rhythms of the milky voice, the soothing lilt and mellow modulations. As my eyelids closed, the other children disappeared, and with them the school and the clock slowly counting on the classroom wall. I felt nestled in old Mrs. Murphy's arms, as if my head were pillowed in the soft plenitude of her grandmaternal bosom. Not quite dozing, almost dreaming, I saw all that old Nokomis invoked: "With the Arrow-maker dwelt his dark-eyed daughter, wayward as the Minnehaha, with her moods of shade and sunshine, eyes that smiled and frowned alternate, feet as rapid as the river, tresses flowing like the water, and as musical as laughter. And he named her from the river, from the water-fall he named her, Minnehaha, Laughing Water."

I pictured Minnehaha as the winsome Indian maiden on the Land O Lakes butter box. With the azure Gitche Gumee in the background, beneath a butter-yellow sky, kneeling on the wild green grass, Laughing Water had two feathers in a headband beaded like her bracelets and the belt around her waist. Her buckskin dress was lushly fringed at the hem, sleeves, and collar, and a necklace of coral, bone, and turquoise hung around her neck. She had long dark braids, dusky bright eyes, and rose-red, smile-parted lips. She held a box of Land O Lakes butter in front of her breasts. And she herself was on that package, holding there a smaller package on which I knew, although it was too small to see, she was surely kneeling and holding up yet another, still smaller, package. Smaller and smaller, all the way in, there must have been millions of Indian maidens on endless boxes of Land O Lakes butter. And each and every girl was Minnehaha, "Laughing Water, handsomest of all the women in the land of the Dacotahs, in the land of handsome women," the Land O Lakes, the land of Sweet Cream in a world of creamy sweet dreams.

Big Doug Shulman, my friend Little Mike's sixth-grade brother, taught me how to undress her. It required putting two horizontal folds in the package, the first one across her waist, just below her necklace, the second one, parallel to it, just above the fringe and just below the beads, on the hem of her chamois skirt. Then, when you folded the bottom part of the package up, suddenly, right where the little package of butter had been, her knees became naked breasts, large and firm with ruddy rose nipples. Next to her were magic words: ***Sweet Cream.*** It still works—buy some Land O Lakes butter and see for yourself.

Thanks to the secret Big Doug Shulman revealed to Little Mike and me, I could, with eyes closed as Mrs. Murphy read, envision the enticing breasts of lovely Laughing Water with the soft leather fringe draped down around and in between them. "Peeping at her from behind the curtain, hearing the rustling of her garments from behind the curtain," I saw them. "Who shall say what thoughts and visions fill the fiery brains of young men? Who shall say what dreams of beauty filled the heart of Hiawatha," the boy resting his head on arms folded across a little desk in the second-grade classroom of Ponce de Leon Elementary School in Beverly Hills?

Once I had learned the trick, I was sure to ask my mother to buy Land O Lakes butter whenever she went to the store. My preference in brands of the dairy product didn't surprise her since she was well aware of my fascination with Indians. Insisting that I had outgrown the cowboy outfit they had given me the previous year, I begged my parents to please, please buy the Indian brave costume in the FAO Schwarz catalog for me for Chanukah.

I rushed to behold the Indian boy in the large mirrors on my mother's dressing room doors, opened so that I could see him from all sides. Like Hiawatha, "he had moccasins enchanted, magic moccasins of deer-skin." From his brightly beaded belt hung a wampum pouch, a leather sheath for a rubber knife, a real fake tomahawk, and, like a scalp taken on the warpath, a lucky rabbit's foot on a key chain. I loved the long fringe on the sleeves, across the chest, and around the back of my brown flannel shirt and down the outside seams of my matching trousers. I liked being an Indian more than being a cowboy because Indian garments had even more fringe than western wear. And cowboy boys weren't as wild and free as Indian kids.

Most marvelous of all was the Indian war bonnet with its sixteen turkey feathers passing for the plumage of an eagle. Raccoon tails dangled down in front of my ears and two thick crimson stripes of my mother's lipstick across each of my cheeks looked to me like real war paint. I looked like Little Beaver. With the mirrored doors at just the right angles to each other, there were enough Indian braves for all the maidens on the infinite boxes of Land O Lakes butter.

On the second night of Chanukah, I unwrapped *The Golden Book of Indian Life*. I'd dress up as an Indian to listen to my mother read from it: "The Indian child had lots of playmates because Indians lived together in large families. It was fun to be an Indian. The small children played about, wearing no clothes at all. They helped with such tasks as bringing sticks for the fire. By the age of about seven or eight (just your age, Lee), they started wearing clothes (just like your Indian costume, my darling). And then the boys began to follow the men, learning how to hunt and fish, while the girls stayed with the women, learning how to cook the food and make the clothes." As she read, I'd sit close to her on the red velvet couch to gaze in pleasing wonder at the drawings on each page. Entranced, I saw the Indians in their feathered bonnets, with war paint on their faces, smoking peace pipes outside their tepees, hunting buffalo on their painted ponies, and dancing their fierce, ecstatic dances.

"You may have heard that Indian languages don't have as many words as English," the book noted and explained: "This is because Indians often lump a number of ideas into one word. One of their words can be a whole sentence in English. Thus, in the Musquakie language, for example, the word *mintutipo* means 'a young maiden who is announcing to the young braves of her tribe that she is ready for marriage by wearing beaded moccasins that have been presented to her by a wise old widow.' On the other hand, Indians have a lot more words for some things for which we have only one word. There are, for example, more than forty words for arrow in Apache, not including expressions for it in smoke signal or finger sign (a rigidly extended finger moving back and forth)."

When she had finished reading, I'd often pull blankets from my bed to construct a tepee behind the couch. Sitting in that tent in my costume, I'd sometimes think about the little girl played by Eve W—— in the opening scene of *Apache Princess*. I would wait for the warriors of my tribe to kidnap her and bring her to my wigwam. I'd try to console her for the loss of her parents by telling her how much fun it was going to be to be raised as an Indian. By moving my rigidly extended finger back and forth, I'd tell her my name: Little Straight Arrow.

In addition to reminding my mother to buy Land O Lakes butter at the store, I'd ask her to get Nabisco Shredded Wheat. I was collecting the Straight Arrow Injun-uity Cards that separated the layers of the large biscuits in the boxes of that cereal. Because I didn't actually like eating shredded wheat, I'd secretly throw out one or two pieces each day so that my mother would have to buy another box containing two more cards.

From those gray cards, with words and images printed in blue, I studied Indian leather and wood crafts and learned how to send smoke signals, pitch a real tepee, and construct a wickiup, how to set an animal trap and put up a spit on which to roast my catch, how to carve a totem pole, and how to make a birchbark canoe and paddle it. The only one of the many Indian skills explained on the cereal cards that I actually tried, however, was number 24 in series 2. It revealed why Indians never get lost: "While traveling in darkness or through strange wooded areas, an Indian will constantly break off twigs so that he can follow his own trail back home." Thus I snapped off branches of plants in the front yards of the homes on my way to school. Even though I knew my way home, I enjoyed the feeling that, like an Indian, I would have been able to return even if I didn't.

One day, right after Mrs. Murphy had finished reading to us, right after Hiawatha had heard from old Nokomis the story of his parents, "learned from her the fatal secret of the beauty of his mother, of the falsehood of his father," Miss Minnette, the upper-school home economics teacher at Ponce de Leon Elementary, and Mr. Gordon, the sixth- and seventh-grade science and math teacher, came to visit us. The girls were asked to stay seated so that Miss Minnette could talk to them about joining the Brownies. The boys were told to rise and, single file, follow Mr. Gordon outside onto the playground, where we were instructed to sit cross-legged in a circle "like Indians at a powwow." In addition to being a teacher at the school, Mr. Gordon was, he proudly informed us, a cubmaster, the leader of pack 48, a group made up of all the dens of Cub Scouts at Ponce de Leon. Standing at attention and in uniform at the cubmaster's side was none other than sixth-grader Frank Hardy, who, Mr. Gordon explained, having joined Cub Scouts in the second grade, had gone on, "diligently following the Arrow of Light," to become a Boy Scout.

"Let's make believe you lived two hundred years ago," the recruitment speech began. "Suppose your father was an Indian chief and your mother was an Indian squaw. You would learn the secrets of the Great Forest. You would follow the tracks of the Wolf." Mr. Gordon was in the midst of telling us how Indian boys our age learned to make arrows, weave blankets, build tepees (and other things already familiar to me because of *The Golden Book of Indian Life* and Nabisco Shredded Wheat), when suddenly he stopped to order Robbie Freeman to run five laps around the playground. He had seen Robbie lean over to whisper to me something I already knew all too well: "Frank Hardy is an asshole."

After announcing that discipline was one of the things we'd learn as scouts, the cubmaster continued: "The Indian boy knew how to survive on his own. 'But I'm not an Indian boy,' some of you might say. That's right, boys, but you can follow the Wolf Trail anyway by joining the Cub Scouts of America. Your cubmaster will show you the way. Your den mother will help you make things. Your cub chief, a Boy Scout like Frank, will teach you to jump like the deer, run like the fox, and build like the beaver. By joining Cub Scouts, you can learn all that the Indian boy learned when he went into the Great Forest. Yes, right here in Beverly Hills, California, you can have all the fun and thrills that Indian boys used to have."

Despite Robbie's advice against it, I enlisted: "I, Lee Siegel, promise to do my best, to do my duty to God and my country, to be square and obey the Law of the Pack." Wearing an Eagle Scout chief's uniform during our initiation ceremony at the year's first meeting of pack 48, Mr. Gordon explained that the Law of the Pack demanded that we "follow Akela, chief of the Webelos Indian tribe. Akela is a Cub Scout term for a good leader. You are going to learn how to become good leaders some day. But, in order to do that, you need to start by learning how to be good followers." He told us to address him as Akela at pack meetings, but never at school: "There I am just Mr. Gordon, an ordinary science and math teacher." Akela led us in the recital of an oath never to reveal any of the secrets we learned in scouting to non-scouts.

There were seven Bobcats in our den: Ricky Rubin was automatically appointed den leader because his mom volunteered to be our den mother. Then there was Buzzy Graham (assistant den leader), Chuck Mandel (treasurer), Larry "Spanky" Feinstein (assistant treasurer), Little Mike Shulman (flag monitor), Leo Roth (assistant flag monitor), and me (I was nothing and had no assistant nothing). That our den leader had changed his name that year from "Dick," as he had been called in the first grade, to "Ricky" suggested that, like me, he had learned the transgressive meaning of "dick."

In order to become full-fledged Wolf Cubs, we, as Bobcats, needed to demonstrate a mastery of twelve of the "achievements" in our *Cub Scout Handbook*. Since proof of an ability to perform those feats was the signature of a parent, I soon had a Wolf Badge sewn on the left pocket of my navy blue Cub Scout shirt. My mother loved me so much that she actually believed me when, handing her the handbook and a pen to sign her name, I swore that I could climb a twelve-foot pole, walk a twelve-foot railing, make a lasso and lasso a milk bottle with it, construct a pair of wooden stilts and walk with them, repair a punctured bicycle tire, send a message in Morse code, and build a bird feeding station and identify five of the birds that came to feed on it.

It was not, however, necessary for me to lie to my mother for all of the achievements. I could, in fact, recite the Pledge of Allegiance and sing both "Cub Scouting We Will Go" and "The Star-Spangled Banner" (at least the first verse). And I did, at one of our den meetings, actually cook a hot dog in strict accordance with the secret method used by the Webelos Indians as delineated in my *Cub Scout Handbook:*

"Carefully stick a frankfurter on the sharpened points of a forked branch and turn over hot coals until done. Do not over cook. Serve inside a roll."

That was eleven achievements. The twelfth had to be done at a Pack meeting in the presence of Akela. We would be called upon to recite the Law of the Pack in Indian sign language. Larry Feinstein (whom we called "Spanky" because, slightly chubby as he was, he looked vaguely like Spanky on the *Little Rascals*) and I went over to Little Mike Shulman's house to practice. Little Mike's older brother Big Doug made fun of us. "That's not real Indian sign language. Let me teach you the real thing. Here," he said, as he gave us the finger. "It means, 'Fuck you, Kimosabe.' Now, let's see you do it."

When the three of us then each extended a middle finger, Big Doug laughed at us: "No, no, that's how girls and fairies flip the bird." Then, tutoring us in how to correctly give the finger, a gesture not unlike the Apache sign language word for "arrow," he explained that the two digits on either side of the rigid, never bent, middle finger had to be tightly curled and lowered "like this, like balls below a stiff dick." The thumb pointed out and the musculature of the hand, the wrist, indeed of the entire arm, all the way up to the shoulder, was fiercely flexed. As if it were one of the achievements, we practiced it until we got our teacher's approval.

Thorough pedagogue that he was, Big Doug asked if we knew what *fuck* meant. Proud to be able to provide an erudite definition of the term as based on my assiduous study of *In the Beginning: A Children's Book about Grown-up Love,* I explained that it was to perform "*coitus* or *sexual intercourse* or sometimes, less formally, just *making love.*"

"No, you little dumb ass," Big Doug said, insisting on capturing the more subtle semantic nuances and rhetorical resonances of the word, "It's when you stick your dick in a girl." Then he told us some dirty jokes including the one about Tom, Dick, and Harry, and another about an Indian: "Did you hear about the Injun who drank so much tea that he drowned in his tepee?"

Spanky, who had laughed heartily over it, tried to tell it at our next den meeting when Mrs. Rubin left the room to get that week's snack, Jell-O with Reddi-wip: "Did you hear about the Indian who drank so much beer that he drowned in his tepee?" After the meeting I explained to Spanky why no one had laughed. The next week, when Mrs. Rubin went to get the Tom Sawyer potato chips and sour cream-date dip, he tried again: "Did you hear about the Indian who drank so much beer that he drowned in his beer-pee?"

By the time I had earned my Wolf Badge, I was becoming disillusioned with scouting since, despite all the promises that Mr. Gordon had made to us on the playground, we didn't learn to do the things, or have the fun and thrills, that Indian boys did and had in the Great Forest. I still couldn't jump like the deer, run like the fox, or build like the beaver. Rather than making bows and arrows, we made name tags by gluing dry alphabet noodles to spell out our names on little pieces of wood cut for us by our den mother from tongue depressors. We varnished them, affixed safety pins to the backs of them, and wore them on our Cub Scout shirts. The closest thing we did to hunting in the Great Forest was, as arranged by Ricky Rubin's mom, going to the San Fernando Valley on a field trip to tour the processing plant of the Pan American Poultry Company. The company ("Putting Thanksgiving Turkeys on the American Table since 1928") was owned by Ricky Rubin's dad. We never, at any of our den meetings, wove blankets, set up tepees, or sent smoke signals to other dens. We just took the roll, read the minutes of the previous meeting, said the Pledge of Allegiance to the flag, collected the weekly dues, ate whatever after-school snack Mrs. Rubin thought we'd like, sang "Cub Scouting We Will Go," and, in turn, each of us announced whatever achievements we had the nerve to claim to have accomplished that week. The only activity that had anything to do with Indians, other than reciting the "Law of the Pack" in Indian sign language or listening to Spanky trying to get the drowning Indian joke right, was when our den went to see the movie *Apache War Smoke*.

Except by dressing up in my Indian brave outfit from FAO Schwarz (and, while wearing it, folding my Land O Lakes butter package), I didn't have much of an opportunity to enjoy Indian ways until I was cast as Lazy Dog in a school play put on that year in celebration of the twenty-fifth anniversary of the founding of Ponce de Leon Elementary School.

Other than the play, festivities included class visits by "very special visitors." The first was the eighth-grade history and Spanish teacher, Mr. Ball, dressed as a conquistador: "*Buenos dias, muchachos y muchachas.* My name is Señor Ponce de Leon and I have a secret to tell you, *uno secreto muy grande,* something I've never told anyone until today. Believe it or not, I really did find the Fountain of Youth in 1513. *Si, es verdad.* If you've been studying your addition and subtraction, you can probably figure out that that was 439 years ago. I've been alive for a very long time boys and girls! So, as you can imagine, I know a lot about American history. That's why I'm here. So come on *estudiantes,* ask me anything you want to know about history. I've lived through all of it."

Since nobody in our class had any questions about history, Ponce de Leon used the opportunity to remind us that we lived in the greatest country of all time ("*Viva los Estados Unidos!*") and to inform us that we were lucky we were not living in the Soviet Union, where kids who thought they were learning history in school were, in reality, only being brainwashed with Communist propaganda.

"*Muchas gracias,* Señor Leon," Mrs. Murphy said with a big smile on her round rosy face and a little applause of her pudgy hands. "It's fun to learn about the history of our country from someone who was there." After Mr. Ball left to go to Miss Ross's third-grade classroom, Mrs. Murphy assured us that he had been dressed "exactly as the real Ponce de Leon would have been when he became the first civilized man to step foot on what is now the United States of America." The outfit, Mrs. Murphy divulged, had been worn by "Pepe Pelotas when he played the part of Hernando Cortes in *Aztec Love Goddess,* a movie musical about the conquest of Mexico." Mr. Ball had borrowed it from the costume department of Eagle-Lion Studio, where he had worked on several occasions as a stand-in for Pelotas. "You've probably seen Mr. Ball in the movies and not even known it," Mrs. Murphy said, explaining that, working as an extra, he had been "a gladiator, a World War II infantryman, the member of a posse, and an Indian twice (once in *Apache Princess* and once, most recently, in *Apache War Smoke*). He had a speaking part in *I Married a Communist,* and he did a swell job." Mr. Ball was just working as a teacher at Ponce de Leon Elementary School until his dream of being a movie star came true.

The next visitor to our class was "Mr. Jim," the janitor, who, having cleaned Ponce de Leon Elementary School since its founding, had been invited to tell us about the early days. "At first it was just called Beverly Hills Elementary," he recalled. "They changed the name to Ponce de Leon during the War."

Donna Young, who everyone thought was smart because she wore thick glasses, raised her hand to ask him why they had changed it.

"I don't know why," Mr. Jim said with a sort of sad look on his face. "I was overseas at the time. I was with the 969th All-Negro Field Artillery Battalion, fighting for our country, and . . . "

Probably fearing that the janitor would be sidetracked from the important business at hand to tell us about his wartime experiences, Mrs. Murphy interrupted: "And you did a swell job Mr. Jim. We won that war. Thank God. And thank you, Mr. Jim, for fighting in the war, for keeping Ponce de Leon so neat and clean for so many years, and for coming in today. I wish we had more time. It's fun to learn about the history of our school from someone who was there."

Our last visitor on that special day, more dressed up than any teacher, with white gloves, a brimmed hat, cat-eye glasses, and a sparkling American eagle jeweled brooch, was waiting near the door, right under the Stars and Stripes. Mrs. Murphy enthusiastically introduced her as Mrs. Ethel Chambers, the wife of our principal, Dr. Gus Chambers, PhD, and a member of the Beverly Hills Board of Education. Mrs. Chambers was going to all of the lower school classes to recruit volunteers to be in a play that she herself had written to celebrate the twenty-fifth anniversary of Ponce de Leon Elementary School. "It's going to be a lot of work," she warned. "But it's also going to be a lot of fun." After she had told the story and described some of the characters, she asked us to raise our hands if we wanted to act in it: "Let's see some school spirit! Come on boys and girls, let's put on a show!"

I raised my hand because there were parts for Indians in it. It was the story of Ponce de Leon, the explorer after whom our school had for some unknown reason been renamed. While Mrs. Chambers's conception of that Spanish seafarer differed from Mr. Ball's, she shared his view of the Soviet Union. "If we were living under Communism," she alerted us, "we wouldn't be able to put on a play like this."

I just recently found a copy of the program stuck in between the pages of *The Golden Book of Indian Life,* one of the books that I recovered a few years ago from a box that was waiting in my mother's basement to be picked up by the Salvation Army.

On the day before the play, all of us involved in it had to stay after school to cross out Babs Cohen's name on the printed programs. We were instructed to put a circle around "Donna Young" and then to indicate, by drawing an arrow, that she was being promoted from her part as a nonspeaking Indian maiden to replace Babs in the role of Laughing Flower. Babs Cohen had come down with mononucleosis, "the kissing disease," the second-grade equivalent, in terms of mystique, of syphilis or gonorrhea.

Casting Laughing Flower had been problematic from the beginning. Mrs. Chambers had tried to convince Rebecca Welles, the daughter of Orson Welles and Rita Hayworth, to play the part. Rebecca looked down as she timidly shook her head to indicate a "no, please no."

"Don't be shy, Rebecca," Mrs. Chambers urged. "I know Orson and Rita would be proud to see you following in their footsteps. As a writer and director, I've been very influenced by your dad. Come on, Rebecca,

Ponce de Leon Elementary School Proudly Presents

FOUNTAIN OF YOUTH!

A musical comedy by Ethel Chambers

Celebrating Twenty-five Years of Education
at the Ponce de Leon Elementary School

One Performance Only!

11:00 on April 1, 1952 A.D.
in the Ponce de Leon Elementary School Auditorium

Director
Ethel Chambers
Choreography and Musical Direction
Ethel Chambers
Musical Accompaniment
Miss Stewart (Piano) and Ethel Chambers (Tom-tom)
Costumes, Props, and Make-up
The Parents of the Actors and Actresses (Thanks Moms!)
Set Construction
Mr. Woodcock and the seventh grade students
in his shop class (Thanks Boys!)
Ushers
Cub Scout Pack 48 (Thanks Bobcats, Wolves, Bears, and Lions!)

THE CAST

Ponce de Leon, *a Spanish explorer*.................... Frank Hardy (sixth grade)
Queen Isabella, *the queen of Spain*............... Connie Feinstein (sixth grade)
Jumping Fox, *an Indian chief*........................ Doug Shulman (sixth grade)
Dancing Tree, *Jumping Fox's squaw* .... Becky Fine (sixth grade)
Laughing Flower, *Jumping Fox's daughter*........... ~~Babs Cohen~~ (second grade)
Lazy Dog, *an Indian boy* .... Lee Siegel (second grade)
Padre Juan Sandiego, *a priest*......................... Jose Zutano (third grade)
Rabbi Jaime Diegostein, *a Jew* .... Marty Mandel (fifth grade)
Conquistadors .... Leo Roth, Robbie Freeman, Buzzy Graham,
Mike Sobel, Leon Owens, Jay Fineman,
Paul Steinbaum (first throug~~h sixth grades~~)
Indian Maidens...................... Patty Shultz, Clover Wiener, Donna Young,
Bridget Kelly, Beatrice Sugarman, Ange~~la Portinari~~,
Vickie Rothberg, Lana Gurdin, Elizabeth Ulm,
Candy Canter (first through sixth grades)
Indian Braves .... David Brent, Mike Shulman, Joe Zimmelman,
Christopher Stagnaro, Ricky Rubin, Chuck Weiner,
Richard Stern, Leo Roth (first through sixth grades)

THE SETTING

1513 A.D. Spain (Prologue) and then a peaceful little village in the New World

PROLOGUE

The Court of Queen Isabella

ACT ONE

Scene One: Indian Songs and Dances
Scene Two: Civilized Man Comes to North America

ACT TWO

Scene One: The Fountain of Youth!
Scene Two: Indian Education

GRAND FINALE

"God Bless America!"

MUSICAL NUMBERS BY IRVING BERLIN & ETHEL CHAMBERS

"Ook-a-looka, Gah-hay-la-kinka" words and music by Irving Berlin
"One Little, Two Little, Three Little Indians" arrangement by Ethel Chambers
"Hoy-yo, Hoy-yo, Hoy-yo" words and music by Ethel Chambers
"Heap Good Injun Education" words and music by Ethel Chambers
(with a little help from our Principal! Thanks Dr. Chambers!)
"God Bless America" words by Irving Berlin, arrangement by Ethel Chambers

SPECIAL THANKS

Dr. Gus Chambers, Ph.D., and the entire Chambers family (who never complained while Mom took time off from her job as housewife to put on this show); our great teachers, Mrs. Murphy, Mr. Ball, Miss Ross, Mr. Gordon, and Mr. Schumann; our dedicated Janitor and Cross Walk Officer, "Mr. Jim" (congratulations on twenty-five years of service!); all the members of the Beverly Hills Board of Education (not to mention our hard-working mayor!); Lou the Good-Humor Man (the sound of your jingle kept our spirits high!); the generous folks at the Pan-American Poultry Company (you put the feathers in our bonnets!); and all the other special people, too numerous to thank individually by name, who helped out (you know who you are!). And, most of all, thanks to everyone who attends—without you, it wouldn't be possible!

show some school spirit." The little girl kept her head down and her mouth shut.

Unable to change Rebecca's mind, Mrs. Chambers turned to Hedy Lamarr's daughter, Denise Lee. After claiming that she wouldn't really mind being in the play, Denise gave the excuse that she wouldn't be available for rehearsals because she had lessons every day after school: horseback riding, tennis, flute, and ballet (classical ballet on Thursdays, water ballet on Fridays).

When the author-director then asked Melinda Marx to be in the show, Groucho's daughter responded that, while she had no interest in the part of Laughing Flower, she might consider playing Ponce de Leon.

"No," Mrs. Chambers explained, "I'm sorry. But you're a girl. Also, we have to take advantage of the fact that we have a very authentic Ponce de Leon costume, generously lent to us for the production by Mr. Ball. And I'm afraid, Melinda, that it's much too big for you even if you were a boy." The costume was a good fit for sixth-grader Frank Hardy, who was as tall for a boy as Mr. Ball was short for a man. Furthermore, the military posture and stentorian voice that he had developed by following the Arrow of Light in scouting made him right for the lead.

"I want to be Laughing Flower," Babs Cohen eagerly announced. "I can do it. My Dad's in show business too." Her father, a Beverly Hills dentist, had, she boasted, "filled one of Rita Hayworth's cavities" and worked on the teeth of Clayton Moore, George Reeves, Liberace, Pepe Pelotas, Jane Russell, and Debra Paget. He had, furthermore, capped one of Gilbert Roland's incisors when the actor broke that tooth by biting on a bullet while Gene Lockhart removed an Indian arrow from his leg in *Apache War Smoke.* That did it—Babs Cohen was chosen.

I was pleased that Donna Young replaced Babs because, as Laughing Flower, she would, during each rehearsal and finally in the show itself, have to hold hands with Lazy Dog, the Indian boy played by me. She was cute even with thick glasses. Although Lee Siegel would have been too shy to hold the hand of Donna Young in the school cafeteria or on the playground, Lazy Dog would, according to the script, boldly take Laughing Flower's hand in his in the Indian village. He would experience all the natural pleasure, if not the heathen passion, to which young Indians were accustomed, pleasures and passions forbidden to Jewish kids in Beverly Hills in 1952. Indian boys and girls, I was convinced, played together more intimately than we did. While it had been dangerously naughty for Clover Wiener and me to watch each other pee, Indians did that freely and mirthfully in the Great Forest and on the Great Plains. Even after they started wearing clothes at the age of seven or eight, they were not embarrassed by nakedness and not afraid of touching one another with the same fingers that they used to speak to each other in sign language. Gleefully, and entirely carefree, they stripped off their amply fringed buckskins to swim together, laughing and splashing in the lakes of the Land O Lakes. At night, after finding their way home through the darkness of strange woods by following the twigs that they had broken off on their way out earlier that day, they cuddled up together under warm bear-fur blankets in wigwams. I envied the unrestrained pleasures kids my age must have had in America before there were schools, before all the rules, before clocks, before bikes replaced ponies and telephones supplanted smoke signals, before there were separate toilets for boys and for girls, before poultry processing plants, Communists, or atomic bombs.

I landed the part of Lazy Dog by telling Mrs. Chambers about the costume that my parents had given me for Chanukah. I claimed it had been hand tailored by Apache women on an Indian reservation. I did, I thought, as I gazed at myselves in the mirrors on my mother's dressing room doors, look like the real thing, at least as authentic as any of the Indians who had attacked the stagecoach station in *Apache War Smoke.*

Wearing an Indian maiden's costume that her mother had, for the sake of the play, bought at Uncle Bernie's Toy Store, Donna was a perfect match for the well-dressed young Indian brave who was me. The moment I saw her at the first rehearsal in her little white moccasins, the word *mintutipo* came to mind. Even with her thick glasses, Laughing Flower was the handsomest of all the girls in the land of Beverly Hills, in the land of handsome girls. That she wore two feathers in her headband and a dress with lots of fringe on it made her the spitting image of what I thought Minnehaha must certainly have looked like as a child in the Land O Lakes (at least if she had worn glasses). Every time I caught sight of the knees below the fringed hem of her skirt, I saw little breasts, nippleless of course, but naked breasts nonetheless.

The best part of Donna's costume was the real mink neck stole that her mother had let her borrow to wear, not for rehearsals, but in the final show. Wrapped around her waist, it was fastened by clamping the mink's mouth onto its tail. The two black beads that were the mink's eyes glistened brightly under the stage lights.

With a large cross, cut out of cardboard and covered with silver glitter, hanging from a string around his neck, Jose "Cisco" Zutano was dressed as Padre Juan Sandiego in a white-collared black gown that he had once worn as a member of Our Lady of Guadalupe's Mexican

Children's Choir in Chula Vista. When his mother was hired by Becky Fine's parents as a live-in maid, Cisco had been enrolled in Ponce de Leon Elementary School. Having flunked each of his three years at the school, he was still in the third grade. But, being the age of a sixth-grader, and every bit as big as Frank Hardy, Cisco had supposed that he would make a good Ponce de Leon. He told Mrs. Chambers he wanted to wear the conquistador outfit that Mr. Ball was lending to us for the play.

Mrs. Chambers patiently explained that, for the part of Ponce, not only were there too many lines for a third-grader to possibly memorize, but there were also too many big words for a foreigner to pronounce. It was, however, because he was a native Spanish-speaker that she did cast Cisco as Padre Juan Sandiego. A little Spanish spoken, the author supposed, would give the production authenticity. Since she herself did not, however, know that language, Mrs. Chambers directed Cisco to improvise his lines: "At three different times in the play, Ponce will ask you, 'What do you think, Padre?' When he does so, just answer with whatever comes into your mind, as long as it's in Spanish, and as long as it's only one sentence."

Mrs. Chambers must have imagined that, since the majority of the children at Ponce de Leon Elementary School were Jewish, it would be appealing to have a rabbi as well as a Catholic priest come to the New World with Ponce de Leon. "Do any of you boys speak Hebrew?" Mrs. Chambers asked at the final casting session in the school auditorium. Fifth-grader Marty Mandel, my friend Chuck's older brother, raised his hand and got the part of Rabbi Jaime Diegostein. "When Ponce asks you the same question, Martin," Mrs. Chambers coached the boy, "when he says, 'And what about you, rabbi, what do you think?' that will be your cue. Answer him in Hebrew. And remember, only one sentence."

Although he didn't know very much Hebrew other than the Four Questions he had been made to recite each year at the family's Passover seder, Marty considered Yiddish close enough. He had been picking up some of that language since his grandmother, an old woman with a number tattooed on her arm, who spoke no English, had come to live with her son's family. The rabbi wore a yarmulke, a tallis, and, cut out of cardboard and covered with gold glitter, a large Star of David on a string around his neck. Although Marty had had a long black beard glued to his chin at each rehearsal, he was clean-shaven for the actual show. He claimed that Moshe, the Mandels' dachshund, had stolen the beard from his room and buried it somewhere in his backyard.

Next to the professionally costumed Ponce de Leon, the other conquistadors didn't look so genuine. Robbie Freeman wore a straw sombrero with an enormous brim upon which was embroidered the word "Tijuana"; Buzzy Graham had a powder blue sailing cap with a shiny black visor; and the others wore no hats at all. Indian headgear was easier to come by, thanks to Ricky Rubin, whose father, as owner of the Pan American Poultry Company in the San Fernando Valley, was pleased to supply Mrs. Chambers with all the turkey feathers she needed to festoon the headbands of every Indian in the show.

The play began in front of the curtain, right after the eighth-grade glee club had sung "The Star-Spangled Banner." Queen Isabella, played by my friend Larry "Spanky" Feinstein's older sister, Connie, wearing one of her mother's satin evening gowns (its top, Spanky informed me, stuffed with wads of toilet paper to fill out the bosom) and a tiara that her cousin Minnie had worn as the prom queen at Beverly Hills High School the year before, dispatched Ponce de Leon to the New World: "I have all the gold a woman could ever hope for. But I want something that gold cannot buy. Youth! There is, they say, a fountain in the New World that flows with a magic water. Those who drink from it, so the legend goes, stay young forever. Ah, youth! Ponce de Leon, bring me water from that Fountain of Youth, if it does in fact exist, and I shall give you gold!"

"Yes, your Majesty," Frank Hardy answered with a courtly bow and scoutly salute, and then, as soon as he and Connie Feinstein had exited to opposite sides of the stage, the curtain went up. Indians were dancing in front of a big tepee set against a backdrop of trees that had been painted the previous year for a production of *Hansel and Gretel.* Accompanied on the piano by Miss Stewart, the upper-school music teacher, and on the tom-tom by Mrs. Chambers, we sang the Indian war chant from *Annie Get Your Gun:*

Ook-a-looka
Gah-hay-la-kinka
La-ha-hoo-way
Hoo-way.

Although we suspected that the song, having been written by Irving Berlin, probably wasn't very authentic, we were confident that our war dance was because Mrs. Chambers had found the directions for its performance on a Nabisco Shredded Wheat Straight Arrow Injun-uity card: "Each brave holds a tomahawk in his right hand. Stealthy steps and furtive glances from side to side suggest an awareness of a lurking enemy. The step is simple. Touch the ground with the ball of the foot, then your heel. Shift your weight and repeat. Ball, heel." She was beat-

ing out the rhythm for us on her tom-tom. "Ball, heel, heel, ball. And now the other foot. Ball, heel, heel, ball. The Indian War Dance is easy to do. Isn't it? And it's fun! Heel, ball, ball, heel. And let's see those furtive glances!"

Our savage song and heathen dance routine were interrupted by the arrival of Ponce de Leon and his men. They said, "*Buenos dias,*" and we said, "*How.*"

"What do you think, Padre?" Frank Hardy asked Jose "Cisco" Zutano, and the priest answered, "*Oye Ponce, vamos a salir a buscar flete por ahi.*"

"And what do you think, Rabbi?" Frank Hardy asked Marty Mandel, and the rabbi answered, "*Gai tren zich.*"

After the Spaniards had sung "One Little, Two Little, Three Little Indians," we, the Indians, sang, "Hoy-yo, hoy-yo, hoy-yo," the lyrics of which were easy to memorize since they consisted only of the two syllables in the title.

Getting down to business and on with the plot, Ponce de Leon informed our leader, Big Chief Jumping Fox, that he was searching for the Fountain of Youth. He wanted to know if the legend of its magic waters was true. If it was, he had many things from over the Great Sea to trade for bottles of the rejuvenating beverage.

"Me need have pow-wow with tribal council," Jumping Fox informed the Spanish explorer. "Come back after lunch."

Big Doug Shulman had to memorize a lot of lines for the next scene, in which a sly Jumping Fox explained to his tribe that he would lie to the Pale Faces by telling them that, yes, the legend of the Fountain of Youth is true and that we owned the land on which it is situated. Then we'd sell them ordinary tap water. When Becky Fine, as Dancing Tree, Jumping Fox's wife, expressed her worry that the White Men might not believe the Indian chief, Big Doug divulged the rest of his crafty plan. Introducing the Pale Faces to his diminutive seven-year-old daughter, Laughing Flower, and her young playmate, little Lazy Dog, the chief would tell the Spaniards that we were over twenty-five years old and married. We looked like second-graders because we had been drinking the magic water since childhood. The chief and his squaw would themselves claim to be over eighty.

Donna and I were holding hands when the conquistadors returned to the stage. "Me live many moons," I nervously recited on cue, "but I drinkum heap good water. Keepum much young. This my squaw, Laughing Flower. These our papooses," I said, pointing to the Tonto doll and the Princess Summerfall Winterspring puppet in the papoose carriage that was strapped onto Donna Young's back.

That Donna had given birth to two of my children meant that, at least twice, I reflected, I must have done to her what was described in the fifth chapter of *In the Beginning: A Children's Book about Grown-up Love.* At least twice, my penis, having become "hard and stiff like a finger, but much bigger," had been inserted into her vagina, where it had "moved in and out with rapid motions until sperm-bearing fluid came out of it." I thought about that every time I saw Donna in her little fringed Indian maiden's skirt. I also thought about it when, sitting cross-legged in the tepee behind my red velvet couch, I'd rehearse my lines over and over again: "This my squaw, Laughing Flower. These our papooses." That Donna also carried in her arms a little teddy bear, wearing a little feathered headband, insinuated that Laughing Flower might have experienced what *In the Beginning* described as "one of the most beautiful experiences a Mother and Father can have together" with a grizzly bear in the Great Forest.

Believing that Donna and I were married and had children (even though, through the magic power of the Fountain, we looked no more than seven years old), Ponce de Leon offered the Indians various products from the civilized world in return for bottles of that water of Eternal Youth: Lincoln Logs, Slinkys, Play-Doh, a Paint-by-Number *Mona Lisa,* Monopoly, a Mr. Potato Head, and lots of Silly Putty.

In our first rehearsal, Jose "Cisco" Zutano asked Mrs. Chambers if they really had Silly Putty in Spain five hundred years ago. The author-director rolled her eyes and shook her head as she explained: "Of course they didn't. Silly Putty was not discovered until after World War II. That's why the audience will laugh. This play is a comedy, Jose, and the idea of Spanish explorers bringing Silly Putty to the New World is funny. But just because it's a comedy doesn't mean that it can't have a serious message about education."

After waiting a second or two for the audience's faint laughter over Ponce de Leon's offer to give Chief Jumping Fox Silly Putty in exchange for water from the Fountain of Youth to subside, the Indian chief exclaimed, "*Kowabanga,* Pale Face! We not wantum trinkets, we wantum White Man education. You teach Injun reading and writing. You give Red Man books, paper, pencils, erasers, pens, and ink. And we give you magic water of youth."

"What do you think, Padre?" Ponce de Leon asked, and the Christian answered, "*A Ponce le gusta que le dan candela por el culo.*"

"And what do you think, Rabbi?" Ponce de Leon asked, and the Jew answered, "*Kush in toches arein.*"

"You've got a deal, Chief," Ponce exclaimed as he shook Jumping Fox's hand. "But you better keep your part of the bargain."

"We not Indian givers, *Kimosabe!*" Chief Jumping Fox insisted, and then, after the Indians had cheered, howling as we slapped our hands over our mouths, he and his wife, Dancing Tree, led us in the song that Mrs. Chambers had composed for the occasion:

We used to use our time and brains
Hunting buffalo on these great plains.
But now we want to learn our a-b-c's
So we can read and write with ease.
Sitting in our tepees, in our feathered bonnets,
We'll be reading all of Shakespeare's sonnets.
Study hard Hiawatha, Cochise, and Geronimo,
'Cause the more you read, the more you'll know.
With reading, writing, and arithmetic, much to our relief,
You can become a doctor or lawyer, not just an Injun chief.
We want to gettum one heap-good school education,
So we won't have to live on some redskin reservation!

In the next scene, a blackboard on which the alphabet had been written was set up in front of our tepee. The conquistadors handed out books from which we read: "See Laughing Duck run. See Jumping Rain play. See Puffing Cat play. Come Spotted Dog, come!"

Having learned to read, the Indians studied the Bibles that Padre Juan Sandiego and Rabbi Jaime Diegostein had given to us. The Holy Scripture made us realize that we had been wrong to lie to Ponce de Leon about the Fountain of Youth. Sorry for what we had done, we confessed the truth to the Spaniards.

"So there is no Fountain of Youth!" Ponce de Leon sighed. It was Jumping Fox's cue to recite the author's message: "Yes, there is a Fountain of Youth, Ponce my friend. But it was you who gave it to us. The real Fountain of Youth is a good education. May all Americans in the future have the opportunity to slake their thirst for knowledge by partaking of its precious waters."

"What do you think, Padre?" Ponce asked the priest, and Cisco answered, "*Oye cabron, te la voy a meter de mira quien viene.*"

"And what do you think, Rabbi?" Ponce asked the rabbi, and Marty answered, "*Oder a klop, oder a fortz.*"

Because it was a comedy and not a true history, Mrs. Chambers didn't feel constrained to depict the actual battle during which the Indians slaughtered most of the Spaniards and wounded Ponce de Leon in the leg with a poison arrow, as a result of which he subsequently died a painful death in Cuba. Instead, right after Jumping Fox's uplifting monologue on education, the play ended with the conquistadors and the Indians joining hands to sing:

Let us swear allegiance to a land that's free,
Let us all be grateful for a land so fair,
As we raise our voices in a solemn prayer

In the middle of the song, Indian brave Ricky Rubin suddenly threw up. The projectile gush of vomit divided the singing cast into two groups: those children who knew that, no matter what happens, the show must go on; and those who did not. As those in the latter group, screaming, groaning, and crying out things like "Yuck!" "Puke!" "Help!" and "Ooooo, Ricky barfed!" ran from the stage, those in the former group continued to sing:

From the mountains, to the prairies,
To the oceans, white with foam . . .

Ricky was in that group. A real trooper, he wiped his mouth with his fringed sleeve and made it all the way through the last line, "God bless America, My home sweet home," before vomiting once more. Ricky Rubin, it turned out, had come down with mononucleosis. Naturally we all assumed that he must have kissed Babs Cohen.

No sooner had the curtain gone down than Mr. Ball rushed to Dr. Gus Chambers, PhD, with a translation of the three lines of Spanish delivered on stage by Padre Juan Sandiego. Everyone knew that, whatever they meant, they must have been very, very dirty because, that very afternoon, Jose "Cisco" Zutano was suspended from school. As a result of missing three weeks of class (one for each Spanish sentence), he flunked again that year.

If Mr. Ball had known Yiddish, Marty Mandel would have been punished as well. Marty's younger brother, my friend Chuck, translated for me after the show: "'Go fuck yourself,' 'Kiss my ass,' and 'It's either a turd or a fart.' My grandmother looks really sweet, but she's got a very dirty mouth."

Cisco wasn't the only person to get in trouble because of the play. Dancing Tree's parents, Mr. and Mrs. Milton Fine, also went to see the principal after the show. Offended by the name that Mrs. Chambers had chosen for the rabbi, they accused the playwright of anti-Semitism.

Apparently concerned that other Jewish parents might also have been upset, Dr. Chambers sent an open letter of apology to the parents of all students at Ponce de Leon Elementary School who he thought

were, or might be, Jewish.

I listened as my mother, after shaking a martini for my father, read the letter to him in our library-bar: "It was out of her genuine admiration for Jews, for all that you folks have accomplished in science, medicine, law, philosophy, education, finance, the arts, and show business, that Mrs. Chambers included a rabbi in the dramatis personae of her play, *Fountain of Youth!* The name 'Jaime,' chosen for that Spaniard of the Hebrew persuasion who came to America with Ponce de Leon, is a perfectly respectable Spanish name, meaning 'James' or 'Jim.' It should not be confused with 'Hymie' as a derogatory term for a Jew. When, in 1950, I was offered the job as principal of Ponce de Leon Elementary School, I was duly informed that I would be dealing with many Jewish boys and girls. I can, in all honesty, inform you that that was one of the things that made the position I now hold most attractive to me. Jews, both Mrs. Chambers and I have always believed, are among the most intelligent of all races. Let me take this opportunity to tell you something that many of you may not know about Mrs. Chambers. Serving on the Beverly Hills Board of Education, Mrs. Chambers has, for the past few months, been doing everything in her power to convince the Board to make both Rosh Hashanah and Yom Kippur legal school holidays at Ponce de Leon Elementary. It is Mrs. Chambers's dream that, in the years to come, Jewish students at our school will not feel that they are missing out on their education on those days when they must go to their synagogues to pray to their God. Mrs. Chambers and I hope that all of us can keep a sense of humor and put this little misunderstanding behind us so that we can get on with the serious business of educating the youngsters of Beverly Hills. Shalom and Mazel Tov!"

My father laughed as my mother refilled his martini glass.

With no more rehearsals for the "one performance only" play, I missed holding Donna Young's hand. But I'd remember the sensation (an incoherent but arousing rush and wave of pleasure, nervousness, ache, timidity, loneliness, misery, and delight) whenever, dressed in my Indian outfit, I looked in the mirror. I'd recollect it every time I folded my Land O Lakes butter package or broke off branches of the plants in the front yards of the homes on my street. And I'd recall it as Mrs. Murphy once again read *Hiawatha* to her second-grade class after lunch. With closed eyes, my head was cradled in arms folded over one another across the little desktop in the classroom of Ponce de Leon Elementary School in Beverly Hills. I could see Donna, the Arrow-maker's daughter, in her white moccasins and fringed dress, with a mink biting its tail around her waist. "Over wide and rushing rivers in my arms I bore the maiden; light I thought her as a feather, as the plume upon my head-gear; cleared the tangled pathway for her, bent aside the swaying branches, made at night a lodge of branches, and a bed with boughs of hemlock, and a fire before the doorway with the dry cones of the pine-tree." Over that fire, strictly following the Webelos Indian secret recipe, on the sharpened points of a forked branch, I carefully stuck a hot dog and roasted it for my lovely little squaw.

Nokomis was chanting ("From the sky the moon looked at them, filled the lodge with mystic splendors, whispered to them, 'O my children, day is restless, night is quiet'") when, all of a sudden, the shrill screech of the Conelrad Red Alert emergency alarm system opened my eyes and transformed old Nokomis back into Mrs. Murphy, turning the soothingly calm voice into one urgent and unnerving: "You know what that means, children. Duck and cover. This could be the real thing."

I fell to the floor under my desk with my hands over my neck in fear that the Russians were dropping an atomic bomb on Ponce de Leon Elementary School.

1953

Russia explodes a hydrogen bomb, the destruction by nuclear detonation of a facsimile of a typical American community is nationally televised, and AM radio dials are marked with triangles at 640 and 1240 to make Conelrad frequencies easy to find; Marilyn Monroe becomes the first woman to appear naked in *Playboy* magazine, and, in the cockpit of an F-86, Jacqueline Cochrane becomes the first woman to break the sound barrier; Jack Webb's *Red Nightmare* and Walt Disney's *Peter Pan* are released; Julius and Ethel Rosenberg are executed in Sing Sing, and Edmund Hillary and Tenzing Norgay conquer Mount Everest; *Sexual Behavior in the Human Female* by Dr. Alfred Kinsey and *Sex Harmony* by an unnamed "Sexologist, Marriage Counselor, Eugenicist, and Lecturer" are published; *Adventures of Superman* and *The Adventures of Ozzie and Harriet* premiere on television; my mother stars in the movie *Phantom from Space,* and Mr. Herbert Gordon, science and math teacher at Ponce de Leon Elementary School, is interviewed in the *Los Angeles Examiner* about his sighting of an Unidentified Flying Object over Beverly Hills; Dr. John H. Gibbon performs the first successful open heart surgery, and Beatrice Sugarman's tonsils are successfully removed by Dr. Maurice H. Feinstein.

She was on her knees, her delicate feet just inches from my face and the graceful curve of her buttocks within easy reach. My heart was pounding with lubbs of desire and dupps of fear as the civil defense siren howled the high-pitched Conelrad Red Alert emergency alarm signal that urgently announced imminent death. With scorn for the freedom and envy of the happiness that American children were so privileged to enjoy, the cold-blooded, iron-fisted Russians would drop a hydrogen bomb on Ponce de Leon Elementary School. As soon as Miss Ross commanded, "Duck and cover," we automatically fell to our knees, assuming a fetal position under our desks in an anticipatory rehearsal for the apocalypse. Our hands were clasped over our necks.

Because my desk was right behind Beatrice Sugarman's, I almost looked forward to Red Alert. Although I don't recall her face as well as I remember her little tushy, she was, as far as I was concerned at the time, the cutest girl in the entire free world, cuter even than Donna Young, Clover Wiener, Gretel Woodcutter, or Eve W——. I gazed in awe at the diminutive posterior, softly swathed in pastel-pink cotton and raised up as if in presentation to me. It was love at first sight.

As Beatrice Sugarman obediently dove to the floor, she was usually demure enough in the face of mass destruction to remember to tuck her dress under her thighs, modestly concealing the anatomical feature that distinguished girls from boys, her from me. Occasionally, however, I'd be blessed by the carelessness of her haste with a glimpse, fleeting but vivid, of white underpants. I was familiar with such undies from long lucubrations over the 1953 Sears, Roebuck catalog, the girls' underwear section of which had as its only competition for my fascination those pages that unabashedly showed the conical-cupped brassieres and open-bottomed girdles that, if only the bomb didn't get us, Beatrice would someday wear. By that time I would have switched from Jockeys to boxer shorts and then, perhaps, we might loll about together, garbed for love in mail-order men's and women's underclothing.

From where the tips of her shoes touched, the soles formed a dainty V out to the spread heels. Sometimes her feet wiggled. Maybe she was nervous, frightened of Communism, radioactive fallout, or death. Or maybe she just had to pee. Or was it possible that little Beatrice Sugarman already knew how to be seductive?

A pale mole on her right calf, just above the turned-over top of her white sock, was dot number one on a connect-the-dots game, the starting place from which unseen things could be made to take shape.

"This could be the real thing," Miss Ross ominously insisted as she took her regimental command post in the classroom doorway. I thought it might really be that real thing each of the several times that Clover Wiener was absent on a Red Alert day—her mother, being a Communist agent (and thus privy to the knowledge of when the bomb was going to be dropped on Beverly Hills), would, in that event, certainly leave town with Myron Spellman and probably take her daughter with her.

If the hydrogen bomb was indeed falling on Ponce de Leon Elementary School, I realized, I would die without ever having examined that special and ineffable part of a girl that so fascinated me. A curiosity, indistinguishable from longing, that had been kindled by the description of "the female sexual apparatus" in chapter 4 of *In the Beginning* ("Sugar and Spice and All That's Nice"), was stoked by the close-up of Beatrice Sugarman's raised buttocks and fanned by her wiggling heels during Red Alert. If this truly was the end, I asked myself, what difference would it make if I just reached out and touched it? All I needed to do was muster the courage to free a hand from its perch on my neck. Like a bird to the crumb, it would hop to the little mole. From there it would nestle into the cozy crevice between the little calves, then squirm forward toward the knees and beyond, up under the soft pink fabric to squeeze in between closed thighs, higher and higher, getting warmer and warmer, all the way up and into the creviced nest, the place of birth, the origin of the world.

Sex, as the instinctual drive to perpetuate life through reproduction in pleasure, embedded and, in various degrees, awakened in each of the eight-year-old children who were curled up fetus-like, was being challenged during each Red Alert by the dark, timeless, obdurate ultimacy of oblivion. It was under my desk in 1953, I think, that I first became conscious of death. The school year had begun with an announcement of it: "Mrs. Murphy died this summer of a heart attack," Miss Ross reported on the first day of class. "Ponce de Leon's beloved second-grade teacher will be remembered and missed." I did remember her, how she had read to us and how, with her mellifluous voice, old Nokomis had told Hiawatha about the Death-Dance of the spirits: "In the frosty night of Winter," she had shown him, "the broad white road in heaven, pathway of the ghosts, the shadows, running straight across the heavens." My friend Neezer died that year too. "Sweet Jesus!" Sally May Carter exclaimed as she broke the news. "Old Neezer's jubilatin' up above tonight!" My friend Chuck Mandel's grandmother, the old woman with the dirty Yiddish words in her mouth and the blue number tattooed on her arm, also died; and so did Ricky Rubin's dad, the "Poultry King of the San Fernando Valley." As the siren shrieked, I understood that my grandparents, Uncle Joe, and both my mother and my father were also going to die someday. And so, I deduced, would I. And since I was going to die, I reasoned, I might as well reach up under Beatrice Sugarman's dress. If this was the end, I told myself, Beatrice probably, with the blinding flash and deafening blast of the bomb, and a monstrous mushroom of gray cloud forming over Beverly Hills, would not even notice, let alone care.

On the other hand, I reflected, if I did rashly allow myself to succumb to temptation, and Red Alert turned out, as it always had before, to be only a drill and not the real thing, I'd be in big, big trouble. If my impetuous hand were given free rein and the hydrogen bomb did not destroy us all, Beatrice Sugarman would probably scream and report me to the teacher. The most dreaded of punishments would then be mine. Miss Ross would send me to the principal's office, and there Dr. Gus Chambers, PhD, would menacingly snarl, "Lee Siegel, this will go on your record!"

Convinced, as we all were, that there was an immutable chronicle of our behavior that, though kept as confidential from us as our IQ scores, followed us for the rest of our lives, I was certain that, if I did what I so yearned to do and we did not all die, my indecent transgression would be preserved forever. I wouldn't be able to get into college or join the army. One day a prospective employer, looking up from my record, across his desk, and into my eyes, would solemnly inform me: "Mr. Siegel, we do not hire your kind here." No woman, at least not the sort of responsible citizen that the well-behaved Beatrice Sugarman was sure to become, would want to marry an uneducated and unemployed man who had not served the United States of America in the battle against the Red Menace. And if I couldn't find anyone to marry me, I might never in my entire life have the opportunity to come to know and love, inside and out, that wondrous thing that was cached beneath Beatrice Sugarman's pink dress and white underpants—the *vagina,* about which I had learned so many interesting things from *In the Beginning:* "At first glance, it doesn't look like very much is there. But there is, in fact, a lot more to a girl's reproductive system than meets the eye." It was amazing to contemplate the fact that there was one hidden under the clothes, in between the legs, of every little girl and every grown-up woman in the whole world. Even Miss Ross had one and—strange but true, believe it or not—so did Mamie Eisenhower! And so, I learned from *Confidential* magazine, did Christine Jorgensen, thanks to medical science.

As the Conelrad siren blasts persisted, I was distracted from thoughts of death, transfixed and transported by the sublime buttocks before which I bowed in reverent obeisance, not daring to do what I itched to do. I could not help but be peeved that the postman had not yet delivered my "Amazing X-Ray Eye-Glasses."

I had clipped the coupon and sent in a dollar bill (to cover the "99¢") to Gags Galore for the glasses that had been advertised on one of the back pages of the issue of *Confidential* that Larry "Spanky" Feinstein, my friend from Cub Scouts, had stolen from his Uncle Mannie. "What this Country needs is a Good Laugh," the coupon pointed out, "And Gags Galore is where to get It!" The magazine itself contained some shocking stuff. After studying the story about Christine Jorgensen, with Spanky and Little Mike Shulman sitting on either side of me on the red couch in my room, I read the testimony of a high school girl claiming that movie star Pepe Pelotas had autographed her underpants. With a naughty smile, the proud teenager held the inscribed panties up for the photographer.

"You Won't Believe Your Eyes!" the advertisement for the glasses promised: "See Through Clothes! Discover the Naked Truth! A Scientific Wonder and Lots of Fun Too! They're Magic! Guaranteed!" Once the X-ray spectacles arrived, even if I didn't get to actually touch the bodily part in question, I'd at least be able to clearly see it through the pink dress and white panties. If they worked as well as the whoopee cushion that I had ordered at the same cost from the same company, with a coupon from the same magazine, I'd be as happy as Clark Kent must have been when he looked on as Lois Lane, unaware of the ocular powers of the seemingly mild-mannered reporter, turned her back to him to bend over and pick up a pencil that had rolled off Clark's desk.

Weeks had gone by and they still hadn't arrived. Hoping, since Gags Galore claimed the glasses were "magic," that they might also be sold at the Hollywood Magic Shop, I begged my mother to take me there. Disappointed to discover that they were all sold out of X-ray glasses, I asked my mother to buy the arrow which, with a wire loop replacing the center of its shaft, could be worn in such a way as to make me look like a victim of one of the Indian attacks in *Apache War Smoke.* Walking back to the car along Hollywood Boulevard with an arrow sticking through my head, I wondered if any of the people on the street who were wearing glasses could see my mother and me naked.

That year, no doubt because of the enthusiasm with which I had beseeched my mother to take me to the Hollywood Magic Shop, I was given Professor Mysto's Hocus Pocus Magic Set for Chanukah, along with a magician's costume—a black top hat and cape, white gloves, and a magic wand—from FAO Schwarz in New York. It seemed appropriate since the festival celebrates a magic trick wherein oil enough for only one day burned for eight. My father proudly told me that "Houdini was a Jew."

I had seen the great Professor Mysto himself saw a woman in half with an electric buzz saw on Ed Sullivan's *Toast of the Town.* The good part was that he had been able to put her back together. If I could saw Beatrice Sugarman in half, I mused, not only would that impress her, but it would give me the opportunity, before putting her back together, to sneak off with her lower half and inspect it without her upper half knowing about it.

Although my magic set did not come with either a buzz saw or X-ray glasses, it did include Professor Mysto's Magic Finger Chopper, a little guillotine with a blade that sliced across two holes, one for a finger and one for a cigarette. When I raised the blade and slammed it down, it seemed to pass right through my finger, miraculously leaving that appendage intact, before slicing the cigarette in half. Practicing with it, I must have gone through more than a pack a day of my father's Viceroys.

My mother loved the trick no matter how many times I showed it to her. I think Sally May Carter did too, even though every time I did it, she'd protest: "Shit boy, don't scare Mama Sally like that. One of these days you gonna mess up and cut that finger off!"

I learned that women like to be fooled more than boys do. When I took my finger chopper next door to show Little Mike Shulman the trick, his older brother, Big Doug, after making fun of my costume ("You look like Dracula"), sneered: "That's stupid. Why don't you put your dick in it? That would make it a lot better." And then Big Doug told us a joke: "So there was this guy who worked as a cook at a restaurant. And one night he comes home and tells his wife that he's been fired: 'The boss came into the kitchen and caught me sticking my dick in the salami slicer.' 'Oh, God,' his wife screamed, 'is your dick okay?' 'Sure,' he told her; and then she asked him, 'But what about the salami slicer?' And the guy answers, 'The boss fired her too!' Get it?"

Words, no less than anything in Professor Mysto's Hocus Pocus Magic Set, I understood, could be used to play tricks and do magic, to cause wonder and laughter. Of all the gimmicks in the kit, next to my finger chopper, I best liked Professor Mysto's Amazing Color Vision Mental Miracle, a cube with a different color on each of its six sides. I could guess which color faced up in the covered box in which the person I was fooling had placed it: "Think of that color. Concentrate," I'd say, to make sure that they would think I was determining that color through mentalism rather than X-ray vision. While Larry "Spanky" Feinstein said he thought the trick was stupid and claimed that he knew how I did it, my mother and Sally May Carter repeatedly seemed to be amazed. "Shit, boy," Sally said with an incredulous laugh, "you read my mind! How'd you do that?"

I liked it when a woman thought I could divine her thoughts. If I had been a little less shy around Beatrice Sugarman, I would have shown the Amazing Color Vision Mental Miracle to her. But even more than wanting her to think that I could read her mind, I wanted to imagine that I really had that power. Kneeling down behind her during Red Alert, I always wondered what she was thinking. Could it be about me or just about death? I wanted to see what was on her mind as much as what was under her dress.

It had been over a month since I had sent away for the X-ray glasses from Gags Galore, and they still hadn't been delivered. Until they arrived, I needed to resort to imagination, a faculty that I would strive to develop and exercise for the rest of my life in matters of love. Since imagination relies on empirical references in the phenomenal world, external realities to mold, enhance, and embellish into inner visions, I required vivid representations of the real thing. Thus I clipped another coupon from *Confidential,* filled it out, and sent it off with three dollar bills for the purchase of *Sex Harmony,* a book with "over 100 graphic illustrations that reveal all. Many of these realistic and detailed pictures were formerly available only to members of the medical and legal professions. Study and grope in the dark no longer!" The ad copy made the tome irresistible:

> This scientific no-holes-barred book will provide you with the key to open the door to a love-filled life. Sexual ignorance leads to fear, worry, disease and shame. Avoid embarrassment on your honeymoon! Be a master in the bedroom and enjoy your life more than you've ever dreamed of! Endow yourself with the knowledge of SEX HARMONY now! All the nuts and bolts of SEX are explained down to the last detail in a language that anyone can easily understand. Over ¼ million copies have already been sold to people just like you! Complete Satisfaction Guaranteed.

The "Partial Table of Contents" was promising: "The Honeymoon. SEX Organs. SEX Secrets of Science. Healthy Mating. SEX and Sanity. Venereal Disease. Eugenics."

Noting that the candid and uncensored book could not be sold to minors, the ad further demanded that customers "State age when ordering." Not quite sure at what age I'd cease to be a minor, I claimed, just to be on the safe side, that I was forty-five years old, my father's age at the time. I also used his name: Dr. Lee Siegel, MD. Since Sally put the mail in the butler's pantry each day, I'd check there first thing after school so that I could intercept it before my father arrived home. I didn't want *Sex Harmony* to fall into the wrong hands.

The arrival of the book compensated somewhat for the no-show on the X-ray glasses. Since it was the exact same size as my half-read copy of *Treasure Island,* I was able to take the cover off the latter to wrap as a disguise around *Sex Harmony.* It wasn't because my parents were in any way puritanical that I concealed my guide to sexual mastery; but for anything to be really thrilling, it had to be illicit.

None of the adventures aboard the *Hispaniola* were nearly as exciting as those I had in bed each night with a flashlight illuminating the pages of *Sex Harmony.* I explored uncharted regions and discovered there treasures the likes of which young Jim Hawkins never dreamed. Just to make sure my parents didn't find it, I hid it, along with a Land O Lakes butter package, inside the stuffing of the red velvet couch in my room. No longer afraid that my mother would read *Once upon a Time: Children's Best Loved Tales* to me, I took that book out of my hiding place and put it on a shelf in my brother's room. I figured the three-year-old was ready to be terrified by "Hansel and Gretel."

I don't know who authored *Sex Harmony,* but he (the unnamed expert identified on the cover as a "World-Renowned Sexologist, Marriage Counselor, Eugenicist, and Lecturer") was, as far as I was concerned, a much better writer than Robert Louis Stevenson in terms of content, form, and style. Reading his discursive poetry out loud to myself (in whispers so that my parents wouldn't discover that I wasn't yet asleep), I especially relished "The Vulva," the first section of chapter 2, "SEX Organs," wherein I learned that

> The two elongated folds of flesh that run down and back from the soft, hair-covered, round mound of fatty tissue over the pubic bone are known as the Major Lips. Toward the anus the Major Lips flatten out to merge with the surrounding flesh. The space between the Major Lips becomes visible only when the lips are parted (SEE FIGURE 13).

I'd repeat the words "Major Lips, Major Lips, Major Lips" as I turned eagerly to figure 13. After staring at it for a bit, I'd flip back, leaving a finger to mark the page with the diagram for quick return, to review and ponder the fantastic description of the Minor Lips that culminated in crucial information: "By spreading apart these pinkish folds of skin, we can see the vaginal orifice, into which the husband will insert his penis at the appropriate time." I learned that the "anus, which is exactly the same in size, shape and function for both men and women, though located in close proximity to the genitals, is completely separate from them. In normal people, the anus, which belongs to the Digestive System, plays no role in achieving SEX HARMONY."

In the Beginning had completely ignored the anus and had not even mentioned the fantastic anatomical button that I read about in *Sex Harmony:*

> Any man who wants to become a master in the bedroom must be ready and willing to acquaint himself with the oft-ignored clitoris. It can play a dramatic part in achieving SEX HARMONY. The clitoris is to be found inside the Major Lips, where the Minor Lips meet just above the urethra (the hole used by women for urination). A knowledge of the clitoris, both what it is and how it works, will come in handy on the honeymoon. Cognizance of the clitoris separates the men from the boys in the bedroom.

The text itself was of a higher quality than its black-and-white illustrations, which were still more interesting than even the color renderings of Long John Silver in my coverless copy of *Treasure Island.* While *Sex Harmony* had literary power, I turned for fine art to a monograph I had discovered among the medical books shelved in my parents' library-bar: *The Reproductive System,* by Dr. Frank G. Lafleur, MD. Although the prose was unintelligible, the artwork was as good as anything my mother, in her attempts to cultivate her child's aesthetic sensibilities, had ever shown me in *Masterpieces of the Louvre.* I did, however, quite like the nude women in that book. I was particularly intrigued by a painting of "Cupid and Psyche," the same couple, I realized, that was depicted on the cover of *In the Beginning: A Children's Book about Grown-up Love:* a winged boy, completely naked, his eyes closed, was kissing a young girl, naked except for the diaphanous wrap around her glowing loins; his hand rested on her chest, just above her bare breast, and the look upon her face—especially the fixed gaze—expressed, I supposed, what real love felt like. But that was just art, and I was interested in the real thing.

In the Beginning was, by its own admission, for kids; *Sex Harmony* was obviously for amateurs; but *The Reproductive System* was for professionals. Unlike *Sex Harmony,* "written in a language that anyone can easily understand," *The Reproductive System* had been composed in a technical tongue with an obscure nomenclature that was difficult even to pronounce: *labia majora, labia minora, mons pubis, glans clitoridis, perineum, rima pudendi, urethra muliebris, Bartholin's glands.* Who, I could not help but wonder, was Bartholin, and what did he do to be so honored as to have things in the vulva named after him?

I was far more compelled by the vulva than by the deep anatomy as illuminated in any of my textual and visual sources. Once you got inside, I had already learned from *In the Beginning,* girls weren't so very different from mice, rabbits, dogs, cats, or even elephants and whales. The graphic indications in both *Sex Harmony* and *The Reproductive System* of all the stuff hidden within women's bodies were made all the more uninviting by the fact that the internal female sex organs were necessarily represented in illustrations of either cross-sections of the female pelvis or of organs removed from the body and on their own. The former insinuated a woman sliced in half from the top of her head down to her crotch, the latter, a woman cut open and eviscerated. The uterus seemed to float in midair, like a headless bird held aloft by pulpy wings in which its lumpy eyeballs, the so-called ovaries, were embedded. All that was left of the artist's model was laid out upon a cold metal dissection table in a laboratory, perfumed with formaldehyde. I tried not to think about it.

But the sweetly scented models for the illustrations of the healthy vulvas so masterfully rendered and gorgeously colored by Dr. Frank G. Lafleur, MD, in *The Reproductive System* were whole, alive, and well, lying comfortably on their backs, probably on soft warm blankets, with their legs spread as their sumptuous vulvas proudly posed for their portraits. I liked thinking about it: naked women from the Louvre provided me with images of their bodies, and I matched up the face of Psyche with my favorite painting in the book of a normal, healthy and happy vulva.

I imagined a white-robed Dr. Frank G. Lafleur, MD, throat mirror over his forehead and stethoscope around his neck, with a palette of oil paints in one hand (glistening blobs of pink, crimson, scarlet, vermilion, puce, primrose, madder, magenta, some white for the highlights, and a little umber for shading), extending his other hand and raising a thumb to check proportions as he scrutinized the winsome vulva, the smile of which was so much more enigmatic than that of Mona Lisa in *Masterpieces of the Louvre.*

Eighth-graders at Ponce de Leon Elementary School were required to do a science project; the winner's project would be entered in competition at the annual California State Science Fair. Five years ahead of time, an ample period for in-depth experimental research, I was determined to investigate "The Vulva." Because my father was a doctor, I supposed that school officials would allow it. I'd get a note of authorization from him, even if I had to forge it, to assure the likes of Dr. Chambers and Mr. Gordon that my project wasn't dirty: "Since Lee plans to go to medical school and become a physician like me when he grows up, work on the vulva will prepare him for the future. I am confident that my son is mature enough to handle the vulva." I'd be gynecology's foremost child prodigy. Maybe I would, in my research, even discover something. Near Bartholin's glands there might someday be Siegel's things: glands, ducts, membranes, or even little lips that nobody else had ever noticed.

In order to view the fantastic vulva in the same position that Beatrice Sugarman's was during Red Alert, I'd turn the medical book upside down so that the thighs in the illustration reached downward, positioning the anus on top and the mons pubis on the bottom, with the vaginal orifice above the clitoris.

The specific pages of *The Reproductive System* that proved most helpful to me in my effort to envision Beatrice Sugarman's vulva were the

ones on which hymens were featured. The chapter in *Sex Harmony* on "The Honeymoon" had convinced me that Beatrice Sugarman had one
 of her own.

Science has yet to determine the physiological function of this delicate membrane at the threshold into the vagina proper that has, since the dawn of civilization, been highly prized as evidence of virginity. Lest the sorts of suspicions arise that are sure to subvert SEX HARMONY and thus ruin a marriage and with it two lives, the modern groom should keep in mind that the absence of a hymen is not irrefutable proof of prior sexual activities on the part of his blushing bride. Many a hymen has been innocently ruptured by such nonsexual activities as horseback riding, cycling, and gymnastics.

Before reading the book, I had only encountered the word for the highly prized evidence of the virginity of Beatrice Sugarman (who, to the best of my knowledge, owned neither a horse nor a bicycle nor parallel bars) as a proper noun—Hymen Weinstein was the name of the rabbi at our synagogue, Temple Beth Israel. Grateful that my parents hadn't decided to name me after the venerable Jewish clergyman, I couldn't help but feel sorry for him, certain as I was that he must have been mercilessly teased as a child once his peers discovered, as I just had, the anatomical meaning of *hymen*. *Hymen* was even dirtier than *wiener*.

While I was exposed to the scientific terminology of female reproductive anatomy by Dr. Frank G. Lafleur, MD, and had a layman's sense of what was what from *Sex Harmony,* I acquired the more earthy vernacular lingo from Jose "Cisco" Zutano, the fatherless son of a Mexican maid-in-residence at the home of Becky Fine's parents in Beverly Hills. Having flunked the third grade three times, this twelve-year-old in a class of eight-year-olds knew all the words for the female sexual apparatus that had been excluded from the dictionary. Although his reading and writing skills weren't very well developed, he knew more than any of us about life, or at least about the act which was, I knew, responsible for creating life.

Although Cisco referred to the hymen as a *cherry,* the rest of the female reproductive system, both the vulva and the vagina, the major and minor lips, the clitoris and even Bartholin's glands, indeed the whole shebang, the entire kit and caboodle, were lumped together into *cunt, twat, pussy, snatch,* or *box*. He boasted that there were ten times as many words for it in Spanish than in English (*tonto, raja, bacalao, chocho, panocha, nido, coño, concha, conejo,* and *almeja,* to name but a few), more terms for it in his native tongue than there were words for "arrow" in Apache. Mexicans knew a lot more about it, and what to do with it, than anyone else. A gringo may have come up with the polio vaccine, Cisco conceded, only to brag that it was a Mexican who discovered Spanish fly.

I relied on Cisco for a critical and analytic gloss on my reading of *Sex Harmony.* Even though it was supposedly in "a language that anyone can easily understand," there were many terms, and indeed concepts, that I did not comprehend. When I asked Cisco if he knew what *eugenics,* the subject of the final and most esoteric chapter in *Sex Harmony,* was, the south-of-the-border savant confidently answered, "Fucking girls."

Cisco had explained *tampon* earlier that year when, after finding one in a drawer in my parents' bathroom and stealing it, I showed it to him, trying to impress him with a claim that it was a stick of dynamite. "That's not dynamite," he laughed condescendingly. "It's what women stick up their butts after they have sex." I subsequently hid the tampon inside the red velvet couch.

Following the example of my teacher, I started using *cunt* and *twat,* Cisco's two favorite words for what many of my third-grade peers were still calling a girl's *weewee* or *peepee.*

"Twat did you say?" seventh-grader Big Doug Shulman said to me and his little brother one day. "I cunt hear you! Get it?" After hearing that joke, *cunt* insinuated to me an inability to do something, and *twat* implied a lack of knowledge. I reverted to the words *vagina* and *vulva* until, several weeks later, Big Doug told another joke: "Do you know what happens to a girl who sits on the toilet seat too long?" he asked. Little Mike and I had to confess that we didn't. "She gets ring around the rosie," Big Doug laughed: "Get it?" Yes, I got it, and ever after that there was a rose under Beatrice Sugarman's dress during Red Alert, a rosy pink rosebud, fragrant and moist with morning dew. There was nothing either clinical or vulgar about it. Her rose by any other name (including *female sexual apparatus, vagina, vulva, cunt, twat, pussy, snatch, box,* or even *peepee* or *weewee,* not to mention all the words for it in Spanish) was still a rose. Its calyx, the major lips around the soft petals of minor lips that puckered into the tender bud that would someday open gloriously wide into a voluptuous crimson blossom exuding luscious honeys and perfumes of sugar and spice and all that's nice.

Cisco traded with me, taking my whoopee cushion from Gags Galore in exchange for his photograph of a naked woman from Tijuana. She had enormous floppy breasts with dark, saucer-sized nipples and a thick shrub of black pubic hair that certainly concealed not a tiny rosebud but rather a large panicle of the rubbery, greenish-white flowers of the Mexican yucca, the plant that rhymed, if you subtracted the final vowel, with the dirtiest word in the English language, the word that Cisco used to translate the first word of the inscription on the illicit photo: "*Chinga Mi Coño!*" I hid the photo with the other illicit materials inside my couch-safe.

Like the heroic bandito after whom he had nicknamed himself, Cisco took delight in challenging repressive rules for social behavior as dictated by strict agents of established authority. He was the sort of intractable rascal who champions individual freedom without even thinking about it because he cannot do otherwise. He was a natural born troublemaker, as careless in his behavior as he was fastidious in combing his hair into a swanky pompadour before the mirror in the boys' bathroom. I loved to watch him do that. Nothing ever seemed to bother him or shake his optimism. He took nothing seriously. I supposed that he probably wasn't even afraid of the hydrogen bomb. A clown by nature and a *pachuco* by aspiration, he couldn't resist putting the whoopee cushion on Miss Ross's chair.

Sighting it before she had even started to sit down, the teacher glowered as she held the inflated rubber bag aloft: "Who does this belong to?" she demanded. All of us sat still and silent. If the person responsible would come to her after school and confess to the crime, there would be leniency. But if no one came forward, there would be an investigation: "And when I find out who did it, I shall report it to Dr. Chambers and it will go on your record." Having once owned the item in question, I worried that Miss Ross might call in the Beverly Hills police or even the FBI and that they would discover my fingerprints on it. J. Edgar Hoover might contact Gags Galore for a documented account of the year's mail-order whoopee cushion sales. Even if that happened and I was accused of the malfeasance, I swore to myself, I wouldn't snitch on Cisco. I'd try to keep my mouth shut, take the blame like a man, letting it go on official record for the rest of my entire life that I had once put a whoopee cushion on a schoolteacher's chair. I felt I owed that to Cisco for all that he had taught me. I was beginning to develop a sense of morality.

No doubt disappointed by the failure of the whoopee cushion prank, the intrepidly mischievous Cisco tried to cause the kids crouched down under their desks around him during Red Alert to break into seditious laughter by making farting sounds with his mouth. Miss Ross shouted over the scream of the siren: "Who's doing that? Stop doing that! This could be the real thing!"

Cisco had probably counted on it that, until the drill was over, she wouldn't budge from her place in the doorway, the position established for teachers by nationally codified procedures for civil defense. But in her zeal to nab the culprit and deal with such flagrant misbehavior, Miss Ross risked life and limb by relinquishing her post. After identifying Cisco, she quickly returned to the doorway, waited for the siren to stop, and then sent my amigo to the dreaded office of the principal, Dr. Gus Chambers, PhD. Not that Cisco cared, but he was suspended from school for a week for making farting sounds during an official Conelrad Red Alert civil defense drill. He had the longest record at Ponce de Leon Elementary School.

From a required in-class reading of *Alert Today, Alive Tomorrow,* a pamphlet on how to survive nuclear warfare published by the United States Department of Defense, I had learned that doorways were the safest place to stand during an attack. Thus I assumed that if and when the bomb landed on Ponce de Leon Elementary School, the teachers would all survive, standing in the many doorways of the remaining framework of the classrooms on both the ground and upper floors. They would gaze down on the rubble under which all of the children would be buried, and Miss Ross would no doubt wave to Mr. Gordon in his doorway down the hall. Rumor had it that there was something going on between them.

Just as they had come the previous year to Mrs. Murphy's class, Miss Minnette, the upper-school home economics teacher, and Mr. Gordon, the sixth- and seventh-grade science and math teacher, visited Miss Ross's class to recruit more Brownies and more Cub Scouts. It was, Mr. Gordon said, not merely something we as children could do for ourselves, for all the fun we'd have and the great things we'd learn, but also, by joining scouts we could help our country, the Land of Liberty, by doing our share in the campaign against the Red Menace. "In camps behind the Iron Curtain, youngsters no older than yourselves are currently being trained to talk, dress, and act like American boys and girls," Mr. Gordon divulged, Frank Hardy in a Boy Scout uniform standing at attention at his side. "They will be used to infiltrate our society for purposes of espionage and then subversion. They'll be in our schools and in our churches, mingling with you at the ballpark and soda fountain. As scouts you will be trained to identify these young Communist spies. Some of them may already be among us." Miss Minnette (with Larry "Spanky" Feinstein's older sister, Connie, in a Girl Scout uniform standing at attention at her side) stared intently at Jose "Cisco" Zutano as Mr. Gordon continued his exposé on the presence of spies in American elementary schools. The stare insinuated a suspicion that the older boy might be a Communist. He had, after all, misbehaved during Red Alert. He was from a foreign country. And why didn't he have a father?

Cisco was, in fact, guilty of spying, but not the kind Mr. Gordon had spoken about. From the maintenance shed near the parking lot behind the school, where Cisco often hid to smoke Lucky Strikes, he had, he swore to God and the blessed Virgin, seen Mr. Gordon walk Miss Ross to her car after school: "First he kissed her. Then he grabbed her ass. And then he goosed her!"

"What did she do?" I asked in astonishment.

"She smiled," he confided. "She liked it. She liked it a lot."

I reckoned that, as a science teacher, Mr. Gordon probably knew the technical terms for all the parts of Miss Ross's reproductive organ, inside and out, but had he ever seen it? Or touched it? Did Miss Ross, I wondered, have a hymen?

Whenever our teacher sharpened a pencil, turning her back to the class, one hand holding the pencil and the other turning the handle on the sharpener affixed to the wall at the side of the blackboard, her ample keister, presumably held firm by a Sears, Roebuck open-bottomed girdle, would swivel vigorously about. A keister, incidentally, was, in my rapidly increasing anatomical vocabulary, what a tushy became when it grew up.

"Jack Webb, the star of *Dragnet,*" Chief Akela (as Mr. Gordon insisted on being hailed at the monthly convocations of pack 48) would be sure to announce before the closing ceremony of each of those meetings, "will be our special guest speaker next month. He will talk to us about the Communist threat and what we can do about it." The next meeting would inevitably begin with an apology: "I'm sorry, Cubs," Chief Akela would say, "but Mr. Webb can't be here tonight. Something very important came up for him at the last moment. But he'll be here next month." And then our cubmaster would introduce whoever it was who would be addressing us on the television star's behalf. One night, actor and Ponce de Leon's eighth-grade history and Spanish teacher, Mr. Ball, who had been lucky enough to be cast as a Mexican narcotics dealer in an episode of *Dragnet,* spoke candidly about his experiences working with Mr. Webb. The next month, when once again Jack Webb didn't show, Mr. Ball, who had played a small part in *I Married a Communist,* told us what it was like to make a movie about Communism. "Mr. J. Edgar Hoover, the director of the Federal Bureau of Investigation himself, visited the set one day," Mr. Ball proudly proclaimed, "and I had the great honor and privilege of shaking his hand."

We were informed that Ben Alexander, who played Officer Frank

Smith, Sergeant Joe Friday's partner on *Dragnet,* had solemnly promised Mr. Ball that he would come to our next meeting if, once again, Jack Webb had to cancel. We had waited over an hour for either Alexander or Webb to show up before Chief Akela, finally giving up hope, led us in the songs that officially concluded each assembly of pack 48: "Cub Scouting We Will Go," "Webelos Are We," "My Country 'Tis of Thee," and "The Star-Spangled Banner."

When Ricky Rubin's father died, Chuck Mandel's mother took over for Mrs. Rubin as our den mother. That she was an Orthodox Jew made our den meetings even worse than the pack meetings. The customary den snack was sure to be terrible—Chuck was the only Cub among us who could stomach either his mother's chopped liver or her carrot kugel. He was also the only boy who sang along with his mother as, in vain, she tried to teach us to sing "Cub Scouting We Will Go" in Yiddish. "Except for the little brims, your Cub Scout caps look just like yarmulkes—*es gefelt mir!*" Mrs. Mandel said with enthusiastic good cheer as we arrived at the destination of the year's first field trip—an Orthodox synagogue on Fairfax Boulevard. In preparation for Chanukah, we had to make little dreidels out of clay. And, of course, at the next den meeting, when they were dry and ready, dreidel we had to play. That game, all of us except for Chuck felt, had nothing on Monopoly or Checkers. It wasn't even as good as Chutes and Ladders.

Chief Akela had issued a regulation that all den meetings had to close with "The Living Circle." He had taught us how to perform the sacred Webelos ritual during one of the many pack meetings while we waited for Jack Webb: "Hold out your left hand with the palm down and the thumb out. Hold the thumb of the boy on your left to form a circle. Hold up your right hand in the Cub Scout sign and, in unison, recite the Law of the Pack. The Living Circle means you are friends and den brothers forever. No member of a Living Circle shall ever betray another."

Despite our cubmaster's proclamation, all of the boys whose hands had formed the Living Circle with mine (even my very best friends, Little Mike Shulman and Larry "Spanky" Feinstein) betrayed me. It was the worst day of my life. And it happened during Red Alert.

The alarm was blasting stridently and, curled up under my desk, I realized that I had to pee. The harder I tried to ignore the feeling, the stronger it became, and with the growing urgency, the screech of the siren seemed to get louder and louder. It seemed it would never stop. The longer it went on, the more urgently I needed to pee. I heard Miss Ross say, "This could be the real thing." The more fervently I struggled, squirming, squeezing, and wiggling my legs, to hold the urine back, the more my bladder seemed to swell, mock, and threaten me. The siren refused to shut up. Unable to contain it any longer, I surrendered. It was the real thing: warm urine soaked my blue jeans, formed a puddle around me, and then turned cold.

As soon as the drill was over, I slipped quickly back into my seat in the hope that no one would notice my wet pants. I prayed against all odds that the kids around me would suppose that the puddle under my desk might be the result of a broken water pipe beneath the wooden floor. Proceeding from the doorway to her desk, Miss Ross made no such mistake.

"Lee," she called. I did not answer. "Lee, I'm talking to you. Come up to the front of the class right now." She repeated it insistently: "Lee Siegel, come here." With no prospect of escape from the horror of the humiliation ahead, I wished the Russians really had dropped the hydrogen bomb on Ponce de Leon Elementary School.

Leo Roth started the ritualistic chant in murmurs with the repetitive rhythm that characterized all teasing: "Lee wet his pants, Lee wet his pants." That's when the boys who had been in the Living Circle betrayed me—they laughed at me. So did the other kids in the class, all of them except Cisco Zutano and Angela Portinari. Even Clover Wiener, who, in the first grade, had taken so much pleasure in my pissing, giggled. I resolved to quit Cub Scouts and never to go back to Ponce de Leon Elementary School.

Miss Ross instructed my classmates to be quiet: "Lee has had a little accident. And all of us can have accidents. Responsible citizens learn from the accidents of others. Responsible citizens remember to use the lavatory before they go into the classroom, even if they do not need to do so. And when they have accidents, responsible citizens are quick to clean up after themselves and get on with their business. Lee, there's no need to feel embarrassed or ashamed. Just go to the janitor's room and get a mop from Mr. Jim to take care of that little mess. I know it won't happen again."

I headed down the empty, locker-lined hallway, but instead of turning right into the janitor's room, I broke into a dash straight ahead and through the door out of the building. I ran as fast as I could across the playground and then along Elevado Street. I stumbled, breathless and crying, up Maple Drive toward home. There were no cars in the driveway—my parents weren't home. Entering the back door, I knew from the sound of the vacuum cleaner that Sally May Carter was upstairs.

Hiding in the basement that had been designated as the family bomb shelter, with my jeans draped over one of the large gas heating units to dry, I waited until three o'clock, the time I normally got home from school.

The next day, after saying good-bye to my parents and Sally May, I pretended to set out for school but instead lurked in the backyard until I could sneak back into our bomb shelter, where I again waited until three o'clock. To pass the time, I had packed my school bag with my copy of *Sex Harmony,* my photograph of the naked Mexican woman, a Land O Lakes butter package, and Professor Mysto's Magic Finger Chopper. If the tampon I had stolen from my parents' bathroom drawer had really been a stick of dynamite, I might have tried to beat the Russians to it by blowing up Ponce de Leon Elementary School myself.

After I had been absent for three days, the school nurse, as was customary given our fear at the time of polio epidemics, telephoned my mother to ask if I had a contagious disease. Polio and Communism were linked in my mind: kids with polio had to live in an Iron Lung, and kids who were Communists had to live behind the Iron Curtain.

My mother had no choice but to insist that I return to school, where I was greeted on the playground by Cisco Zutano. Wrapping an arm affectionately around my shoulder, he swore to God and the Virgin, "*reina y madre de misericordia,*" that, if I wanted him to do so, he would "kick the shit" out of Leo Roth for teasing me. "And if any of the other boys bring it up or make fun of you, just let me know. Cisco will take care of everything. And don't let Miss Ross bother you. She's a dirty old cunt." Yes, I agreed, relishing Cisco's rhetorical use of one part of her body to refer to the whole person. She was nothing like the immaculate young rose, my Beatrice Sugarman. The good news was that Beatrice had not been at school on the day I wet my pants during Red Alert. "Beatrice Sugarman," Miss Ross had announced, "is in the hospital. She's having her tonsils taken out."

Because Larry "Spanky" Feinstein's father had, so Spanky boasted, performed the tonsillectomy, I was able to find out where to send a get-well card. Searching the stationery box in a drawer of my mother's desk, I chose the perfect one. There was a painting of a rose, glistening with dew, on the front of the card, and inside, words that captured my feelings perfectly: "In this time of sorrow, know that my heart is with you." I was too shy to sign the card with anything but, "A Secret Admirerer" [*sic*]. There was another card in the stationery box with a drawing of praying hands beneath the words "*Our Sympathy*" on the front and, inside, a poem: "Death be not proud, though some have called thee mighty and dreadful, for thou art not so," it declared. "One short sleep past, we wake eternally, and death shall be no more." I wanted to send that one to Neezer or to Mrs. Murphy, but I was well aware by then that there was no place to mail it to.

I was so worried that Beatrice Sugarman might die that, kneeling down at the side of my bed each night, I prayed for her. In my great concern for her, I examined the tonsils in a painting of an open mouth by Dr. Frank G. Lafleur, MD, in *The Digestive System,* a book shelved in my parents' library-bar in between *The Reproductive System* and *The Nervous System.* Except for the presence of teeth behind the major lips and the absence of an anus on the chin, the image was reminiscent of the well-studied icon rendered in similar colors in *The Reproductive System.* The uvula was especially suggestive of something or other I had encountered during my gynecological research. I tried to assure myself that the excision of Beatrice Sugarman's tonsils then was no more life-threatening than the removal of her hymen would be in the future on her honeymoon.

I vowed that, if she survived surgery, and if the Russians did not drop the bomb on Ponce de Leon Elementary School, I would someday take her on that honeymoon. My assiduous study of *Sex Harmony,* having made me a "master in the bedroom," would provide me with "the key to open the door to a love-filled life."

Beatrice Sugarman did recover from her operation and was soon back at school. During the next Conelrad Red Alert drill, as the alarm signal resounded in short, rapid, high-pitched tones, I, having remembered to use the lavatory before class, was happy (even though my X-ray glasses still hadn't arrived from Gags Galore) to once again have the esteemed tushy before my eyes and within my reach.

The first time I had seen it, I was about the same age as Dante when he first beheld *his* Beatrice. And his Beatrice was about the same age then, in 1274, as my Beatrice was in 1953. The Italian poet recollected the epiphany in *La Vita Nuova,* his book of love: his vital spirit, no less than my own, 679 years later, "began to tremble so violently that I felt the vibration alarmingly in all of my pulses. . . . From then on Love ruled over my soul." And just as Dante never spoke a word to his beloved Beatrice, I, to the best of my recollection, never actually talked to Beatrice Sugarman. She was no more aware of my adoration than the Florentine girl was of Dante's. Nor did she ever realize that the little buttocks that she covered with a pastel-pink cotton dress had aroused in me a sentiment that the visionary author of the *Divine Comedy* assessed as nothing less than "the Love that moves the sun and other stars."

In Chapter Three, Remember The Meaning of Romance

1954♥1955

When Tom stepped forward to go to his punishment the surprise, the gratitude, the adoration that shone upon him out of poor Becky's eyes seemed pay enough for a hundred floggings. Inspired by the splendor of his own act, he took without an outcry the most merciless flaying. . . . [After going to bed that night] Tom fell asleep at last with Becky's latest words lingering dreamily in his ear: "Tom, how could you be so noble!"

Mark Twain, *The Adventures of Tom Sawyer*

In this stage of the family romance, the child, having learned about sexual processes, tends to picture himself in erotic situations and relations.

Sigmund Freud, "Family Romances"

1954

President Dwight D. Eisenhower adds the phrase "under God" to the Pledge of Allegiance to the American flag, and Premier Nikita Khrushchev creates the Committee for State Security in the Soviet Union; Dr. Jonas Salk inoculates children against polio, and Swanson introduces the TV Dinner; *Beulah* goes off the air, and *Sheena Queen of the Jungle* comes on; *Lord of the Flies* is published, and my mother reads *In the Beginning: A Children's Book about Grown-up Love* to my brother; live coverage of both the Miss America beauty pageant and the Scripps Howard spelling bee are broadcast on national television; "How Much Is That Doggie in the Window?" hits the number-one spot on the music charts, and both *Lassie* and *The Adventures of Rin Tin Tin* premiere on television; Louis Lapine's *Commie Sex Siren* and Andrew Svenson's Hardy Boys novel *The Wailing Siren Mystery* are published; Marilyn Monroe marries and divorces Joe DiMaggio, and Charlie Chaplin leaves America; the Army-McCarthy hearings are broadcast, and Connie Feinstein wins the Ponce de Leon Elementary School Citizenship Award for her essay, "What Freedom Means to Me."

Beatrice Sugarman, Donna Young, Clover Wiener, Eve W——, and Gretel Woodcutter were little girls, cute but childish; Connie Feinstein, my friend Spanky's eighth-grade sister, was—as attested to by a brassiere—a woman, beautiful and mature. Bewitched by that womanhood, I couldn't help falling for her. Not only did she have breasts but she was also a civil defense leader, a flag monitor, and winner of the coveted Ponce de Leon Elementary School Citizenship Award. And, as if that weren't enough, she had received an honorable mention for the project on the effects of radioactive fallout that she had submitted for the Ponce de Leon Elementary School Eighth-Grade Science Fair.

I had become especially fascinated by eighth-grade women after Becky Fine, a friend of Connie's, left Ponce de Leon to go to boarding school in Switzerland and rumor ran rampant that she was pregnant. That proved it—eighth-grade girls had sex.

In the fourth grade I no longer looked forward to Red Alert since Beatrice Sugarman's desk was on the other side of the classroom and I was behind Larry "Spanky" Feinstein. I preferred Yellow Alert. Not only did I get to leave school early, but my emergency evacuation unit was led by Connie Feinstein.

As soon as we heard the slow, deep-droning groans of the Conelrad alarm system announcing a Yellow Alert, we put our books and papers away in our desks as we had been trained to do. Obediently we rose and, in silence, marched mechanically out onto the playground, where, in alphabetical order, we formed single-file lines in groups determined by the direction from Ponce de Leon Elementary School in which we lived.

Two civil defense monitors from the eighth grade were assigned to each group, one at the front of the line and one at the end. Connie Feinstein, at the head of my unit, and Frank Hardy, taking up the rear, each had a yellow civil defense helmet, dark safety goggles, a red vinyl vest, a whistle, a list of students, and extra copies of *Alert Today, Alive Tomorrow*. It was their job to make sure that we kept our line straight and our mouths shut. Hardy's scout uniform gave him added authority.

Maybe, if I had looked up and seen a Russian plane overhead and a bomb falling out of the sky, I would have had the gumption to defy the rules and break the mandatory silence: I would have said good-bye to my friends Little Mike Shulman, Spanky Feinstein, Robbie Freeman, Chip Zuckerman, Cisco Zutano, and Chuck Mandel and even to Leo Roth, whom I still didn't like. I'd tell Ricky Rubin that I was sorry that I wasn't going to be able to pay back the five dollars I still owed him for the copy of *Swedish Sunbather* magazine. Given our imminent death, I might even have confessed to Connie Feinstein that I had a crush on her.

On Yellow Alert days, children in Beverly Hills were enjoined to direct members of their family, as well as any domestic servants residing in the home, into their shelter and there to solemnly review with them the life-saving information in *Alert Today, Alive Tomorrow*, the government pamphlet that Miss Bartz, our fourth-grade teacher, had duly distributed to us:

> Our best life insurance, given the threat of nuclear warfare, may be summed up by four words: ALERT TODAY, ALIVE TOMORROW. All you need is a properly stocked shelter, a desire to survive, common sense and, to keep your spirits up, a sense of humor. Family members should drill together with diligence, reviewing survival plans on a regular basis in order to be prepared for attack and to know what to expect in its aftermath.

My parents were rarely at home in the afternoons and Sally May Carter, usually muttering "Sweet Jesus, boy, if we're gonna die, we're gonna die," always insisted that she had too much housework to do to take time out for a civil defense drill. So whenever I arrived home from Yellow Alert, it was always just me and my brother Robert, then a kindergartener, who descended the stairs into the basement to prepare for attack. I was able to lure him into coming with me by offering him access to the pornography that I kept hidden inside the red velvet couch in my room. I'd transfer it to a brown paper bag and, with Robert following close behind me, carry it down into the bomb shelter. "This could be the real thing," I'd warn the four-year-old.

My illicit collection of smut was admittedly a modest one: a 1950 copy of *Titter* magazine that I had bought from Big Doug Shulman for three dollars; a glossy edition of *Swedish Sunbather* that Ricky Rubin, who had taken up shoplifting after his father died, had stolen from Martindale's bookshop and sold to me for five bucks; and *Commie Sex Siren,* a novel by Louis Lapine that Larry "Spanky" Feinstein had swiped from his uncle Mannie, an alcoholic widower whose library of dirty books included almost all of the Louis Lapine classics of erotic espionage. I had taken proud possession of the literary masterpiece in exchange for the 1954 Marilyn Monroe calendar that I had gotten from Chip Zuckerman in trade for *Sex Harmony.* As I had replaced the jacket on *Sex Harmony* with that from *Treasure Island,* so Chip disguised *Commie Sex Siren* as *The Wailing Siren Mystery,* in which the Hardy Boys, by breaking up a gang of South American smugglers, foil the funding of a Communist revolution. Because of the name of the older of the heroes in the series, I hated the Hardy Boys mysteries. I didn't consider *In the Beginning* (because it was for kids), *The Reproductive System* (because it was a medical book), or *Masterpieces of the Louvre* (because it was art) dirty enough to take along with the saucy stuff that I'd peruse with my brother after school on Yellow Alert days in our basement bomb shelter.

I'd usually start with *Titter,* "America's Merriest Magazine, a Mirthquake of Girls, Gags, Giggles, and Gayety." Although the girls rendered on the cover were as alluring as any of the women in *Masterpieces of the Louvre,* those in the black-and-white photographs on the inside were, while vastly intriguing, somewhat intimidating. These were women who would obviously be a lot more interested in rugged GIs who had seen action overseas in World War II than in little Jewish boys in Beverly Hills who were afraid of World War III.

One of the most fascinating layouts in my edition of *Titter,* "Girls' Rough and Tumble Fight," featured a wrestling match between a blonde in a white bra and panties and a brunette in a black bra and panties. Both wore spiked high-heel shoes, up-to-the-elbow gloves, and long, rolled stockings. Although neither of the girls had anything on Bobo Brazil when it came to brawn, they both seemed to know even more holds than he did.

In "Naughty School Girl," another *Titter* photo essay, a teacher a lot stricter than Miss Bartz was spanking a girl with freckles, pigtails, frilly undies, and big breasts. She must have flunked many more times than Cisco Zutano, I reflected, to still be in school at her age. "What," the copy asked, "could she have done to deserve such a spanking?" A lot more than talking during Yellow Alert, I figured. Whatever it was, it would certainly go on her record. My advice to her would have been to quit that school and enroll in the Wayne Academy, which was advertised in the back pages of *Titter:* "Get your education at home the easy way! No classes to attend! Study only when you want to! Your chances of getting ahead in life are better with a High School Diploma from Wayne! People with an education are admired and respected."

While I had been able to mask *Titter* with a cover from *Boys' Life,* I couldn't find anything the right size to fit over *Swedish Sunbather,* the magazine that declared itself dedicated to "Healthy Living in a Natural Way." Robert preferred it to *Titter* both because some of the girls in that publication were about his own age and because, unlike the any of the women in the pin-up publication, the Scandinavian sun worshipers were completely nude (except sometimes for tennis shoes, roller skates, climbing boots, and the occasional hat, baseball mitt, or knee pads). It disappointed him, however, that there was, due to the photographers' careful attention to poses, angles, and focus, not a patch of pubic hair to be seen. The closest thing to it was the goatee on the smiling face of the Swede whose photograph was featured on the "Message from the Editor" page of the magazine.

I had mixed feelings about the photographs of naked Swedish men, women, and children playing Ping-Pong, croquet, volleyball, and softball, swimming, having picnics, reading books and magazines, and doing other everyday things, even praying in an all-nude church. It reminded me uncomfortably of the upsetting recurrent dream that I had been having: Miss Bartz, looking as stern as the teacher in *Titter,* would call me up to the front of the classroom to write the words BE ALERT, STAY ALIVE on the blackboard. No sooner would I have finished and turned around to face the class than I'd realize that, in getting dressed that morning, I had forgotten to put on my underwear and jeans. I'd try to pull my boldly blue-striped T-shirt down over my penis but, as soon as I did so, the kids in the class would notice that I was naked from the waist down. They would burst into jeering laughter, and I'd wake up gasping for air and shivering with shame, desperately wanting to transfer from Ponce de Leon to either the Wayne Academy or an elementary school in Sweden, where, I imagined, it was not so unusual for a kid to show up in class without his pants on.

While Robert studied the photographs in *Swedish Sunbather,* I'd read to him from my favorite book, *Commie Sex Siren.* It was the kind of novel that you want to read again and again, a page-turner that keeps you on the edge of your seat. Like the Bible, *A Tale of Two Cities, Moby Dick, Anna Karenina,* and the *Communist Manifesto,* it begins with a line that you can never forget: "'Wow, what a body,' said United States Intelligence Agent Dick Steele as he gazed at the naked form writhing on the bed like a female satyr in heat." Agent Steele knew that she was the Commie spy (code name "Jezebel") who had stolen top-secret US plans for an unmanned airborne hydrogen superbomb (code name "Armageddon"). At first read, Dick Steele's assignments seemed more enviable than Herbert A. Philbrick's in *I Led 3 Lives,* but having sex with lots of beautiful women, I soon learned, wasn't always what it was cracked up to be:

"Why Marika?" Dick asked himself. "Why did Jezebel have to turn out to be a gorgeous dame with cherry lips, limpid eyes, hair of gold, pert breasts, and loins that drip with milk and honey?" Using sex, woman's most powerful weapon throughout time for the domination of the male, Marika Semenova's objective was to liquidate every Tom, Dick, and Harry who refused to bow down before the unholy trinity of Marx, Lenin, and Stalin. Agent Steele knew that he had to exterminate her. Yes, like it or not, that was his job. "But business," Dick told himself as he lay down next to the panting nympho, "will have to wait until morning."

"That's great," Robert remarked and, turning back a few pages in *Swedish Sunbather* to reinspect the photographic coverage of "Good Clean Fun in the Midnight Sun," he told me that he loved it when I read to him. The threat of nuclear holocaust brought Lee and Robert Siegel as close together as David and Ricky Nelson.

Sometimes, down in the basement, as I perused *Titter,* I'd imagine Connie Feinstein in spiked high-heels, up-to-the-elbow gloves, and long, rolled stockings in a rough and tumble wrestling match with a Russian girl in red panties and a red brassiere with a hammer and sickle embroidered on each cup. Connie wore her yellow helmet and dark safety goggles, and her vinyl civil defense vest covered her breasts. Why, I wondered, since it was my fantasy, was Connie always wearing that vest and undies as well? But, no matter how hard I tried, I could not at the time picture her without them.

I had had a crush on Connie ever since the first Yellow Alert drill of the school year. But it wasn't until several months later that I fell truly in love with the gorgeous eighth-grader with cherry lips, limpid eyes, hair of brown, pert breasts, and loins, I mused, that surely dripped with milk and honey. It happened on a Saturday morning in the bomb shelter of the Feinstein home on Arden Drive and, as is typical of love, it happened by surprise.

Spanky had invited me over on that fateful day to listen to his newest party record, swiped from his uncle Mannie, of "a farting contest between world champion Lord Windesmere and cabbage-loving challenger Paul Boomer." The last time I had gone to the Feinsteins', it had been to hear a Redd Foxx album (also stolen from Uncle Mannie). I had stared at the phonograph as I listened to the jokes: "How does a French girl hold her liquor?" the comedian asked, hesitated, and then answered the riddle: "By the ears." Although I didn't get it, I forced a chuckle to make it seem that I did as Spanky laughed so hard that he had to hold his crotch to prevent himself from wetting his pants. When I told the joke to Robert in the bomb shelter, he didn't get it either. But it did make Sally May Carter laugh a little and, when I asked her why it was funny, she laughed again: "Shit, boy, you're too young. But you'll understand someday. Don't you worry, you'll get it. I promise." Looking forward to the day when I'd know enough about sex to understand why the joke was funny, I hoped that the Russians didn't drop the bomb on us at least till then.

Spanky loved dirty jokes, the dirtier the better. He'd memorize them off the records filched from his uncle. "So this guy wakes up one morning and discovers that he has a red ring around his dick," my pal began with a big grin. "He goes to the doctor, and the doctor prescribes some cream. A couple of days later the guy calls the doctor and says, 'I'm cured, Doc. That cream worked great. What was it?' And the doctor answered, 'Lipstick remover.' Get it, Siegel? Do you get it?"

"Yeah," I said, but, because I hadn't laughed convincingly enough for Spanky to believe me, he insisted that I explain it to him.

Even more than verbal jokes, Spanky loved practical jokes, and he had an enviable collection: wind-up Yakity-Yak chattering teeth, a squirting pen filled with disappearing ink, a peanut can out of which sprang what was supposed to be a snake, cigarette stink loads, fake vomit, a hand buzzer, and a book titled *Shocking Sex*, which, when opened, delivered a mild electric shock. Falling for it, I didn't think the shock so mild or the joke so funny.

Spanky tried to sell me a piece of Who Done It? Doggie Doo Doo for a dollar. He had an extra, sent to customers as a special bonus gift from Gags Galore for all purchases over ten dollars. It reminded me that the X-ray glasses I had ordered the year before still hadn't arrived. "You're getting a good deal, Siegel, on this dog shit," Spanky pitched.

"If it doesn't look like the real thing, I don't know what does. The Japs are great at copying things. You'll get a lot of laughs with it. I sure have with mine."

Connie, by Spanky's own proud account, had often been the butt of her brother's practical jokes. She had fallen for it when he put his Who Done It? Doggie Doo Doo on the pink carpet in her bedroom and, since the Feinsteins didn't have a dog, she thought her brother had actually defecated on her floor. He was capable of just such zany shenanigans. Spanky could hardly stop laughing long enough to give me a full report on the other pranks he had played on Connie: he had put no-tear toilet paper in her bathroom, offered her a stick of gum that, when removed from the packet, sharply snapped down on her finger, and taken a picture of her with his squirt-gun camera. But the one that made him laugh the hardest as he boasted of it was the prank he had most recently played on his sister—he had dusted her supply of Kotex sanitary napkins with Itchy-Twitchy itching powder from Gags Galore.

After opening the door for me on that Saturday morning when I rode my Schwinn over to the Feinstein house to hear the farting record, Connie told me that Spanky (whom she called "Larry") wasn't home: "He slipped in the bathtub and split his chin open," she announced with a gleeful grin. "My mom took him to the emergency room. My dad's going to sew him up. He's a surgeon, you know. I hope the little jerk bleeds to death."

In an effort to prolong the conversation, I told her that I thought she was doing an excellent job as a civil defense monitor: "During Yellow Alert I always feel that when the bomb really does fall, we'll be okay because you're leading us. You make nuclear attack a lot less scary."

"I love Yellow Alert," Connie confessed, smiling with obvious gratification over my compliment. "Helping kids prepare for a Soviet attack gives me the opportunity to do something important for America. Because of my training as a civil defense monitor, Mom and Dad asked me to personally arrange and stock our bomb shelter." It was the first time she had ever spoken to me other than when, while leading my line along Elevado during Yellow Alert, she had shouted, "Siegel, no talking!"

She was so proud of her bomb shelter that, when I disclosed that her brother, much to my disappointment, had never shown it to me, she graciously invited me into the house and down into her refuge from the apocalypse.

"Look around," she said. "We've got everything a family needs to survive." That there were four cots, each with a blanket and pillow, made me ashamed to realize that my mother, unlike Connie Feinstein, didn't seem to be taking nuclear holocaust seriously enough. We would be sleeping on the concrete floor of our basement. Although my mother had put a few cans of Green Giant corn in the shelter, there was no can opener. While we did have a roll of toilet paper, there was no toilet. Mom had remembered that we'd need a battery-powered radio, but she had forgotten spare batteries. Our bomb shelter was a disgrace. Survival was going to be tough for the Siegel family.

The Feinstein shelter, on the other hand, had a Deluxe Chem-O-Matic Sanitary Human Waste Disposal Unit, a complete set of Melmac molded dinnerware, a Geiger counter, the *World Book Encyclopedia,* and, in accordance with the government's advisory material, a prominently displayed Bible "to provide inspiration and keep spirits high during the possible weeks or even months of confinement." There were huge bags of beef jerky, large vats of Cheez Whiz, industrial-size jars of maraschino cherries, a ton of marshmallows, cartons of Chesterfield cigarettes, cases of Dr Pepper, and countless boxes of Cracker Jack, Barnum's Animal Crackers, Abba-Zabas, M&M's, and Brach's Party Mix. A cardboard box of Kotex sanitary pads that I noticed in the corner with the cartons of toilet paper, Kleenex, and paper party napkins was a reminder of both Connie's womanhood and Spanky's sense of humor.

When Connie showed me their extensive medical supplies, I was abashed, given that my father was a doctor, that all we had in our first-aid kit was Band-Aids, Phillips' Milk of Magnesia, and some Aspergum. Connie advised me to remind my mother to supply our shelter with tranquilizers: "You'll need plenty of them to ease the strain and monotony of life in a shelter. And these are my mom's diet pills; you can gain a lot of weight when you're cooped up for weeks or even months without any exercise. Boredom will be the biggest problem." To combat that ominous ennui, Connie had stockpiled some Palmer Paint-by-Number kits including what she described as "two of the greatest masterpieces ever painted": Leonardo da Vinci's *The Last Supper* and *Looks Like Four of a Kind,* C. M. Coolidge's classic depiction of dogs playing poker.

"Recreational supplies," Connie explained, "may not seem so important, but they are. Things like Slinkys, Silly Putty, jigsaw puzzles, and Monopoly can keep you from going insane during what could be a very long time underground. Survival in the aftermath of nuclear attack is serious business, but that doesn't mean you can't have any fun. I've got some hand puppets to keep our spirits up." She slipped her hand into the head of what, with its large drooping ears, big nose, and tan, black, and white markings, appeared to be a beagle: "Woof, woof," the dog said in a low voice. "There won't be any electricity after the bomb falls, and that means no TV. But you can still have fun, kids, by putting on your own puppet shows. Woof, woof!"

"That was great," I said, and it made her smile. "Your lips hardly moved at all. Larry is really lucky to have you for an older sister. He'll realize just how lucky he is when the bomb falls on Beverly Hills and you put on a puppet show for him."

"I hate Larry," she glowered. "He's a jerk. I hope that, when the Russians do drop the bomb, he gets locked out of the shelter and that the radiation makes his skin blister and peel off." She smiled at the thought and then made what almost seemed like a profession of affection: "I wish you were my little brother. I wouldn't hate you like I hate Larry."

Having noticed how much she relished flattery, I let her have it: "And you've done a great job on this shelter. I love this place. You've got everything down here."

The smile remained on the lovely lips even as they parted in speech: "Yeah, if the Russians were to attack us right now, if the hydrogen bomb were to fall on Los Angeles today, you and I would be okay." It was those words, I think, that did it to me. I imagined us alone together there for weeks, even months. We ate Cracker Jack and drank Dr Pepper garnished with maraschino cherries. While she painted *The Last Supper*, I worked on my Dr. Frank G. Lafleur, MD, professional paint-by-number vulva portrait. As I amazed her with illusions from my Professor Mysto's Hocus Pocus Magic Set, she amazed me with her beauty. We might not read the Bible very often, but, with her hand in the beagle's head and mine in a German shepherd, we put on a puppet show for each other in which the two dogs rubbed their noses together: "Woof, woof!" For the first few weeks, she slept on one cot and I on another. But then, one night, because I was cold, she invited me to cuddle up next to her to keep warm.

Wishing I could stay in the Feinstein bomb shelter with Connie longer, I was gravely disappointed when she said that she had to go. It made me jealous to hear that she was meeting Frank Hardy at Beverly Park where, every Saturday afternoon, he drilled Attila, his rigorously trained Doberman pinscher, one of those perfect dogs that are always alert and ever eager to obey the commands of a master: sit, shake, roll over, fetch, play dead, and sic 'em.

Not only was Frank Hardy a civil defense monitor like Connie, he also raised and lowered the flag with her outside Ponce de Leon Elementary School on Mondays. There was clearly something going on between them. And I imagined that he had a big dick and hairy balls like some of the ones in Frank G. Lafleur, MD,'s *The Reproductive*

System. And because he wasn't Jewish, I speculated, that hefty penis wasn't very clean.

Since, unfortunately, Frank Hardy lived several houses down the block from us on Maple, I'd run into him walking Attila only too often. He'd usually call out to me: "Hey, Siegel, you little pussy, come here. I want to talk to you." I'd always keep walking, reminding myself that, if Frank let Attila off his chain and barked that most terrifying of all commands ("Sic 'em!"), I must not try to run away. That only makes Dobermans more vicious. My only hope for survival would be to stand still and pretend I wasn't afraid.

I wished I could somehow trade lives with Rusty, the lucky master of Rinty on *The Adventures of Rin Tin Tin,* who, as an honorary corporal in the United States Cavalry, got to wear a really cool uniform, ride a horse, and live in a fort in the Old West. If Frank Hardy had ever called him a "little pussy," Corporal Rusty would merely have yelled "Yo-o-o-o ho, Rinty!" and the amazing German shepherd, after chasing off a terrified Attila with his bark, would have leaped into the air and onto Frank Hardy, knocking him over, pinning him to the ground, and keeping him there until he apologized to me. Connie Feinstein would stand behind me, smiling in loving admiration as I, at the end of my episode, knelt down and hugged my beloved dog.

For Chanukah that year I asked my parents for a United States Cavalry outfit just like Rusty's, which I had seen in the FAO Schwarz catalog. I also wanted a dog, a German shepherd like Rusty's. But my father had a prejudice against them, soberly explaining to me that the Nazis had used them in the concentration camps to keep Jews in line and that "Adolf Hitler owned a German shepherd." So he bought a beagle for me because, he enthusiastically proclaimed, "David Ben-Gurion owns a beagle."

Our dog, Mr. Gus, may not have been anti-Semitic, but, for whatever reason, he didn't seem to like us. The animal's entire waking life was dedicated to trying to escape from the Siegel house. Because Mr. Gus would howl all night, as if screaming for other dogs in the neighborhood to rescue him from captivity, my mother had Sally May Carter put Miltown in his Kal Kan. It was only when he was in a state of sedation that I dared pet our dog. In prescribing the tranquilizers for Mr. Gus, Dr. Wiener had noted that the medication had "done wonders for Bullet the Wonder Dog."

Mr. Gus had been given to me on the first night of Chanukah. Sally May Carter dragged the growling dog by force into the library-bar right after I had lit the menorah. The moment Sally let go of his leash, Mr. Gus bounded toward our Chanukah tree, sniffed it, raised his leg, and urinated on it. He was squatting, about to defecate under the tree, when Sally grabbed his leash and yanked him into the backyard. That night he ran away for the first time. And in the morning I had to go with my mother to the Hollywood Humane Society to pick him up.

The only thing about Mr. Gus that made me proud was that his balls were bigger than Attila's. Otherwise he was in no way a gratifying pet. I was too embarrassed to ever walk him because, if he saw any other dog on the street, he'd howl, and the sticky red tip of his penis would poke out of its sheath. It did the same whenever he came into my room, where he'd immediately hump the arm of the old red velvet couch. Afterward he'd usually crap on my floor, and Sally May Carter, grumbling "This is the shittinest dog I've ever seen," would have to come clean it up. The thought of being cooped up with Mr. Gus in our bomb shelter was one of the most frightening of all the prospects of nuclear war.

Whenever Mr. Gus escaped, my mother and Robert and I would have to run down Maple Drive after him, pathetically pleading at the tops of our voices, "Here Mr. Gus! Here boy! Mr. Gus, come home! Please, Mr. Gus! Here boy!" That made him run faster. The only person who could ever catch him was Sally May Carter, and he'd only come to her if she was waving a slab of red meat. We had to chase after our dog a lot, and whenever Frank Hardy saw us, he'd laugh mockingly while Attila barked as if cheering the fleeing beagle on to freedom. "Hey Siegel, I don't think your dog likes you. That's because you're a pussy."

One, two, or three days after one of Mr. Gus's successful escapes, there would inevitably be a telephone call from someone in some faraway place like Torrance, Hawthorne, or El Segundo who had found him and dialed the Crestview number on his dog tag. And then I'd have to get in the Cadillac with my mom to go and pick up the renegade canine.

On one of those forays, we pulled up in front of a ramshackle house in East Los Angeles. In the unmown front yard there was laundry hanging on a line, two broken-down cars and sundry auto parts, a bike on its side, lots of unidentifiable junk, and a kid about my age playing with Mr. Gus. No sooner did the dog see us emerging from the Cadillac than the hair on his back stood on end and he growled. Suddenly bolting away from the boy, he scurried through a hole in the screen door and into the house. A woman in a tattered and food-stained apron, with a yellow bandana around her head, came out to ask if we were sure he was our dog. She wanted to see identification.

As I dragged a whining, snarling, gasping Mr. Gus to the Cadillac, his choker collar almost strangling him to death, the woman, the boy, and a gathering group of neighbors looked on, no doubt supposing that we abused Mr. Gus. "White folks," I supposed they were thinking, "don't even treat their dogs nice."

I was tempted to go along with it when Larry "Spanky" Feinstein suggested that we dust the arm of the velvet couch in my room with Aaaachoo Sneezing Powder from Gags Galore so that the dog would get a big noseful of it when, before humping the couch, he took his usual fevered precoital sniff.

Not only did I get a beagle rather than a German shepherd that year for Chanukah, I got a gorilla costume rather than the cavalry uniform I had asked for. On the second night of the Jewish festival, as I ripped the green ribbon and red wrapping off the package, my mother forewarned me that FAO Schwarz had been out of cavalry outfits in my size: "I tried to get a Royal Canadian Mounted Police costume, but they were out of them too. You've already had the Indian, cowboy, and magician's outfits. The only costumes they had in stock that would fit you were the chef, the devil, and the gorilla."

While the body of the gorilla wasn't very impressive (just a chocolate-brown flannel jumpsuit that zipped up the back and slippers and gloves adorned with synthetic black fur), the realistic gray rubber mask with a black head of hair was spectacular. Looking at myself through the little eyes of the massive simian face in the door mirrors in my mother's dressing room, I couldn't help pounding my chest and roaring as fiercely as Mighty Joe Young had when his Edenic life in darkest Africa with the beautiful Terry Moore was threatened by the arrival of a Hollywood producer on safari. Connie Feinstein looked, I mused, a little bit like Terry Moore.

On the third night of Chanukah, my father told me to remove the ape mask before saying the blessing. But, as she poured his martini from the silver shaker, my mother cajoled him into letting me wear it, reminding him that Chanukah is a children's festival. If my mother had bought the FAO Schwarz devil costume, he probably wouldn't have agreed to it, but my father finally did give in on the ape. My parents, my brother, and Sally May Carter watched as a gorilla, lighting the candles in the menorah, recited: "Blessed art thou, O Lord Our God, King of the Universe, who wrought miracles for our ancestors in days of old at this season." Having learned about evolution that year in Miss Bartz's class, I understood that some of those ancestors had, in fact, been apes.

Because Mr. Gus would snarl and bare his teeth whenever he saw me in the gorilla outfit, I didn't dare wear it unless I was certain that he was tied up in the backyard.

"You've got the worst dog in the world," Spanky said with what seemed like genuine pity. He had been afraid to sleep over at my house ever since waking up there in the middle of the night to discover Mr. Gus doing to his leg what the beagle so enjoyed doing to the arm of my couch. But, not holding me personally responsible for my dog's wanton behavior, Spanky did occasionally invite me to spend the night at his place. And in the hope that I might see Connie, I always accepted. If I were really lucky, she might let Spanky and me watch her favorite television show, *I Led 3 Lives,* with her. The grim introduction to each episode of the program still echoes in my ears as a gloomy dispatch from a bleak world on the brink of nuclear war: "This is the fantastically true story of Herbert A. Philbrick, who for ten frightening years did lead three lives: average American citizen, member of the Communist Party, and counterspy for the FBI."

Arriving to sleep over at the Feinsteins' on the Saturday that the stitches were removed from Spanky's chin, I asked where Connie was, only to learn, much to my dire disappointment, that she was spending the weekend at citizenship camp. Spanky was happy she was gone: "We can watch *Rin Tin Tin* instead of *I Led 3 Lives* tonight."

Mrs. Feinstein let us stay up to watch *Your Hit Parade,* but, even though I could hear Snooky Lanson singing "How Much Is That Doggie in the Window?" I couldn't see him very well because of what was supposed to be a water tap coming out of the center of the television screen. Much to his own amusement, Spanky had attached a Phoney Phaucet, his newest gag from Gags Galore, by its rubber suction cup to the TV screen.

No sooner had Mrs. Feinstein turned out the lights, instructing us to be quiet and go to sleep, than Spanky started telling me the usual jokes. He had finally gotten the one about the Indian who drowned in his tea-pee right. Because I wasn't laughing, he must have thought I was asleep.

"Wake up, Siegel," he whispered, standing in the darkness at my bedside. "Come on, get up. I've got to show you something. Come on, come with me. You're going to love this. But be quiet. Don't let my parents hear us. If they catch us, they'll kill us."

Nervously, but admittedly excited by the adventure, I followed him in absolute silence down the dark hall into Connie's room and from there into her bathroom, where Spanky had some fascinating things to show me: "This is one of her Kotex pads. And look, here's some of the lipstick remover that she gives to Frank Hardy to use on his dick." He opened a wicker clothes bin to show me a few impressive Peter Pan brassieres, an intriguing Perma-lift girdle, and several white Spun-lo panties. Turning a pair of the underpants inside out, he choked on a muffled guffaw: "Look, Siegel, there's one of her pussy hairs." The single delicate curlicue of fine dark hair stood out in splendor against the white rayon. "She's got a really hairy box," Spanky whispered with naughty glee.

Falling loose from the panties, the tiny hair floated angelically down onto the sink, and Spanky, tossing the laundry back into the basket, said we'd better get back to bed.

There was still a lump in my throat from the wondrous vision of that curly little hair on the white porcelain sink. Tossing and turning, I was anxious and worried that Frank Hardy might also be spending the weekend at citizenship camp. Like Connie, he was very enthusiastic about things like citizenship.

"Psssst, Feinstein, are you still awake?" I whispered. There was no answer. I asked it again, and once more, and, still not getting a response, I sat up to muster my mettle. In spite of my fear of getting caught by the Feinsteins, I then did the most daring thing I had done since climbing over the wall into Mr. Myron Spellman's backyard. Again, I dared to do what I did because of love.

Tiptoeing out of Spanky's room, I crept down the dark hall and through Connie's bedroom into her bathroom. I knew just how United States Intelligence Agent Dick Steele must have felt when he snuck into Marika Semenova's hotel room in Stockholm. Daring to turn on the light, I discovered, much to my consternation, that the pubic hair was no longer on the sink. Getting down on my hands and knees, keeping my eyes close to the yellow tile floor, I, with perseverance, finally found what I was risking getting into so much trouble to search for. Wrapping the delicate little strand of hair in a piece of Connie's soft pink toilet paper, I put it in the pocket of my flannel pajama top and made my way cautiously back to bed. With Connie Feinstein's pubic hair in my possession, I felt as triumphant as Agent Dick Steele must have felt when he recovered the microfilm of the plans for an unmanned airborne hydrogen superbomb from the bathroom of the Hotel Svensk.

Returning home in the morning, I could tell something was wrong. Sitting on the red velvet couch in my room, my mother had the same expression on her face that she had had in *Phantom from Space* when, playing the part of an astronomer at the Griffith Park Observatory, she informed her family that an invisible creature from another planet was on the loose in Los Angeles. "Lee," she said somberly, "I have something to tell you." The sad news was that she and my father had sent

Mr. Gus to live on a beagle ranch in Washington state, where, my mother assured me, he'd be better off, "running free with other dogs
 in the country. He'll be happy there."

I don't really know why I broke into tears, sobbing as Rusty, more understandably, would have done if Lieutenant Rip Masters ever told him that Rin Tin Tin had been sent to Washington. "I miss Mr. Gus," I cried. "I love Mr. Gus." Putting her arm around me, stroking my hair with her hand, and kissing me on the forehead, my mother tried to console me: "And Mr. Gus loves you too, my darling."

That week, during Yellow Alert, as I silently marched in the single-file line along Elevado, there was some solace for my inexplicable sorrow over the loss of Mr. Gus in the secret and illicit pleasure that I derived, now that I had in my pocket one of her pubic hairs laminated between two pieces of Scotch tape, from just looking at Connie Feinstein at the front of the line. The hair was a magic fetish giving me an occult power to vividly envision that lusciously hirsute private part of Connie Feinstein that, I had learned from Dr. Frank G. Lafleur, MD, was technically named the *pubes.* I could picture it as I, with my hand over my heart, pledging my allegiance to one nation under God, watched her and Frank Hardy raise America's star-spangled banner. Now when I imagined her wrestling with the Russian girl, she no longer wore panties. With closed eyes, I gazed in awe at the soft lush grass of a misty meadow in which I longed to loll.

Inspired as I was by Connie Feinstein's *pubes,* I spent hours sitting at my desk, usually dressed in my gorilla outfit, sketching it, starting with a faint upside-down triangle and then patiently penciling in the precious little hairs one by one. Thumbing through *Masterpieces of the Louvre* to see how the masters had rendered it, I could not, despite all the nude women there, find a single painting of pubic hair. There wasn't any in *Titter* or in the Scandinavian nudist magazine either. So, with nothing other than the goatee on the face of the editor of *Swedish Sunbather* and the sundry renderings of flocculent *montes veneris* above the *pudendi feminini* in *The Reproductive System* to guide me, I relied on my own inner visions to create my works of art.

When Spanky invited me to come along with him and his uncle Mannie one Sunday to the Santa Monica pier amusement park, I declined, not because I didn't want to go but because the prospect of finding Connie at home without Spanky there that day promised more of a thrill than any merry-go-round, Ferris wheel, or bumper car could. With Connie's pubic hair in my pocket, I'd show up at the Feinsteins' as if I thought Spanky would be home and then, when my beloved informed me that her little brother had gone out with their uncle Mannie,

I'd tell her that I hoped she could spare another copy of *Alert Today, Alive Tomorrow,* adding that, inspired by her example, I was currently trying to restock my bomb shelter: "I'd like to look at yours again."

My plan worked as well as anything ever devised by Agent Dick Steele. Connie was pleased to escort me into the basement and, once down there, she cordially asked if I wanted anything to eat: "Some Cracker Jacks, animal crackers, or beef jerky? We've also got a big supply of Fanning's bread and butter pickles." Tempting as such delicacies might have been under ordinary circumstances, amorous excitation had taken away my appetite.

As we sat across from each other on military-green canvas cots, Connie recounted some of her favorite episodes of *I Led 3 Lives.* After the fifth or sixth one, there was an abrupt silence during which she disarmed me with a bewitching smile, and then, all of sudden and out of the blue, she said something wonderful: "I'm glad you came by today. Of all of Larry's friends, I like you the best. You're the only one who really seems to care about civil defense." Utterly touched and enthralled, I responded by telling her that, not only was she a superb Yellow Alert monitor, "but you also do a really great job of raising the flag. It makes me proud to be an American."

The moment I said "raising the flag," her happy expression shifted into one pained and serious. Connie rose from her cot and sat down next to me. My breathing became heavy and my hands trembled as she announced that she had something that she wanted to tell me, a dark secret, "something really shocking, something I haven't told anyone. I hope it won't make you think I'm bad." She made me promise never to tell.

What could it be? I wondered. What could be so shocking? Was it possible that a mature eighth-grade woman with *pubes* on her *mons veneris* could have a crush on a little fourth-grade boy? Was she going to confess to that? What in the world could make me think that Connie Feinstein was bad? Was she going to admit to some naughty impulse to do something in her bomb shelter that kids weren't supposed to do? Simultaneously shaken by fear and desire, anxiety and eagerness, and all sorts of other hitherto unknown emotions, I suddenly had a weird premonition that she was going to announce that she wanted to fondle me. I had recently overheard my parents talking about our neighbors, the Benzingers, who, my mother said, had just fired their maid because they caught her "fondling" their seven-year-old son, Ben. Although I wasn't quite sure exactly what fondling entailed, I was interested in finding out. I understood that it caused both shame and pleasure, and shameful as it might have been, I was enticed by the as yet obscure pleasure. I wanted to know what Ben Benzinger knew. And if Connie Feinstein taught me, I swore to myself, I'd never tell a soul (not even Little Mike Shulman).

She disappointed me, however, and it upset my stomach when I tried to swallow the terrible-tasting jealousy that she served up to me: "I can't believe I'm actually going to tell you this, but I've got to tell somebody. I feel so guilty. I've got to get it off my chest. Frankie and I did something really bad in the janitor's room, where the flag is stored. It was just last Monday. I didn't want to go along with it, but Frankie insisted, and because he's my boyfriend, I did what he said."

I feared that she was about to reveal that Frank Hardy had kissed her, perhaps fondled her, and maybe even—God forbid!—run his fingers through the soft, curly pubic hair to which I felt I, and I alone, had a right of access. Frank Hardy might even have moved his erect penis in and out of her vagina with rapid motions until sperm-bearing fluid came out of it! Connie Feinstein, like her friend Becky Fine, might be pregnant!

"I'm so ashamed of myself," she continued. "Frankie and I had lowered the flag as usual and taken it to the janitor's room, where we always refold it into a neat triangle according to government standards and federal regulations. With the last fold, I let go of it, thinking that Frankie had the flag firmly in his grip. At the exact same moment, he let go too, assuming that the flag was securely in my hands. Oh, God! There it was on the floor of the janitor's room—the Stars and Stripes, our nation's banner of freedom!"

I was relieved.

"Well, you know what that means!" she said as if I'd care. "According to federal law, an American flag that has touched the ground must be burned. Frankie and I knew that, and we were upset. He said it was my fault, and I argued that it was his, but whoever's fault it was, we both knew that we'd both be disgraced by what had happened. We had failed our country. I felt that it was our duty as American citizens to confess the truth. But Frankie said that if we did, Dr. Chambers wouldn't permit us to continue as flag monitors. We wouldn't be allowed to lead Yellow Alert drills anymore or attend citizenship camp. Not only that—Frankie would be given a dishonorable discharge from Scouts. He convinced me to keep quiet about it. 'It'll go on our permanent records,' he said, 'and that means I won't be able to join the air force when I graduate from high school.' So I haven't told anyone except you. But I still feel bad about it. I went along with it because Frankie's my boyfriend. But I'm not sure that he made me do the right thing. What do you think? Do you think we should have told?"

Since when you're in love with a woman, you naturally always try to tell her what she wants to hear, true or not, I swore on the Bible in her basement that I thought she had done the right thing. She took my hand in hers to thank me. That she had revealed her deepest, darkest secret to me, and that she was still holding my hand, gave me some hope that she liked me. Even though she was four years older than I, we were, I felt, perfect for each other. Frank Hardy was all that stood between us. Once he was out of the picture, whenever I slept over at Spanky's house, I'd be able to sneak through the darkness into Connie's room late at night.

Of course, deep, deep down, I knew that nothing would ever come of it, but a knowledge that the fulfillment of love will never come to pass has never stopped anyone from falling in love. On the contrary, impossibility is the fuel of the most puissant transports of love. True love is when you can't help it. I loved Connie Feinstein. And it was that love that drove me to do the terrible thing I did.

I got the idea from an episode of *I Led 3 Lives,* one of Connie's favorites, in which a concerned mother reported it to the authorities that her daughter's boyfriend was a Communist. The mom had become suspicious when, after starting to date the boy, the girl had begun saying that she hated war and wished America would ban the atomic bomb. After an investigation by Herbert A. Philbrick, the boyfriend was sent to a rehabilitation camp where he was treated for the "infection of Communism." And the girl returned to her senses.

Sitting at my desk in my gorilla outfit, I composed a note to Connie Feinstein in which I reported that Frank Hardy was a Communist. In another episode of the same show, I had learned a trick used by spies to prevent notes from being traced back to them through their handwriting: Herbert A. Philbrick cut the needed letters and words out of printed material to paste his message together. Addressing the envelope was easy. The first name was embedded right there in the title of ***Confidential*** magazine, and the surname was snipped from a caption in *Titter:* "It doesn't take an **Einstein** to figure out what makes this gal such a bombshell in the bomb shelter!"

The words of the message itself were cut from *Alert Today, Alive Tomorrow, Swedish Sunbather, Commie Sex Siren,* and the dust jacket to *The Wailing Siren Mystery* that disguised *Commie Sex Siren* as a Hardy Boys book:

I believed that the American flag, cut from *Alert Today, Alive Tomorrow,* gave the note credibility and exigency. Once the message was in her hands, Connie would realize that any loyal American would, any time that hallowed flag ever touched the ground, immediately report it to the authorities. She might even suspect that Frank Hardy had dropped the flag intentionally as a subversive act: each day the innocent children of Ponce de Leon Elementary School were pledging their allegiance to a flag that, unbeknownst to them, had been desecrated. It would also probably occur to her that Hardy's inside knowledge of our Yellow Alert strategies put him in a position to provide the Kremlin with valuable information.

Cautious not to be seen as I did it, I slyly slipped the envelope into the Feinstein mailbox when I went over to Spanky's house a few days later under the pretext of wanting to listen to his *Pardon My Blooper, Volume 2,* record.

At first, even though I knew that Corporal Rusty would have been ashamed of me, I felt good about what I had done. I figured that, if Connie believed it, not only would she break up with Frank Hardy in fear of the Communist infection but she might also report him to the FBI, and that J. Edgar Hoover might then send my rival to that camp where the traitorous teenager in the *I Led 3 Lives* episode had been rehabilitated.

But then I started to worry. What if the FBI investigated it? They might search my house. If so, they'd be sure to check my room, and there they might even think to look inside the red velvet couch, where they'd discover not only a tampon, a photograph of a naked Mexican woman, and a Land O Lakes butter package but also, with words incriminatingly cut out of all of them, *Titter, Swedish Sunbather,* and, in the jacket of a Hardy Boys mystery, *Commie Sex Siren.* They'd also find an envelope containing a small, dark, curly hair between two pieces of Scotch tape.

I'd be in very big trouble. Not only would it go on my permanent record, I would also be sent to a reform school or a foster home. And when the judge at juvenile hall asked me why I had done it, he probably wouldn't understand my answer: "I did what I did because of love."

In that state of worry, love didn't seem to me worth all the trouble people could get into for its sake. But I didn't learn the lesson. In the years that followed, I would get into trouble a lot over love. Most of the times it almost seemed worth it.

1955

"Rock around the Clock" and "The Ballad of Davy Crockett" compete for the number one spot on the music charts, and one out of every two Americans watches Mary Martin fly on television in *Peter Pan;* actor Pepe Pelotas has a heart attack while playing Captain Hook in a touring production of *Peter Pan,* and President Dwight D. Eisenhower has a heart attack while playing golf in Denver; Walt Disney opens Disneyland, and Ray Kroc opens the first McDonald's hamburger stand; Vladimir Nabokov's *Lolita* is published in Paris after being turned down by four American publishers, and the Revised Standard Version of the Holy Bible is the bestselling book in the United States in the category of nonfiction; *Titter* magazine goes out of business and *Good Housekeeping* celebrates its seventieth anniversary; the Ford Motor Company introduces the Thunderbird, and James Dean is killed in the crash of his Porsche Spyder; both Albert Einstein and my grandfather, Albert Roth, die; and both Don the Beachcomber Exotic Cocktail Mixes and Hawaiian Punch frozen concentrate are marketed nationally.

Through a haze of tropical rain on the window, fern, bamboo, ti, and birds of paradise, fleshy fans of banana leaf, primordial purple vulvic orchids, and the crimson phallic protuberances of anthuria all glistened with the delicate droplets of intermittent jungle showers. Heady perfumes of pikake, plumeria, and ginger and the spicy fragrances of a ceremonial feast were in the air. Through affable chatter laced with mirthful laughter, I heard a susurrus wash of foamy waves upon a beach, dulcet ukulele melodies, and a honeyed voice in lilting song. I looked up at the bamboo beams under the woven palm frond ceiling at what seemed to be the silhouette of a gecko in the lambent green glass globe lamp hanging in the overhead fisherman's netting of our grass shack, an alcove in Don the Beachcomber South Seas Restaurant on McCadden Place, just above Hollywood Boulevard. No matter what the weather was like in Southern California, it was, by the grace of an automatic sprinkler system, always sure to drizzle every fifteen minutes on the life-like rubber flora outside the windows of Don the Beachcomber's paradise.

Upon walls of woven grass matting and tapa cloth hung the shields, spears, and shark-tooth barbed fighting clubs of South Seas warriors.

There were mounted swordfish and marlin, gaping shark jaws, and paintings that, to my taste, deserved a place in *Masterpieces of the Louvre.* Mona Lisa would have been a lot more fetching, I thought, if Leonardo da Vinci had asked his model to replace her blouse and shawl with a garland of flowers and then painted the portrait on black velvet with a gushing waterfall or crashing ocean waves, a blazing sunset or bright full moon, in the background. Don the Beachcomber's masterpieces depicted voluptuous bare-breasted wahines dancing the hula, casting out fishing nets, or languorously leaning against sloping trunks of palm trees, balancing trays of pineapples, bananas, mangoes, and papayas on their heads or bathing in a moonlit grotto or the shimmering pool at the foot of a waterfall.

"Aloha, Dr. Siegel," said Mr. Lee, the suave Chinese maître d', wearing an immaculate white linen suit, a pale pink silk shirt, and flowered tie, his shiny black hair slicked back, as he offered a cordial bow and a decorous smile. At the entrance to the restaurant, guarded by a large statue of the great god Tiki, there was a glass display case of bamboo tubes with the names of celebrities and good customers burned into them. I was proud that one was engraved DR. AND MRS. LEE SIEGEL, M.D. It contained the plastic ivory chopsticks that would be ceremoniously presented to us by Mr. Lee just before our meal was served.

Enthroned in the expansive, flabellate-backed cane and woven wicker queen's chair at the head of the irregularly shaped, smoothly polished koa table, my mother sipped a gardenia-garnished Scorpion and my father, with his Viceroy burning in an abalone shell ashtray, quaffed a Zombie from a ceramic Tiki goblet. Robert and I, dressed for the occasion as adults in matching white sport coats, sucked on the Flex-Straws in our Keiki Pi-Yi's, a nonalcoholic version of a libation normally concocted of four kinds of rum, brandy, curaçao, passion fruit liqueur, pineapple juice, guava nectar, grenadine, orgeat syrup, bitters, and a secret ingredient that Trader Vic was dying to figure out. Served in a hollowed-out pineapple and garnished with an orchid, pineapple slice, maraschino cherry, mint sprig, piece of sugar cane, plastic Tiki stirrer, bamboo back scratcher, and a little paper umbrella, the drink looked as great as it tasted.

When Robert and I asked if we could have our Pi-Yi's flaming like a Pele's Passion, Kilauea Killer, Lava Flow, or Flaming Bastard, Mr. Lee politely explained that it was 151-proof rum that ignited those drinks; but, he consoled us, he'd ask Chico the bartender "to put a few extra maraschino cherries in them."

The food at Don the Beachcomber was as good as the grog and the art: pupu platters of shrimp fried in coconut batter, spring rolls that we were allowed to pick up with our fingers, and skewers of pineapple and chicken, all served with condiments in little porcelain butterflies— ketchup, mustard, and mango chutney, as well as plum, hot chili, and sweet-and-sour sauce.

We were never allowed to order either the spare ribs or the bacon-wrapped rumaki, and much to my embarrassment, my father would always insist on loudly asking Mr. Lee about the spring rolls: "There isn't any ham, bacon, or pork in these, is there? We don't eat ham, bacon, or pork. We're Jewish."

The religion of the god Tiki, at least as I understood it from eating at Don the Beachcomber and seeing the South Seas adventure movie *Bird of Paradise,* appealed to me more than the religion of my forefathers. I preferred the little black wooden ruby-eyed Tiki idol dangling on a leather neck cord that I had bought at the Don the Beachcomber gift shop to the silver Star of David on a silver chain my father had given me for my tenth birthday, along with a certificate documenting that a tree had been planted in my name in Israel. While he may have hoped that I would one day visit the Holy Land to see my tree, I dreamed of voyaging to the South Seas to loll barefoot under a palm tree, staring out to sea like Don the Beachcomber on the cover of the restaurant's souvenir matchbooks. While on isles holy to the great god Tiki, grass-skirted, bare-breasted wahines danced the hula, drinks were served flaming, and pineapple came sacramentally with everything you ate, in Israel, I surmised, women in military uniforms danced the hora, old men with long beards drank Mogen David wine, and rumaki was illegal.

I did not feel that my preference for Tiki, the fun-loving god of Don the Beachcomber, Trader Vic, and Mr. Lee, to Yahweh, the straight-laced god of Abraham, Isaac, and Jacob, was in any way heretical. The movie *Bird of Paradise* had provided me with a connection between the religion of my birth and my faith of choice. In that film, actor Maurice Schwartz, uncle of my classmate Bucky Schwartz and a member of the congregation of our synagogue, Temple Beth Israel (where I had seen him the previous Yom Kippur), had very convincingly portrayed the Kahuna, the Polynesian equivalent of the Kohen Gadol, or High Priest. When Luana, played by Debra Paget (who went on to be Jewish that year in *The Ten Commandments*), proclaimed her passion for Johnny, a Gentile shipwrecked on her island paradise, by dancing the hula for him, Kahuna Schwartz went into a religious tizzy: "The White One brings disaster to our island! Madame Pele is angered." Madame Pele, irascible Volcano Goddess that she is, threatened to destroy the island with an eruption unless the first-born daughter of a Kahuna was sacrificed. And so Debra Paget, who, like us, had her own personal engraved bamboo chopstick holder at Don the Beachcomber, had to save her people by jumping into a volcano. "I have loved and been loved," she said, after kissing Johnny one last time. "I am ready to die." That, I thought, was true love—yes—the real thing.

The most thrilling scene in the movie took place underwater when suddenly, as the White One and Luana were playfully swimming together in a lagoon behind a waterfall, a giant clam clamped its powerful jaws-like shell down around Debra Paget's delicate foot. With an endless stream of bubbles coming out of his mouth, Johnny struggled to pry the clam open with his bare hands. Of course, I was one of only a few who knew that it was really the foot of my former swimming coach, aquatic stuntwoman Fitta Knullaman, and not Debra Paget's, that had been caught in the clam. After the White One got the foot out of the clam, he lay with Luana in exhaustion on the beach. That was very, very sexy.

There was an enormous clamshell, just like the one in the movie, for sale in the gift shop of Don the Beachcomber, and I wanted my parents to buy it—a bargain, I reckoned, at twenty bucks. But even more than the gaping shell of the man-eating clam, the shrunken human head with long straight black hair, its eyes and mouth sewn up with raffia, was what fascinated me. That it cost a hundred dollars assured me that it was the real thing. Who, I wondered, had the little head belonged to, and what, I tried to imagine, had he done to end up with his head for sale in a restaurant gift shop in Hollywood?

My father always gave Robert and me a two-dollar bill each to spend in that shop, where we could browse enchanted no matter how long our parents continued to drink and smoke, talk and laugh. On the way from the table to the shop, we'd always stop to give the ship's wheel a turn and ogle the woman with the torpedo-like naked breasts. She was a cutwater figurehead who, when formerly ornamenting the prow stem of a sailing ship, had undoubtedly stared straight ahead, stalwartly smiling through tropical typhoons. After retiring to Don the Beachcomber, she had obviously been given a paint job: the long flowing tresses of her carved hair were bright yellow, her wide-open eyes bright blue, her smiling lips bright red, her full-blown flesh bright pink, and the flowing robes wrapped around her loins were like a sheet snatched from a lover's bed, bright white. When Robert dared me to reach up and touch the breasts, the protruding nipples of which were painted with the same crimson as her lips, I swore I'd do it for a buck. He bargained me down to fifty cents, just enough for me to buy one of the small dried seahorse key chains in the shop. When I turned around from copping the furtive feel, I blushed with embarrassment to discover that Mr. Lee had seen me. "Oh, I was just trying to see if . . . ah . . . ," I hemmed and hawed, trying to come up with a good excuse for my indecent behavior. The Chinese maître d' let me off the hook with a polite smile and the explanation that it was an old custom: "Sailors would rub them before boarding a ship for luck, to keep them safe on the high seas." Now that we had learned that fondling a woman's breast was good luck, Robert asked me to lift him up: "I want to be safe too."

Robert and I loved the shop, inspecting with eyes and fingers all the wonderful souvenirs of the South Seas: white candles that magically dripped many different colors of wax; brightly hued little rocks that when placed in a bowl of water would grow into fantastically shaped miniature stalagmites; lots of Tikis, of course, in every size, on their own or decorating anything with enough space for embellishment; there were sharks' teeth, swordfish swords, dried blowfish, painted starfish, scrimshaw, and curios made of coconut and turtle shell; ukuleles and bamboo flutes; flowered shirts and dresses, silk robes and grass skirts; paintings of women on black velvet; Don the Beachcomber Exotic Cocktail Mixes with which to make your very own Fog Cutters, Cobra Fangs, Vicious Virgins, Wicked Wahines, and Zombies at home, as well as Tiki-adorned goblets from which to sip them, Tiki-topped swizzle sticks with which to stir them, and Tiki-embossed coasters upon which to place them. There were chopsticks and painted fans for sale, and shells of every shape, color, and size, some small enough to be strung on a string and worn around the neck, others large enough to be held up to the ear and hear in them the sound of distant South Seas waves. And one was big enough to clamp down on the foot of a South Seas princess. But most fascinating of all, there was that shrunken human head.

The salesgirl, a demure young woman from somewhere far away, always wearing a silver-embroidered red silk dress with a slit up the side, told us about it more than once. "After the headhunters cut the head off," she explained with a curiously sangfroid smile, "they take out the skull, sew up the mouth and eyes, and then fill it with sand. When they boil it, the head keeps its shape as it shrinks while the sand gets pushed out through the nostrils and the ears. The headhunters drink the broth in which they've boiled the head. They believe that it is an aphrodisiac. And having a shrunken head, they think, brings them good luck." I had to explain to Robert that an aphrodisiac was "something that gives you a boner." I wanted that head more than ever.

Going out with my parents to dinner at Don the Beachcomber gave me a taste of adulthood, and it was delicious. I wanted to be an adult as soon as possible. My parents always seemed to have so much fun. They could go to Don the Beachcomber to drink flaming drinks every night if they wanted, and stay up as late as they pleased even on school nights.

Although they took my brother and me along to Don the Beachcomber, we stayed home with Sally May Carter to watch television when they went to Chasen's or Romanoff's, Ciro's or the Mocambo, or other places without gift shops. I'd often lie on their bed watching them get ready: my father, in his black socks and white broadcloth boxers, his pastel-blue shirt open, paused after putting in one of his cuff links to take a sip of a martini; my mother, wrapped in a pink silk robe, sitting at her dressing table, pinched a small clamp-like instrument down on her eyelashes to curl them up.

On one of those nights, we watched *Peter Pan.* I hated it when Peter, a boy supposedly about my age played by a woman, sang, "I won't grow up! I'll never grow up, never grow up, never grow up! I'll never grow a mustache, or a fraction of an inch, 'cause growing up is awfuller than all the awful things that ever were." The song made no sense. Didn't Peter realize that in a few years Wendy Darling, once she had boobs, pubes, and used Kotex, would be a lot more interested in a guy like Don the Beachcomber, who had both a mustache and a few good inches on Mary Martin, than in any kid in tights, even if he could fly? I wanted to grow up more than anything and as soon as possible. The person who wrote that perverted song was, I figured, lying, or had forgotten about the ache of childhood. Did he not remember being teased by peers, being afraid of older, taller boys like Frank Hardy, being made to run punitive laps around a playing field by teachers, being told by parents to "be quiet and go to sleep" at night and to "wake up and go to school" in the morning, being ordered by adults to do what he didn't want to do and not do what he did want to do? Had he forgotten the stifled yearnings, the tug of ineluctable cravings, the gnawing confusion and unfocused anxiousness that are caused by a lack of a knowledge, ability, opportunity, and freedom to discover and establish repeated release and substantial relief from a yet-to-be-understood, but already very overwhelming, desire?

Chuck Mandel, who because his family was Orthodox was already, three years before the event, studying Hebrew for his bar mitzvah, had put it simply: "I can't wait for my bar mitzvah because once you're bar mitzvahed, you're a man. And then you can smoke, and drink, and gamble, and have sex with girls. You can do pretty much anything you want except eat pork, work on Saturdays, or have a Christmas tree."

Yes, I too longed to be an adult, but I knew I had to be patient, that I had been sentenced, as if for some crime or sin, to spend the early years of my life incarcerated behind the bars of childhood. The crime had, I sensed, something to do with sex. And a significant part of the punishment was being made to go to school.

Because my parents were concerned that almost every morning over breakfast I declared, sometimes with tears, that I hated school and didn't want to go, they decided to invite the principal of Ponce de Leon Elementary, Dr. Gus Chambers, PhD, and his wife, Ethel, author of the unforgettable play *Fountain of Youth,* to dinner. They would talk about my problems as if there were a solution. I was pleased that my parents were going to take the Chamberses to Don the Beachcomber and that, having been treated to dinner at the best restaurant in the world, the principal might do his best in the future to keep it off my permanent record when and if I got into trouble (which, I feared, was likely since I was very interested in forbidden things like switchblade knives, flaming drinks, pornographic literature, breasts, pubic hair, vulvas, and rumaki).

In my pajamas and robe, with mukluks on my feet and my hair neatly combed with Brylcreem, I went, when summoned, downstairs to the library-bar to say hello and goodnight to the principal and his wife. Dr. Gus Chambers, PhD, had a goatee just like the one on the puss of the editor of *Swedish Sunbather,* and Mrs. Chambers wore glasses very similar to the ones perched on the nose of the strict teacher who spanked the naughty school girl in *Titter.*

After eating the olive from her martini, Mrs. Chambers told my parents that she had given up playwriting to devote her creative energies to the composition of educational materials: "I've just begun research for a book, *Facts of Life and Love for the American Teenager,* in which I'm going to deal frankly with a subject that's been kept far too hush-hush. Young people today have so many questions about growing up, about how their bodies will change and how those changes will affect their feelings. They want to know about dating, courtship, and—I'm sorry, there's no other word for it—sex. It's going to raise a lot of eyebrows, but I want to introduce into our curriculum a study unit on the facts of life here in Beverly Hills. I'm prepared to put up a fight!"

In the midst of her polemic, Robert, then a first-grader at Ponce de Leon Elementary, came running across the living room to leap into the air and down the two stairs into the library-bar, shouting, "I can fly! I can fly!"

With a smile to indicate his amusement over the consummate cuteness of my irrepressible sibling rival, Dr. Chambers, realizing that

Robert's behavior had been inspired by *Peter Pan,* confessed that he and Mrs. Chambers too had watched the show and had been impressed by the fact that almost everybody in America was tuned into the broadcast, "doing and enjoying the same thing at the same time. It gives me hope that, as Americans, despite our many differences, we make up one united United States. I'd like to propose a toast to America, land of the free and home of the brave."

As the four martini glasses clinked together in honor of our country, Robert pretended to sprinkle fairy dust on Dr. Gus Chambers, PhD. And then he sang "I Won't Grow Up."

Once Robert had finished the song, the school principal turned to me to ask what my favorite subject was. "Except for P.E., of course," he added with a grin to make a joke, which wasn't funny to me since I hated physical education as much as I detested science and math.

My answer ("I like reading") seemed to impress the educator. "Reading is very important," he pontificated. "Not enough youngsters these days, when there are so many shows on television, enjoy reading as much as they should. What have you been reading lately?"

"*The Wailing Siren Mystery.* It's a Hardy Boys Mystery," I blurted out, the first book title I could think of, having seen it that very day on the dust jacket wrapped around *Commie Sex Siren.*

Removing a large volume from the bookshelf, Robert handed it to Mrs. Chambers: "This is my brother's favorite book. He shows it to me a lot." It was Dr. Frank G. Lafleur's *The Reproductive System.* And my brother knew exactly where to open it in order to show Mrs. Chambers the full-page spread of a vulva. Flustered in my struggle to contain my rage, I made it worse by stammering, "Robert's lying. I've never looked at those dirty pictures."

After the adults had left for the restaurant, Sally May Carter, while effectively preventing me from killing, maiming, or even just slightly injuring my younger brother, could do nothing to stop me from shouting at him: "You dirty little mother-fucking son of a bitch." To which he, protected by Sally May, giggled, "Since I'm your brother, your mother is a bitch too."

Having cried myself to sleep, I woke up in the morning dreading school even more than usual. My misery, however, was at least temporarily assuaged when, upon going downstairs for breakfast, I saw what was on the kitchen counter. I could hardly believe it. I was thrilled. It was, much to the horror and disgust of Sally May Carter, right there in our very own house, under a glass display bell—the shrunken human head from the Don the Beachcomber gift shop!

Sitting at the kitchen table in his bathrobe, with a cup of coffee and a toasted bagel, the daily consumption of which was for him a eucharistic affirmation of our Jewish heritage, my father did not look up from the *Los Angeles Examiner* as my mother told the story with an indulgent smile: "Papa had had a few too many Zombies," she began and recounted that after dinner they had gone into the gift shop, where Dr. Chambers had been startled and amply impressed by the shrunken human head.

"That looks like the real thing to me," the school principal had said, and for some reason, he knew all about them: "They're not from the South Seas, of course, but from the Amazon. It's the Jivaro Indians who are the head hunters and shrinkers. There are lots of fakes on the market, made from monkey or goat heads. But that looks authentic. You can tell it's human by the detail and complexity of the folds in the ears. Yes, sir, if that head isn't the real McCoy, my name's not Dr. Gus Chambers, PhD. It's a steal at a hundred dollars. A real collector's item."

And so my father, his resolve weakened by Zombies, impulsively splurged on the shrunken head that I had so often, without any luck, begged him to buy. The story, however, was not over, and the happiness the human head had afforded me was substantially compromised by the subsequent denouement. My father had done something that embarrassed me even more than Robert's showing a twat to Mrs. Chambers. On the way back from Don the Beachcomber, he had taken the principal of my elementary school and his wife to the Largo Club to see Candy Barr perform striptease.

"No!" I cried out, choking on the shock and shame of it. "Tell me you didn't. I can't believe you'd do that! How could you? I'm never going to school again! You've ruined my life."

My father looked up from the newspaper with a smile: "They loved the show. What Candy Barr did impressed Dr. Chambers a lot more than Mary Martin's flying. His eyes were popping out of his head." He calmly took another bite of his bagel, laughed, and then continued to read about racial unrest in the paper. Robert thought it was funny too, and my mother didn't seem the slightest bit upset.

Forced to go to school, I avoided Dr. Chambers and tried to make the best of things by taking advantage of an opportunity to brag to my friends that I owned a shrunken human head. Looking at it as displayed in a glass bell in our library-bar, none of them believed that it was real.

"They sell them down in Tijuana for five bucks," Little Mike Shulman scoffed.

"Yeah," concurred Robbie Freeman, who always seemed to know what he was talking about. "They make them out of monkey heads."

Larry "Spanky" Feinstein added that he had bought a rubber shrunken head for one dollar from Gags Galore. "It looks as real as yours," he claimed, "and it's washable. They're made in Japan. The Japs are great at copying things."

My friends were more interested in looking at Frank G. Lafleur's depictions of female genitalia in *The Reproductive System* than at the real head of a real man, shrunken by real savages in the Amazon. That they didn't believe me when I swore the head was real was understandable since we often lied to one another.

Coming up from our bomb shelter, where we had been enjoying my pornography collection one afternoon, Robert and I were surprised to find our father in the kitchen, home from work so early and holding our mother in his arms. She was crying and he was silently stroking her hair. She had just learned that her father had passed away.

That summer my mother decided to take our widowed grandmother to Hawaii. A vacation in the islands would provide a little sweet pleasure after the bitter sadness experienced over the loss of someone so loved. The good news was that Robert and I were going to get to go along. Sally May Carter exclaimed that, with us gone, she'd have to take a vacation, "Shit, I ain't stayin' alone in this house with Dr. Siegel! A man's a man no matter what's the color of his skin."

Although my parents traveled a lot (yet another thing adults could do whenever they wanted), my only experience of a foreign land had been a family excursion to Tijuana one weekend. During my six hours south of the border, I was thrilled with a sense that there was sin and crime and, above all, sex in the air. Pimps, prostitutes, striptease dancers, nymphomaniacs, and Spanish fly manufacturers, not to mention drug dealers, bandits, and Communist revolutionaries, were, in my imagination, lurking in every shadow. That made it scary, and that made it fun. Although I knew it would be difficult to recognize her in clothes, I had kept my eyeballs peeled for the wanton woman in the photograph that Cisco Zutano had given me in trade for a whoopee cushion. I saw the neon sign for the famous Blue Fox, where Larry "Spanky" Feinstein swore that his uncle Mannie had sworn to have seen a show in which a woman had sex with a donkey. Even though Spanky hadn't believed that my shrunken human head was real, I suspected that his shocking story might be true. When it came to sex, I already knew, anything was possible.

Just as they always let us go to the gift shop at Don the Beachcomber while they continued to drink rum drinks, so my parents allowed Robert and me to go out to the street market in front of Hernando's Hideaway while they finished their margaritas. I had to act fast to buy what I wanted before they came out to look for us. Utterly astounded that they'd sell such dangerous things to a kid, my heart was pounding excitedly as I counted out the cash for a switchblade knife, brass knuckles, a rawhide bullwhip, and some cherry bombs. These articles were subsequently added to the cache of contraband hidden in the red velvet couch in my room.

Robert spent all of his money on a small portrait of President Dwight D. Eisenhower painted on black velvet. Eisenhower had recently had a heart attack, and, Robert explained, "If he dies, this painting is going to go way up in value."

Before leaving Tijuana, my father couldn't resist letting the street photographer take a picture of his wife and two sons to be proudly displayed along with all the others that decorated the walls of his medical office at Twentieth Century-Fox Studio. The photographer posed us before a painted backdrop depicting a cactus desert. He put large a sombrero on my head and one on Robert's, draped serapes over our shoulders, and helped my mother adjust a florid floral mantilla. Robert was seated on an old donkey. I wondered if the animal had ever worked at the Blue Fox.

Six months later, displayed next to that framed photograph, there was a new one in which the hats on our heads were woven out of palm fronds. There were garlands of flowers around our necks, and there was a parrot rather than a donkey. It was perched on Robert's shoulder. The painted backdrop showed a beach, palm trees, and Diamond Head in the distance. The photograph, taken at Don the Beachcomber in Waikiki, the Hawaiian version of the original authentic South Seas restaurant in Hollywood, was included in our Special Holiday Luau Package. We were also allowed to keep both the leis that had been given to us with a kiss upon arrival and the hollowed-out pineapples in which our Pi-Yi's were served.

"Aloha," the master of ceremonies in the flowered shirt shouted with considerable gusto and then encouraged us to repeat it: "A-lo-haaaaa! It means hello, good-bye, and I love you." He taught us ancient native customs: whenever you put a flower lei around someone's neck, you are required to give that person a kiss; you wear a flower behind your right ear if you are available, one behind your left ear if you already have someone you love; to appease the Goddess Pele, you throw a bottle of gin into a volcano. He also told us there was evidence that the Polynesians were the lost tribe of Israel and that it was the missionaries who made "the wahines of our islands cover up their naked bodies. And thus the muumuu was born."

In addition to the shrimp fried in coconut batter and chicken with pineapple on bamboo skewers, I had, because my father wasn't around, the illicit, but rather exiguous, pleasure of eating some of the pig that had been cooked in an underground pit. As the meal was consumed, women in muumuus waved their hands rhythmically in the air as they sang songs about "soft breezes sighing and night birds crying where palm trees sway and sweet breezes play, down by the sea in Waikiki, where moonlight beams bring love's sweet dreams, on this isle of love, our Aloha Land."

An enormously fat woman strumming a ukulele so tiny that it practically disappeared into her hefty bosom sang, "Princess Papuli has a papaya and she loves to give it away; but all of the neighbors say that while she gives you the fruit, she hangs on to the root." I didn't know exactly why it was dirty, but I could tell that it was because all of the adults, even my grandmother, although still in mourning over the loss of her husband, laughed. Later that night, as I was trying to fall asleep, I heard her in the bathroom of our hotel room weeping.

As the dessert of pineapple-coconut cream cake was brought to us on banana leaves, a chorus of little girls, some as young as Robert, the oldest not much older than me, came onto the stage dressed in green grass skirts, with little bras made of coconut shells, flower leis around their necks, and hibiscus blossoms behind their right ears. There was one girl, the third from the right, who looked a lot, I supposed, like Luana would have looked when she was ten. The emcee sang as they danced:

I love a pretty little Honolulu hula-hula girl;
She's the candy kid to wiggle, hula girl.
She will surely make you giggle, hula girl,
With her naughty little wiggle.
Someday I'm gonna try to make
This hula hula girlie mine.
Her oni-oni motions
Stir up my emotions.
Yes, I've gotta make that little hula-hula girl mine!

And my emotions were indeed as stirred up as any exotic tropical drink, and flaming at that, so much so that I'd look for my little Honolulu hula-hula girl as I sat on the beach in front of the Moana Hotel each morning, as I ate papaya for breakfast in the Banyan Court, as I went with my mother and grandmother shopping at the marketplace on the other side of Kalakaua. I assured myself that if I spotted her, I'd have the courage to walk right up to her and say, "Aloha." And if she then offered to dance the hula again, this time just for me, this time where palm trees swayed and sweet breezes played, down by the sea in Waikiki, where moonlight beams would bring love's sweet dreams, I'd make sure that, before she did, I threw a bottle of gin into a volcano so that Madame Pele wouldn't get pissed off.

Although I never found her, the little hula-hula girl of my reveries, or any other girl for that matter, and despite the fear of giant clams that I felt whenever I went swimming in the ocean, I liked Hawaii. The intermittent rains were almost as gentle (although not as regular) as those outside Don the Beachcomber, and the sunsets were almost as beautiful (although not as bright) as those painted on velour at the Hollywood restaurant. Those paintings had given me hope that I might run into some bare-breasted wahines in the South Seas. Because of the Christian missionaries, however, the only naked boobs that were to be seen anywhere in the islands were the floppy white whoppers of my grandmother, hanging all the way down to her waist, exposed as she changed into or out of her bathing suit in the room she and my mother shared with Robert and me.

Inspired by our Waikiki vacation, my mother decided to redecorate our pool house as a Hawaiian hut.

My grandmother, moving down to Los Angeles from Wenatchee, Washington, brought along with her Debbie B. Toyland, a snow-white toy French poodle, as playful and cute as Rin Tin Tin was obedient and courageous.

Because I knew how sad my grandmother still was over the loss of her husband, I did a portrait of Debbie to give to her as a present. She was, after all, the only woman in the world whose naked breasts I had actually seen in person. First I drew what looked exactly like Connie Feinstein's pubes, and then, at the point at the bottom of the triangle of curly hair, I placed a big black dot for the nose, and just above and on either side of that nose, identical black dots for the eyes (too high or too low, too wide apart or too close together, and the quintessential cuteness would be lost). Then an upside-down T for the lips and enigmatic smile, a few whiskers, a little goatee, some curly hairs for the ears, and she was almost done. All I needed to do was use my pink colored pencil for the little bow in her hair, and there she was—Debbie B. Toyland. I planned to buy some white and pink paint and some black velvet to do another portrait of the dog, a more elaborate painting that would include not only Debbie B. Toyland's pink bow but also her pink, rhinestone-studded leash and even the pink cashmere sweater, monogrammed *DBT*, that she wore in inclement weather.

"Debbie's in heat," my grandmother announced. "We'll have to put a pair of Damsel-Doggie Modesty Panties on her when we walk her. Otherwise a male could get to her." Finally, once my grandmother had explained "heat" to me (and I had inspected that moist, swollen little plum between Debbie's hind legs), I understood what Louis Lapine had meant when he wrote that Communist agent Marika Semenova was "writhing on the bed like a female satyr in heat." "She's ready to be impregnated and receptive to being mounted by a male," my grandmother said. "And smelling it, a male will do anything to get to her."

After she had promised to take me to Don the Beachcomber for dinner, it was hard to refuse a widowed grandmother's request that I walk Debbie B. Toyland. I was no more than three doors away from our house when I heard the dreaded voice and terrible derision: "Hey, Siegel, you little pussy, bring that little mouse of yours over here. I want to feed it to Attila." And Attila, no doubt picking up the scent of Debbie B. Toyland's heat and responding to the olfactory call to love, barked with ferocious passion.

After graduating from Ponce de Leon Elementary School, Frank Hardy had gone on to the Golden Eagle Military Academy, and he was so proud of his ROTC uniform that he was wearing it that day, even though it was a Saturday. I was afraid that he'd release Attila and that the Doberman would, much to his master's amusement, pounce on the French poodle, rip her from my grip, and carry her off in his powerful jaws, her rhinestone-studded pink leash dragging behind them. He'd tear off her modesty panties and have his way with her.

Turning back toward home and walking fast (but not running, since that, I reminded myself, made Dobermans attack), I suffered a humiliating razzing: "Come back here, Siegel, you little fairy. That's a faggot dog."

When I told Spanky Feinstein about the terrifying encounter, he shrugged his shoulders and, instead of offering words of support or understanding, commented, "Well, she is kind of a faggot dog. I'd never walk a poodle, especially not one in panties with a pink bow in her hair."

Spanky liked to come over once our pool house had been transformed into what I referred to as "Lee the Beachcomber": a Hawaiian hut with grass matting on the walls, a fisherman's net overhead with dried starfish and glass balls in it, a giant clamshell filled with rubber tropical fruit, cane and bamboo furniture, scenic paintings on black velvet, potted palms, abalone shell ashtrays, blowfish lamps, Tiki-god-handled bottle openers, mugs, stirrers, napkins, and, best of all, a real human shrunken head. In that setting I told Spanky about the enormous waves on which I had ridden a surfboard in Hawaii and about beautiful Luana, the hula-hula girl who had been my sweetheart on the Isle of Love. "The girls there have to let you kiss them if you give them a lei. It's an ancient Hawaiian religious custom. Hawaiian women went around naked until the Christian missionaries made them wear muumuus. Luana, being the daughter of a Great Kahuna and worshiper of Tiki, is not a Christian, and so she doesn't wear a top except when she goes to school. Just a grass skirt and a flower lei. We swam together every morning in a pool behind a waterfall."

Although Spanky probably didn't believe anything I told him about Hawaii, he seemed to be changing his mind about the shrunken head. "Yeah, it looks real," he said. "Can we take it out of the case? I'd like to hold it." As soon as I let him do that, he grinned to say, "Yesireee, this head feels like the real thing."

When we went in for a swim, Spanky left the head in the hibiscus-print upholstered seat of the rattan rocking chair in which he had been sitting while examining it. Debbie B. Toyland had followed us to the pool house, where, as usual, she acted cute in the hope of getting human attention and a share of any candy we might happen to have on us. She especially liked M&M's.

After getting out of the pool and drying off, we went into the pool house to change, only to discover the miniature white poodle nestled into the Hawaiian rattan rocker with clumps of black hair scattered around her. She had eaten the face of the shrunken human head, devouring everything but the pate of long straight hair and the knots of raffia that had sealed shut the eyes and mouth of the relic.

Not only was I upset to have lost my hundred-dollar head, I was worried that I'd get in trouble for not taking better care of it. Spanky offered to give me his rubber shrunken head from Gags Galore to replace the real one in the glass display bell on the chance that my parents wouldn't be able to tell the fake one from the real thing. I had more faith in a simple lie. I told my parents that little Debbie, after jumping up onto the bar and knocking the glass bell over to get to the head, had run off with it. By the time Spanky and I had found her it was too late. "Being in heat," I sighed, "is really making her act crazy."

My grandmother took Debbie to Dr. Wiener, who, prescribing Pepto-Bismol and Miltown for the dog, consoled the owner: "Dogs are natural scavengers and omnivores. If Debbie had grown up in the wild, human flesh would have been an occasional part of her diet." I imagined a pack of poodles, Debbie among them, watching a tribal battle from the Amazon underbrush, waiting to rip their dinners from the bodies of slain warriors. Once Debbie had eaten the head, I never again allowed her to lick my face.

The best part of fixing up the pool house was that whenever we went to Don the Beachcomber, my father would give Robert and me extra money to spend in the gift shop on decor. We could always use a new Tiki god, if not in the form of the actual idol, at least adorning an ashtray, shot glass, or napkin. And I had an additional twenty bucks the night my grandmother took Robert and me to the restaurant, money to buy party favors for my upcoming eleventh birthday party, a real Hawaiian luau in our house.

My grandmother invited a depressed Mrs. Snook to join us for dinner at the Polynesian restaurant. Mrs. Snook was visiting from Wenatchee, where she had formerly worked as a clerk-typist at my grandfather's Coca-Cola bottling works. Although she was, we were told, one of the most pathetic women in the world, it turned out that she was not quite pathetic enough. All of her many tragedies had something to do with love and sex: her fourteen-year-old daughter was pregnant and didn't know who the father was; her older daughter had stolen Mrs. Snook's diamond engagement ring, hocked it, and given the money to a Fuller Brush man, who subsequently abandoned her (a trauma for which she was hospitalized in the psychiatric ward of Wenatchee's Seventh-day Adventist hospital); her oldest son, a hairdresser at the Wenatchee Palace of Beauty, was arrested for indecency, lewd behavior, and solicitation at the Temple of Adonis, a men's bathhouse in Seattle; her husband, a shoe salesman, after infecting her with a venereal disease that he had picked up in a Pullman brothel, ran off with Wenatchee's Apple Blossom Queen; Mrs. Snook's eighth-grade son had been arrested by juvenile authorities for molesting a fifth-grade girl; and the girl's father, furious that the boy's punishment consisted of no more than compulsory weekly counseling with a county social worker, vengefully set the Snook house on fire. As undaunted by her calamities as Job, Mrs. Snook boarded a Greyhound bus in Wenatchee to come to Hollywood so that, by appearing on *Queen for a Day,* she could win back some of the home appliances she had lost in the fire and be given enough in cash prizes to buy a new diamond engagement ring.

I had seen the show, on which a mustached Jack Bailey would interview four tearful women about their respective tragedies. At the end of the program, Bailey would hold his hand over the head of each contestant in turn, and the one who, according to the live audience's judgment as registered on the Queen for a Day Applause-O-Meter, was the most pathetic would be draped in a sable-trimmed red-velvet robe, crowned Queen for a Day, and given prizes.

Mrs. Snook, convinced that, by being such a loser, she was sure to be a winner, had asked my grandmother, the only person she knew in Los Angeles, to drive her to the television studio for the interview at which contestants were chosen. Not only was Mrs. Snook not crowned Queen for a Day, she was not even considered sufficiently pathetic to appear on the show. Maybe Mrs. Snook's story wasn't sad enough, or perhaps American television just wasn't yet ready for a tale of prostitution, adultery, illegitimacy, homosexuality, venereal disease, and child molestation, all in one dose. "The show's fixed," Mrs. Snook declared as we turned off Hollywood Boulevard onto McCadden Place, "and Jack Bailey wears a toupee."

Since one of the prizes for all Queens for a Day was dinner with Jack Bailey at Don the Beachcomber, my grandmother, out of pity for Mrs. Snook, decided that, before dropping her off at the Greyhound bus station, there would be some consolation in taking her to that restaurant. Debbie B. Toyland, being small enough to hide in my grandmother's big purse, came along too. She loved the rumaki that my grandmother slipped to her under the table.

Robert and I were coached to be jolly with Mrs. Snook because, my grandmother divulged, "she could be suicidal." Sitting next to me in the back of my grandmother's new pink and white Packard Clipper, my brother whispered in my ear: "Tell her that joke about the guy with the red ring around his dick. That ought to cheer her up."

We were almost finished with dinner, and Mrs. Snook, installed in our table's queen's chair, had just ordered her fourth Pele's Revenge, when who should come into the restaurant but Jack Bailey with an old woman wearing a sable-trimmed red-velvet robe and a crown. No sooner were they seated than Mrs. Snook stood up and, announcing that she had to "have a word with Jack," went over to their table. My grandmother couldn't stop her.

At first we couldn't hear what she was saying to the queen and the television host, but when Mr. Lee approached the table and took hold of her arm to escort her away, Mrs. Snook's voice became loud enough for me to hear the word *fuck* more than once.

Several waiters had joined Mr. Lee in his attempt to calm Mrs. Snook and return her to our table when, all of a sudden, she broke loose from their grip, lunged forward to grab the Queen's flaming Lava Flow, and threw it on Her Majesty of the Day, thereby setting her regal sable-trimmed red-velvet robe on fire. There were screams as customers jumped up from their seats; waiters were running, trays overturned, drinks dropped, and, inside the purse under our table, Debbie B. Toyland was barking. Mr. Lee wrestled a moaning and sobbing Mrs. Snook to the floor and pinned her down with his knee between her breasts. Jack Bailey, as reported the next day in the *Los Angeles Examiner*, had heroically risked being burned himself by pulling the flaming robe off the Queen's shoulders and throwing it to the floor, where busboys stamped out the fire.

Once the police had taken Mrs. Snook away, Mr. Lee went from table to table, apologizing to all of the customers except us. I was so embarrassed that I didn't turn the ship's wheel, rub the figurehead's breasts, go to the gift shop, or ever want to return to Don the Beachcomber.

Even though I hadn't bought the Polynesian favors for my birthday party that night, the luau in our Hawaiian pool house seemed authentic enough without them: we drank Hawaiian Punch out of ceramic Tiki mugs garnished with pineapple slices and maraschino cherries; we ate shrimp fried in coconut batter and skewered chicken with pineapple; and served on banana leaves, there was a pineapple-coconut cream cake decorated with a palm tree in green and brown icing and, in blue icing, Happy Birthday Lee.

I was sorry that Little Mike Shulman couldn't come to the party and disturbed when my mother told me the reason why. One night earlier that week, when the Shulmans were out to dinner, Little Mike's older brother, Big Doug, had stolen the family's second car, a new Buick Roadmaster. After picking up his girlfriend, Mona Leaseman, and driving up to the top of Mulholland Drive with her to make out, he had missed a turn. The car went off the road and plummeted into a ravine. Big Doug had broken his neck and was being operated on the weekend of my party. Although we didn't know the Leasemans well enough to attend Mona's funeral, my mother asked me to sign the sympathy card that would be sent with the flowers to her parents.

Robbie Freeman wasn't at the luau either because he had been sent, earlier that year, to boarding school in Switzerland. All my other friends, however—Buzzy, Ricky, Cisco, Chip, Spanky, and Chuck—were there, as was my newest pal, Lance Finkel, whose parents were getting a divorce, and Leo Roth, who was invited even though I didn't like him because my parents were friends of his parents. There were lots of cute girls too—Donna Young, Bridget Kelly, Denise Lee, Patty Schultz, Candy Canter, Babs Cohen, Lana Gurdin, Elizabeth Ulm, and Suzie Krasny.

Other than when, at one point in the party, all of the kids who were swimming jumped out of the pool screaming in terror because Spanky Feinstein had floated a few plastic Who Done It? Doggie Doo Doos in the water, it was a pretty good luau. The highlight for me was the arrival of Suzie Krasny in an authentic cellophane grass skirt and a little coconut-shell bra. I had never before noticed how really cute she was. Really, really, really cute.

I had greeted the girl guests to my Hawaiian hut by saying "aloha" and placing a lei of paper flowers around each of their necks. And, in accordance with Hawaiian custom, as explained to them by my mother, I was required to kiss each one of them lightly on the cheek as I did so. When I said "aloha" to the other girls, it just meant "hello" when they arrived at the party and "goodbye" when they left. But when I said "aloha" to the little Beverly Hills hula-hula girl in the cellophane grass skirt and coconut-shell bra, both times it was Hawaiian for "I love you."

In Chapter Four, You Break Up, But You Give Her Just One More Chance

1956♥1957

By and by she gave up, and let her hands drop; her face, all glowing with the struggle, came up and submitted. Tom kissed the red lips and said: "Now it's all done, Becky. And always after this, you know, you ain't ever to love anybody but me."

Mark Twain, *The Adventures of Tom Sawyer*

A small minority are enabled by their constitution to find happiness in spite of everything, along the path of love. But far-reaching mental changes in the function of love are necessary before this can happen.

Sigmund Freud, *Civilization and Its Discontents*

1956

In the United States, the Atomic Energy Commission explodes the world's first airborne hydrogen bomb, the phrase "In God We Trust" is adopted as the national motto, and *I Led 3 Lives* goes off the air; Debra Paget appears in both Cecil B. DeMille's *The Ten Commandments* and *Love Me Tender* with Elvis Presley, and Jayne Mansfield appears in Frank Tashlin's *The Girl Can't Help It;* burlesque artiste Candy Barr is arrested for shooting her drunk husband, and actor Pepe Pelotas is convicted under the Mann Act for transporting a Beverly Hills High School senior girl across state lines for immoral purposes; the US Department of Agriculture identifies four official basic food groups, and Certs, the first candy breath mint, is introduced; Marilyn Monroe marries playwright Arthur Miller, and motion picture producer Irving Finkel divorces former Miss America Marsha Monroe; the California chapter of the National Society for Rabbit Protection and Welfare is formed, and Bugs Bunny stars in *Rabbit Romeo;* Li'l Wally Jagiello, the World's Polka King, appears on *The Lawrence Welk Show,* and Elvis Presley appears on *The Ed Sullivan Show;* the United States hockey team loses the gold medal to the Soviet Union at the winter Olympics, and Americans Bobby Byrd and Carol Summers win the fox-trot gold medal in the International Harvest Moon Ballroom Dance Competition at Madison Square Garden.

"I adore Elvis," Suzie Krasny sighed. "I love his long hair and big dark eyes, the way his nose twitches and his upper lip quivers. I love how he wiggles and shakes, and hops around and jumps about. He's so cute. He is so cool. I'll always love Elvis."

"I guess he's kind of cool," I conceded in an effort to ingratiate myself, "at least for a rodent."

An affronted Suzie snapped back at me in indignant defense of her beloved pet: "Rats and mice are rodents. Rabbits aren't rodents. They're lagomorphs. Elvis is a purebred, long-haired Mini Lop lagomorph."

While most Jews hide only the afikomen at Passover seders for their children to find, the Krasnys hid, in addition to that piece of matzah that symbolizes the paschal lamb, chocolate eggs wrapped in brightly colored foil as emblems of the assimilation of Jews into the American way of life. Whichever of their four children, Matt, Mark, Luke, or Suzie, retrieved the most eggs was awarded a grand prize. Suzie, the oldest of the Krasny kids, as the winner in 1956 (5716 on the Jewish calendar), had received the Pesach Bunny. The Passover egg hunt, Suzie explained, had been instituted as a Krasny family tradition in response to her brother, Matt, who had, in the midst of asking the Four Questions at their seder the previous year, complained that it was more fun to be a Christian than a Jew: "They've got the Easter Bunny and chocolate eggs, and all we've got is Elijah and kosher macaroons."

In order to assure his offspring that Judaism could be as much fun and just as cool as any other world faith, Mr. Seymour Krasny, a musical director at Warner Brothers, composed a song for his family to sing right after "Had Gadya":

Here comes Moshe Shmattentail
Shleppin' down the bunny trail,
Hippity shmippity, hoppity shmoppity
Our Messiah's on his way!
Bringin' ev'ry Jewish girl and boy
A basketful of Pesach joy—
Matzahs and chocolate eggs, oy vey!—
All the things to make your Seder
Bright and gay!

During the presentation of her rabbit research for Mr. Gordon's sixth-grade science class, Suzie (who had changed her lagomorph's name from Moshe Shmattentail to Elvis Krasny) sang the song right after proclaiming that "bunnies should play a more important part in Jewish holidays. 'Rabbit' comes right after 'rabbi' in the *World Book Encyclopedia.*"

Elvis peered nervously through the screened side of his Porta-Bunny carrier as Suzie read her report: "Rabbits symbolized love, romance, and fertility to the Egyptians, Babylonians, Greeks, Romans, and the Musquakie Indians of Northern Illinois." After informing us of the keen intelligence, vast capacity for affection, deep sensitivity, clean habits, good humor, and adorable manners of rabbits, Suzie proudly announced that she had recently been elected secretary-treasurer of the children's division of the newly formed California chapter of the National Society for Rabbit Protection and Welfare, a group dedicated to banning the slaughter of rabbits for meat, pelts, or lucky feet. She concluded by inviting any of us who might be interested in receiving a newsletter, attending a meeting, or making a donation to see her after class.

I had no particular fondness for rabbits, and I still had the lucky rabbit's foot that I had received for Chanukah a few years earlier as an accessory to my FAO Schwarz Indian brave outfit. Nevertheless, I told Suzie that I'd love to go to a Rabbit Protection and Welfare meeting with her sometime. I had had a crush on her ever since my eleventh birthday party luau, and just recently, by luck or fate, we had been paired up on the basis of our respective heights as dance partners at the Bobby Byrd of Beverly Hills Dance Cotillion. So I offered to help Suzie carry Elvis home from school.

My assignment for the section of the class that Mr. Gordon devoted to animals had been to report on raccoons, the encyclopedia entry for which would have come right after "rabbit" if not for the article on "rabies." I plagiarized most of my paper from my parents' *Encyclopaedia Britannica,* which was shelved not far from the complete works of Dr. Frank G. Lafleur, MD. In that adult reference work, I discovered a fabulous fact about the flesh-eating, tree-climbing North American nocturnal mammal whose striped bushy tail so handsomely festooned Davy Crockett's cap:

> The raccoon penis contains an elongate bony structure known as the baculum. Since raccoon ovulation is not periodic, but induced by copulation, the penis bone serves the survival of the species by prolonging the duration of intercourse. Raccoon penis bones have been prized by some American Indian tribes as good luck charms.

Right after Suzie's presentation, Little Mike Shulman read his report on the vulture (which I realized would come right before "vulva" in a good encyclopedia). And then it was my turn to deliver my raccoon paper. The moment I uttered the phrase "raccoon penis," the class broke into wild laughter, prompting an appalled Mr. Gordon to jump up from his desk, rush toward me, rip the essay out of my hands, and sentence me to ten laps around the playing field after school. I think he had disliked me ever since I had quit Cub Scouts. Reporting to the teacher after class, I made a desperate plea for him to commute that sentence on the grounds that I had merely been presenting information from the *Encyclopaedia Britannica,* arguing that surely nothing in that venerable compendium of knowledge could be dirty.

But Mr. Gordon was a strict judge. "Listen, young man, it's not that I have anything against either the *Encyclopaedia Britannica* or raccoon penises, or that I personally consider penises, raccoon or otherwise, with or without bones in them, dirty. I don't, because I am a scientist. But teaching science isn't my only responsibility here at Ponce de Leon. No, it's also my duty to keep order in the classroom. We can't learn unless there's order. And I know that you knew darned well that as soon as you said 'raccoon penis,' not to mention 'penis bone,' it would make the others laugh and disrupt the educational process. A science class is no place for clowning around. It's not *what* you said, but *why* you said it that was wrong. Think about that as you run those laps this afternoon."

With Elvis in his Porta-Bunny on her lap, Suzie sat on a playing field bench watching me run my punitive laps as she waited for me to help her carry Elvis home. Finally, we set out along Elevado together. I cavalierly told her that I thought Elvis was cool and that her report was edifying: "Having a real rabbit in the room as we learned all of those fascinating facts about them was really great. I wish I could have brought a male raccoon to class."

"Don't let his Porta-Bunny Travel Hutch swing so much," Suzie ordered as we walked along together. "Carry him carefully. I don't want Elvis to vomit. It doesn't take much to make him sick. And I hate it when he throws up."

Once I had apologized for my egregiously inattentive handling of Elvis, Suzie acknowledged my classroom disgrace: "Even if you had brought a raccoon, Mr. Gordon would have punished you for saying 'penis.' He's a dork."

It was thrilling to hear a cute girl say "penis," even though I knew that, while she could do so in reference to animal genitalia, it would have been too saucy for her to talk about a human penis, mine or that of anyone she personally knew. She could say "penis," furthermore, because we were only eleven years old. Once she went through puberty and had breasts, penis talk would become dangerous. But while she could say "penis," she would never, at least not in the presence of a boy, have said "cock," "dick," or "prick" any more than Cisco Zutano, so admired by his male classmates for his command of dirty language, would ever have used the word *penis*. He taught me some of the Spanish words for the organ in question. There were hundreds of them, both feminine and masculine: *reata, verga, chuperson, picha, arma, pinga, polla, rabo, pedazo, tonsilo, nabo, morrongo, carajo, pito,* and *picho,* to name but a few. Appropriately, they had as many words for the penis as they did for the vagina. "Spanish," Cisco boasted, "is a romance language."

It practically took my breath away when Suzie continued to use the potent word for which I had been so severely punished: "It was wrong of Mr. Gordon to get so hot under the collar over *penis*. It's just a word. It's the word doctors and nurses use. It's in the dictionary. Penis. Penis. Penis." My hands were shaking, my knees were weak, and, almost unable to stand on my own two feet, I practically dropped Elvis's Porta-

Bunny Travel Hutch. I wondered if she knew what she was doing to me.

"Because of what happened to you just for saying 'penis,'" Suzie persisted, "I'm glad I didn't tell the class about how rabbits mate. I would have had to say 'bunny penis.'"

"So, how do they mate?" I asked ingenuously, and she answered, whether consciously or not, coquettishly: "Just like us. I mean, you know, just like human beings, except they do it from behind. Isn't that cute?"

When we arrived at Suzie's house, Mrs. Krasny offered us an after-school snack and, even though our choices included all of the most popular gastronomical delicacies of the era (Hawaiian Punch and Kool-Shake, Laura Scudder's potato chips with party dip, Skippy peanut butter and/or Cheez Whiz on Ritz crackers, Sealtest Triple-Treat ice cream with Reddi-wip, and Kraft Tuna-Cheesewiches), Suzie announced that all she wanted was a carrot. As an amorous courtesy, I gallantly said that I too would have only a carrot. What was good enough for Suzie and Elvis was good enough for me.

We took Elvis up to Suzie's room, the walls of which were adorned with portraits of Peter, Bugs, and other illustrious lagomorphs, as well as autographed photographs of Perry Como and Pat Boone, for whom Mr. Krasny had written songs. Just as she could say *penis* because we were only eleven, so could she have me up to her room unchaperoned. Once she was wearing a brassiere and using Kotex sanitary pads, there would have to be guardians of her chastity.

When I asked where his cage was, it offended Suzie as much as when I had referred to Elvis as a rodent: "I'd never keep Elvis Krasny cooped up. Bunnies have feelings too. How would you like to live in a cage? My room is Elvis's room."

Once released from his Porta-Bunny Travel Hutch, Elvis hopped his way toward the bathroom, where Suzie proudly showed me "his potty." Putting what remained of her carrot in the litter box for him, she noted with a happy smile that "he likes to eat while he poops. Isn't that cute?"

After doing what Suzie thought was so adorable and then scrambling up the little ramp into Suzie's bed, Elvis nestled among her collection of teddy bears. "I used to have a stuffed rabbit, but I got rid of it because it scared him. It made him throw up. He thought it was a dead rabbit—a real one."

Yearning to hear my girlfriend say the magic word again, I redirected the conversation: "I've been thinking about what you said earlier about *penis*—you know, about it being in the dictionary. Is it really?"

When, in order to get a dictionary from her mother, Suzie left me alone with Elvis, I sat down on the bed next to him. The rabbit looked up at me with an expression that said, "Please don't throw me in the briar patch." It seemed to me that if he was anywhere near as intelligent, perceptive, and sensitive as Suzie claimed rabbits to be, Elvis would sense that his rival for his mistress's affection didn't think it was even slightly cute that he liked to shit and eat at the same time.

"Yes, *penis* is here," Suzie exclaimed excitedly as she returned, open dictionary in hand. "*Penis* is in between *peninsula* and *penitence. Penis.* It's from the Latin *penis,* which means 'tail.'" She smiled. "Like in Peter Cotton*tail.* '*Penis.* A male organ of copulation.' Yes, *penis* is in Webster's. That proves it—there's nothing wrong with *penis.*" The presence of the rabbit notwithstanding, it was rapturous to be sitting on her bed listening to her say "penis" no less than six times (even though one of those times it was just the Latin word for "tail"). I noticed a soft pink and white bunny-adorned flannel nightgown hanging on a hook on the back of her half-closed door. It was about as much sex as an eleven-year-old could hope for.

Pubescent passion tempted me to inform Suzie that *dick, cock,* and *prick* were in the dictionary too (I had looked all of them up). But, even though none of those words were defined in the dictionary as "a male organ of copulation," I knew that uttering them would amount to a major transgression of the limits of what a nice boy could say to a nice girl, even one with undeveloped breasts. I had to be content with *penis.*

"Do you want to hold him?" Suzie asked. "He's very cuddly." In spite of her insistence that rabbits were lagomorphs, Elvis was still just a rodent to me. Although I had no interest in handling a rabbit, I played along to please my girlfriend and prolong the delight of the day.

"No!" she suddenly screeched as my fingers wrapped around his ears. "Never, never, never ever pick up a bunny by his ears. Imagine someone trying to pick you up by your ears! Pick him up just like you'd want to be picked up. I'll show you." Tenderly she ran one hand under his belly and, gently stroking his back with her other hand, Suzie lifted Elvis as lovingly as any rabbit, or male member of any species, including raccoons and human beings, could ever want to be picked up. Holding him in her arms and softly caressing him, she kissed his long ears and spoke baby talk to him: "I wove my wovewy widdle wabbit." She looked up at me to say, "He loves it when I talk to him like that."

In hopes of hearing her say "penis" again, I asked how she knew Elvis was a boy. In her response, something even more thrilling than "penis" came out of Suzie's mouth: "I've sexed him. Would you like to watch?" God knows I did.

"Come here, sit next to me. I'll show you how to do it. The easiest way to sex your bunny," she explained, "is to hold him with the palm of one hand around the back of his head, with your thumb in front of the ears like this, so that he's lying on his back on your lap, like this." Submitting to the demonstration, a languorous Elvis was belly up between her legs. She continued: "Clamp his ears very gently between your knees, like this. You've got to be gentle. Being sexed can make him nervous, and when Elvis is nervous, he throws up."

"And you hate it," I added in anticipation of the inevitable, "when he throws up."

Suzie was leaning forward so that the rabbit's lucky little feet were propped up against her someday-to-develop breasts. Being sexed as lovingly as any creature could ever want to be sexed, Elvis looked happy.

"With your other hand," Suzie continued in a soothingly soft voice, "use your thumb and this finger to gently press on either side of this spot, here, what my bunny owner's manual calls the 'genital vent.' If the bunny's a boy, there will be something known as a 'tubular protrusion.' See, there it is—the tubular protrusion. Isn't it cute? It contains his penis. If Elvis was a girl, there'd be what the book calls a 'slit-like organ.' I've been thinking of getting a girlfriend for Elvis. The problem is that my parents say that if I get a girl bunny for him, then I have to have Elvis fixed so that we don't have a houseful of baby bunnies. The Egyptians, Babylonians, Greeks, Romans, and the Musquakie Indians of Northern Illinois didn't consider rabbits symbols of fertility for nothing. Rabbits love to mate. I don't know what to do. What do you think Elvis would like more: to have a girlfriend and be castrated (that's what my book calls it) or to have testes (that's what my book calls them) but not ever have a girlfriend? You're a boy, you ought to know. What do you think?"

Not caring one way or the other about Elvis's balls, I seized upon the opportunity to say something that I considered sweetly romantic: "He doesn't need a girlfriend, Suzie—he's got you to love him. He's a lucky lagomorph."

She smiled and closed her eyes. There was a moment of silence and adolescent self-consciousness, an entanglement of fear and desire, ache and trembling, and all of a sudden—I couldn't help it—I leaned over and kissed Suzie Krasny on the lips, something I wouldn't have had the nerve to do if I had thought about it. I couldn't help it. Love had made me do it. Suzie seemed less surprised by what I had done than I was. With her eyes still closed and Elvis still belly up in her lap, she sighed a sigh that seemed to say, "Again." And as my puckered lips touched her mouth, I felt her lips, supple and warm, open slightly. "Sex," I thought to myself, "is even better than the books say it is."

Handing Elvis to me, Suzie stood and, walking to her dresser, on which there was a new Webcor Coronet High Fidelity record player, said she wanted me to hear her favorite song. "I adore Elvis," she sighed. "I love his hair and long sideburns, the way he moves, and his blue suede shoes."

After positioning the stylus on the spinning forty-five, she rejoined me on the bed. As if in appreciation of the privacy lovers naturally yearn for, the singer's namesake squirmed out of my lap to hop off to the bathroom. Surrendering to the impetuous impulses of love, I put my arm around Suzie's shoulder and kissed her again, softly first and then more robustly, and again, and didn't stop kissing her until the song was over.

Love me tender, love me sweet,
Never let me go.
You have made my life complete
And I love you so.
Love me tender, love me true,
All my dreams fulfill.
For, my darling, I love you
And I always will. . . .

For her twelfth birthday, I gave Suzie *The Complete Rabbit Encyclopedia*. It was a book I could hardly resist buying for her after turning, as I stood in the hobby, garden, and pet book aisle of Martindale's bookshop, to *M* for "mating," the entry for which was more sexy than anything in *Commie Sex Siren*. Before giving her the book, I read it over while in bed in my pajamas at night, imagining her in her pink and white flannel nightie, cuddled up in bed with Elvis and reading the same luscious words. I turned over a corner of the page in question just to make sure she didn't miss it. I had read it so many times that I practically knew it by heart:

Like human beings, rabbits, because of their high level of social organization, exhibit an elaborate pattern of sexual behavior. The mating of rabbits is a ritual dance that commences with the male pursuing the female. In the course of getting closer and closer to the object of his desire, the male holds his hind feet rigid. Because the rabbit's hind feet are longer than its fore feet, this has the effect of raising the animal's hindquarters, causing the tail to perk up stiffly like a flag. This arouses the female. The male turns his back on his partner, lopes off a few paces, and then promptly rejoins her. This exhibition, repeated three or four times, serves to further stimulate the female by enabling her to smell his secretions and to see his white rump. Once the male is close enough to her, he squirts a jet of urine over her. In reaction to this exhibition of excitement, the female presents her own swelling rump to her mate so that, by mounting her from behind, he can commence with copulation. Once penetration has been achieved, the female passively submits to the powerful, rapid thrusting of the male's pelvis. After ejaculation, the male disengages to scamper off and away from the female.

That last line of the juicy vignette seemed so disconcerting that I was tempted to either cross it out or add a note in the margin: "Dear Suzie, I'd never scamper off and away from you."

I'd think of that passage on Thursday evenings when we danced the Bunny Hop at the Bobby Byrd Dance Cotillion. We were lined up behind each other—boy, girl, boy, girl—each of us holding on to the waist of the person in front of us. We began kicking sideways with the right foot and then jumping forward—one, two, three—and then kicking with the left foot, and then jumping again, forward, backward, forward, forward, forward: dada dada dada, da da da. Like a male rabbit presented with his mate's swollen hindquarters, I was behind Suzie with my hands just above her hips. The sumptuous organza of multilayered petticoats made her skirt flair out in such a way that, as I jumped forward, entering into that soft, enfolding spread, I'd think of the powerful, rapid thrusting of the pelvises of male rabbits in the wild.

In learning how to dance at the Bobby Byrd Cotillion, we were supposedly becoming young ladies and gentlemen, who, like rabbits with their high level of social organization, exhibit an elaborate pattern of mating behavior. As Bobby Byrd himself put it: "There's nothing like dancing to teach us what it is that makes a man, what it is that makes a woman, what it is that makes them different from each other, and what it is that makes them the same. Dance," he'd inevitably add, "rhymes with romance. So, hey, come on young ladies and gentlemen, let's dance, dance, dance!"

There were mirrors all along one side of Studio A, the ballroom where we tried to learn to fox-trot, mambo, rumba, waltz, swing, and cha-cha-cha. For the sake of mastering the basic box step, there were numbered shoe soles painted in white on the floor in one corner of the room, with dotted lines and arrows indicating the moves. Looking across the room at Suzie, I longed for an opportunity—a quick, clandestine moment in the darkness of the parking lot perhaps—to kiss again the lips that were glossed cherry red for cotillion.

"Okay young ladies and gentlemen, join your partners and, hey, let's dance, dance, dance," Bobby would say, and his assistant, Miss Summers, would lower the needle onto the Ray Conniff record: "The box step! One, one, two, one, one, two, three. That's it! Now open the box." There was inevitably some juvenile male snickering whenever Bobby Byrd said "box." Although as boys we could insinuate our fond familiarity with raunchy references, the girls necessarily pretended they didn't know why we laughed. As for Bobby Byrd, he thought it was because we were having so much fun.

The world was forever different after the Sunday night in 1956 when Elvis Presley appeared on *The Ed Sullivan Show* and it was announced that he could not be shown from the waist down. Threatened by the transformation of our society that Elvis heralded, Bobby Byrd, with the mute assistance of Miss Summers, was struggling to preserve the manners of a neater and cleaner past, when teenagers in America were primly polite and respectably respectful young adults in dress suits and evening dresses, dancing the fox-trot and aspiring to become as happily wholesome as the Cleavers and the Nelsons. This would require the sublimation of all sexual energy into the process of training to become those good citizens. Rock and roll mocked that sublimation with promises of purer and more passionate pleasures. Elvis Presley was, at least in Bobby Byrd's world, more dangerous than Nikita Khrushchev. The teacher boasted that he and Miss Summers had given private dance lessons to Richard and Pat Nixon to prepare them to cut up the rug at the 1953 Presidential Inaugural Ball. "Dick was stiff," he said as if he didn't know it would make the boys snicker, "but Pat was a natural."

In addition to Ray Conniff numbers, the Bobby Byrd musical canon included the melodies of Hugo Winterhalter and the songs of Gale Storm, Doris Day, and Patti Page. Bobby loved Perry Como's "Hot Diggity Dog Ziggity Boom" and anything by Pat Boone, but especially "It's Too Soon to Know." Just to show us that he wasn't the square he really was, he allowed "See You Later, Alligator" (but not "Rock around the Clock") by Bill Haley and His Comets. "The Green Door" was forbidden after a rumor spread that it was about a brothel. Usually during our break, when we had chocolate ice cream, graham crackers, and Hawaiian Punch, Bobby Byrd had Miss Summers play novelty songs like "The Flying Saucer, Part One," or "The Flying

Saucer, Part Two," to assure us that even though "learning to dance is hard work, it can be one heck of a lot of fun too."

While both Fats Domino and Little Richard were simply never heard in Studio A, Elvis "the Pelvis" Presley was actively and vociferously denounced there. "Dancing isn't just primitive gyrations, uninhibited shimmying, savage shaking, rude rocking, and raucous rolling à la Elvis," Bobby Byrd told us. "It's a matter of practice and control, of poise, grace, and flair." And in order for us to practice those skills, he had each of us warm up by walking around the dance floor with a book balanced on our head. The book just happened to be *Dance! Dance! Dance!* by Bobby Byrd, and it was available for purchase.

Bobby Byrd divulged a fundamental terpsichorean formula: "My own dance teacher, the one, only, and fabulous Caesar Ruiz, used to say that the secret of dancing is in pretending while you dance that you're in love, in love not only with your partner but with the whole world! So, okay young ladies and gentlemen, let's try it again. And remember, you're in love with everybody in the whole wide wonderful world. So, hey, let's dance, dance, dance!"

"Hey, kids," Bobby Byrd squealed once "Que Sera, Sera" had finished and we (some of us wondering whether we'd someday be happy or someday be rich) had returned to our seats (boys on one side of the room, girls on the other), "if you really want to, and you set your mind, heart, and both feet on it, someday you'll be able to dance like me." And then, the moment Miss Summers lowered the phonograph armature onto the spinning record, he pirouetted around the dance floor for us, loudly chanting, "One and a two, and a one, two, three."

In fact, none of the boys wanted to dance like Bobby Byrd; to have done so would have been to be a fairy in the eyes of male peers. I personally wanted to dance like Elvis Presley, whom Suzie Krasny so adored. If I could dance like him, the girls at the Bobby Byrd Dance Cotillion wouldn't be allowed to look at me from the waist down once I was on the dance floor. I wanted to dance like the cool teenagers who were old enough to go to Rock 'n' Roll Nite at the El Monte Legion Stadium—"Be there or be square!" the ad on the radio exclaimed. They had sideburns and ducktail hairdos, Zippo lighters and switchblade knives; they smoked cigarettes and drank beer; and they necked and petted and a few even went all the way with their girlfriends in the backseats of customized hot rods. While we, well-to-do Reform Jewish kids in Beverly Hills, were purebred Mini Lop domestic bunnies, those guys, all of them down-and-out Gentiles, lots of them Mexicans and Negroes, were wild rabbit bucks spraying their urine, waving their tails, scattering their scent, and doing mating dances made up of primitive gyrations, uninhibited shimmying, savage shaking, rude rocking, and raucous rolling. They wore black leather jackets and motorcycle boots during the day, and at night, when they went out dancing, they wore rogue trousers, white sport coats, and blue suede shoes with taps on them so that their girls could hear them coming.

I was certain that I'd be able to dance like those naturally cool guys and at least a little bit like the definitively cool Elvis the Pelvis if only my mother would buy me the pair of blue suede shoes that were in the window of the Beverly shoe store on Beverly Drive. Suzie had said she loved those shoes.

Because I felt sorry for the shoe salesman who, though a grown man, had to kneel down in front of a young boy for the sake of a meager living, I forgave him for ogling my mother's legs as he tied the blue suede tasseled laces into bows for me.

"Okey-dokey, young man," he said to me, sneaking a peek under my mother's dress as she uncrossed her legs to stand up. "Let's see if those shoes fit as good as they look. Come along, Mrs. Siegel, let's take a look into the X-ray Shoe Fitter." He had a slight accent that I guessed might be German.

The thing I loved best about shopping for shoes was looking at the bones in my feet wiggling in the fluoroscope. Every time I passed the shoe store, even without my mother, I'd go in and try on a pair of shoes just so that I could step up onto the raised platform, put my feet into the holes in the X-ray machine, press my eyes against the viewer, press the button that sent hundreds of Roentgens up through my feet into my undeveloped testes, and see my wiggling toes. Unaware at the time that the X-ray machine rivaled the Russian atomic bomb in its potential to contaminate American children with radiation, I could have looked at my feet for hours.

My mother and the shoe salesman stood close together on the other side of the X-ray Shoe Fitter, looking into the two viewers that allowed them to also enjoy the wondrous spectacle of my playfully squirming phalanges through blue suede, white rayon sock, pink skin, and blood-red muscle. These episodes with the fluoroscope never failed to remind me that the X-ray glasses that I had ordered in 1953 from Gags Galore still, after three years, hadn't arrived.

"Okey-dokey, Mrs. Siegel," the salesman said with unnatural glee, "the shoes fit like a glove." Noticing that he was paying more attention to my mother than to my shoes, I felt compelled to mention that my father was a doctor: "He has a big X-ray machine. He can X-ray every part of the body."

Checking myself out in the mirrors on the closet doors in my mother's dressing room, I was confident that when Suzie danced with me in those blue suede shoes, she'd fall as head over heels in love with me as I was in love with her. Running a black plastic pocket comb through my Brylcreemed hair, I softly sang her song.

When at last my dreams come true,
Darling, this I'll know:
Happiness will follow you
Everywhere you go.

The moment Bobby Byrd heard the taps on my blue suede shoes as I entered Studio A, before Suzie even had the chance to see my new footwear, the dance teacher accosted me in a snit: "I love tap dancing as much as anyone in the world! God knows I do," he snapped. "But if you want to wear taps, you'll have to enroll in my Wednesday night tap class, which meets in Studio B. On this floor we do not wear taps. We don't want scratches." He made me take off my shoes and leave them unattended in the Young Gentlemen's Lounge. "Just pretend," he suggested, forcing a smile to show that he was not as angry as he really was, "that you're at a sock hop. Hey, sock hops are fun!"

It hurt when Suzie stepped on my white rayon socks. But that wasn't the worst of it. After the perfunctory good-night Bunny Hop, as the girls fetched their purses from the Young Ladies' Lounge, I, anxiously hoping for a clandestine parking-lot kiss, went to put on my prized and cool blue suede shoes. No sooner had I slipped in my right foot than I felt the cold goo. Looking down, I saw the chocolate oozing out over the top edge of the shoe, and I realized that I was the butt of a practical joke. Better that somebody would have knocked me down, stepped on my face, slandered my name all over the place, even stolen my mom's car or put my allowance in an old fruit jar. I was devastated that someone had put ice cream in my blue, blue, blue suede shoes. Not only were my cool shoes ruined, but everybody, including Suzie Krasny, would laugh at me, just as they had when I wet my pants in the third grade. To avoid that humiliation and prevent my personal tragedy from becoming their collective comedy, I ignored the feeling in my right shoe and slipped my left foot into the other shoeful of melted ice cream. I pretended that nothing had happened.

"Hi, Siegel, how's it going?" Leo Roth asked with a big grin. Since we normally never spoke to each other, I suspected that he was the culprit. So that no one would notice the brown chocolate that was spreading up the ankles of my white socks, I stood in the darkest place in the parking lot to wait for my mother to pick me up. Fortunately I had a handkerchief to wipe off the ice cream that had spilled over the tops of the shoes; unfortunately the ice cream from that handkerchief was then in my white sport coat pocket. As soon as I climbed into the backseat of my mother's Cadillac, I burst into tears.

"What," I asked myself as I lay in bed that night, "would Elvis do if somebody put chocolate ice cream in his blue suede shoes?" But, of course, that could never happen. Robbie Freeman, the coolest guy I knew, had pointed that out: "Would Elvis ever go to dance cotillion? Fuck, no." Robbie, who had just come back from a year at boarding school in Switzerland, who had gooseneck handlebars on his bike, and who wore a black turtleneck sweater under a blue shirt with the collar up, wasn't taking dance lessons. "Dance cotillion," he proclaimed, "is for fairies. James Dean never went to dance cotillion."

"Yeah," Lance Finkel, the second most cool guy I knew (even if he did go to dance cotillion), agreed. "Bobby Boyd is definitely a homo."

"No he's not. He just acts like a fairy," argued Larry "Spanky" Feinstein, who had begun insisting that we no longer call him Spanky ("I swear to God, I'll kick the shit out of any asshole who calls me 'Spanky'—it's a fairy name"). "Last Thursday night, the night you had to dance in your socks, Siegel, I left my wallet at dance cotillion and was halfway home before I realized it. My mom drove me back to get it, and I went straight to the boy's lounge to look for it. I turned on the light and there they were—Miss Summers and Bobby Byrd. She was on her knees with his dick in her mouth. Bobby Byrd screamed as the light went on, but I think I turned off the light before they recognized me. I swear to God, Miss Summers was giving Bobby Byrd a blow job!"

"That doesn't mean he's not a homo," the urbane Robbie explained. "Homos like blow jobs."

"I'd like a blow job," Lance Finkel insisted, "and I'm not a homo." Chuck Mandel said he wanted one too, "and I'm not a homo either. I'm praying to God that I get a blow job for my bar mitzvah."

Lance lit a cigarette and held it between his lips as he talked: "I'm going to get one this summer when I go to France with my pop. The girls over in France love giving blow jobs. I'll probably get more than that. French people fuck like jackrabbits. And they love American guys because, in World War II, we saved them from Hitler and Communism. French guys fight with their feet and fuck with their faces."

"I don't get what you mean," Chuck confessed.

"The French do a kind of foot boxing called 'savant.'" Little Mike Shulman explained.

"Yeah, I know," Chuck said, "I get that part."

Laughing at Chuck, Lance then told us that his dad had informed him that "blow jobs are better than sex because you don't have to wear a rubber."

Little Mike Shulman, who had been silently shuffling the cards during the discussion of fellatio that evening in my Hawaiian hut pool house, ended the colloquy with an announcement: "Five-card draw, deuces and one-eyed jacks wild." We all felt sorry for Little Mike since he was often unable to come to our Saturday night poker parties. Since his older brother, Big Doug, had become paralyzed from the neck down, Little Mike had to stay at home with the quadriplegic whenever their parents went out. When the bet came to him, he folded and asked my brother Robert for a drink.

Robert was our bartender and banker, selling us the chips and serving the cocktails—Canada Dry crème de menthe straight up, on the rocks, or mixed with Coke, 7-Up, Dr Pepper, or White Rock ginger ale out of the big bottle with the beautiful little bare-breasted girl on the label. "This stuff is good," Larry exclaimed after downing a straight shot of it. "It tastes like Certs."

Because we were too young to drive and to date, playing poker and talking about sex (talking as dirty as we knew how) was the most exciting thing we could think of to do on a Saturday night.

Lance told Robbie, who had supplied us with a full pack of Lucky Strikes, that he ought to switch to Chesterfields: "I read a scientific medical report that said smoking Chesterfields is good for your nose, throat, and lungs. My pop smokes them. So does Jack Webb, George Reeves, Tyrone Power, Mr. Woodcock, the seventh-grade shop teacher, and Jonas Salk, the doctor who discovered the cure for polio. He wouldn't smoke them if they were bad for you."

Larry said he had read that all cigarettes are good for you: "Yeah, because they cause pleasure, and a medical research team at Harvard has discovered that it is a psychological fact that pleasure is good for your disposition, and that it is a biological fact that a good disposition is good for your physical health. People who have a lot of pleasure live longer no matter what brand of cigarette they smoke."

"Elvis Presley doesn't smoke," Chuck Mandel insisted as he shuffled the cards in preparation for his deal. "That's what I read in *Photoplay.* Elvis doesn't drink either. And he loves his parents a lot, especially his mom. He's dating Debra Paget. That's what I read. Five-card stud: aces, deuces, one-eyed jacks, kings, and sevens wild. Sevens have always been lucky for me."

Lighting up a Lucky, then picking up his hand and fanning it out, Robbie noted that "James Dean smoked three packs a day" and said that he didn't believe that Elvis really didn't smoke or drink. "They just say that because they know that a lot of kids want to be like him, and they don't want us to smoke or drink."

"That's right," Lance put in, placing an extravagant bet of ten ten-cent chips (bluffing I figured). "That's because they don't want us to have fun. I'm sure Elvis smokes and drinks and everything else. I'll bet you that he's probably fucked a thousand girls. Hey, Siegel, have you fucked Suzie Krasny yet?"

"If I was Elvis," Larry (apparently uninterested in my answer) piped up (seeing Lance's bet and raising him five), "I'd fuck a different girl every night."

"If I were Elvis," Chuck Mandel said as he folded, "I'd go back to school and go on to college so that I could get a good job if my singing career didn't work out."

"Did you hear that Elvis the Pelvis has a brother?" Larry asked. "Enis. Get it? Elvis the Pelvis, Enis the Penis."

"I wonder if Elvis is circumcised," Chuck remarked as he carefully counted his few remaining chips. "He isn't Jewish. That's for sure."

I bragged that Elvis, who was filming *Love Me Tender* at Twentieth Century-Fox at the time, had gone to see my father at the studio infirmary.

"Did he have the clap?" Robbie wondered.

"No, he had warts on his hands," I divulged. "He told my dad that he got them because he had put some toads in a burlap bag and killed them."

"Too bad he didn't have VD," Little Mike said as he lay down his hand of five wild cards and spread them out for us to see. He raked in his winnings: "Your father could have told you whether he's circumcised or not. I'll bet he isn't. And I'll bet he's got a huge dick."

"Speaking of dicks," Chuck announced, "I've started to get some hair on mine. Well, not actually on it. Kind of above and around it."

It was Lance Finkel's deal: "Five-card stud, low ball, deuces, one-eyed-jacks, and nines wild." And as the cards were dealt, more cigarettes were lit, and another round of crème de menthe was served up by Robert, Larry told us a story that Cisco Zutano had told him: "There was this twelve-year-old girl in Tijuana who was a virgin. Her stomach started getting bigger and bigger, and so her mother took her to the doctor, and, you'll never believe it, the rabbit died. Yeah, the little virgin was pregnant. So her family thought it was a miracle, you know, like the Virgin Mary, because nobody had ever fucked her. She still had a cherry, but she was pregnant." He paused to see Robbie Freeman's bet and turn over the next round of cards: "The word began to spread about the pregnant virgin, and people started to visit her. They'd kneel down and pray to her. They're very religious down in Mexico. A priest announced that Jesus Christ was going to be born again in Tijuana. But then a doctor, investigating the miracle, figured out what had really happened."

Little Mike, who had won the hand, shuffled the cards for his deal and asked what all of us wanted to know: "So what really happened?"

"The family was real poor, so poor that they had to share their hot water. And it turns out that the girl would always take a bath after her brother, in the same water. And the brother would jack off in the bathtub. That's how she got knocked up."

"That explains Christ. His mom's brother probably beat off in the river where they bathed," Chuck said as he picked up his hand. "What's wild?" he asked and then repeated the boast that he was growing pubic hair.

I asked Larry what he had meant by "the rabbit died."

"God, Siegel, you dumb douche bag," Larry groaned as he drew three cards. "Don't you know anything? If you inject a girl's piss into a rabbit and the rabbit dies, it means that the girl is pregnant."

"So be careful, Siegel," Lance joked. "If Suzie Krasny pisses on that stupid rabbit that she brought to Mr. Gordon's class, and it dies, you might be a father."

Everybody laughed.

Suzie's rabbit did die, but the death had nothing to do with sex, pregnancy, or me. Elvis had succumbed, Suzie sobbed, to "Encephalitozoon cuniculi." His symptoms had included lots of throwing up. "I always hated it when he threw up," she sighed. "He also had diarrhea, a floppy neck, and twitching ears, and he walked in circles like he was drunk." Suzie had read in *The Complete Rabbit Encyclopedia* that the disease was caused by a parasite that is passed from mother rabbits to their offspring at birth.

I went to pay my solemn respects at the burial ceremony in the Krasnys' backyard. It was the first time I had ever been to a funeral. Suzie had made a marker for the grave:

✡

R.I.P.

ELVIS KRASNY

1955–1956

GONE BUT NOT FORGOTTEN

♥

"Elvis dedicated his short but sweet life to making others happy," her eulogy began. "He was gentle and kind. He loved everyone he met. Elvis was a saint." The announcement of the canonization of Elvis made Suzie's brother Matt snicker, which made Mark giggle, which made Luke roll on the ground in uncontrollable convulsions of laughter, which made Suzie scream: "I hate you. I hate all three of you. I hope all of you die like Elvis. But he's in heaven. You—all three of you—are going to hell." Unable to continue the tribute to the deceased loved one, she ran up to her room, locked the door, and, so Luke later told me, wouldn't come out for three days. She didn't show up at school for a week and missed two Thursday night dance cotillions in a row. Hoping to console her with my kisses, I rode my bike over to her house, only to be told by her mother that she wasn't seeing anyone, not even her best friend, Candy Canter.

Finally, three weeks after Elvis had gone to the great hutch in the sky, she returned to cotillion, and we practiced the box step together once more. I wore brown penny loafers. Whispering in her ear as we danced, I told Suzie that I was heartbroken by the rabbit's untimely death: "Elvis Krasny was the cutest little Mini Lop lagomorph I ever saw. He was really cool."

I remembered seeing my mother cry when her father died the year before. And just as my father had taken his beloved wife in his arms then, so I held Suzie Krasny in my arms as we danced to the singing of Pat Boone:

Does she love me? It's too soon to know.
Can I believe her when she tells me so?
Is she foolin'? Is it all a game?
Am I the fire or just another flame?
A one-sided love would break my heart.
She may be just acting and playing a part.

The tragic loss of Elvis seemed to bring us closer and love seemed to be offering some solace against the sting of death. I imagined that Suzie had come to terms with her sorrow as we danced, and I supposed that being in my arms helped.

But then it happened, all of a sudden, at the end of the evening, in the midst of a dada dada dada, da, da, da: bursting into tears, Suzie Krasny broke loose from the line of boys and girls and ran sobbing out of Studio A.

The final Bunny Hop had been too much for her.

1957

The Soviets launch the satellite *Sputnik* into orbit around the earth, and Jayne Mansfield announces her engagement to former Mr. Universe Mickey Hargitay; Marilyn Monroe stars in *The Prince and the Showgirl,* and Brigitte Bardot stars in *And God Created Woman;* Elvis Presley goes to prison in *Jailhouse Rock,* and my mother kills a rancher with an ax in *The Lone Ranger and the Lost City of Gold; I Was a Teenage Werewolf* is released, and Eve W——'s mother stars in *Love Affair with a Vampire;* Art Linkletter's *Kids Say the Darndest Things!* tops the nonfiction bestseller list, and Grace Metalious's *Peyton Place* tops fiction; police serve a warrant for the arrest of Lawrence Ferlinghetti for publishing and selling Allen Ginsberg's *Howl,* and Ku Klux Klan members kidnap Willie Edwards Jr. and, alleging that he has flirted with a white woman, force him to jump to his death from a bridge; *Leave It to Beaver,* Dick Clark's *American Bandstand,* and the United States Senate Rackets Committee hearings debut on television, and both the *Howdy Doody Show* and *Your Hit Parade* go off the air; dancer Candy Barr is arrested on drug charges, and Carol Summers is arrested for arson after the Bobby Byrd Dance Cotillion is destroyed by fire; the State of California charges *Confidential* magazine with conspiracy to commit criminal libel and disseminate obscene material, and Lance Finkel is expelled from Ponce de Leon Elementary School.

Warmly misted in billowing steam, she stood stirringly still and sexily silent next to the open door of my shower. With one knee bent coquettishly and a hand propped up on her voluptuous hip, a soft shoulder brazenly tilted forward to make a sumptuous offering of her flamboyant breasts, the lusciously tempting fruit of a cardinal knowledge. Ripe-swollen, candy-apple red lips were prettily parted as if in readiness to kiss, smile, sigh, or whisper my name. As my pajama bottoms fell to the tile floor, I uttered hers. "Jayne Mansfield," I said. "Good morning, Jayne." And I closed the shower door behind me.

As soon as she had arrived from Locklace Glamour and Pin-up Photographs, I taped her to my bathroom wall. The advertisement for the "Life-Size Real-Color Poster of Hollywood's Most Titillating Love Goddess and Explosive Sex Bomb" avowed that it had been "taken totally in the NUDE" and that it exposed "ALL you could want to see and MORE than we can show here!" A scant irradiant red bikini did, however, conceal three things I would have liked to have seen. Since it was illegal in America not to tell the truth in advertising, I believed that either the two pieces of the bathing suit had been painted over the blowup poster of the original photograph or that it was the photographer who had been "totally in the NUDE" when the photo was taken. In any case, it was just as well that her nipples and pubic hair were concealed, as they might have been a bit too raunchy for Sally May Carter when she cleaned my bathroom.

"Real Color" referred to the three hues that had been used, slightly off register, to tint the black-and-white piece of cheesecake: a wash of fleshy pink for her skin; a uniform shade of a lurid red for her lips, fingernails, toenails, and that bikini, which presumably did not exist in the real world; and, for Jayne Mansfield's illustrious platinum blonde hair, canary yellow. At least her breasts were, as advertised, approximately "Life-Size."

"Wow! What a body!" I exclaimed, quoting United States Intelligence Agent Dick Steele as I dried myself, confident that Jayne Mansfield was not then nor ever had been a member of the Communist Party. I'd glance over at her as I brushed my teeth, and with my terry towel wrapped like the animal skin around Johnny Weissmuller's loins, I snarled, "Me Tarzan, you Jayne."

Although the poster wasn't really very sexy in an arousing way, it blatantly represented arousal as it insinuated the fulsome joys of a fantastic world in which sexual desire went unharnessed. It was for me a travel poster for a lush terra incognita where a gorgeously naked woman might merrily offer her body up to a fun-loving boy, initiating him into manhood more effectively than any bar mitzvah ever could.

I had ordered Jayne with a coupon cut from *Confidential,* a magazine to which I had easy access ever since my grandmother had moved to Beverly Hills. To keep abreast of the truth about what was really going on in Hollywood, she had started subscribing to the tabloid that swore to contain "No Fiction—All Fact, Uncensored and Off the Record." She even made a donation of one dollar to the American Civil Liberties Union in support of the legal defense of *Confidential* against the United States Post Office's efforts to ban the sending of the magazine through the mail on grounds of obscenity.

The cover of the issue in which I had found the ad for the Jayne Mansfield promised to divulge "The Secret Sex Life of Davy Crockett" and to expose the presence of "100,000 Insane Teachers in America's Elementary Schools." Inside, a story called "Stars at Midnight" provided "a peek into the bedrooms of Hollywood after the servants have gone to sleep." Liberace, Marilyn Monroe, Huntz Hall, Debra Paget,

Mamie Van Doren, and Phyllis Allbright were among those enjoying enviably scandalous sex lives. "Fun with Dick and Jayne" was the title of a piece on Jayne Mansfield.

I proudly invited Chuck Mandel, Larry Feinstein, and Lance Finkel over to see Jayne Mansfield. Upon entering my bathroom, Chuck immediately offered to buy her for ten dollars.

"That's what I paid for her," I explained, "plus postage and handling." When Chuck bid twenty, I advised him to order one of his own, and I cut another Locklace Glamour and Pin-up Photographs coupon from *Confidential* magazine for him.

Chuck had been the first boy in our class to go through puberty. In the sixth grade, his voice had become deep, his skin blemished, and, although his body stopped growing taller, his penis grew impressively fatter and longer. At first he had been eager to display it. But by the seventh grade, he finally realized that none of his peers really cared to see it, at least not after the first time.

He wanted the poster because, he confessed, he was in love with Jayne Mansfield. "I saw *The Girl Can't Help It* seven times," he boasted. "It's a million times better than *The Ten Commandments,* which I saw three times. Jayne Mansfield should have played Nefretiri in *The Ten Commandments.* Jayne Mansfield! Get it? Mans-field. She's a man's field! She's the most beautiful woman in the world. I've read everything that's been written about her in *Photoplay.* I think about her all the time, even at Hebrew school and in synagogue. Sometimes, when I'm lucky, I get to dream about her."

Lance Finkel couldn't resist: "So, you want the poster so that you can look at her when you jack off?"

That an offended Chuck swore to God that he did not masturbate was supposed to be plausible since he was an observant Jew in an Orthodox family. But, taking note of the incredulous expressions on our faces, he amended the testimony: "Well, not anymore." He hesitated: "No, not very much." He hesitated again: "And never on Shabbis! And, anyway, my feelings for Jayne are not just physical. They're spiritual. She's exactly the kind of lady I'd like to marry someday. My parents would want her to convert, of course, but I wouldn't care. It doesn't bother me that she's a Gentile. I'd take her just as she is."

Gazing at her on my bathroom wall, Chuck seemed to be trying to muster the courage to touch her. He sighed: "Oh, God, she's so gorgeous. She's the perfect woman. Not only does she have a forty-one-inch bustline, but she's also a devoted mother, a music lover, an excellent cook (especially barbecue), and, even though she's a Christian, she has always been good to the Jews."

"What the fuck are you talking about?" challenged Larry as he lit up one of the Viceroys from the pack that I kept hidden in my red velvet couch. "What has Jayne Mansfield ever done for the Jews?"

"Well, for example," Chuck said in vehement defense of his beloved, "last Chanukah she invited both Jeff Chandler and Eddie Fisher to her home for an all-kosher barbecue. I read about it in *Photoplay.* It was a really cool story. After her father, Herbert, died when she was just three years old, her mother, Vera, married Harry 'Tex' Peers. Tex taught Jayne how to barbecue. And she's great at it. She makes her own barbecue sauce from scratch."

Larry scoffed: "Jayne Mansfield's a boob. She's just a poor man's copy of Marilyn Monroe. Monroe's the hottest broad ever. And she actually married a Jew, a guy named Henry Miller who wrote a really depressing play called *Death of a Sailorman.* She married him! That means she's had sex with him. She's had sex with a Jew! Did Jayne Mansfield have sex with either Jeff Chandler or Eddie Fisher, or any other Jews for that matter, at her Chanukah barbecue? I don't think so. No, Mansfield married Mr. Universe, a goy if there ever was one. She only likes musclemen, and there are no Jewish musclemen. Anyway, even if she wasn't an anti-Semite, I doubt Jayne Mansfield would ever let a little Yid with acne fuck her, no matter how big his shlong was."

While the direct reference to Chuck's height and dermatological condition, despite the nice compliment to his penis, would have been cruel in another context, insults exchanged between seventh-grade boys at Ponce de Leon Elementary School were understood as expressions of camaraderie, the harsher the friendlier, a way of saying, "I like you so much that it's okay for me to abuse and humiliate you."

"You're an asshole, Spanky," Chuck countered in the same spirit of amicable hostility. "And you don't know what you're talking about. There have been lots of Jewish musclemen. Samson for example. He was a Jew. Furthermore, if Marilyn Monroe was such a good piece of ass, Joe DiMaggio wouldn't have dumped her. Besides, her tits are smaller than Jayne's."

It was, in this courtly battle of two errant knights, each asserting the superiority of his own lady over the inamorata of the other, Larry's turn to parry and thrust: "Mansfield dyes her hair. Marilyn's blonde hair is real. And don't ever call me Spanky again, zit face, or I'll kick the shit out of you. I swear to God I will."

Aware, since I had boasted of it, that my father had been Marilyn Monroe's doctor at Twentieth Century-Fox Studios, they turned to me to settle the dispute. "What color is the hair on Marilyn Monroe's pussy, Siegel?" Chuck asked. "What did your father tell you?"

Since apparently Mr. Mandel reported to his son every detail of his work as president and manager of Mandel's Mail Order Ladies' Wear International, Chuck found it hard to believe that my father would not have discussed Marilyn Monroe's pubic hair with me. After all, Chuck pointed out, he had told me about Elvis's warts.

"Come on, Siegel," urged Larry, tossing the butt of his Viceroy into the toilet. "Get your dad to fill you in on Marilyn's muff. Or, better yet, you could hide in his office sometime, behind a curtain or under a table or something, and take a picture of it. I'd give anything in the world to see that box. I'll bet twenty bucks that the hair is blonde."

"That's sick," Chuck said, returning to the fray. "It shows that you don't really care about Marilyn Monroe. You're an asshole, Feinstein. I'd never talk like that about Jayne Mansfield. I respect her. I care about her."

"Don't tell me that you wouldn't like to see her pussy, Mandel," Larry scoffed.

"Only if she wanted to show it to me," Chuck solemnly avowed. "Only if she really cared whether or not I liked it."

I asked them to leave the bathroom so that I could take a piss, and when I emerged, Chuck and Larry were reclining on my king-size bed and Lance Finkel, who had been silent during the Mansfield-Monroe debate, was seated on the old red velvet couch. It was his turn: "Neither of you know diddly about women," he was saying. "The sexiest sex kitten ever, not just in America, but in the whole fucking universe, is, hands down, B. B., the one and only Mademoiselle Brigitte Bardot."

His father, so Lance claimed, had taken him to see *And God Created Woman,* getting him into the theater by telling the ticket lady that he was sixteen. Like all of us, Lance lied a lot. But we were supposed to forgive him since Lance had problems: "Be nice to Lance," our parents would tell us. "His parents are divorced." Lance smoked Chesterfields like his dad, a movie producer who drove a Corvette, wore Hawaiian shirts, and went out on dates with younger women. Lance spent weekends with him in Malibu. Ever eager to show us the French magazines that Mr. Irving Finkel had smuggled into the United States and kept in a drawer by his bed "with his French ticklers and Ramses rubbers," Lance bragged, "He's got a ton of rubbers."

When Larry asked if that was because he wore "a rubber when he beats off with the magazines," Lance was quick to defend patriarchal honor: "Pop doesn't need to jack off. He's fucked half the starlets in Hollywood. Last weekend Phyllis Allbright stayed over, and I could hear them going at it all night."

"Who's Phyllis Allbright?" Chuck wondered.

"You know, the chick who plays Beaver's teacher on *Leave It to Beaver*. She's kind of square on camera, but that's just acting. She's hot in real life. Pop told me that she's a great fuck."

Mr. Finkel had taken his son with him to Paris the previous summer. "I saw that dance in France," Lance claimed, "you know, the one where the women wear no pants." He also crowed to having "fingered" a French girl who looked just like Brigitte Bardot, "but younger and more stacked." That verbal form of the absolutely innocent noun was the dirtiest word in our vocabulary, dirtier even than *fuck*, and to use dirty words was to have a good time.

We knew that Lance was lying as usual when, after Chuck asked the girl's name, the best thing he could come up with on the spur of the moment was "Fifi. Yeah, Fifi. Mademoiselle Fifi DeGaulle. She's a freshman at Paris High."

As a boy in the seventh grade, you were a man not in terms of what you had ever actually done or even wanted to do with a girl, but in terms of what you could, with dirty words and a working imagination, convince other boys you might have done given the opportunity and sufficient anatomical development.

"So, okay, Siegel, which one do you think is the best—Brigitte Bardot, Marilyn Monroe, or Jayne Mansfield?" Chuck asked, hoping I'd cast a vote for the woman in my bathroom. Larry rephrased the question: "Yeah, if the three of them really were in your bathroom, which one would you choose?" Lance further refined the query: "Imagine that Jayne Mansfield, Marilyn Monroe, and Brigitte Bardot are all here right now, and all of them are naked—which one are you going to fuck first?"

Although I would have been quite happy to settle for any of the three movie stars, I didn't want to take sides with one of my friends over the other two, so I avoided answering the question by asking if it would be possible to include Suzie Krasny in the group of nudes from which to select a favorite.

"Why in the world," Chuck asked, "would you want to boink Suzie Krasny when you could have Jayne Mansfield?"

"Because she's my girlfriend," I explained, "and I have a feeling that she'd be more interested in me than the others would be." Since an arsonist had torched the Bobby Byrd Dance Cotillion, I no longer had the opportunity to dance with Suzie. And since she no longer invited me up to her room, I no longer had the opportunity to kiss her. Nevertheless, I still considered her my girlfriend, and the fact that she gave me one of the loaves of banana bread that she had baked in Miss Minnette's home economics class made me confident that she thought of me as her boyfriend. Banana bread was, in the seventh grade at Ponce de Leon Elementary, a symbol of a girl's love. While Lance had received a loaf from Donna Young, and Larry, one from Candy Canter, no girl gave banana bread to Chuck Mandel. "I don't like banana bread anyway," he shrugged, "and, even if I did, my doctor says it's bad for your skin."

Ever since she had started wearing a brassiere, Suzie had been coquettishly dotting the i in her name with a little heart. I rarely talked to Suzie at school because boys usually sat with boys and girls with girls both in the cafeteria for lunch and in the auditorium for assemblies. Sitting with a girl in either context paradoxically insinuated that you might be a fairy. But sometimes on a Friday or Saturday night, if she had a girl (usually either Candy Canter or Donna Young) spending the night, she'd telephone me and, with her friend snickering in the background, she'd tell me what was really going on at Ponce de Leon Elementary School, "No Fiction—All Fact, Uncensored and Off the Record": "Angela Portinari started her period. Beatrice Sugarman went out with a high school boy when she was in Palm Springs with her parents last weekend. Laura Landy wears falsies. Clover Wiener is in love with Leo Roth, and Carrie Katz has a crush on Chip Zuckerman. They made out in the Katzes' bomb shelter, and she let him put his hand down her bra. Carrie's kind of a nympho. But the big news—and this is really secret, so you've got to swear to God that you'll never tell anyone—is that Lance Finkel's mother went out on a date with George Reeves. My mom saw them together at Nate 'n Al's delicatessen. Mrs. Finkel and Superman!" I suppose that by now the statute of limitations on my oath before God is up.

Lance and Larry were spending the night at my house on the Friday Suzie made this particular revelation, but Chuck had gone home before sundown for the Sabbath. "I'm worried about Chuck," Lance said with uncharacteristic compassion. "I think he believes in God, a God who, for some reason, doesn't want us to eat bacon, lettuce, and tomato sandwiches."

In the morning, when I got up to pee, I was startled by the sight of Jayne Mansfield: a heart with a dagger through it and the name "Lee" within it had been tattooed on her arm. There was a cigarette in her mouth, a Star of David on a chain around her neck, and a comic strip bubble above her head to indicate that she was saying, "FUCK ME!"

"Who did that?" I asked with substantial annoyance. "Spanky, I mean Larry," laughed Lance, and Larry laughed, "Shit head, I mean Lance."

Coming by a few days later to see the poster of his beloved and to inform me that he had ordered one of his own from Locklace Glamour and Pin-up Photographs, Chuck actually seemed upset to find Jayne Mansfield so violated: "Like Elvis, Jayne doesn't smoke," he said defensively. "She doesn't drink either. And Jayne Mansfield would never swear like that. It's disgusting. Larry and Lance are fucking assholes."

The Jayne Mansfield–Marilyn Monroe–Brigitte Bardot debate came to mind when one day, flipping through my mother's *Masterpieces of the Louvre* for nude women and happening upon a sculpture of the three Graces, I was relishing the vivid nakedness of the two-thousand-year-old Greek girls who were identified as the "attendants of the Goddess of Love, a triple incarnation of beauty and of the joy of love. They made any man they visited completely happy." Thalia had to be Jayne because her name meant "Abundance," and B. B. was definitely Euphrosyne, who was said to represent "Jollity." That left Aglaia, "a manifestation of Splendor," for Marilyn Monroe. No less than the ad for my Jayne Mansfield poster, the description in the art book promised more than the black-and-white picture of the girls with their heads and feet missing actually delivered: "With their sensually sinuous bodies enlaced in voluptuous dance, their frankly erotic display has inspired artists ever since. This classic sculpture is a celebration of the beauty of the female nude and all the joys of physical love." In order to help the Graces live up to such racy characterization and to bring their stone flesh to life, I got my colored pencils. After softly shading their bodies approximately the same pink that had been used for Jayne Mansfield's flesh by Locklace Glamour and Pin-up, I sharpened a bright red pencil for the nipples. The Grace on the right, the fleshiest of the three, the only one whose breasts were fully exposed, her knee bent exactly like the one on my bathroom wall, was easily recognizable even without her head as Thalia/Jayne Mansfield. The middle Grace, facing away from me, had to be Euphrosyne/Brigitte Bardot, whose cute little tushy was as celebrated as Jayne's big boobs. That left the one on the left to be Aglaia/Marilyn Monroe. Taking a stand on the hair color question, I colored in Aglaia's pubic hair yellow and Miss Abundance's burnt umber.

The effect was so pleasing that I went on to the Venus de Milo and, in the Locklace spirit, used the same red for her nipples, lipstick, and the toenails on her one remaining foot. I used the same yellow for both the hair on her head and the lock that I made to curl up from behind the top of the sheet around her hips. The Goddess of Love, I figured, certainly wouldn't dye her hair. If she had arms, I mused, she might look a little like Miss Pinchas, my blonde Hebrew teacher.

During my work on the remaining female nudes of classical antiquity in *Masterpieces of the Louvre,* I took particular pleasure in coloring in the sexy parts of Psyche on sculptures of her with Cupid. As a couple they reminded me of me and Suzie Krasny. If only I had wings and a foreskin, I might, I reckoned, with my curly hair, look a little like Cupid, and Suzie's breasts were promising to develop into ones about the size and shape of Psyche's. Two red dots, and a little bit of burnt umber, and I could see almost "ALL you could want to see and MORE" of the Goddess who, according to my mother's book, represented "the Mind."

Since *Masterpieces of the Louvre,* shelved between the *Encyclopaedia Britannica* and the complete works of Dr. Frank G. Lafleur, MD, was never consulted by anyone but me on my quests for depictions of naked girls, I wasn't worried that my artwork would be discovered. My mother hadn't looked at the book in years. Proud as I was of the way my coloring job had so effectively transformed old art into new porn, I showed my creations to my brother, Robert. While he had to admit that they were pretty good, he said that he thought that my friends were doing a better job on Jayne Mansfield in my bathroom. "You should definitely add a few FUCKS," the seven-year-old advised.

"FUCK" had by then been written at least ten times on the poster, in bubbles of statement and thought and in new tattoos all over her body, and one big FUCK floated in its own dimension over the figure. Jayne had, thanks to my friends, grown lots of black hair: first a mustache, then a goatee, and then a full beard and Hasidic payes; there was chest, leg, and arm hair; and, of course, thick bushes of fur had begun to sprout lush and rank out from under and up over the top of her bikini bottom. It almost made Chuck Mandel weep.

One day, insisting on walking home with me after school, Chuck informed me that his mother had opened the large envelope that arrived in the mail addressed to her son from Locklace Glamour and Pin-up and discovered his "Life-Size Real-Color Poster of Hollywood's Most Titillating Love Goddess and Explosive Sex Bomb." She had destroyed the idolatrous image of the goddess, so adored by Chuck, in an anger as ardent as that felt by Moses upon discovering the Israelites dancing around the golden calf at the foot of Sinai in *The Ten Commandments.* Mrs. Mandel also cut off Chuck's allowance, grounded him, and sentenced him to five extra hours of Hebrew each week. Jayne Mansfield's unrepentant lover appealed to me for help. Yearning for another copy of the poster, he wanted it sent to my house so that it wouldn't be confiscated. And since he no longer had an allowance, he also wanted to borrow ten dollars "plus postage and handling."

Again I found a coupon and ad for the Jayne Mansfield portrait in one of my grandmother's copies of *Confidential* and clipped it for Chuck. As I did so, I noticed another advertisement on the same page of the magazine:

"Wow, what a difference between being the boss of my very own woodworking shop and my old job as a foundry laborer," says Efraim Harris, Professional Woodworker and graduate of the Woodwork Trade School of America. "No more dusty hard work or worries about money and layoffs for me." Right at home in your spare time you can do what Efraim Harris and hundreds of other WTSA graduates, fellows just like you, have done. With the growing shortage of expert woodworkers in America, there's a well-paying job waiting for you. Or if, like Efraim Harris, you're sick and tired of working for a boss, then woodworking offers you a golden opportunity for a new and independent life as a self-employed woodworker.

The ad further implied that being a professional woodworker made you more attractive to women: if you were married, your wife would stop nagging you about all the bills; if you were a bachelor, you could have practically any girl you wanted. "A National Survey has shown that ninety percent of American women admire self-employed professionals," the advertisement proclaimed. "Imagine the ways in which, with your new skills and all that extra cash in your pockets, you'll be able to earn the respect of the missus or impress that special sweetheart." I supposed that I should have been grateful that, as a student at Ponce de Leon Elementary School, I would never have to pay the tuition required to enroll at the Woodworkers Trade School of America in order to enjoy what the ad promised to be "the fascinating, comfortable, and happy life of a professional woodworker." I was learning woodworking for free in the wood shop class that all of the boys in the seventh grade were required to take from Mr. Woodrow "Woody" Woodcock.

While I might be willing to admit that I may have embellished a few things in this chronicle (and I might even confess to having lied once or twice), I swear it's true that (as unbelievable as it may seem) the wood shop teacher at Ponce de Leon really was named Woodrow "Woody" Woodcock. Why, I wondered, would anyone with a name like Woodcock get a job teaching young boys who, as anyone would surely know, would, anywhere in the English-speaking world, invoke the name in hilarious mockery? At Ponce de Leon, however, if you laughed, or even grinned, when the name was said, or if you stressed the second syllable when you said it yourself, you were ordered to run ten laps around the playing field. Mr. Woodcock was a tough guy.

While fighting in the Korean War, Mr. Woodcock had lost a leg in the battle at Chinju. And he was damn proud to have given that limb as an offering in the battle against Communism. While recovering from his combat injury in the Los Angeles Veterans' Hospital, he had himself carved his own prosthesis out of wood. He showed that leg off to us as a symbol of his patriotism, his manliness, and his skill as a professional woodworker. He had carved the words GOD BLESS AMERICA into the calf.

"A leg," he said with a wistful smile, "is a small sacrifice for an American to make for the sake of his country." And then he asked an ethical question of the class: "If you were told that by giving up one of your limbs you could prevent the spread of Communism and thereby ensure world peace, freedom, and democracy, which one of you would do it?"

All of us raised our hands to indicate that we would.

A tattoo—**WOODY★US ARMY**—was visible through the curly white hair on Mr. Woodcock's muscular right forearm. We suspected that other tattoos were concealed under his clothes—probably a bare-breasted hula girl on the thigh above his amputation, one who'd wiggle when he flexed his leg muscles. I fancied that on his chest he might have a Venus de Milo who had given up her arms in order to prevent the spread of Communism in ancient Greece.

While the seventh-grade boys at Ponce de Leon Elementary were learning how to cut, drill, sand, nail, and (ten laps if you laughed when you said it) screw in Mr. Woodcock's wood shop class so that we could make wooden tie racks, the seventh-grade girls were learning how to sift, stir, knead, and beat in Miss Minnette's home economics class so that they could bake banana bread for their future husbands. This separation of the boys and girls into separate classes also provided an opportunity for lessons in "Health and Hygiene." While all of us, in the segments of both home economics and wood shop devoted to those lessons, were required to read *Facts of Life and Love for the American Teenager,* any discussion of its contents (which included information about such touchy subjects as brassieres, girdles, menstruation, testicles, erections, masturbation, and what it called "grown-up hair") in mixed company would have resulted in the running of many thousands of laps around the playing field.

That such subjects were addressed at Ponce de Leon Elementary attested to the progressiveness of the Beverly Hills Board of Education.

Less fortunate Negro, Mexican, and working-class Gentile kids would have to figure sex out on their own by trial and error.

The book, meant to prepare us for high school courtship and romance, had been written by Ethel Chambers, the wife of our principal, Dr. Gus Chambers, PhD, and published by Chambers and Chambers Publications. It had been endorsed by *Parents* magazine as "a frank but thoroughly clean discussion of the problems that may shock some but will help Dick and Jane know how to get along properly with members of the opposite sex." Despite the lesson that she should have learned from the response to her play, *Fountain of Youth,* about Jewish sensitivities to Gentile characterizations of Jews, she did not, in her book, shy away from a discussion of circumcision as a Jewish practice:

> All baby boys are born with a cap of skin, known as the **foreskin** or **prepuce,** around their penis. It acts as a protector. For religious reasons people of the Jewish faith have been cutting them away for thousands of years. Thanks to the many Jewish doctors in America, this practice, known as **circumcision,** has, in modern times, been discovered to have hygienic value. Circumcision prevents a cheesy sebaceous substance, known as **smegma,** from accumulating under the foreskin. Cancer of the vagina is, furthermore, less common among the wives of men who are circumcised. Thus most Christians in the United States now choose to have their male children circumcised like Jews.

That passage introduced *prepuce* and *smegma* into the vocabulary of boys at Ponce de Leon. When arguing over who was the sexiest, Marilyn Monroe or Jayne Mansfield, Larry Feinstein would call Chuck Mandel "smegma face," and Chuck would come back at him with "prepuce head."

Facts of Life and Love for the American Teenager was divided into "Chapters for Girls" (to be read in home economics), "Chapters for Boys" (to be read in wood shop), "Chapters for Boys and Girls" (to be read by all of us), and "Chapters for Parents." The girls' chapters included such sections as "The Menstrual Code," "How to Say 'NO,'" and "Do You Have to Pet to Be Popular?" The boys' chapters covered such issues as "How Your Penis Works," "Self-Abuse," "Nocturnal Emissions," and "Taking 'NO' for an Answer."

Of course, since we were sure we knew how our penises worked, the boys were immensely more interested in reading the girls' chapters than those about us. I learned in one of those chapters that "foundation garments such as the elastic panty girdles that give a girl such a grown-up feeling should be washed frequently" and that "dusting a little deodorant powder on a menstrual pad helps keep it sweet." I was pleased by the thought that Suzie Krasny, no doubt unable to resist the boys' chapters, had read that "Down through history the penis has been known as *the* male organ. It hangs in front of the scrotal sac suspended from the lower abdomen. When excited, it can become hard and stiff. In that state it is called the 'erection.'" Although Suzie no longer talked to me about penises as she had in the sixth grade, at least, I figured, thanks to *Facts of Life and Love for the American Teenager,* she was probably thinking about them.

The chapters we read in common were a testimonial to the scope and limits of the open-mindedness of Ethel Chambers and the Beverly Hills Board of Education:

> Even normal persons have distracting thoughts about sex from time to time as well as dreams in which sex may play a role. These should not be a cause for alarm or concern. They are but symptoms of one's maturing sex endowment and will pass as suddenly as they have come without undue strain or difficulty. Persons who deliberately stimulate such thoughts with shady stories and lewd pictures, however, have the added burden of keeping under proper control the excitation that builds up under those circumstances. This can cause serious mental problems.

What we all wanted to read about didn't come until page 238:

> The sexual union of a man and a woman is called **intercourse,** or **mating,** or the **marital relation** or simply the **sex act.** Among the youth of today, it is popularly known as "going all the way." It is a straight-forward procedure. While other positions are possible, most commonly the man lies on top of his wife. Once his penis has become erect, he inserts it into the vagina and moves it in and out until, due the stimulation it receives from that action, the ejaculation of semen occurs. This is usually followed by a period of rest and often sleep.

I remember the page number because it became a code word for *fuck.* Two-thirty-eight was even funnier and dirtier than sixty-nine. Every time the clock in the wood shop struck thirty-eight minutes after two, everybody would snicker. "What are you boys laughing about?" Mr. Woodcock would ask, but because he couldn't figure it out, he couldn't make us run laps.

"Listen, guys," Mr. Woodcock confided during the sex education segment of wood shop, "I know that sex seems funny, but I can assure you it isn't. Take it from me—this book is no joke. Sex is a serious business. We didn't have books like this when I was your age. I had to learn about sex the hard way." Despite the dread of laps, it was hard not to grin, let alone not to break into laughter, when he said things like that, things like: "Let's talk about masturbating man to man, without any beating around the bush," "Don't worry about wet dreams. Even I had them when I was a kid," and "The female sexual organ is a hard nut to crack."

Although Mr. Woodcock didn't give us the details of his experiences in war, we sensed that not only had he killed his fair share of North Korean soldiers but that he had also probably cracked the nuts of just as many South Korean prostitutes.

Because of the shock of it, no one giggled or even grinned when, one day, Mr. Woodcock actually said "fuck" in wood shop. It was not, however, in reference to page 238 of *Facts of Life and Love for the American Teenager* but rather to the appearance of the word as repeatedly scrawled with a permanent black laundry marker upon the walls of Ponce de Leon Elementary School. No sooner would those walls be repainted than the word would reappear.

"Someone here," Mr. Woodcock declared, "is sick. When the little kids in the first and second grade who are just learning to read see that word—F-U-C-K—they're going to sound it out. Fuck. That's right boys, you heard me—fuck! And then they'll start saying it. What is that going to do to their lives?" Our teacher looked directly at Cisco Zutano as he spoke: "This isn't Tijuana, no sir—this is Beverly Hills. We're going to clean up this filth, and you boys are going to help." Issuing us laundry markers of our own, the former army sergeant gave his newly drafted troop our orders: "Every time you see that word, I want you to take out your marker, and change the *F* into a *B*, like this." After demonstrating the orthographic emendation, he continued: "Then turn both the *U* and the *C* into *O*'s. We're going to change every single FUCK here at school into BOOK. It will remind kids that they should read more."

The campaign was even less successful than the US Army's at Chinju: we all started saying "Book you" to each other; statements like "Let's go to the library and get a good book" became hilariously dirty; "I asked Beatrice Sugarman out on a date," Lance Finkel joked, "and she said she was all booked up."

One day, as I was turning a FUCK into a BOOK, I realized that I recognized the handwriting from my poster of Jayne Mansfield. Either Lance Finkel or Larry Feinstein had to be the vandal.

I wondered what the word for "fuck" was in Hebrew, the language, Miss Pinchas told me, that God spoke. Even though I had little interest in learning the holy tongue of the Torah or finding out what God had to say in it, I enjoyed the lessons each Thursday after school because Miss Pinchas, a former paratrooper in the Israeli army, was very pretty and, sitting next to me at my desk, her leg would occasionally touch mine. Every time it did, I'd picture the breasts of Venus de Milo beneath her blouse.

Miss Pinchas, who had come to Los Angeles from Israel in the hope of becoming a movie star, had worked for a film company in Jerusalem dubbing American movies into Hebrew. She had provided the voice of Marilyn Monroe as Lorelei, the little girl from Little Rock, in *Gentlemanim M'hadifi Blondinyot.* She had arrived in Hollywood the year before, just in time to get a bit part dancing around the golden calf in *The Ten Commandments.* Meeting her in the commissary at Twentieth Century-Fox, my father got the idea of hiring her, as a native Hebrew speaker, to prepare me for my bar mitzvah.

Shortly before the end of the school year, a crime was committed at Ponce de Leon that made the big FUCKS on our walls seem like little misdemeanors. Mr. Woodcock, we were informed by Dr. Chambers, PhD, with Mr. Ball, Mr. Gordon, Mr. Schumann, and Mr. Jim standing at attention in a row behind him at an emergency assembly for grades six through eight, had (as was his custom in order to rest up for his night job as a watchman at Bekins Van & Storage) been taking a nap after school in the office he had set up in the wood shop. It was natural for him to remove his prosthesis when he slept. Someone had entered the shop and stolen Mr. Woodcock's leg. Dr. Chambers believed it was an inside job.

Perhaps it was to live up to the assertion in a spelling lesson years before that he was our "pal" in the office that our princi*pal* took an understanding approach to the situation: "We are all capable of playing foolish pranks when we are young. But often what you think is just a little prank at the time actually turns out to be a serious crime. I want the youngster who stole Mr. Woodcock's leg to return it. I know, since you're all good kids here in Beverly Hills, that the one of you who has the leg is feeling bad about it. Naturally, you feel guilty. It's called 'having a conscience.' Once you return the leg, you'll feel a lot better. If the student who has the leg will come forward with it, I promise that I will do my best to make sure that it does not go on your record."

When, after a week, no one had returned the missing limb, Dr. Chambers called another assembly: "Because I understand that whoever has Mr. Woodcock's leg might not believe that I won't punish him for what he has done, I've decided to put a special box in the school parking lot where you can leave the missing body part without anyone noticing."

When, after another week, no one had deposited the leg in the parking lot box, there was yet another assembly, at which Dr. Chambers, PhD, gave a sterner speech: "I'm sad to say that whoever stole Mr. Woodcock's leg has no conscience. As a Doctor of Educational Psychology, I can inform you that the lack of a conscience is a symptom of the criminal mind. Once a person with a criminal mind—what we in the field of psychology call a 'sociopath'—gets away with something, he is sure to go on to commit other, more serious crimes. He starts by stealing a leg, then it's something bigger, like a car! Yes, and then, in no time, he's robbing banks. We also know from scientific studies of the criminal mind that the hoodlum who has gotten away with something always needs to tell someone. Because he wants his buddies to think he's a big shot, the sociopath is sure to boast of what he has done. Thus I am certain that one or more of you, innocent as you are, knows who the criminal is. I want you to do something good, not only for Mr. Woodcock and for Ponce de Leon Elementary School, but something good for yourself and for the criminal as well. I want you to come to my office and identify the thief. I know there's a lot of pressure on you not to tell on your friends. We used to call it 'tattling' or 'snitching' when I was in school; the youth of today call it 'finking.' I know you probably think finking is bad. But it isn't. If it weren't for finking, a lot of the criminals in our prisons would still be on the loose. And finking can also be a way of helping your friend. Once we know who the miscreant is, we will, I promise you, do everything in our power to rehabilitate him. Think about it: what if you know who the thief is, but you don't tell? Twenty years from now, you might read that he has been gunned down by police in a shootout during a bank robbery. All because you thought you shouldn't fink on a friend! Yes, kids, you'll be doing him a favor by turning him in. And I can assure you that I won't tell anyone who it was who told me who stole the leg."

When, after yet another week, Mr. Woodcock still had no right leg to stand on, Dr. Chambers tried yet another strategy. He offered a reward to anyone who reported the identity of the culprit: no laps for the rest of the school year, straight A's in wood shop and physical education, a year's pass to the La Brea Tar Pits, free Eskimo Pies at lunch for a week, and an autographed copy of a book that Dr. Chambers, PhD, himself had written, *Kids of Today, Citizens of Tomorrow.* Like *Facts of Life and Love for the American Teenager,* it had been published by Chambers and Chambers Publications and endorsed by *Parents* magazine.

At the next weekly assembly, an infuriated Dr. Chambers was making no bargains: "Okay, this has gone far enough. I've called in the Beverly Hills Police Department. They're going to throw the book at whoever stole Mr. Woodcock's leg. And whoever knows about it and has not reported it will be considered an accessory to the crime. I can assure you punishment will be severe."

Despite the combined efforts of the Beverly Hills police, a private detective hired by Mr. Woodcock, and a retired FBI agent who occasionally bowled with Dr. Chambers, the crime remained unsolved. In the meantime, Mr. Woodcock, apparently uncomfortable in his commercially manufactured prosthesis, had become more and more depressed. The soldier who by his own account had "kicked" so much "Commie ass in Korea" had been devastated by an elementary school student in Beverly Hills. While the loss of his leg of flesh had been an honor, the loss of his wooden leg had been a disgrace because, while the North Koreans were supposed to hate him, the boys at Ponce de Leon were supposed to admire him. There was whiskey on his breath and, when I asked him what grade of sandpaper I should use to finish off my tie rack, he, without even touching the wood, mumbled, "It's smooth enough." He had, furthermore, lost all pedagogical enthusiasm for explaining the *Facts of Life and Love for the American Teenager.* "Just read it," he muttered. "Read the book if you want to pass the fuckin' final exam."

I can still remember a few of the questions on that exam:

What hangs down in front of the scrotal sac suspended from the lower abdomen of boys and men?

a) the tampon
b) the male organ
c) the tonsils
d) the ovaries
e) all of the above

Cisco Zutano protested getting that one wrong, arguing that it was a trick question because there are times when male organs don't hang down and also because in Spanish, he claimed, "*el tonsilo*" was one of many words for the penis. It was ironic that the only boy in the class who might really have ever gone all the way with a girl was the only one to fail the sex test.

I got an A on the exam. But even though I got the following one right, I had mixed feelings about my answer:

Feelings of sexual attraction for which of the following are not out of bounds?

a) an older person of the same sex
b) an older person of the opposite sex
c) a person of the same age of the same sex
d) a person of the same age of the opposite sex
e) all of the above

I circled *d,* which applied to Suzie Krasny, and not *b,* which applied to Miss Pinchas, because I had become well aware of the difference between a correct answer and a true answer. I had read the chapter called "Crushes Out-of-Bounds" in *Facts of Life and Love for the American Teenager:*

There are many older women, even some who are married, who are lonely and hungry for affection. Such a woman may find herself enjoying and being flattered by the attention of *a young and inexperienced boy* [italics mine]. One day she considers the boy just a promising student. The next day she finds herself in an improper embrace that puzzles and dismays both her and the boy and leads to further emotional involvement that will be seriously harmful to the mental health of both of them. It could ruin their lives forever.

Based on my reading, I also knew the correct answer (as well as the different, true answer) to the following:

A boy who has frequent sexual thoughts about an older woman should

a) discuss it with parents, teachers, or clergyman
b) relieve himself with masturbation
c) go on a date with a girl his own age who has a bad reputation
d) ignore it, tell no one, and keep it bottled up inside of him
e) all of the above

When, prior to my Hebrew lesson one day, I went into our library-bar to contemplate the breasts of Venus de Milo in *Masterpieces of the Louvre* in anticipation of the arrival of Miss Pinchas, I was startled and unnerved to discover that it was not shelved in its usual place between the *Encyclopaedia Britannica* and the complete works of Dr. Frank G. Lafleur, MD. I couldn't find it anywhere. It wasn't until after Miss Pinchas left that afternoon that I discovered what had happened to it. It was in my mother's hands as she entered my room. No sooner had she seated herself on the red velvet couch and opened the book to the three Graces than I was swearing to God that I hadn't done anything wrong and knew nothing about it. My brother, Robert, had, it turned out, finked on me.

"Robert's lying," I claimed. "I didn't do it. I swear to God, I didn't do it."

My mother tried to convince me that Robert had only shown her the book because, impressed as he was by his older brother's artistic talent, he was proud of me. "Robert looks up to you. But don't worry, darling," she said with a gracious smile of maternal affection. "I'm not angry with you." She informed me that if we had lived in ancient Rome and saw that same marble relief of the three Graces there it would have been painted just as I had colored it. And the nipples of the Venus de Milo would have been red as well. My mother had accepted my defacement of her book as art restoration. She always appreciated my artistic endeavors and even thought my wood tie rack was beautiful, even though it hadn't been sanded very smooth and all of the prongs for the ties were slightly crooked.

My mother would certainly have been less pleased by my friends' embellishments of my Jayne Mansfield poster than she was by my enhancements to the sculpted nudes in *Masterpieces of the Louvre,* but she didn't have occasion to go into my bathroom since it was Sally May who cleaned up in there. Sally May's reaction was frank: "Shit, boy, why'd you go and do that to that pretty girl? That's Miss Jayne Mansfield. She deserves some respect."

The defacements were, even to the limited aesthetic sensibilities of a twelve-year-old boy, offensive: FUCK had, by that time, been written on it more than it had been scrawled on the walls of Ponce de Leon Elementary School; and, intruding upon the photo from the edges of the poster, there were five penises, each with hefty, hairy testicles hanging from them, all squirting the seminal emissions that I had read about in *Facts of Life and Love for the American Teenager* onto the desecrated body of Jayne Mansfield. It broke Chuck Mandel's heart.

Given his ardent enthusiasm for all things dirty, I figured Lance was probably responsible for at least 50 percent of the filth drawn and inscribed on the poster in my bathroom. Smut delighted, amused, fascinated, and enthralled him. Thus, when he showed up one day to show me something "really bitchin', I mean the coolest thing you've ever seen," I assumed it would be the latest sample of French pornography swiped from his father's collection. But, in fact, it had nothing to do with sex. It was Mr. Woodcock's leg.

Even though I was amply impressed with his daring, I asked him to take it away, confessing that I didn't want to get in trouble for being an accessory to the crime. Perhaps it was because all of his friends—Chuck Mandel, Larry Feinstein, Chip Zuckerman, Robbie Freeman, Little Mike Shulman, and even Leo Roth—had had exactly the same reaction that he decided to get rid of it. It might have been concluded that he had a conscience since, rather than burning the leg in an incinerator, he rather nobly decided to return it.

Maybe that would have been taken into account when Mr. Jim, the school janitor, caught him on the night he threw it over the fence into the playing field. Maybe, since he was trying to restore the leg to its rightful owner, they would have gone easy on him. Maybe Dr. Chambers would have merely suspended him rather than expelling him; maybe—if only Lance hadn't carved FUCK so large and deeply into the calf of the leg right next to GOD BLESS AMERICA. With a chisel, Mr. Woodcock subsequently changed that FUCK into BOOK.

Lance took it in stride that he was being sent to a boarding school in France: "I'll be able to see Fifi again. Not only do French girls like to fuck like jackrabbits, but you're allowed to smoke in school." Happy not to have to take Hebrew anymore, he didn't care that he wouldn't be having a bar mitzvah: "Religion is a crock of smegma," he declared. "If there weren't any religion, we could do all the things we'd like to do. People thought up God and religion to prevent us from having too much fun."

With Miss Pinchas sitting next to me going over the Torah portion I'd read the following year, I was thinking about Lance's theological insights when my Hebrew teacher suddenly switched into English from the language spoken both by God and, thanks to Miss Pinchas, by Marilyn Monroe in *Gentlemanim M'hadifi Blondinyot:* "Excuse me, Lee. I'll just be a moment. I need to use the powder room."

No sooner had she crossed the bedroom, entered my bathroom, and locked the door behind her than I realized that, with her skirt up around her waist and her panties down around her ankles, sitting there on my toilet, she was looking at my "Life-Size Real-Color Poster of Hollywood's Most Titillating Love Goddess and Explosive Sex Bomb."

As soon as the bathroom door opened, I began to apologize: "Oh, God, I'm so sorry about that disgusting picture in there. It belongs to my brother, Robert. He sent away for it and then drew and wrote all over it. He taped it up on my wall this morning. He's really a naughty kid. My parents are worried about him. They're afraid that he is becoming a sociopath."

"They shouldn't worry," Miss Pinchas smiled. "Robert's such a cute little boy and good too. I can tell that by his smile. He reminds me of the Beaver. *Ta'azov et ze le Beaver* is very popular in Israel now."

Once my lesson was over and Miss Pinchas had gone, I peeled the poster of Jayne Mansfield off the wall and ripped it up. Putting the pieces of it into the incinerator by the alley, I recollected something I had read in *Facts of Life and Love for the American Teenager:* "Like every other source of power, the sex urge must be harnessed or it will run wild and become destructive."

Unharnessed sex urges had destroyed Jayne Mansfield and they were getting to me. But at least the book offered hope:

> Don't worry about those embarrassing thoughts that sometimes go through your head. Just take control of your sex drive, before it takes control of you. And remember, if properly harnessed, the sex urge can enhance your life by lending its power to love, thereby augmenting the great joy and happiness that true love has to offer every human being.

That sounded pretty good to me. All I had to do was figure out what "properly harnessed" meant.

By Chapter Five, She Loves You, And All Your Dreams Come True

1958♥1959

So endeth this chronicle. It being strictly a history of a boy, it must stop here; the story could not go much further without becoming the story of a man.

Mark Twain, *The Adventures of Tom Sawyer*

With the arrival of puberty, changes set in which are destined to give infantile sexual life its final, normal shape. The activity of the sexual instinct has hitherto been derived from a number of separate instincts and erotogenic zones, which, independently of one another, have pursued a certain sort of pleasure as their sole sexual aim. Now, however, a new sexual aim appears, and all the component instincts combine to attain it, while the erotogenic zones become subordinated to the primacy of the genital zone. . . . The new sexual aim in men consists in the discharge of the sexual products.

Sigmund Freud, *Three Essays on the Theory of Sexuality*

1958

The National Aeronautics and Space Administration and the John Birch Society are founded; *Explorer 1,* the first US satellite to successfully orbit the earth, is launched, and Americans discover that television game shows are fixed; Elvis Presley is drafted into the United States Army, and Jerry Lee Lewis, after releasing "Great Balls of Fire," marries his thirteen-year-old cousin; Ricky Nelson sings "A Teenager's Romance" on *The Adventures of Ozzie and Harriet,* and Carol Lynley stars as a pregnant teenager in *Blue Denim;* Jayne Mansfield poses in the nude for *Playboy* magazine, and Brigitte Bardot appears in *Love Is My Profession;* Cocoa Puffs are introduced by General Mills, and the Jolly Green Giant promotes canned vegetables on television; *The Lone Ranger* and *The Roy Rogers Show* go off the air, and *Sea Hunt* comes on with an episode in which Fitta Knullaman appears as a female escape artist whose underwater stunt goes awry; James Van Allen discovers a belt of radiation around the earth, and Billy Hunter wins the All-California Elementary School Science Fair; the Monotones record "The Book of Love," and I become a Son of the Commandment.

"In tribal societies," Mr. Schumann, our eighth-grade social science and physical education teacher as well as the coach of the Ponce de Leon Elementary School softball team, explained, "boys officially become men by passing tests of strength, endurance, courage, and knowledge. These tests are called," he paused to write the phrase on the blackboard, "*puberty rites.*" Anything on the blackboard was likely to be on our own tests of knowledge: *tribe, clan, family, society, race, initiation,* and *incest taboo.* Such terms as *puberty* were defined in our textbook, *The Story of Man:*

Puberty is when human beings first become capable of sexual reproduction. While the genital organs of both boys and girls mature during this period, only the girls begin to menstruate. Other characteristics of adulthood, such as pubic hair on both males and females, facial hair on males, and the growth of breasts on females, also begin to appear. While the age at which puberty occurs is usually around fourteen in boys and twelve in girls in America, primitive people tend to mature more quickly.

Anyone who laughed when Mr. Schumann, in reviewing our reading assignment, uttered words like *pubic hair, genital organs,* or *menstruation* would be punished: boys were made to run laps and girls, to tidy up the classroom. Larry Feinstein was ordered to run ten laps for snickering when Mr. Schumann said *homo sapiens.*

I learned that if I had been a member of one of the northern tribes of Central Australia, my own puberty would have been recognized and celebrated by my being publicly subjected to kicks, blows, and lashes with stinging nettles, after which a medicine man would ceremonially give me a sacred bull-roarer, which I would vow never to show to either women or younger males. Had I been a Musquakie Indian adolescent, I would have undergone a fast followed by a solitary period of wandering in the wilderness that would last until the spirits of my ancestors appeared in a dream to reveal the identity of a *mintutipo* girl of our tribe with whom I would be required to copulate as a ratification of my new status as an adult male. Among the Narangga, following prolonged orgiastic feasting, ecstatic dancing, and trance journeys, sexual intercourse would also mark the completion of passage into manhood. If I were an Amazonian Jivaro Indian, I would be shrinking my first human head (probably unaware that it could end up in the gift shop of a Polynesian restaurant in Hollywood).

While among the Reform Jews of Beverly Hills in 1958 the male puberty rite included a revel with both feasting and dancing, the ritual never culminated in sexual intercourse. Although I had dreamed more than once of Candy Canter, I would not, unlike my Musquakie counterpart, be required to copulate with her. I did, however, invite her to be my date at my bar mitzvah at the end of the year. I knew that Suzie Krasny was no longer my girlfriend when I read the letter she wrote to me from the Hillel Horseback and Hebrew Summer Camp to tell me that she wanted "to be friends." That phrase, I realized, is the kiss of death—"I want to be friends" means "I can't stand you."

Had we been kids in Azimba Land, after having my face scarified, my torso painted, and my penis circumcised and striated, I would have been given a spear by my father. Thus branded and armed, I would have appeared before Candy's father, who, in order to secure my father's allegiance and promote tribal solidarity, would have given me not only his daughter but also a kid goat and a woven basket of yams as well. The girl herself, in preparation for the event, would have undergone a puberty rite that would have included the ceremonial braiding of her hair and piercing of her ears, as well as a clitoridectomy. Although Candy did have her hair done at the Beverly Beauty Parlor for my bar mitzvah party, her vulva certainly went unmutilated. Her parents wanted her to wait until after her Sweet Sixteen party to have her ears pierced and to wait until her wedding night for sexual intercourse. The only thing that made being a Jewish boy better than being Azimban was that I got circumcision over with at a very early age.

Bar mitzvah parties in Beverly Hills provided a training ground in which Reform Jewish youngsters attempted to master adult courtship manners and learn the meaning of romance. Boys wore dark dress suits, and the cuff links in our white shirts matched the tie clips for the ties we hung on the wooden racks that we had made in wood shop. The girls sported high-heel shoes and nylon stockings held up by fastener straps on their girdles. The skirts of their cocktail gowns were spread out by plush petticoats of crinoline or organza. They learned how to apply cosmetics—lipstick to make their lips lush, rouge for flushed cheeks, and mascara to make young eyes brightly beguiling. We drank soda pop from champagne glasses and, at Larry Feinstein's bar mitzvah bash, the girls were given chocolate cigarettes and the boys, bubblegum cigars.

Nine months before my own rite of passage, Clover Wiener had agreed to be my date for Chip Zuckerman's bar mitzvah party at the Sportsman's Lodge in Van Nuys. With their bar mitzvah invitations, all of the boys, following the custom of Southern Californian Reform Jewry, were provided with a list of the girls who had been invited so that each of us could ask one of them to be his date for the party.

Just as boys in the Murrumbidgee tribe have two of their lower incisor teeth knocked out at puberty, and just as members of the Kedah-Semang tribe have their teeth filed into sharp points, so, in the same spirit, as a Jew in Beverly Hills, I had metal orthodontic braces attached to my teeth. Rather than making me feel as fierce as I supposed adolescent Murrumbidgee and Kedah-Semang warriors did when they flashed their choppers, however, my braces made me self-conscious, especially since Clover Wiener's braces had been removed in the seventh grade. It was daunting that she was more physically developed than I. While such characteristics of manhood as a mature sexual organ and pubic hair were not yet manifest in me, signs of female puberty—notably big boobs—were marvelously blatant on the womanly body of Clover Wiener. That figure had turned out even better than I had imagined it would when we were taking swimming lessons together seven years earlier. My awareness that she was capable of sexual reproduction was so intimidating that I considered merely inviting her to be my date at Chip's bar mitzvah party to be as much a test of manly courage as anything done by my peers in Azimba Land. Having realized a few years before that it was very unlikely that her mother really was a Communist, I was not afraid to accept when Mrs. Wiener volunteered to drive us to the Sportsman's Lodge.

Outside the dining room of the lodge, there was a trout pond from which diners, provided with fishing poles, could catch their entrées. The pool was so full of fish that no customer, no matter how inexperienced a fisherman, would have to settle on just the salad bar for dinner. Like the Yupik youths of Northern Alaska, who, we had learned in Mr. Schumann's class, become men when they kill their first seal, and like the Makah boys of the Pacific Northwest, who attain manhood by spearing a whale, so we, Jewish boys in dress suits, with yarmulkes on our heads and fishing poles in our hands, stood around the pond at the Sportsman's Lodge, fishing in a tribal observance of Chip Zuckerman's bar mitzvah.

Each boy had to catch two trout, one for himself and one for his date. In the excitement of the ritual battle of man against nature, Clover grabbed my arm and, jumping up and down, cried out, "Catch me a big one! Come on, Lee, I want a big one." Apparently Clover wasn't aware that all of the trout in the pond were the same size. She seemed satisfied enough with the fish thrashing about on the end of my line, desperately wiggling in resistance to the imminence of sacrificial death. And when, about half an hour later, what was claimed to be that very fish, beheaded, cleaned, skinned and boned, dressed with almonds, lemon, a dollop of tartar sauce, and a sprig of parsley, was served to her, she gobbled it up. I thought of the adolescent males of the !Kung tribe of Namibia, who offer a cut of the flesh from their first kill to a girl of their tribe; eating it marks her consent to initiate him into the mysteries of adult sexual experience.

The scene reminded me of our adventure in Myron Spellman's backyard years before. And when she excused herself, saying she had to go to the "powder room," I remembered gazing at her as she sat on the toilet to pee before me. I recalled how Clover and I had watched Howdy Doody making love with Muffie and the other girls. And the memories were arousing. As soon as Clover returned from the bathroom, I invited her to take a walk with me out by the trout pond.

"Do you remember the day, when we were kids, that I brought my Howdy Doody dummy over to your house?"

"No," she responded without any indication of interest in hearing about it.

"Remember how we snuck over the wall of the Spellman house and stole the gold fish?" I asked.

"No," she answered again.

"Do you remember reading *The Little Mermaid* to me and what I read to you?"

Again: "No."

"But you do remember coming to my house for swimming lessons?"

"Was that your house?" she asked.

"Do you remember anything about me from when we were little kids?"

"Yes," she blushed, "but it's kind of embarrassing. I don't want to say."

I guessed that she was probably remembering us in her bathroom and that, like me, she might be thinking that, since we had already, as six-year-olds, been so familiar, we might as well now explore some of the ways in which twelve-year-olds could be intimate. I was ready to give her a kiss and feel her up both over and under the top of her party dress. We were halfway around the pond and alone except for the couple that I could hear necking in the bushes. All I needed as a signal for me to make my amorous advance was for her to tell me the embarrassing memory. I had to insist before she finally gave in.

"Okay," she said with slight smile. "The thing I remember best about you as a kid is when we were in the third grade. You wet your pants, and Miss Ross made you come up to the front of the room. I felt sorry for you. I was just glad it wasn't me. Do you remember that?"

"No," I said and asked Clover if she'd like to go back inside and dance.

"Sure," she answered, "but can I ask a favor? There's something I'd like you to do for me. Can I ask you?"

The request rekindled my hope. On the chance that she was about to ask me for a kiss, I said, "Sure. Anything."

"Okay, I'd like to dance with Leo Roth," she confided. "But he's been ignoring me all night. I think that's because I'm your date. But if you'd tell him that it would be okay with you if he danced with me, I'm sure he'd ask me. Would you do that?"

"Sure," I said, realizing that, like Suzie Krasny, Clover Wiener wanted us "to be friends." Disappointed, I walked her back to the Sportsman's Lodge dining room, where the Four Sportsmen were singing "All I Have to Do Is Dream."

While Leo Roth danced with my date, I talked to Candy Canter about her plans for the upcoming Ponce de Leon Elementary School Eighth-Grade Science Fair.

The bar mitzvah party was the culmination of a ceremony that had begun in a synagogue on that Saturday morning. Among Reform Jews, that more formal aspect of the puberty rite demanded that the initiate demonstrate before the congregation and guests his ability to read a passage from a sacred book written in a strange script and ancient language, making it seem as though he might actually know the meaning of any of the words he was uttering. This solemnity was followed by a speech in which the bar mitzvah boy conventionally mouthed sentiments that epitomized the moral values of the elders of his tribe. "I want to thank the God of my forefathers, Abraham, Isaac, and Jacob," Chip Zuckerman proclaimed, "the God whose commandments I so happily accept on this occasion of my bar mitzvah, for the many blessings that He has given me." Those blessings included "being a Jew and living in America, having great parents and cool friends who are too numerous to mention by name."

It had been the duty of the Zuckerman's maid to stay up night after night during the months prior to the ceremony in order to play the tape recording of a Hebrew reading of the Torah and Haftorah portions over and over again for a soundly sleeping Chip. It was an exercise in "Somnoeducation," a field of investigation into human cognitive processes in which Chip's father had been involved as a psychology instructor at Santa Monica Junior College. That research had resulted in Professor Zuckerman's establishment of Brain Sells, Inc., a Beverly Hills advertising agency providing commercial enterprises with access to the unconscious minds of consumers. The company was in the vanguard of the development of the controversial methods of marketing by subliminal persuasion.

It was irrelevant that the housekeeper who sang gospel songs at the Torrance Baptist Church each Sunday could probably have recited the Hebrew text quite as well as the boy standing in front of the congregation of the Beverly Hills synagogue on the Saturday of Chip's bar mitzvah: the point, as Chip explained in Mr. Gordon's General Science class, was not that learning in sleep was necessarily more effective than learning while awake. Rather, it was that "sleep is the best mental state in which to memorize things that are so boring that they would put you to sleep if you tried to memorize them while you were awake, stuff like 'The Midnight Ride of Paul Revere,' 'If,' by Rudyard Kipling, and the Torah. Because of somnoeducation," Chip announced, "being asleep doesn't have to be a waste of time."

"Subliminal Advertising: Bane or Boon to Mankind?" Chip had announced when it was his turn in Mr. Gordon's class to propose a project for the 1958 Annual Ponce de Leon Elementary School Eighth-Grade Science Fair. It was an event that, because of the successful launch of *Sputnik* by the Soviets the previous year, had become even more important than the All-Beverly-Hills Elementary Schools

Softball Championships. That the Communists had put a satellite into orbit before us implied that while American kids were playing baseball, going to the movies, watching television, and dancing to rock 'n' roll music, our girls learning how to bake banana bread and our boys how to make tie racks, Commie kids had been assiduously studying science. All work and no play may have been making them dull, but it had also given them the edge on us in the space race and, therefore, in the arms race. National security was being threatened by a lack of rigor in science programs in the American school system. It was time to get serious. And nothing was more serious than science. All boys were required to have slide rules.

"Science," Mr. Gordon solemnly informed us, "is the Latin word for knowledge." His expression was lofty, his tone, serious. "And knowledge is power. And power is freedom." The teacher smiled reassuringly. "And freedom is happiness."

Cisco Zutano raised his hand to ask, "And happiness is . . . what?"

Mr. Gordon didn't trust the sixteen-year-old eighth-grader with long sideburns and a ducktail. "I'll pretend I didn't hear that!" the teacher snapped in consternation before regaining the composure to continue his address: "Whoever wins the gold medal here at Ponce de Leon will have his, or even—yes, young ladies—*her,* project entered in the All-California Science Fair in Sacramento. And if you win there, you'll receive a one-thousand-dollar college scholarship from Westinghouse and an all-expense-paid visit for you and a companion to the Lockheed Missile Systems Labs in Sunnyvale, California. And your project will go on to the Nationals. The winner there will visit the White House to shake hands with both President Dwight D. Eisenhower and Vice President Richard M. Nixon."

"I'd like that," Chip Zuckerman said as if his project on subliminal advertising had a shot of being entered in the Nationals. The big win would give his father an opportunity to speak to Ike and Dick in defense of the marketing technique that "left-wing paranoiac eggheads at the National Association of Broadcasters" were trying to ban from America's airwaves.

Chip's project report divulged that the Soviets were as far ahead of us in the development and application of subconscious persuasion as they were in the space race and the stockpiling of intercontinental ballistic missiles. "Like atomic energy," the Zuckerman display decreed, "subliminal advertising can be used either for good or for evil." It argued that subliminal advertising should not be banned, but rather restricted, licensed by a department of the United States Government to ensure that it was not used, as it was behind the Iron Curtain, for indoctrination. Such an "Office of Unconscious Operations" would, in cooperation with the FBI, prevent subliminal advertising from falling into the hands of Communists here in America and, at the same time, guarantee that it was employed only to market wholesome, American-made products.

There were illustrations of the brain and photographs of such pioneers in the field as Sigmund Freud, Ivan Petrovich Pavlov, and Professor Charles Zuckerman. The display itself consisted of the testing equipment that had been used in the Zuckerman experimental research: a miniature soda fountain that offered a choice among three soft drinks (Coca-Cola, Canada Dry Spur cola, and White Rock cola) and a tape recorder that, with the push of a button, played a one-minute instrumental version of "Love Is a Many Splendored Thing," the lyrics to which practically everyone in America in 1958 knew as well as they knew the Pledge of Allegiance. Wherever the word *love* would have come in the song, "Coke" was softly whispered by a sexily silky, barely audible voice that was hardly distinguishable in timbre from the violins. During the sixty seconds of music, the soothed mind registered the subliminal message: "Coke is a many splendored thing . . . Coke is nature's way of giving . . . Coke is the reason to be living." And then, when it was time to select a beverage: "Nine out of ten people chose Coke."

Given the popularity of Coca-Cola as instilled by conventional, non-subliminal advertising, the Zuckerman conclusions raised questions in the critical minds of the astute judges: "Would the experiment have worked if the subliminal message had been either that Canada Dry Spur cola is nature's way of giving or that White Rock cola is the reason to be living?"

It made Chip bitter to have received only a bronze medal for all of his father's hard work. It was a disgrace to have been beaten out by a Gentile (Billy Hunter) and an absurdity to lose to a girl (Angela Portinari).

All three medal winners received a copy of Dr. Chambers's book, *Kids of Today, Citizens of Tomorrow,* a subscription to *Scientific American* magazine, and a certificate signed by the esteemed judges (Mr. Schumann, Mr. Gordon, Dr. Gus Chambers, PhD, and, through the influence and efforts of Mr. Ball, none other than television star Jack Webb). In addition to that, the second-place winner, namely, Angela Portinari, was given a book of coupons good for admission to all of the science and technology displays in Disneyland's Tomorrowland. In presenting the silver medal to Angela, Mr. Gordon decreed before the assembly that "there's going to be a lot of room in science for the women of tomorrow, which is to say, the girls of today. Who better than the housewife to help us determine the ways in which science and technology can improve life in the American home? Even the most advanced scientific research can benefit from the feminine touch."

Angela Portinari's project, "The Miracle of Concrete," hardly seemed either feminine or the result of advanced scientific research. Her father's involvement in it was as apparent as the contribution of Professor Zuckerman to Chip's project. I estimated that about 90 percent of all the eighth-grade science projects had been done by the parents of the students who submitted them. The figures were about the same for the composition of bar mitzvah speeches.

Angela's father, Angelo Portinari, something of a celebrity after his appearance on national television in 1952 for questioning by Estes Kefauver's Special Committee on Organized Crime in Interstate Commerce, was owner-director of Portinari All-American Concrete, a company dedicated to the manufacture of materials for the building (licensed exclusively to Portinari All-American Construction) of "domiciles that are comfortable, attractive, inexpensive, and best of all, resistant to atomic blasts!"

Within a glass display case, in front of a large and familiar photograph of a monstrous mushroom of radioactive cloud, there was a miniature model of a Portinari house. There were blueprints, floor plans, cubes of Portinari All-American Concrete, and samples of such modern nonpermeable materials as the Glosheen, Congoleum, and Fiberglas that were used for the fixtures and furnishings in Portinari homes: "With an ordinary garden hose, the entire house, inside and out, can be cleansed of atomic ash in a jiffy!" There was also a comprehensive history of both concrete and atomic energy.

"These homes are protected with a money-back guarantee," Angela's text promised, "to safeguard occupants from atomic blast pressures expected at distances as close as one-thousand feet from ground zero of a bomb with an explosive force equivalent to 50,000 tons of TNT. There's no need to be afraid of tomorrow if you live in a Portinari blast-resistant concrete house today."

Poor loser that he was, Chip Zuckerman spread the rumor that Angela had been awarded the silver medal only because her father had intimidated Mr. Gordon with threats to put his feet in Portinari concrete and throw him off the Santa Monica pier unless the girl's project received a medal.

Angela herself did not, according to Chuck Mandel, feel worthy of the award: "She thought my science project was better than hers," Chuck confided. "She wanted to give me the silver medal and that stupid book by Dr. Gas Chambers, and she offered to pass on her copy of

Scientific American each month." Although he turned the medal, book, and magazine down, he did accept her invitation to Tomorrowland. After visiting Autopia, the Clock of the World, Monsanto's Home of the Future, and the Hall of Chemistry, Chuck, in the heavenly darkness of the Moonliner, had mustered the courage to invite Angela to be his date at his own bar mitzvah party. And, much to Chuck's amazement, she accepted the invitation. "It was probably because of my science project," Chuck sighed. "She thinks I'm kind of a genius."

In my own opinion Chuck was a nice guy but no genius, and his project, while perhaps the most impressively sad of the science fair entries, was hardly worthy of a medal, a magazine subscription, coupons for Tomorrowland, or even an autographed copy of *Kids of Today, Citizens of Tomorrow.* It was called "Acne" and proved little more than that there did not seem to be any effective cure for acne, at least not for Chuck Mandel's.

Chuck, who had started to go though puberty in the sixth grade, before any of the other boys in our class, had, at that time, in addition to not growing any taller (while his dick got bigger and bigger), become afflicted with extreme pustular dermatitis and sebaceous facial cysts. His science project consisted of a display of samples of the many dermatological treatments he had tried without success: creams, lotions, salves, soaps, poultices, plasters, pills, and injections. And behind each of the medications, there were two photographs of Chuck's face, one before treatment and one after. His expression in all of the more than twenty photographs of the persistently acne-ravaged face was the same: pained, hopeless, and starkly self-conscious. The attainment of physical manhood and the ability to sexually reproduce had been a disgraceful humiliation for Chuck. That his "genital organ" (as it was called both by Mr. Schumann in social science class and in the textbook *The Story of Man*) had matured into quite an impressive shlong did not seem to be much of a consolation to the short Orthodox Jew with badly blemished skin.

The most startling feature in Chuck's display was the presence, in the line of medical cures, of a mezuzah. Chuck was wearing a yarmulke in the two photographs behind the holy amulet. The photos showed him both before and after his bar mitzvah, before and after he had prayed with all his heart to Adonai for a miracle. It had seemed reasonable to have faith that the God who had the power to part the waters of the Red Sea could easily cure Chuck Mandel's acne.

According to Chuck's account, Angela maintained that the acne project should have received the gold medal because it had scientifically settled a debate that had been going on for thousands of years:

she believed that Chuck Mandel had proved that God does not exist. And, unlike most of the students in the eighth grade, he had done it on

his own, without the help of his father or mother.

"At first," Chuck told me, "Angela figured God hadn't helped me because I'm a Jew and he's still pissed off because we killed his son. So she started to pray to Christ for me in church, to ask him to heal me just like he cured those lepers in the Bible. They were Jewish too." That there still was not the slightest improvement in Chuck's chronic dermatitis cinched it for the confirmed Roman Catholic girl: there is no God, and Jesus was, like Chuck Mandel, just an ordinary Jewish guy (although he was probably taller than Chuck and blessed with better skin).

Apparently it did not occur to Angela that the experiment did not necessarily disprove the existence of God (nor the divinity of Christ) but only demonstrated his (or their) utter lack of interest in both Chuck Mandel's acne specifically and the 1958 Annual Ponce de Leon Elementary School Eighth-Grade Science Fair more generally. In spite of Angela's revelation, and without confessing it to her, Chuck himself maintained a belief in God, albeit a merciless one.

Except for Chuck and Angela, everyone at Ponce de Leon thought that the Mandel bar mitzvah had been the worst one of the year: the excruciatingly long ceremony was mostly in Hebrew, and the girls couldn't sit with the boys; at the party in the hall adjoining the synagogue proper, there was only kosher food, and the girls were not permitted to dance with the boys. Angela clapped her hands as she watched an ever self-conscious Chuck dance with his father, Mendel, his uncles, Milton and Morris, and a few bearded men from New York whom nobody seemed to know. The music for the party was provided by an old man in a dirty suit and dark glasses with an accordion, on which he enthusiastically played what seemed to be only endless variations on "Hava Nagila."

While in the Old World, based on the geographic area in which their traditions had developed, Jews were divided into the Ashkenazim and Sephardim, in the New World, the two camps were the East Coast Jews and the Californians. Chip Zuckerman's bar mitzvah had been as Californian as Chuck Mandel's was Eastern. Because the Eastern Jews (with New York as their Jerusalem and outposts of the nation in places like Chicago, Milwaukee, St. Louis, and Cincinnati) still lived close to their zadies and bubies, they knew some Yiddish and often had to attend shul. As California Jews, we only went to synagogue on the High Holy Days and for bar mitzvahs, and the only Yiddish words most of us knew were *shmuck, putz, toochis, keister, shtoop, goy, shiksa, chutzpah*, and *oy vey*. Our strictest observance of Levitical dietary laws had us eating lox and bagels and corned beef on rye at Nate 'n Al's delicatessen every once in a while. While we could order Oscar Mayer wieners at the ballpark, we had Wilno kosher hot dogs at home. We were not supposed to eat ham, bacon, or pork, but there was nothing wrong with lobster or crab; and everybody at Chip's bar mitzvah, except Chuck Mandel, had wolfed down the Sportsman's Lodge shrimp cocktails that were served while we waited for our trout to be cooked.

When Angela, in thanking Chuck for inviting her to his bar mitzvah, said that she had never imagined "that religion could be so much fun," he seized on the chance for another date with her by asking her to come with him to my bar mitzvah party. It was on that occasion, three months later, that he danced with her for the first time. But, afraid that physical contact with his acne might disgust Angela, he did not dare to make it cheek to cheek. All the love he had felt for Jayne Mansfield was transferred to Angela Portinari. And the following year, when we were freshmen at Beverly Hills High School, Chuck had sex with Angela. Immediately afterward his acne began to clear. I imagined two photographs of Chuck, one labeled "before," the other, "after"; and in the latter, there was a radiant smile on an unblemished face. The photos were mounted on a Portinari All-American concrete wall behind a bed upon which Angela lay naked, eager and open for Chuck Mandel.

Just as Chip Zuckerman had whined about Angela getting the silver medal only because her gangster father had threatened Mr. Gordon with reprisals if she didn't, so he bemoaned being beaten out for the gold by Billy Hunter, "that little goy, only because Mr. Gordon is an anti-Semite. He resents it that Jews are so much better at science than everybody else. Most of the scientists at Los Alamos were Jews. It's thanks to us that America has the atomic bomb, psychoanalysis, movie studios, and subliminal advertising."

That Billy Hunter, the class genius, having skipped three times, was only ten years old made his accomplishment even more impressive. The display was elegantly simple: there was a fresh tomato (aptly labeled "fresh tomato"), a mushy squished blob of tomato (informatively labeled "tomato after being frozen and thawed"), and a tomato that looked just like the fresh one (intriguingly labeled "tomato after Hunterization"); and there was an appliance (proudly labeled "Hunterizer") with two gauges and two valves. Billie explained his invention to the class: "When a fruit or vegetable is frozen, the liquid within each of its cells expands, thus breaking the cell membranes within the piece of produce. When thawed out, given the loss of structure provided by the walls of its cells, the fruit or vegetable turns to mush. To prevent this natural internal pulpifaction, I have developed the Hunterizer, an apparatus in which, as the temperature is gradually reduced, the air pressure is gradually increased so that freezing can take place without any rupturing of the cell walls. Likewise, during thawing, the air pressure in the compartment is decreased to prevent an implosion of the cells as temperature is increased. Thus, by means of Hunterization, fresh produce can be frozen indefinitely for storage and shipping, and thawed out with no loss of character or quality." He had calculated the requisite ratios between air pressure and temperature for five different sizes and weights of tomatoes.

After presenting the gold medal to the prodigy with the announcement that the Hunterizer would be entered in the All-California Science Fair, Dr. Gus Chambers, PhD, proudly shaking Billy's hand, declared that "Hunterization offers a hope to American families that they will be able to enjoy fresh fruits and vegetables even in a nuclear holocaust."

By winning the All-California Fair, not only did Billy receive a Westinghouse thousand-dollar college scholarship and an all-expense-paid visit for him and a companion to the Lockheed Missile Systems Labs in Sunnyvale, California, but he was also, once executives at the Green Giant Company got wind of the Hunterizer, flown to Le Sueur, Minnesota, to meet the Jolly Green Giant.

"He was tall," Billy reported in Mr. Gordon's science class, "but not that tall, not an actual giant, but over six feet. At least he was painted green, and he did say 'Ho, ho, ho' a lot."

The company must have paid Billy well for the rights to Hunterization because no sooner had he returned to Beverly Hills than he bought a Ford Thunderbird convertible. Mr. Hunter, an employee of the RAND Corporation who was out of town on business much of the year, consented to release the funds for the sports car from the trust that had been established for Billy by the Green Giant. There was even enough money for Billy to engage a chauffeur to drive him to school, as well as to the UCLA computing laboratory, his psychoanalyst, his judo class, and the various homes where he gave private chess lessons. He hired none other than Jose "Cisco" Zutano for the job.

The 1958 Ponce de Leon Elementary School Eighth-Grade Science Fair brought the ten-year-old who had skipped three grades together with the sixteen-year-old who had flunked three times. But as Billy's science project had earned him kudos and cash, Cisco's effort brought castigation and an end to his academic career.

Called upon by Mr. Gordon to inform us as to the nature of his project, Cisco announced it to be "The Effects of Marijuana." After emending the title to "The Dangers of Marijuana" and giving his approval to the proposal, our science teacher reminded us that marijuana was being smuggled into the country by drug dealers working for the Kremlin. The Communists were trying to turn young people in America into dope fiends so that we would lose our initiative, our interest in science, and our love of freedom and appreciation of democracy.

Hoping that he might get to visit the Lockheed Missile Systems Labs or even, if he worked really hard, that he might get to shake the hands of Dwight D. Eisenhower and Richard M. Nixon, Cisco went all out on the project. His display included some marijuana leaves and three little rolled cigarettes labeled "Reefers." Suspecting that the samples might be the real thing, Mr. Gordon turned them over to the Beverly Hills Police Department. His suspicions were confirmed. Despite protestations that he had exhibited the marijuana so that kids, learning what it really looked like, would be able to turn it down, Cisco was sent for rehabilitation to Santa Monica Juvenile Hall. Upon his return to Ponce de Leon, he was informed that, since he had missed a month of school, he would have to repeat the eighth grade. Having turned sixteen, however, Cisco had the legal right to drop out of school. Although he exercised that right, we continued to see him behind the wheel of the T-bird each morning when he dropped Billy off at Ponce de Leon and each afternoon when he picked his employer up. Cisco had taken the car to Tijuana to have it reupholstered with white tuck-and-roll leather and repainted candy-apple red.

Cisco accompanied Billy to the Lockheed Missile Systems Labs in Sunnyvale, and Billy went along with Cisco on Saturday nights to cruise Hollywood Boulevard. They were the best of friends; neither had siblings, and just as there was no Mr. Zutano, there was no Mrs. Hunter. Calling his new pal "Billy the Kid," Cisco taught the boy how to smoke cigarettes and roll reefers; and Billy the Kid taught the *pachuco* how to play chess and use a slide rule. They came together to my bar mitzvah party in the Thunderbird.

When it had been my turn to tell the class what I was planning to do for a project for the science fair, I didn't know what to say. Although as a third-grader I had been certain that, as an eighth-grader, I'd do my science project on the female reproductive system, now, five years later, I realized how naive I had been in imagining that, even with a note from my father, I could get away with working on the twat. In any case, at the age of twelve, I was no longer as interested in the vagina as an isolated and discrete feature of the female sexual apparatus as I had been when I was seven or eight. Although I was well aware that Candy Canter had one, I thought less about it than about her bounteously burgeoned breasts, they being so much more immediately apparent and imaginably attainable than anything below her waist. I had been enthralled by the impression those secondary characteristics of female sexual maturity had made upon me as, while Clover Wiener danced with Leo Roth, we danced close and slow to "Love Is a Many Splendored Thing" at Chip's bar mitzvah, the fingers of my right hand slyly resting on the satin dress fabric over the clasp of the brassiere that symbolized her womanhood. Since, unlike Candy, I had not yet undergone the physical changes of puberty, I felt unprepared to deal with the vulva. But I was ready and eager for breasts. I dreamed I saw Candy Canter in a *maidenform bra*.

It might have been the subliminal message in the song that made Candy, once the music stopped, so eager to get a Coca-Cola from the Sportsman's Bar Mitzvah Bar. As she fished the maraschino cherry out of it, she told me about her project for the upcoming science fair: "Food in Outer Space: What Man Will Eat on the Moon." After devouring her own cherry, she asked if she could have mine: "Maraschino cherries are my favorite food in the world except, of course, for roasted marshmallows. So, what are you doing for the fair?"

Given Candy's conversation, I tried to impress her by answering that, although I had not yet worked out the specifics, I too was working on nutrition, "maybe something on maraschino cherries or marshmallows." As one wholeheartedly uninterested in science, I actually had no idea what I was going to do. But to admit that, and not to be enthusiastic about the upcoming science fair, might have made me less of a man in Candy's eyes. In Mr. Gordon's mind, it would have been tantamount to promoting a Communist takeover of America.

Desperate for a project and willing to settle for anything on nutrition, I turned to my brother, Robert. Although he was only in the third grade, he so loved science that he had already, just for the fun of it, dissected a rat that had been killed in a trap set in our basement bomb shelter. He had studied the complete works of Dr. Frank G. Lafleur, MD —not just *The Reproductive System* but *The Nervous System, The Respiratory System,* and most pertinently for my purposes, *The Digestive System* as well. His teacher, Miss Ross, had expressed her belief that he was destined to become a doctor like our father.

Robert had what seemed like a very good idea for my project, but because it would require a lot of work, I offered to give him anything I had if only he would do the whole thing for me. He wanted my copy of *Swedish Sunbather* magazine as well as my rawhide bullwhip, my slide rule, and ten dollars in cash. As Esau offered his birthright to his younger brother Jacob for a pot of lentils, so I gave all that Robert demanded in return for a science project. I further agreed to give him another ten bucks if I won a medal, another twenty if I went on to the state level, and, if I won the National Elementary School Science Award, I would do everything in my power to take him to Washington, DC, with me to shake the hands of President Eisenhower and Richard Nixon.

For my project Robert set up two cages, each furnished with a little treadmill, a feeding bowl, an upside-down piped water bottle, and a plush carpet of wood shavings. Robert put five mice in each cage. In order to prevent the rapid reproduction that would have taken place if mice of both genders had been together, only males were purchased for the experiment. While Group A was given a well-rounded diet and vitamin supplements in their water, Group B was offered only Cocoa Puffs to eat and their water bottle was filled with Coca-Cola.

With all the dedication of a professional research scientist, meticulously measuring the amounts of the nutrients ingested by the mice of both groups, Robert kept precise records in a notebook with my name on it. My brother weighed our little subjects each day, fed them, cleaned their cages, and recorded his observations on their demeanor and behavior. Jonas Salk couldn't have done a more thorough job.

The mice on the well-rounded, vitamin-rich diet gained weight and lived lives that, at least for rodents, seemed generally idyllic: they ate, drank, rooted around in the wood shavings, played on the treadmill, and slept cozily curled up together. Although the mice in Group B also put on weight at the beginning, they soon began to lose what they had gained and more. They never ran on the treadmill. Their only exercise or play consisted in constantly and frantically attempting to mount each other sexually. If the weaker males tried to resist the larger ones in those futile efforts at mating, they were bitten and abused until they surrendered. Robert explained the results of my scientific research to me: "If you eat Cocoa Puffs and drink Coca-Cola, you'll become a homo."

"And you'll get acne," Chuck Mandel added. "Cocoa Puffs are really bad for your skin."

Chip Zuckerman insisted on explaining why Cocoa Puffs had been selected for the experiment: "General Mills has started using subliminal advertising. Just look at the package. Look at the picture of the cereal in the bowl. What do you see?"

"A bowl of Cocoa Puffs with milk on them."

"No, no, Siegel, look at the shapes. Look here. Don't you see? The two tits? And here's her head, and her stomach, and here are the legs. Don't you see the naked lady?"

"No," I answered in all honesty.

"Yes, you do," Chip argued. "You just don't know that you do. That's

why it's called 'subliminal.' Squint a little bit and you'll see her. She's there. And look over here. Look at what's supposed to be the reflection of light on the bowl. What does that look like?"

I didn't know.

"Sure you do, Siegel," he laughed. "Look carefully. It's a cock. See, here's the head, and there are the two balls. Don't you get it? When people look at the box, even though they aren't consciously aware of it, they see the big boner on the edge of the bowl above the naked girl in the Cocoa Puffs. And that's what makes people choose Cocoa Puffs over other cereals. The subliminal images are picked up by a part of the brain known as the 'unconscious.' That's what controls us. The unconscious is where the sex drive is. While the conscious mind sees milk, the unconscious sees jizzum. The picture on the box stimulates the sex drive, causing a desire, as you stand there in the breakfast food aisle of the grocery store, that makes Cocoa Puffs irresistible. This isn't my opinion, it's a scientific fact. It's like Land O Lakes butter. People buy it because of the Indian chick's tits."

Wondering whether or not the packaging might actually stimulate Candy Canter's sex drive, I gave her a box of Cocoa Puffs under the pretext that I thought she might want to consider including the breakfast cereal in her project on food in outer space.

"Obviously, since there's no gravity in outer space," she informed me, "the cereal wouldn't stay in the bowl once you were up there. People on the moon are going to have their meals in pill form." Sorting thousands of M&M's into piles of single colors and placing them in plastic boxes, Candy labeled each container to indicate which color M&M was supposed to be a pill for what food: green was "green beans," red was "maraschino cherries," orange was "oranges," yellow was "banana bread," and the brown ones were divided into two groups, one "steak" and the other "chocolate" (with each M&M in the latter group representing an entire package of M&M's in pill form). The box of steak pills was marked Ⓚ for "Kosher."

Aware that Angela Portinari had won Chuck Mandel's heart by telling him that she thought his science project was the best in the fair, I tried the same lie on Candy. "Really?" she asked, taking the bait of flattery as eagerly as the trout in the pond at the Sportsman's Lodge had swallowed the little red salmon egg on my hook. Having already learned the ways in which lies, in matters of romance, are not necessarily lies, I swore that it was true. Even though I actually thought her science project was absolutely ridiculous, the avowal that I thought she should have won the gold medal and gone on to the state level was simply a way of saying things that were true but unutterable: "I have a crush on you" or maybe even "I love you," not to mention "I'd really like to fondle your boobs."

Pleased by my praise of her scientific endeavors, she accepted the invitation to be my date at my bar mitzvah, and, among Reform Jews in 1958, when you asked a girl to be your date at your own bar mitzvah for the celebration of your transformation from boyhood into manhood, it was the Beverly Hills equivalent of appearing with a spear, scarred face, painted torso, and striated penis before the father of a girl in Azimba Land.

"Candy Canter's hot," Larry Feinstein said as if I needed his approval. "Great tits. I planned on asking her myself. But since you've beaten me to it, and it is your bar mitzvah, I think I'll invite Carrie Katz. She may not be quite as cute as Candy, but she's even more stacked." Carrie Katz's science project on yeast had been even more stupid than Candy's on space food; it was, however, at least less stupid than Suzie Krasny's on "The Psychological Problems of Domestic Rabbits and How to Cure Them."

That he was a good athlete (Ponce de Leon's best softball player both at bat and on the mound) and a slick dancer (the winner, with Beatrice Sugarman, of the 1956 Bobbie Byrd Cotillion Ballroom Dance-O-Rama Dance Competition) gave Larry an enviable self-confidence. All of the baby fat that formerly inspired us to call him "Spanky" had turned to muscle. He wore white buck shoes, which he continually spanked with a little buck powder bag, and he carried a Trojan in his wallet just in case, unlikely as it was, the opportunity to use it might present itself in the near future. He gave me a packet of three of those rubbers for my bar mitzvah: "Don't ever use Ramses," he warned. "Ramses was that asshole pharaoh who persecuted us in Egypt. You know, Yul Brynner." I hid them in the red velvet couch in my room.

For "The Spleen: Pro or Con?" his entry in the Ponce de Leon science fair, Larry had, with the guidance of his father, a Beverly Hills general surgeon, performed a splenectomy on a frog. It was meant to demonstrate that we don't need our spleens, and so we should have them, like our tonsils, routinely removed. "Doctors of yore," the display elucidated, "identified the spleen as the source of ill-will, bad-temper, and melancholy." There was a very large drawing of a very big spleen, and a very small jar in which a very tiny spleen floated about in formaldehyde. Larry might have won a medal if the frog had survived surgery and shown any signs of an improved disposition.

While modest about his scientific achievements, Larry considered himself a savvy womanizer. The recent appearance of hair on his pubis and in his armpits assured him that his bar mitzvah truly did mark a passage into manhood. He swore to God that he had felt up Beatrice Sugarman in the bushes by the trout pond at Chip Zuckerman's bar mitzvah and Laura Landy at Chuck Mandel's in the women's gallery of the synagogue, and he was planning the same for Carrie Katz at mine, in my Hawaiian hut. "Don't even try to get any titty from Suzie Krasny," he warned Chip in regard to his date for my party. "She wears falsies and so there's no way."

Turning to me, he smiled. "Candy, on the other hand, is a piece of cake. Leo Roth used to feel her up every day after school, when they were flag monitors together, in the janitor's room where the flag's kept. Mr. Jim caught them." Even though I didn't believe Larry, it made me dislike Leo Roth more than ever.

Larry made me the beneficiary of his expertise in the ars amatoris: "Since it's your bar mitzvah, Siegel, there's no way that she, as a Jew, can turn you down. There's something in the Talmud about the bar mitzvah boy getting everything he wants on the day of his bar mitzvah. But you've got to know what you're doing. Make sure you play plenty of slow songs at the party so you can dance close with her. As you do, wrap your arm tightly around her, breathe softly on her neck, and push your chest against hers. Reach around her back and touch the edge of the cup of her bra. That's called 'foreplay.' It might help if you slip an aspirin into her Coke. Then play some fast songs, enough of them to get both of you hot and in a sweat. Then, saying you need some fresh air, you take her outside. 'Candy,' you say, 'there's only one thing I really want for my bar mitzvah.' Give her a moment to wonder what you have in mind and then say, 'It's that you'll go steady with me.' Then you take your ID bracelet off and put it on her wrist. If she accepts it, it means she'll let you kiss her. Do it a couple of times. Not too fast and not too hard. Girls love gentleness and tenderness. Once she's relaxed, you can go straight for the tits. Since she is, at that point, going steady with you, and since you're the bar mitzvah boy, she has no right to stop you. Next, you've got to get her bra off."

Larry offered to teach Chip and me the art of unfastening a brassiere clasp: "If you fumble around and can't get it unhooked smoothly, you'll draw attention to what you're doing and break the rhythm of the make-out. Then you're fucked. The girl will think about what's going on. She'll worry that you're going to tell your friends that she's a nympho, and she'll stop you. It's got to be smooth."

In order to master the technique, Larry had stolen a brassiere from his sister, Connie, then a senior at Beverly High with big breasts who had, we figured, probably lost her virginity. I still had one of her pubic hairs stored in the red velvet couch in my room.

Connie's undergarment was a spectacular pink nylon stitched-cup Peter Pan "Hidden Treasure" bra with "Magicups" and a challenging "Holdfast Clasp" with four hooks and eyes. Putting on the brassiere (with a softball in each cup) over the shirt of his Ponce de Leon Elementary School softball uniform, Larry challenged Chip and me to try to unfasten it "with one hand, as quickly and smoothly as you can. Once you've got the bra off, you can try your hand at the girdle. Just hope she's not wearing a Perma-lift Full Pantie Girdle. They'd be a challenge for Houdini."

While Chip and I took turns practicing unclasping his brassiere, Larry confided that, ever since his bar mitzvah, he was having wet dreams almost every night. In those dreams, he boasted, he had had sex with seven Playboy centerfold models, all of whom he could name, give you their measurements, and tell you their hobbies. He had also dreamed of making love to Brigitte Bardot, Princess Grace of Monaco, Jayne Mansfield, Carol Lynley, and Tricia Nixon.

"Who's Tricia Nixon?" Chip asked.

"The daughter of the Vice President of the United States," Larry bragged. "We did it in the White House. That was quite an honor. Believe me, she was a great fuck."

For over a month before my bar mitzvah, I practiced making out with Candy more diligently than I practiced my Torah reading. Each night, my pillow, the same pillow that had, over the years, played the parts of Gretel Woodcutter, Eve W——, Clover Wiener, Donna Young, Connie Feinstein, and Suzie Krasny, was now Candy Canter. She lay quietly next to me in bed as I rehearsed lines that I had composed to win her heart. When I embraced her, she surrendered as easily and completely as only a pillow can. I kissed her softly at first and then more passionately before reaching up under the pillow case that was her blouse to tenderly touch the lumps of down that, in my nocturnal reverie and adolescent imagination, would have felt exactly like Candy's breasts if only they had nipples.

My bar mitzvah was less than a week away, and my body was still not exhibiting the characteristics of puberty described in *The Story of Man* and *Facts of Life and Love for the American Teenager.* I prayed to the God whose commandment I was about to become the son of to make it happen, if not miraculously during the bar mitzvah ritual, at least by the time I went to Beverly Hills High School, where all of the boys were required to take showers together and some of the girls might

start to put out.

Dressed in a navy blue Plateau men's suit, a Countess Mara tie from my handmade wooden tie rack, and a blue velvet yarmulke on my head, I mounted the dais at Temple Beth Israel primed to become an adult Jewish male. On my wrist I wore the sterling silver ID bracelet that I had been given the previous Chanukah, the bracelet that would soon make Candy Canter mine.

I was a little worried that Rabbi Hymen Weinstein would be upset that my father had invited, among his other friends and patients from Twentieth Century-Fox Studios, Yul Brynner to the ceremony. But afterward, when the actor shook hands with the rabbi, who was standing next to me in the reception line, I overheard Weinstein say, "You were great as Pharaoh in the motion picture, but Heston was *gornisht*—why didn't they cast a Jew?"

I have no recollection of the portion of the Torah that, thanks to Miss Pinchas, I read that Saturday morning in 1958 at Temple Beth Israel. I don't remember very much at all about the ceremony other than that Yul Brynner was there and that I gave a speech that sounded a lot like Chip Zuckerman's (except that I thanked my parents rather than his for being so great). I also recall that Rabbi Hymen Weinstein, whose chin had three little pieces of white toilet paper, each with a red dot of blood in the center, marking where he had nicked himself shaving, gave a sermon that sounded a lot like the one that the rabbi at Chip Zuckerman's synagogue had given (except that he congratulated me rather than Chip on becoming a Son of the Commandment). While both rabbis insisted that becoming a man had something to do with being morally responsible for keeping the commandments and being mature enough to want to study the Torah, neither said a word about what really mattered: sex.

Although neither of the rabbis acknowledged it, I knew there was lots of screwing in the Torah. Having seen *The Ten Commandments,* I was certain that, even if Charlton Heston didn't actually feel up Anne Baxter on the screen, Moses, in the ancient Egyptian reality that they enacted, had surely played around with Princess Nefretiri's knockers by the time he went through puberty. And there was no doubt in my mind that he had gone all the way with her before being banished from Egypt. I hoped that my bar mitzvah party, held at my home, could be more like the orgy scene in the movie, when my ancestors danced around the golden calf, than like either Chip Zuckerman's bar mitzvah party or (God forbid) Chuck Mandel's.

I opened the gifts from my parents before the party: a gold Star of David, a Timex watch, a Rand McNally World Atlas, and a Parker 51 fountain pen, as well as 250 dollars in US Savings Bonds with a matching amount in State of Israel Bonds. I also received a Motorola Royal High Fidelity Portable Record Player with a Magic Mind Diskchanger.

Looking bewitchingly beautiful in her strapless, pale blue satin cocktail dress, Candy Canter, after duly congratulating me on having become a man that morning, presented me with a gift that she considered very special, something she believed I would cherish—not the usual tiepin, cufflinks, key chain, or wallet—but all of the containers of all of the M&M's that had represented space food in her science project.

Given the job of playing the records at the party, Robert, dressed in the FAO Schwarz gorilla suit that I had handed down to him, had been instructed to include one slow song before and after every three or four fast ones. After dancing semifast to the Monotones' "Book of Love," I held Candy close to me as the Teddy Bears sang "To Know Him Is to Love Him." Keeping Larry's counsel in mind, I wrapped my arm tightly around her, breathed lightly on her neck, pressed my chest against hers, and slowly moved my fingertips closer and closer to the edge of the cup of her bra. The romantic mood was sabotaged when Robert suddenly put *Pardon My Blooper* on the turntable and pumped the volume all the way up.

"Robert's so cute," Candy remarked. "He reminds me of the Beaver."

I would have socked him if I hadn't needed him to play the three fast songs for the dances that would, according to the plan, get Candy sufficiently hot and sweaty to accept my invitation to go outside for some fresh air. "Yakety Yak," "Splish Splash," and "Great Balls of Fire" did the trick.

Charmer that I was intent on becoming, I pointed out the full moon to her and remarked how meaningful it was to know that someday people up there on that very moon would be nourishing themselves with pills that looked like M&M's. Then, thanking her once more for the wonderful gift and looking around to make sure that we were alone, I readied myself for the first kiss.

All of a sudden I panicked: What if she wasn't wearing a Perma-lift bra but rather a Maidenform bra like the ones I had often scrutinized in the magazine ads? What if the clasp on her bra was different from the one I had practiced on? I could bungle the whole thing, exposing myself, on the very day that I was supposed to have become a man, as an innocent when it came to making love. I tried to convince myself not to be afraid of her bra—I told myself to be a man.

She was talking about how much she had learned from doing the science project, saying that she planned to study nutritional science at college someday, "not only to become a good housewife, but also to get hired by the National Aeronautics and Space Administration and be sent into outer space. I really want to go to the moon. There's going to be a lot of room in science and on the moon for the women of tomorrow." She agreed with me that she should have won a medal: "Angela didn't deserve a prize. Her father did all the work. But I sorted and packaged all those M&M's by myself. Other than paying for them, my parents didn't help me at all."

The complaint gave me a segue back into the business at hand: "Well, Candy, I can't give you a silver medal for your scientific research, but I can give you something else made of silver, something you deserve just for being who you are. It's my ID bracelet. I'd like you to go steady with me."

Candy smiled, closed her eyes, and gracefully extended her right arm. The moment was charged with romance. No sooner had I taken my ID bracelet off and fastened it around her wrist than she tilted her head back and slightly parted the lips that glistened so lusciously in the moonlight. When, daring to hold her as close to me as I had on the dance floor, I kissed her, she sighed dreamily. I kissed her again. That she put up almost as little resistance as my pillow made me bold enough to ask her if she'd like to see our pool house: "It's decorated like a Hawaiian hut." And when she murmured yes, I savored the magic word of surrender. "Larry Feinstein may be a lousy frog surgeon," I thought to myself, "but he seems to know about women. His plan is working."

As soon as we had entered the pool house I kissed her again and, anxious to get at the clasp on her brassiere, I felt for the zipper on the back of her cocktail dress. But the moment I began to unzip it, Candy pulled away from me.

Cursing myself for having moved too quickly, I tried to kiss her again, as gently and tenderly as Larry had advised, in an attempt to start over and proceed more suavely and with greater finesse to the breasts.

"Don't," Candy ordered. "I can't. At least not until after my Sweet Sixteen party. It's not that I don't want to. But if I let you do that, I'll get too excited. And if I get too excited, I might want to go all the way. And if I go all the way, I could get pregnant just like Carol Lynley in *Blue Denim* and like Becky Fine a few years ago. Remember what happened to her? I'd have to quit school and go to Switzerland. I'd have to take care of the baby. And so I wouldn't be able to go to college and become a nutritional scientist. And if I don't become a space dietician, I won't be able to go to the moon. The folks at the National Aeronautics and Space Administration are not going to let just anybody go up in a spaceship."

And so, because Candy Canter wanted to go to the moon someday, I wasn't able to undo the clasp on her brassiere at my bar mitzvah party, and not being allowed that conquest, I felt I had yet to make the passage into manhood. So eager was I to experience that transformation that, for the sake of it, I would have consented to kicks, blows, and lashes with stinging nettles as inflicted by aboriginal tribesmen in Central Australia. And then, once the medicine man had given me a sacred bull-roarer, a girl of my tribe, as chosen by an aged shamaness in a dream, would follow me into the wilderness. We would make love for the first time beneath a canopy of stars and, in that holy act, I would feel one with her and with the universe as well.

1959

'Twixt Twelve and Twenty, Pat Boone's guide to dating, sex, and love, tops the national nonfiction bestseller list, and Ethel Chambers's *Facts of Life and Love for the American Teenager* goes out of print; *Hawaiian Eye* debuts on television, and *The Adventures of Rin Tin Tin* goes off the air; pantyhose stockings are introduced, and guerrilla forces led by Fidel Castro overthrow Cuban dictator Fulgencio Batista; Vladimir Nabokov's *Lolita* is published in America, and D. H. Lawrence's *Lady Chatterley's Lover* is banned from being sent through the mail by the United States Postal Service; Little Rascal Alfalfa is murdered in a bar in the San Fernando Valley, and Mack Charles Parker, a black man charged with raping a white woman, is abducted from his jail cell by a white mob and lynched in Mississippi; both George Reeves, the star of *Adventures of Superman,* and Dr. Gus Chambers, PhD, the principal of Ponce de Leon Elementary School, commit suicide by shooting themselves in the head; Buddy Holly is killed in an airplane crash, and Frank Hardy enlists in the US Air Force; movie theater seats are wired for Percepto to give audiences a mild shock during showings of *The Tingler,* and teenage murderer Charlie Starkweather is executed in an electric chair in Nebraska; Eve W—— plays her mother's character as a teenager in *She Came from Another World,* and my mother appears in a negligee in *Wake Me When It's Over;* Dion and the Belmonts release "A Teenager in Love," and the Monotones sing "The Book of Love" on Dick Clark's *American Bandstand;* Gregory Corso publishes *The Happy Birthday of Death,* and I decide to become a writer.

"In the beginning sex created heaven and earth." That was the first line of my *Book of Love,* a chronicle of the sexual life of an American boy in the 1950s that I, at the age of fourteen, began writing with the Parker 51 I had been given for my bar mitzvah. The second line, "Sex created misery right after it created mirth," had been dictated by my determination to write the memoir in rhymed couplets. "Birth" had been a close second to "mirth" and far ahead of "berth," "worth," "girth," "dearth," or the capital of Western Australia. This book is a revision of my first attempt at literary composition.

A woman had kindled my resolution to become a writer. She worked at Martindale's bookshop, where I had gone to buy *The Adventures of Tom Sawyer,* a reading assigned by Mr. Webster, the teacher of my freshman English class at Beverly Hills High School. In addition to that purchase, the zaftig salesgirl urged me to buy a new volume of poetry, *The Happy Birthday of Death.* She enthusiastically ranked its author, Gregory Corso, as "our greatest living poet." Wearing black tights under a black wool skirt, without makeup or any adornment other than an Indian turquoise necklace hanging heavy between the ample breasts under her black turtleneck sweater, her mien conjured up daydreams of late-night casual beatnik sex on grimy bare mattresses in candlelit rooms smoky with marijuana, jazz, and poetic melancholy. She introduced herself as Erato, "the Passionate One, a Greek nymph, a daughter of Memory, the muse of love poetry. It's the name Gregory gave me—Gregory Corso."

She had met the man she considered America's premier troubadour the year before, she recounted, while driving down to L.A. from Berkeley. When she picked up the hitchhiker on the road just outside of Gilroy, she had had no idea who he was. They had stopped at San Estribo Beach for something to eat and drink, and then, a few hours later, at a Texaco station in Lompoc, while she was in the ladies' restroom, he had written a poem for her. She opened the book I had just bought to show it to me:

To breathe in Neptune's cup
Dodge gale and tempest
Feel the mermaid up
To stay to bind my hair
On the sea-horse's stirrup.

"Neptune's Cup," she explained, "was the name of the restaurant and bar where we had fish and chips and beer. 'Gale' and 'mermaid' refer to me—my name, as I had told him, was Gail Merman. I was driving a '53 Dodge, and *estribo* means 'stirrup' in Spanish. Get it? When I dropped Gregory off in Hollywood, he said that he wished he could give me money for the gas, food, and beer and the carton of Camels he had asked me to buy for him at the Texaco station. But, like all of the greatest poets in history, he was broke. 'This poem is all I have to give you, Erato baby,' Gregory said as if it wasn't enough that he had already given me a very precious gift—the understanding that, as a woman, I have the power to inspire men to write poetry. That's when I decided to change my name from Gail to Erato. By the way, Gregory did not, as the poem might cause you to imagine, even try to feel me up—not literally. But he did *feel* me, and felt that I was *up,* if you know what I mean. He knew how I felt and he touched me, not my breasts, but the heart within my breast. That's what poetry is all about—touching people, feeling them and making them feel. Have you ever written any poetry?"

"Yes, sure," I lied, "lots."

"Women," Erato Merman divulged, "can't resist a man who writes poetry. Women love men who are sensitive and creative." That did it—at that very moment, I decided I would become noticeably sensitive and creative, and that I would write poetry so that I could touch women, feel them, and make them feel me.

When, at a poker party a few weeks earlier, while we were all talking about the pros and cons of possible future livelihoods, Larry Feinstein had remarked that "according to my uncle Mannie, writers get a lot of pussy," it hadn't registered. But when the muse Erato said essentially the same thing, it changed the course of my life. I wouldn't be writing this now if not for her back then. Good night, Miss Merman, wherever you are.

Late at night, by the light of a Magic Color drip candle purchased at the Don the Beachcomber gift shop and placed in a raffia-wrapped Chianti bottle, I'd take a swig of the Italian Swiss Colony wine I had stolen from my grandmother's apartment, light a Viceroy, uncap my Parker 51, and then, inspired by the oracular utterances of my tutelary muse, Erato, the Passionate One, and in the hope of mystical afflatus, I'd close my eyes and take a deep breath to invoke images of all the girls with whom I had ever been in love. It all began, as in the book of Genesis, with Eve:

Is it destined that first love shall be the last,
That passion's future is encrusted in its past,
In cells barred with memory and no word of leave,
So that unknowingly I have searched for Eve
In every girl I've met and dream I've dreamed?
        To answer I must ask:
        "Will Eve be now what then she seemed?"

It felt fated that I met Eve W—— again, after nine years, in Don the Beachcomber. "Aloha," said Mr. Lee, the Chinese maître d', still in a white linen suit and pale pink silk shirt, still standing next to the great god Tiki. Because it was her birthday, my grandmother had the honor of sitting in the fan-backed queen's chair. As my father was ordering the tropical drinks and exotic appetizers, and in doing so reminding the Filipino waiter that, since we were Jewish, our meal could not contain any ham, bacon, or pork, my mother waved to friends who, having just arrived at the restaurant, were being escorted to their table by Mr. Lee.

"Oh, I must congratulate her on the new movie," my mother announced enthusiastically. "Look, her daughter's with her. Come with me, Lee. You remember her daughter, don't you? Eve? Little Eve!"

Although I wouldn't have recognized the gorgeous young woman, I had never forgotten the cute little girl under my kitchen table, so radiant with a gustatory delight that was amplified by the exquisite rush of yielding to temptation as she closed her lips around a forbidden rum baba. The memory had been a foundation stone for the construction of love's marvelous mansions in the heavens of my imagination.

In turn I shook the hand of her mother, her mother's latest fiancé and costar in *She Came from Another World,* the actress Debra Paget, and her date, who was introduced as a writer. And then finally there was Eve. I didn't want to let go of the warm fingers that had once upon a time meandered in a slow circle against the dark back of the red velvet sofa in my room. But, while I remembered her, Eve didn't seem to know me from Adam.

"It's been ages," her mother said. "You must come over to the house. Yes, come Sunday afternoon for cocktails. And you come too, Lee. I know Eve would enjoy that."

By the time my mother and I had returned to the table, the shrimp fried in coconut batter had disappeared, most gobbled up by Robert and the rest having been fed to Debbie B. Toyland, who was cached in my grandmother's purse under the table. I couldn't have cared less—my appetite had been taken away by the sight of Eve across the room, the feeling of the warmth of her fingers lingering in my palm, and the thought of shaking her hand again on Sunday. Watching her lips, warmly aglow with the soft light of the blowfish lamp hanging in the fishnet above her, part for a piece of rumaki, I was bewitched. As the simulated rain outside the window behind her began its automated drizzle on the lushly lifelike tropical plants, I fantasized that outside, beyond the rubber foliage, there was a real jungle and in it a real lagoon in which she and I might swim at night beneath a real moon as luminescent as the one in the painting on black velvet that hung on the grass-matted wall behind Eve.

After Mr. Lee had brought the pineapple-coconut cream cake (Debbie B. Toyland's favorite dessert) with the single candle in it for my grandmother and we had sung "Happy Birthday," Robert asked if we could go to the gift shop while the adults continued to drink. My father gave each of us a two-dollar bill.

On the way to the shop, Robert, as always, stopped to rub the bright crimson nipples on the carved naked breasts of the cutwater figurehead, foreplay to his subsequent flirtation with the gift shop salesgirl who, uniformed in a silver-embroidered red silk Chinese dress with a slit up the side, was always sure to tell me: "Your little brother is so cute."

It seemed like some sort of Polynesian shamanistic thaumaturgy wherein something that is envisioned materializes, or something wished for immediately comes true, that suddenly, right there in the gift shop, no more than ten feet away from me, looking, without acknowledging my proximity, at the array of brightly colored silk sarongs, was Eve.

Sidling toward her under the pretext of inspecting the curios for sale, I took a deep breath, cleared my throat, and dared to speak: "Hi."

"Hi," she answered, without looking away from the Hawaiian-flowered Chinese-silk sarong that she was so gently fingering.

"I'm going out to the parking lot to have a smoke," I remarked with all the nonchalance I could feign, then hesitated, and then, with the intractable nervousness of hope embarrassingly evident in my voice, I asked whether or not she might want to join me: "I've got a whole pack of Viceroys."

When Robert insisted on coming along with us, I took him aside to convince him with my two-dollar bill to keep shopping for South Seas souvenirs. "Your little brother's so cute," Eve commented as we slipped outside.

Once we had taken refuge in a spot in the shadows of the parking lot where we wouldn't be seen, I produced the pack of cigarettes I had swiped from my father. Explaining that she was trying to cut down on her smoking, Eve said she'd just have a few puffs of mine. The uncontrollable trembling of my hands made it difficult to light the match torn from the matchbook, on the cover of which Don the Beachcomber was reclining under a coco palm on a sandy seashore.

"Here," Eve said, "let me do it." Taking the cigarette out of my mouth to place it between her lips, she lit a match, and sparks from the fire that danced in the dilated coal-black pupils of her eyes and on the luscious ruby-red gloss of her lower lip lit the fuse of feeling that would combust my heart.

"Do you know how to French inhale?" she asked. "I do. I'll show you."

As her lips parted, white smoke curled out from between them and up into her nostrils. Her eyes closed in languid pleasure as she exhaled. Returning the cigarette, anointed with her lipstick, to my lips, she taught me: "Take the smoke into your mouth, but don't inhale it into your lungs. Now open your mouth, not too wide, and suck the smoke in through your nostrils. That's it, suck."

I coughed up the smoke when Eve dispassionately asked, "Do you know how to French kiss? I do. I'll show you." Taking the cigarette back out of my mouth to drop it on the pavement and crush it out with a swivel of her high-heel black patent leather shoe, the girl stepped close enough for me to nervously wrap my arm around her waist and accept the invitation made by the simultaneous closing of eyes and opening of lips. Eve inhaled my breath, sucked in my tongue, and swilled my spirit. As if being held underwater by a giant clam in a South Seas lagoon, I couldn't breathe. But I did not want to be released. As if from the bends, hallucinating sunken galleons full of treasure, I ached to dive deeper down. I would have drowned in Eve.

"Hey, you guys," Robert shouted. "Mom and Dad have been looking for you. Come on. It's time to go home. Lee, it's a school night and you've got homework. You better come in," he giggled, "as soon as your boner goes away."

That night I wrote the poem in which I wondered if every girl upon whom I had ever had a crush had merely been a surrogate, an available temporary distraction and diversion from Eve. Charting the ten-year history of those infatuations, the story of my childhood would, I planned, have its climax in Eve.

I took that poem and a new one that I had written about Clover Wiener to Martindale's bookshop to get Erato's opinion. The muse felt that both sentiment and insight had been compromised by hackneyed rhymes and facile comprehensibility:

I thought I was in love at the ripe old age of six,
When I was just a new dog trying to learn old tricks.
It never did occur to me to give the little girl a kiss
Since I thought making love was watching Clover Wiener piss.
When after raising up her skirt, she'd squat to take a pee,
I had a vision of the blessed virgin, love's divine epiphany.

Clover Wiener was still trying to swim and probably, I figured, still pissing in the pool. Since qualifying for the Beverly High girls' swim team required no aquatic acumen, only a B grade average, Clover was given the opportunity to compete in extramural competitions, and, although she never won a ribbon, she was at least able to finish every event except a 200 meter breaststroke race against Hollywood High that proved just half a lap beyond her limit.

I joined the boys' swim team, not, like Clover, with any enthusiasm for swimming, but simply because it was the only sport that did not require a shower after practices or meets. Since I had not yet gone through puberty, I didn't want to be seen naked by the other guys. The only pubic hair I had was Connie Feinstein's, laminated between two pieces of Scotch tape and still hidden in my red velvet couch.

But, even if I didn't have a pubic hair of my own at the beginning of my freshman year in high school, I did have a mustache. When purchasing it at Max Factor's House of Cosmetics on Hollywood Boulevard, I had been assured that it was "a professional facial hairpiece just like the ones real actors wear in the movies." I patiently waited for the spirit gum to become sufficiently tacky to secure it. I then pressed the mustache onto my upper lip. I tried on my bar mitzvah suit and, standing in between the mirrors on the open closet doors in my mother's dressing room, I decided to wear it, even though the legs of the pants and the sleeves of the coat were too short to accommodate a recent surge in the pituitary secretions that stimulate adolescent growth. Donning one of my father's fine old felt fedoras and my own new cool Cool-Shade sunglasses, I set out on foot with Chip Zuckerman for Carl's Market. Because he looked no older than fourteen, Chip waited outside as I, after a lighting up a Viceroy, marched confidently into the store and straight to the liquor section. After selecting a fifth of Don the Beachcomber Jamaica Rum and a bottle of his Authentic Scorpion Exotic Cocktail Mix and then picking up copies of *Playboy, Man's Life,* and the *Wall Street Journal* at the magazine rack as well as a five-pack of White Owl cigars from the tobacco stand, I sauntered to the cash register. The clerk laughed at me: "Nice costume, kid. Come back on Halloween and I'll give you some candy."

Chip tried to cheer me up: "We could try again somewhere else. Maybe it'll work if you put a little gray in the mustache and in your hair. And I'll come into the store with you and say, 'Please, Dad, buy me some M&M's.' Oh, don't worry about it. Fuck it. Let's go over to my place. My parents have plenty of booze around the house. My mom drinks so much, they can't keep track of it."

Over cocktails of Old Grandad and White Rock cola garnished with maraschino cherries, we talked about love. After complaining that although his girlfriend, Donna Young, would let him slip his hand under her bra, she wouldn't let him undo its clasp, Chip asked me about Candy Canter. While the truth was that she would start to cry whenever I tried to feel her up (pathetically sobbing, "I want to, but I can't. I promised I wouldn't."), I assured him that I had been taking her bra off ever since my bar mitzvah party and that I was making serious headway on her Playtex Living Pantie Girdle.

Since, by the time I had run into Eve at Don the Beachcomber, Candy was not showing much promise of making the lies I was telling about her come true, I telephoned her to ask her to return my ID bracelet. Bursting into tears, she hung up the phone and, a few days later, I received in the mail, along with my silver bracelet, a proclamation that she was relieved to be rid of "the most insensitive and dishonest guy in the world. All you care about is SEX, SEX, SEX! It's perverted!" Breaking up with her was like losing Mr. Gus—I couldn't figure out why it made me sad.

A week later, Candy went on a date with Robbie Freeman to see the movie *Gidget,* during which, according to Robbie's sworn testimony, he discovered, in the darkness of the Grauman's Chinese Theatre, that she was not wearing a girdle, panty hose, nor anything else to impede exploration of the virgin field of a terra incognita. What had been thought to be a no-man's-land turned out to be potentially arable, and Robbie was hoping to plow, sow, harrow, and harvest it before winter.

The kisses exchanged in the parking lot of Don the Beachcomber, like the magic kisses that awakened and transformed the heroes and heroines in the stories I remembered from *Once upon a Time: Children's Best Loved Tales,* seemed to have stimulated hormonal processes that promised to help my penis and testicles catch up with my mind and heart in their readiness for true love. I attributed the subsequent, long-awaited appearance of a fine hair on my pubic region to those kisses. Like Elijah the Prophet, Elijah the Tishbite, the lone hair heralded the coming of a new age in the fulfillment of the ancient prophesy of Dr. Isaiah Miller:

> When a boy is about thirteen or fourteen, his testes will wake up, ready to do an important job. At this time, the boy will notice that hair has begun to grow on the pubic region. Since the testes will then remain awake even while the boy is sleeping, the boy may begin to find a strange substance on his pajamas or sheets in the morning. This substance is called a *seminal emission.* The boy should not be disturbed, afraid or ashamed of this. No, he should be proud of it! It means that he is becoming a healthy and virile man, capable of *sexual reproduction.*

I had faith that by Rosh Ha-Shonah, our new year, or by Chanukah and the Christian new year at the very latest, God would have finally answered my prayers and made of me a healthy, virile, hairy man with hard-working testicles.

Instead of doing the French homework due the next day in Madame Cramouille's class, I rehearsed my French inhale before the mirror in my bathroom in preparation for the Sunday visit to Eve's mother's house. When the day finally arrived, I was distraught to discover that Eve was spending the weekend with her father in Brentwood. While the adults drank champagne, Robert and I went for a walk in the garden. I picked the spots where, if only she rather than Robert had been with me, I would have French kissed her. As we left, Eve's mother gave me their telephone number: "I know she would love to hear from you. She was sorry she couldn't be here today."

After the week it took me to get up the backbone to make that call, my overeager finger made three mistakes in dialing. The moment I finally heard her voice, without any of the usual hellos, how-are-yous, and what-have-you-been-doings, I got right to the point by inviting her to be my date on the coming Saturday for a party at Little Mike Shulman's. Although he had, in a sudden spurt of adolescent growth, become the tallest boy in the freshman class at Beverly High, he was still Little Mike.

When, telephoning the next night to find out if Eve's mother had given her permission to come to the party and to say that my mother had agreed to drive me to pick her up, I was told that her mother's driver would deliver her. I telephoned the next night to confirm the plans, and the next to reconfirm. When she answered the phone the next night, I didn't know what to say. After an excruciating moment of silence, I resorted to a "What are you doing?"

"Nothing," Eve sighed. "I'm supposed to be doing my English homework. But I hate studying. I hate English. I hate school."

"Me too," I assured her, pleased to establish that we had something in common, even if it was hatred.

"But I like reading," she told me. "Not the stupid stuff they assign at school like *The Waste Land,* by T. S. Eliot, but good stuff like *The Prophet,* by Kahlil Gibran. That's my favorite book. Kahlil has put my feelings into words. He knew what love is. If only he weren't dead, I'd visit him. I wouldn't care that he is so much older than me, or that he is a foreigner. I would offer my virginity to the man who has taught me what true love is. And then he'd probably write a poem about me."

Trying to conceal the shock that her candor caused me, I confessed that I hadn't read the book but swore that I'd really like to. Wistfully divulging that she kept it at her beside to read each night before going to sleep, she insisted on reading:

> Then said Almitra, "Speak to us of Love." And he raised his head
> and looked upon the people, and there fell a stillness upon them.
> And with a great voice he said:

When love beckons to you follow him,
Though his ways are hard and steep.
And when his wings enfold you yield to him.
Like sheaves of corn he gathers you unto himself.
He threshes you to make you naked.
He sifts you to free you from your husks.
He grinds you to whiteness.
He kneads you until you are pliant;
And then he assigns you to his sacred fire.
Think not that you can direct the course of love,
If it finds you worthy, love directs your course.
Love has no other desire but to fulfil itself.
But if you love and must needs have desires, let these be your desires:
    To melt and be like a running brook that sings its melody to the night.
    To know the pain of too much tenderness.
    To be wounded by your own understanding of love;

Assuring Eve that the passage put my feelings into words too, I added that "I really liked that part about the corn" and went on to mention that, as a matter of fact, I planned on becoming a poet myself. When she asked who my favorite poet was, I was unable on the spur of that moment to think of the name of any poet except the author of the book next to the phone on my bedside table: "Gregory Corso," I answered, randomly opening *The Happy Birthday of Death.* I read to Eve:

Fried shoes.
Like it means nothing.
Don't shoot the warthogs.

Eve, after a moment of silence, responded, "I don't get it. What's it supposed to mean?" I tried to explain that she wasn't supposed to get it, that the meaning of it "like the meaning of life itself, is that it has no meaning."

"Life," Eve disagreed, "does have meaning, lots of it, when you're in love. That's what Kahlil says."

"I see what you mean," I said, not wanting her to have second thoughts about our upcoming date.

Delivered to my door by her mother's chauffeur on the night of the Shulman party, Eve, herself a beautifully wrapped package, presented a gift to me with tantalizing words: "Don't unwrap it now. Wait until later tonight."

It wasn't actually Little Mike's party, but his older brother Big Doug's eighteenth birthday celebration. Little Mike's buddies had been invited because Big Doug, paralyzed from the neck down ever since the car accident a few years before, didn't have any friends. Rather than going to school, he had been privately tutored at home by a Miss Sullivan, an old woman who was the spitting image of her famous cousin Ed. Having worked for over twenty years as a teacher for various Hollywood studios to provide an education for child actors unable to attend regular academic institutions, the spinster was responsible, the Shulmans were proud to say, for the scholastic accomplishments of such stars as Lee Aaker of *The Adventures of Rin Tin Tin,* Jerry Mathers of *Leave It to Beaver,* and Stuffy Singer, who had played Donnie Henderson on *Beulah.*

Clover Wiener was the very big Little Mike's date; Chuck Mandel was there with Angela Portinari, Larry Feinstein with Suzie Krasny, Chip Zuckerman with Donna Young, and Robbie Freeman brought Candy Canter. In introducing Eve, I was gratified to sense from their frostiness that Clover, Suzie, and Candy were all jealous.

After Little Mike had wheeled Big Doug into the dark living room, the lights were suddenly turned on and we yelled, "Surprise! Surprise!" It brought tears to Big Doug's little eyes.

The party was catered by Trader Vic, who had become more popular in Beverly Hills than his competitor Don the Beachcomber by coming up with the idea of kosher rumaki, with beef braten replacing the bacon around the water chestnut and chicken liver. There was a Tiki bowl of fruit punch, which, if you followed Little Mike into the bathroom, became the mixer for a stiff South Seas rum grog that he called "Doug's Dynamite Delight."

As he poured the booze into my cup, Little Mike pitched for a donation: "I'm taking up a collection for my brother's surprise birthday present. It's a hooker. I need a hundred bucks. That's what a decent blow job is going for these days. Big Doug won't be able to feel it of course, but at least he'll be able to watch her giving it to him. So, I'm asking each of my friends for eighteen bucks because he's eighteen today and because eighteen's a sacred number in Judaism. If you and I, Chuck, Larry, Robbie, and Chip chip in eighteen dollars each, that makes one-o-eight. A hundred for the blow job and an eight-dollar tip. Cisco's got the girl all lined up and swears she's a humdinger. You remember Cisco, from school? The Mexican. Cisco Zutano. I ran into him at Thrifty's. He was buying rubbers, a ton of them. When I invited him to the party, he said he couldn't make it, but that's when he came up with the brilliant idea for the blow job. He said that if I really love my brother, I'd want that for him. And I do love Big Doug, even if having to take care of him all the time has ruined my life."

After Big Doug had blown out the eighteen candles on a devil's food cake, everyone stood around him, looking at him, trying to smile but not knowing what to say other than "Happy Birthday." A staunchly sober Miss Sullivan, with the support of a progressively tipsy Mrs. Shulman, insisted that we liven up the party with a game of charades, the boys against the girls.

In going first, Eve displayed all of the thespian talent that had made her appearances in both *Apache Princess* and *She Came from Another World* so convincing: after tugging on her earlobe to indicate "sounds like," she hobbled around the room on her knees until finally Angela Portinari yelled out "midget," and then, after shouts of "fidget" and "digit," Candy Canter screamed, "*Gidget!*" Big Doug had seemed distracted during the game, not paying much attention as Chip Zuckerman acted out *The Waste Land.* But when Little Mike took the floor with the second word in *Moby Dick,* it made Big Doug drool with laughter. As she wiped the saliva off her son's chin, Mrs. Shulman scolded, "Please, Mikey, there are girls present!"

Once her teammates had somehow guessed that Clover, lying on her stomach on the floor and puffing out her cheeks, was supposed to be a fish, she was finally, after more than three excruciatingly long minutes, able to convey the fifth word of *The Adventures of Huckleberry Finn* by pointing to her feet.

It was my turn: movie, five words, fifth word. Widening my eyes into a mad glare, panting and flaring my nostrils ferociously, menacingly baring my teeth and chomping my jaws, I raised my hands, their fingers clenched like claws, over my head and lumbered toward Eve with lupine bloodlust apparent as I ogled her naked neck. "Werewolf?" Little Mike conjectured. Yes! And, as I emphatically pointed at myself, Larry Feinstein triumphantly shouted, *I Was a Teenage Werewolf!*

As if the game of charades hadn't been enough to remind the quadriplegic birthday boy how abject he was, a sloshed Mrs. Shulman announced that it was time to dance. Miss Sullivan pushed Big Doug's wheelchair out of the area of the living room that had been designated as the dance floor and Mrs. Shulman lowered the lights while Little Mike stacked the forty-fives on the record changer. From the penumbral sidelines, Big Doug watched me dance with Eve, holding her close and breathing on the neck from which, had I really been a werewolf, I would have surely sucked the life out of her as she softly sang along with the hi-fi:

Love me tender, love me sweet,
Never let me go.

You have made my life complete,
And I love you so.

"Let's go outside," I whispered, and, as soon as the song was over, I led Eve into the garden. We ambled toward a darkness beyond the driveway where, as I kissed her, I could hear Elvis singing about his shaking hands and weak knees and hardly being able to stand on his own two feet, putting my feelings into words no less than Kahlil Gibran had done with Eve's.

I asked Eve if she'd like to come next door, back to my place, to see the pool house: "It's decorated just like Don the Beachcomber."

No sooner had the bamboo beads that hung over the doorway fallen from our shoulders, than, with arms closing around her, I dared to kiss her, then again, more and more voraciously, again and again, with open lips, open heart, openly anxious to open the clasp on her brassiere. Standing in the darkness, exactly where I had been with Candy Canter on the night of my bar mitzvah party, I felt for the zipper on the back of the aqua organza cocktail dress. The moment she realized that it was being unzipped, Eve sighed a sound that I translated "yes." Still kissing, I worked on the complicated hook-and-eye system of the brassiere.

"Here, let me help," Eve cordially offered. But then, as she stepped away from me to unfasten the bra, she happened to notice the Magic Glow-in-Dark hands of the Kookie Kokonut Klock on the bamboo bar. "Oh, it's almost midnight. My chauffeur will be waiting outside the party. We've got to go back." She laughed as she turned for me to zip her dress back up, "This is just like Cinderella."

An hour or so later, after lighting the candle in the Chianti bottle on my desk and taking a swig of Italian Swiss Colony wine, I opened Eve's gift—Kahlil Gibran's *The Prophet* inscribed "May the words of the Prophet inspire you." I read the pages that had had their corners folded over by the lovely fingers that had almost unclasped her bra for me that night. I then uncapped my Parker 51 and, taking another shot of wine, began to work on the canto of my *Book of Love* that dealt with the year when all I could think about was Beatrice Sugarman's little vulva:

Then said Lee, "Speak to us of the Twat." And as Beatrice Sugarman,
in crouching down beneath her desk, raised up her butt,
the great voice of the Conrelrad civil defense siren seemed to speak:

When the twat beckons you, follow,
Though her ways are wet and slippery.
And when her major and minor lips enfold you, yield.
Like a sheaf of corn, she will gather you into herself,
Threshing, sifting, and kneading you to make you pliant.
Think not that you can direct the course of the twat;
If she finds you worthy, she directs your course.
The twat has no other desire but to fulfill herself.
But if you think about the twat, let these be your desires:
    That your penis moves in and out of a vagina with rapid motions
    Until it melts like a running brook that sings its melody to the night.

Just as in Miss Ross's third-grade class at Ponce de Leon Elementary School, I was again sitting behind Beatrice Sugarman in Mr. Webster's freshman English class at Beverly High. The diminutive tushy that had been the object of contemplation during Red Alert civil defense drills had matured into the sumptuous hips of a carnal woman whose correspondingly outstanding breasts, held aloft under a pastel pink angora sweater by a scaffolding of nylon cup, strap, stay, and band, had earned the admiration of boys and the envy of girls. Aloof from her freshman classmates, the impressively built Beatrice was going steady with Johnny Fox, president of the junior class.

"Johnny Fox is a prick," Robbie Freeman declared, and "Yeah," Chip Zuckerman elaborated, "a real asshole," to which big Little Mike Shulman added, "What a cocksucker!" Chuck Mandel threw in "*shaigetz*" as if being a Gentile was as demeaning as being a penis, an anus, or a practitioner of fellatio. "He's not a goy," Little Mike informed Chuck. "His parents are members of my congregation. They changed their name from Fuks to Fox." Jewish or not, we didn't like him: not only was Fox junior class president and starting quarterback on the Beverly High football team, he also got straight A's and drove Beatrice Sugarman to school each morning in a Corvette.

Having no idea of how fervently I had once prayed for her recovery from her tonsillectomy, no clue that I was the secret admirer from whom she had received a get-well card, Beatrice never even looked at me as I stared at her sashaying to her place at the desk in front of mine in Mr. Webster's class. A little mole on her right shoulder, just above the low collar of her angora sweater and below the flip-curl of her "does-she-or-doesn't-she?" blonde hair, reminded me of the matching one on her calf that, once upon a time, had, in captivating me during bomb alerts, kept my mind off death.

After asking for a show of hands to check that we all had our copies of *The Adventures of Tom Sawyer,* the teacher prepared us for reading

the book by telling us about the life of Samuel Clemens. Mr. Webster, who reminded me of Elvis (not Presley, but Krasny—Elvis Krasny, the dead lagomorph with beady eyes, big ears, a small pink nose, and lips that constantly twitched), informed us that the book had originally been written for adults. "It is *not* a boy's book, not at all," the author had, according to Mr. Webster, emphatically insisted in a letter to his friend, William Dean Howells. "It's meant for mature readers with liberal minds and a healthy tolerance for racy jokes." Howells had, however, Mr. Webster continued, "with the full support of Mrs. Clemens, convinced the writer to edit the manuscript, expunging all potentially objectionable passages, so that there was no risk of it being banned."

That gave me the idea for my paper "Whitewashing *The Adventures of Tom Sawyer,*" in which I argued that Tom Sawyer had sexual intercourse with Becky Thatcher in chapter 31 of the book:

Just like girls here at Beverly High who lie to their parents by saying they are sleeping over at a girlfriend's house when they want to stay out all night with some guy, so Becky told her mother that she was spending the night with Susy Harper in order to have sex with Tom Sawyer in McDougal's cave. That cave, described by the writer as having "an opening shaped like the letter A" (cf. *The Scarlet Letter*) is a symbol of the womb as is made clear by the bushy growth above the opening to it (obviously representing pubic hair) and the fact that the cave is dark and damp (just like the female anatomical cavity in question). The candle that Tom carries into the cave is a phallic symbol (see Freud), and its flame symbolizes Tom's burning passion. The meaning of the white wax dripping down that candle that is held erect in Tom's hand is also obvious.

At the entrance to the cave, Becky and Tom eat "wedding cake," a symbolic act indicating that they are ready to do what a bride and groom do after their wedding, i.e., what is technically known as "coitus," or "sexual intercourse," or, less formally, just "making love." One of the passages that was deleted so that *The Adventures of Tom Sawyer* would not be banned would have come right before the following paragraph:

> How long afterward it was that Becky came to a slow consciousness that she was crying in Tom's arms neither could tell. All that they knew was, that after what seemed a mighty stretch of time, both awoke out of a dead stupor of sleep.

That this clearly indicates that Becky and Tom have just had sexual intercourse is attested to by expert on sexual intercourse Ethel Chambers, who, in her informative book, *Facts of Life and Love for the American Teenager,* scientifically explains that "coitus is usually followed by a period of rest and often *stupor* or *sleep* [italics mine]."

Without the actual missing paragraph to prove my contention, I composed it myself, authenticating it with a footnote in which I claimed to have found the passage in question in one of the ten volumes of *The Complete Uncensored Letters of William Dean Howells* (edited by Louis Lapine, Harvard University Press, 1945). Howells, I reported, had written to Twain to say that the book could not be read by boys "nor by womenfolk, nor even by men if they are at all decent" unless he were to cut the following paragraph:

When Becky lay back, her legs spreading slightly, her dress slipped down her thighs so that, by the light of his candle, Tom noticed that she wasn't wearing any undergarments. The appendage that had since birth indicated that he was a boy suddenly declared that Tom Sawyer was a man. And then he did just what any man, given the same situation, would have done. And Becky, putting up no resistance, became a woman in his arms. After it was done, Tom, as he buttoned his trousers back up, spoke tenderly to her: "Now that we've made love, Becky, you ain't ever to do it with anybody but me."

I figured that Mr. Webster would give me an A on the paper, both because he was very keen on symbolism and because he considered himself liberal in regard to sexuality—it was daring in 1959 for a teacher to assign *The Scarlet Letter* and Andrew Marvell's "To His Coy Mistress" to high school freshmen. My essay was, however, returned gradeless. The teacher commented in red pencil:

Please bring the cited volume of *The Complete and Uncensored Letters of William Dean Howells* to me as I have not been able to find it in any library. If my suspicions that you may have fabricated this are correct, Mr. Siegel, you shall receive an F on this paper. If, however, you can actually produce the passage in question, I shall give you an A for the paper, and for the course as well, to acknowledge the significant discovery of something that has, to the best of my knowledge, gone hitherto unnoticed in the annals of scholarship on American literature. As I consider forgery an egregious literary crime, I do hope that you will be able to prove my suspicions groundless.

I remained in my seat after class, waiting for Beatrice Sugarman to finish complaining to Mr. Webster: "If I don't get at least a B in this class, I can't be on the cheerleading squad." She broke into tears: "That may not mean anything to you, but school spirit is the most important thing in my life." Once she had stomped out of the classroom, it was my turn. Pretending that my feelings had been hurt by the teacher's accusation, I told him that my parents had all ten volumes of *The Complete and Uncensored Letters of William Dean Howells* at home and that, of course, I would bring in the volume in question.

Returning to my desk to retrieve my essay, Parker 51, notebook, copy of *The Adventures of Tom Sawyer,* and Cool-Shade sunglasses, I noticed something on the floor beneath Beatrice's desk and, picking it up, discovered it to be her essay. On the front page of it, right by the title, "Love in Elizabeth Barrett Browning's *Sonnets from the Portuguese,*" Mr. Webster had written her grade in red pencil: C. I couldn't resist taking it with me.

After reading the paper, it was my humble opinion that Mr. Webster had been generous in his assessment of Beatrice Sugarman's expository skills. "Love, according to Webster," the paper began, is "a strong affection for or attachment or devotion to a person or thing." In a footnote, citing the page on which "love" had been so defined in her dictionary, she wrote, "It wouldn't surprise me if you, Mr. Webster, were related to this Webster, since both of you know so many big words and are so good at spelling." Beatrice had copied out all of the lexical definitions of "love," including "in tennis, a score of zero" and "in theology, God's benevolent concern for mankind." Then, having defined her terms, Beatrice articulated her insights:

> Elizabeth Barrett Browning understood that it doesn't matter if you lose at tennis, or any other game for that matter, when you're in love. Because when you're in love, you kinda feel God's benevolent concern even if you don't know that's what you're feeling at the time. It's how I feel when I'm with my boyfriend. Just like Elizabeth Barrett Browning knew that she'd love Robert Browning "better after death," I also know that I'm going to love my boyfriend even more after death because I couldn't love him any more in life than I do already. That's why Elizabeth Barrett Browning is my favorite writer of all the ones we've read in this class. Thanks for assigning her, Mr. Webster! If she were still alive today, I'd like to be her friend. I know that we would get along really good together because we think a lot alike. And Robert would probably like to hang out with my boyfriend, John Fox, junior class president.

I couldn't resist writing a poem on the back of Beatrice's paper. Laboring late into the night with a red pencil and as much zeal as I imagined Elizabeth Barrett Browning had ever put into any of her sonnets,

I did my very best to capture in words the feelings that Beatrice Sugarman's body inspired. I signed the composition "Mr. Webster":

How do I long to fuck thee? Let me count the ways:
I yearn to fuck thee to the depth and breadth of thy cunt
And then my prick, when hard, upright, and blunt,
Shall move my mind to reward thee with straight A's.
I want to fuck thee freely, and then to change thy grade.
I want to fuck thee purely, and squeeze thy beauteous ass.
I want to fuck thee and believe thou needest to get laid.
So—if God approves and thou dost hope or wish to pass,
I shall fuck thee in my office, right after English class.

The next day, after apologizing to Mr. Webster for having forgotten to bring in the Howells book and promising to remember it the next day, I returned the essay to the floor where I had found it and then watched as Beatrice noticed it, picked it up, and without looking at it, stuffed it into her purse.

I might have been flattered that my literary talent was sufficiently impressive to cause Beatrice to imagine that a literature teacher with a degree (he often reminded us) in English from Harvard University was the author of the sonnet, if it had not been the case that Mr. and Mrs. Sugarman also believed it to be the work of the man who had forced their innocent daughter to read *The Scarlet Letter* and "To His Coy Mistress." The outraged Sugarmans stormed the office of Dr. Rottler, the principal of Beverly Hills High School, demanding that Mr. Webster be fired.

After a subsequent comparison of handwriting samples had exonerated the teacher and indicted me, I was dropped from the boys' swim team, suspended from school for one week, and informed that I would be readmitted only after my parents had come in for a consultation with both Dr. Rottler and Mr. Webster.

While vehemently articulating his condemnation of my grave and heinous act, Dr. Rottler showed concern for my well-being by questioning my mother and father about my behavior at home: Did that behavior suggest antisocial attitudes, unnatural or excessive interests in sex, or any other tendencies that might warrant professional counseling? My mother expressed a confidence that I was, at least for a teenager, relatively normal.

Before adjourning the meeting, the principal asked Mr. Webster if he had anything to add or any questions to ask. "Yes," the teacher said, turning to my parents. "Do you, Dr. and Mrs. Siegel, happen to have a copy of *The Complete and Uncensored Letters of William Dean Howells* in your home?" Neither my mother nor my father had ever heard of Mark Twain's friend.

The punitive break from school gave me extra time to work on my *Book of Love.* That my sonnet to Beatrice had aroused such a sensational response encouraged me to continue to play around with the a-b-b-a-b-b-a-c-c rhyme scheme that, according to Mr. Webster, "Elizabeth Barrett Browning found the most powerfully effective for a poetic elucidation of the vicissitudes of passionate love." I used it to write about Connie Feinstein:

In '54 I fell in love with eighth-grade girls
Who mascaraed their eyes, lipsticked their lips,
Brassiered their breasts and girdled their hips,
Tamponed their twats and wore strings of pearls,
Who caused me to stammer and make Freudian slips,
Hardening more than my struggle with coming to grips
With visions of crotches, so fluffy with curls.
Loving Connie Feinstein gave me the despair
Of having to settle for just one pubic hair.

Still laminated between two pieces of Scotch tape, Connie Feinstein's pubic hair remained hidden in the red velvet couch in my room. I began to use it as a bookmark in the leather-bound notebook, a Chanukah gift from my parents, in which I was writing my epic autobiographical poem. I started storing that book in the couch too, not because it was about sex but because it was, for the time being, private. When it was done, however, I planned to show it to Erato, and if she liked it, I would send it to a publisher who would, I hoped, make it available to all the English-language-speaking girls in the world.

While maintaining my trust in the truth of Erato's dictum that "women can't resist a man who writes poetry," I discovered that men aren't always so inclined. "Hey, Shakespeare," Johnny Fox snarled, hovering behind my seat in the cafeteria, where I was eating lunch with Larry Feinstein and Chuck Mandel on my first day back at school, "I'm going to cut your balls off for giving that poem of yours to my girlfriend. And then I'm gonna hang your nuts from the rearview mirror of my car like furry dice."

"He might do it," Larry said. "He can be a real asshole when he wants to." Because Larry was on the football team, he spoke with an authority that came from taking showers with Fox after practices and games.

"He's got a really big dick," Larry divulged while picking the little cubes of bologna out of his Mexican Delight, "and I've noticed that the bigger a guy's dick is, the more of an asshole he can be. You know, like John Dillinger. Have you ever noticed that assholes like being assholes? Maybe that's because assholes get a lot of pussy. It amazes me that Fox gets such good grades because, from what I've been able to observe in the shower, the general rule is that the bigger the dick, the lower the grades."

"You're full of it, Feinstein," Chuck protested. "I've got a big dick and my grades are pretty good and I'm not an asshole." Because the kitchen staff at Beverly High did not uphold Jewish dietary laws as strictly as Mrs. Mandel thought they should, Chuck brought his lunch from home. After offering to trade half of his chopped chicken liver on rye for the little pile of bologna on the side of Larry's plate, Chuck (ever sanguine since Angela Portinari had started going steady with him) tried to reassure me: "Don't worry, Fox won't really cut your balls off because, if he did, he'd have to go to jail. It's illegal in America to cut somebody's balls off."

"Yeah," Larry mumbled through a mouthful of chicken liver on rye, "but that would make him a hero in Bea Sugarman's mind. And he's the kind of guy who wants to be a hero. That's why he's on the football team. Getting arrested for cutting off Siegel's balls to avenge Sugarman's honor would make him the biggest hero at Beverly High. Girls love guys who do shit like that for them, who take big risks for their sake and put love above the law. The jury, especially if the defense attorney made sure it was stacked with women, would acquit him on the grounds that it was a crime of passion. They could easily be convinced that the defendant, young Mr. Fox, a straight-A student, not to mention president of his class with a bright future ahead of him, was so powerfully in love with Miss Sugarman, whom he hoped to marry after graduating from college and serving in the Armed Forces, that he could not restrain himself from ensuring that justice was done."

At that point Larry stood and paced in front of us like a lawyer before a jury: "Overwhelmed by love, Mr. Fox meted out the punishment that seemed most appropriate given the trauma caused to his beloved by the obscene, immoral, lewd, and perverted offense of Mr. Siegel. The castration will surely be applauded by anyone who has any moral standards or any concern for protecting the innocence of the young ladies of Beverly Hills, California. You may call Mr. Fox's state of mind at the time 'temporary insanity,' but I call it 'true love.' I shall not bring exhibit A, Mr. Siegel's so-called poem, into evidence. Thus I spare you, ladies of the jury, the shock and revulsion that Miss Sugarman had to suffer on its account. So too, I spare you, gentleman of the jury, the feelings of anger and fury that have brought Mr. Fox into this courtroom today. Thank you. I rest my case."

Chuck applauded: "That was great, Feinstein. You should become a lawyer. Lawyers make a lot of dough and they get a lot of pussy."

As we headed from the cafeteria to the parking lot to get in a quick smoke before Madame Cramouille's French class, Larry told me that I could come to his house on Sunday if I wanted help for Monday's English test: "I'll tell you the stupid shit about T. S. Eliot that Webster told us in class while you were out on suspension. But I can't guarantee it'll be quiet around there. Connie's coming home for the weekend, and so there's probably going to be a lot of shouting and screaming."

Connie fought with her parents every time she came home from college in Berkeley, where she had joined the Young People's Socialist League. She would accuse her parents, Larry reported with perverse delight, of trying to force her "to conform to the demands of an economic system in which the needs of the people are subjugated to a desire for profit." In response, the Feinsteins would threaten to not support her unless she would "stop listening to Communist propaganda and going to meetings, and start concentrating on your studies and going to class." Connie was particularly angry with her parents for refusing to give her the money she needed to go to Cuba to join Fidel Castro's revolutionary army.

It had all started the previous spring when, according to Larry's account, Connie had come home for Passover. Over the first cup of wine, Connie had proclaimed that "religion is the opiate of the people"; over the matzah she had declared that "religion is the sigh of the oppressed creature."

"That's Christianity you're talking about," Uncle Mannie had insisted. "That's not Judaism."

Refusing to cooperate in the responsive reading of the Haggadah, she had come up with Four Questions of her own: "Why would I want to eat matzah, a symbol of persecution, the bread of slavery, and in eating it suggest that I am willing to stomach the oppression of the masses? Why would I praise a god invented by power-hungry capitalists in order to oppress workers, Negroes, women, and children? Why would I pretend that we have been made to gather here for any other purpose than the perpetuation of capitalism? Why would I want to uphold these stupid traditions that exist only to make us conform and submit to authority?"

"Please, honey," Mrs. Feinstein had pleaded, "Pesach is supposed to be a festive holiday that brings the family together."

"Don't you get it, Mom?" Connie had responded, "The family institution only reinforces a social division of labor that perpetuates the domestic subjugation and economic dependence of women. You're a victim of capitalism too, Mom. You're Dad's slave. Can't you see that?"

"One more outburst like that out of you, young lady," Dr. Feinstein had shouted, "and you'll go up to your room."

"My uncle Mannie was already pretty drunk when he arrived for the seder," Larry had recounted with considerable amusement. "He kept saying, '*A sof! A sof!* Let's get on with it, or we'll never get to the meal. We haven't even gotten to the ten plagues and the second glass of wine.' Connie stormed out. My mother broke into tears and my father moaned, 'What have we done wrong?' And then Uncle Mannie, trying to cheer the family up, started humming *da-da-yaynu.*"

When, having accepted Larry's offer to help me study for our English test, I arrived at the Feinsteins' on Sunday afternoon, I found Connie, whom I hadn't seen for over a year, outside the house, sitting on the curb in front of a hedge with her head cradled in crossed arms. I was able to spot her despite the camouflage military jacket. "Connie," I asked, "is that you?"

She looked up, and it startled me that she wasn't nearly so beautiful as I had once imagined she would turn out to be. The high school girl who formerly went to the Beverly Beauty Salon on a weekly basis no longer had a hairdo, manicured nails, or makeup on her face. But even though she wasn't very pretty, there was something sexy about her. I asked if she remembered me and was pleased that she did: "Yeah, Lee Siegel, a friend of that fucking conformist pig brother of mine."

I wanted to be nice to her as I had, after all, once been in love with her and, sentimental guy that I was, having one of her pubic hairs meant a lot to me: "I'm sorry things aren't going better. Larry told me. It's really a shame that your parents aren't more understanding."

"It's not surprising," Connie said with a grimace. "Not if you've read Marx. My parents are upset because I refuse to be brainwashed into participating in the capitalist system and upholding the ideals of the bourgeois family in which, as Marx pointed out, parents exploit their children in an effort to accumulate wealth. You and I are nothing more to our parents than articles of commerce and instruments of labor. That really pisses me off."

"Me too," I claimed in the hope of offering her the feeling that at least one person in an unabashedly capitalistic and bourgeois Beverly Hills understood her.

"I hate my parents," Connie declared with a disturbing conviction. "I can't believe what they did. While I was in the shower this morning, they went through my duffel bag. They were looking for drugs, but they found my diaphragm. The idea of me making love freaks them out

even more than the idea of me shooting smack. That's because virginity increases the value of a daughter as a commodity to be sold into that institutionalized form of prostitution known as marriage. Marriage enforces a social division of labor in which women are fundamentally defined and made economically dependent by their childbearing role. In a bourgeois society, where monogamous marriage is the norm, love is perverted into something possessive, something that demands dependence and the repression and restriction of our natural sexual instincts. True love is free love. And free love is true freedom."

When I assured her that I too was pissed off about all the sexual repression in America, Connie suggested that I read *The Communist Manifesto:* "We can discuss it when I come home again from Berkeley for Chanukah."

I had a hunch that if I read the book and could talk about the nefarious ways in which the bourgeoisie were trying to force us to repress our sexual instincts so that they could have more capital, I could probably have sex with Connie. Pinko chicks, I had learned from reading *Commie Sex Siren,* put out. Communism, I imagined, might allow my childhood fantasies about my friend Larry's older sister to finally come true. If Connie Feinstein and Karl Marx were right about true love, I could still love Eve without having to repress any of the sexual desire that I felt for Connie.

I went to Martindale's to buy *The Communist Manifesto* for myself and *Sonnets from the Portuguese* for Eve. Erato insisted that I also buy *Howl,* by Allen Ginsberg, and Jack Kerouac's *On the Road.*

Had I left *The Communist Manifesto* out on my desk with my other books, the text would have been harmless, something that might be assigned in Mrs. Rottler's modern history class, but hidden within the stuffing of my red velvet couch with my pornography and rubbers, my switchblade knife, cherry bombs, cigarettes, and wine, not to mention Connie Feinstein's pubic hair and my autobiography in progress, it became subversive. And subversiveness was thrilling.

No sooner had I emerged from Martindale's with the four new books in a bag under my arm than I heard a familiar voice call from a car parked on the other side of Little Santa Monica: "Hey, Siegel! Siegel, *amigo,* how the fuck have you been doin'?" It was Cisco Zutano behind the wheel of black-primered '57 Chevy two-door, lowered in the front, nosed and decked, with baby moon hubcaps, dual exhaust, and a black eight-ball necker knob on the steering wheel that matched the gear shift. Striped serape blankets were draped over the seats. I hadn't seen him since my bar mitzvah party. I jaywalked over to tell him his car was "really bitchin'."

As irrepressibly cheerful as ever, Cisco, after inviting me into his car, offering me a Lucky Strike, and lighting both of our cigarettes with a slick Zippo double move, explained that he was waiting for Becky Fine: "Remember her? She went to Ponce, but she was a lot older than you. Then her parents sent her to school in Sweden or Switzerland, or Swaziland, or somewhere like that because they didn't want anybody to know their little girl was pregnant. The kid's four years old now—a boy."

Cisco made a confession: "I didn't admit that I was the father back then because knockin' up a chick when you're only in the fourth grade is not so good. I would have been expelled from Ponce de Leon forever. But now I'm proud of it. I love my Bequita and my *muchacho* with all my heart. I want to marry her and raise our boy. But her parents think that she's too good for a beaner like me. Who the fuck cares? I don't have the money to do right by my boy right now anyway. I don't have anything but this car. I'm living in it. A friend of my mother's who manages a restaurant in East L.A., La Polla Borracha, lets me park in his lot overnight. That's where I sleep. And I use the toilet there in the morning. But I'm happy—I've got everything I need right here in the glove compartment." He insisted on showing me: Lucky Strikes, Zippo lighter fluid, Ipana tooth paste, a toothbrush, Listerine mouthwash, Jeris antiseptic hair tonic, Especia Añeja cologne, and lots of rubbers that weren't rubber but, as Cisco explained with an enthusiastic smile, genuine lubricated lambskins. "Take one, *amigo*. Try it out. You'll like it better than the rubber ones. More feeling. Once Becky gets her college degree and starts raking in the dough, I'm going to stop using them. I want more sons. At least seven of them."

I had always admired Cisco. I envied his mirthful negligence, confident exuberance, feeling for romance and disorder, and his irrepressible displays of pomp and passion. It seemed like it would be fun to be him if only you didn't have to sleep in a car and use the toilet in a Mexican restaurant. He was undaunted: "My Bequita's living with her parents so that they can support her and babysit my Pancho while she goes to classes at UCLA. They don't know she sees me. When we go out at night, she has to tell them that she's studying at the library. She's going to be a psychologist and, once she gets her degree and starts making some money, we're going to get married and buy a big hacienda with a swimming pool for the boys and a pool table for me. There's big bucks to be made in psychology with all the fuckin' locos walking around these days."

Asking Cisco how his pal, Billy Hunter, was doing, I was informed that the prodigy had received a scholarship to go to Cal Tech: "'Billy,' I tell him, 'Billy, if all you do is study, you'll turn into a faggot.' But he doesn't listen to me. If he's so fuckin' smart, why should he study? It's stupid people who should study. But you know how it is—people who are geniuses in school are usually idiots in life. So how are you doing, Siegel? Not studying too much I hope. You Jews study too much."

He seemed proud of me when I boasted of being suspended from Beverly High, pleased for me when I told him I had a girlfriend, but clearly disappointed in me when, after asking me if she was a "good fuck," I had to admit I didn't know.

He slapped my knee: "I've got to teach you how to get a girl to give you what you want, what a man needs and deserves. Learn from the master—Don José Cisco Zutano, *el Maestro de Amor. El Galon Imperioso!*"

In order to tutor me, he explained, he needed to meet Eve. So I accepted his proposition that (provided Eve and I could get permission from our respective mothers) he and I double date on Friday night.

As the sun set and the Jewish Sabbath began, I could hear the honking horn of the '57 Chevy outside. No sooner had Cisco pulled away from the curb, laying a substantial patch of rubber on the street in front of my house as he did, than he asked me how much money I had on me: "Look, Siegel, let's face the facts. You're a rich Beverly Hills Jew, and I'm nothing but a poor Mexican wetback. But I'm trying to save up some money to make something of myself. It's not for me. It's for my *muchacho.* I want him to look up to me. If that's going to happen, I've got to fix up the car. It is, after all, my home. I got to fill the holes in the body left from taking off the chrome. And I want to get red, white, and blue Naugahyde upholstery. Red, white, and blue because it's patriotic. God bless America! Plus I need cowl-mounted bulls horns, a candy-apple red paint job with flames, scallops, and pinstriping. Little Panchito will love that. Listen, *amigo,* I'm doing all the driving tonight, and your girlfriend lives all the way out in Hollywood. Gas isn't free even in America, you know. And I've bought two six-packs of beer for us, not the cheap shit but Miller High Life—the champagne of bottled beers. Not to mention that I'm going to give you lessons in the art of love. And I gave you a deluxe lubricated skin. They cost twice as much as rubbers. What more could I be doing for you? And what, my *amigo,* are you doing for me? What the fuck is in all of this for Jose Cisco Zutano?"

He wanted fifty dollars. But, accepting that all I had was thirty, he agreed to let me pay him the remaining twenty later. After picking up

Becky in Beverly Hills and then Eve in Hollywood, we drove straight to the Olympic drive-in. I wouldn't have recognized the girl who had played Dancing Tree in *Fountain of Youth!* in the woman who snuggled up next to Cisco in the front of the Chevy, kissed him on the cheek, whispered something in his ear, and giggled.

As soon as Cisco had found a parking space to his liking, he sent me to the concession stand: "Two hot dogs, with everything on mine but no onions on Becky's, two slices of pizza pie, popcorn with extra butter, Jujyfruits for me, M&M's for Becky. You can get the Eskimo Pies later. I don't want them to melt." Since I was broke, I had to borrow the money for the food from him. After Eve ordered a box of Brach's chocolate-covered cherries, I realized I didn't have enough cash to get anything for myself.

By the time I returned to the car, the Pepé Le Pew cartoon was over, Cisco had moved into the backseat with Becky, and the feature, *The Tingler,* had just begun. I sat behind the wheel of the '57 Chevy with my arm wrapped around Eve as she washed down her chocolate-covered cherries with a bottle of Miller High Life.

Cisco could not contain his excitement: "You're gonna love this movie, *amigo,* I promise. I've seen it four times already, twice with Percepto." Vincent Price, with a mustache resembling the one I had bought at Max Factor's, played an insane pathologist out to prove that there is some sort of minuscule organism that grows on our spines when we are afraid and that only when we scream does the organism shrink back down. "So," Cisco explained, in case we weren't following, "if you're afraid and can't scream, the fuckin' Tickler will crack your spine and kill you!"

In order to test his hypothesis, the mad scientist plotted to terrify an old deaf-and-dumb woman who just happened to be the projectionist in a movie theater. Immediately after scaring her to death, Vincent Price performed an autopsy.

"Now it gets good," Cisco exclaimed. "Get ready!" The Tingler, a creature that looked like an elongated lobster with a few extra claws, after slithering out of the woman's back and escaping from the clutches of Vincent Price, crawled in silhouette across the movie screen, which suddenly went blank. In a regular walk-in movie theater, Cisco insisted on telling us, an ominous voice would have announced, "The Tingler is loose in this theater. Scream, everybody, scream! I repeat: the Tingler is loose in *this* theater. Scream for your lives!" When the drive-in movie screen went blank, the voice came through the speaker hanging next to me on the halfway-down window of the Chevy: "The

Tingler is loose in this drive-in. Honk your horns, everybody, honk your horns! I repeat: the Tingler is loose in *this* drive-in. Honk for your lives!"

"Honk the fuckin' horn, Siegel. Honk!" Cisco commanded. "Don't let the Tickler get in my car!"

After the honking of hundreds of car horns had finally shrunk the fugitive Tingler, I put my arm around Eve again and then, tenderly stroking her hair, moved my fingers under her chin to gently raise her face up for a kiss. In the middle of that kiss, the sudden sound of Cisco's moaning made Eve self-conscious. She straightened up to watch Vincent Price perform another autopsy on another deaf-mute as Cisco's moans became groans, more and more embarrassingly vehement: "*Aye, aye, si, si, si.*" Trying to ignore it, I opened another beer for Eve and one for myself. Becky started sighing, "Yes, yes, oh, yes, oh, yes," as Cisco's grunting and sobbing became louder and louder still: "*Si, si, si. Me gusta, me gusta. Si, si, si. Mas. Si, si.*" "Yesssssss," Becky screeched, and Cisco cried out, "*Oye, Bequita! Santa Maria! Reina y madre de misericordia! Ohhh, ohhh, estoy por acabar! Siiiiiiiii!*" He whimpered and then, following a brief moment of silence, spoke up with characteristic good cheer: "How do like the movie so far, *amigo?* It's even better when you see it in one of the theaters where the seats are wired with Percepto to give you a shock."

After we had dropped off Eve in Hollywood and then Becky down the street from her parents' house in Beverly Hills, Cisco reminded me about the money I owed him: "Twenty, plus the fifteen you borrowed for the food. Great movie! If you want, you can come with me to see it again next week in East L.A., dubbed into Spanish. It's even better in Spanish. Bring your girlfriend along. She's a nice girl with big, beautiful *tetas,* and—what's even more important, take it from me—she's nuts for you. *El Galon Imperioso* can always tell. Yeah, if I don't know women, my name's not Cisco. And I can promise you that you won't have any trouble getting her to let you fuck her. Just tell her you love her. That always does the trick if you can say it like you mean it."

After reaching into his shirt pocket for something, then holding out whatever it was in his closed hand, he continued: "And if that doesn't work, try this." His hand slowly opened. "The best fuckin' reefer money can buy. *La mejora! La hierba Mexicana!* One puff of this shit will turn your little virgin into the horniest whore you've ever fucked—*mas puta que las gallinas!* It's worth twenty bucks, but I'll give it to you for ten, *amigo.* And when you do fuck her, use a French tickler. It'll drive her crazy. She'll think you're the best fuck she's ever had. That's my secret. I've got one for you in the glove compartment. The real thing—*hecho en Mexico*—and never used! Only two bucks. Take it."

Having a marijuana cigarette in my possession so thrilled me that, each day after school, I'd take it out of the red velvet couch to inspect it. I'd roll it between my fingers, sniff it, and practice holding it between my lips. Robert was so impressed with the precious contraband that, whenever our parents went out, he'd ask to have a look at it. I was so proud of having something so illicit and subversive that I invited Chip, Robbie, Little Mike, Chuck, and Larry over to see it. Larry wanted to buy it for twelve dollars, and Chip was willing to pay twenty, but I wouldn't sell it for anything. I planned on smoking it with Eve when the time was right, when I felt she was ready to go beyond the law with me, to French inhale a smoke that would transport us to an Eden of our own cultivation.

Allen Ginsberg smoked marijuana, I realized upon reading the book that Erato had urged me to buy. So did the best minds of his generation, poets who, like me, "were expelled from the academies for publishing obscene odes on the windows of the skull." *Howl* influenced me in writing my *Book of Love* to abandon Elizabeth Barrett Browning's a-b-b-a-b-b-a-c-c rhyme scheme but to continue the use of the word "fuck":

SIGH

I saw the cutest girls of my generation go through puberty
dragging themselves through the streets of Beverly Hills
looking for strapless cocktail dresses to wear to cotillion
  and bar mitzvah parties.
Angelheaded chicks with sweet snatches, ready to smoke pot,
  and ripe to fuck. . . .

On the Saturday afternoon that her mother's chauffeur dropped Eve off, I was especially happy because my parents had driven down to Palm Springs and taken Robert with them. Except for Sally May Carter, I would be alone with Eve.

Unzipping her black capris and unbuttoning her floral calypso blouse to strip down to the bright red bikini that she was wearing under them, Eve startled me with the matter-of-factness with which she announced that she couldn't go in swimming: "I'm having my period. I'll just sunbathe."

Without changing out of my Levis and Beverly High Boys' Swim Team T-shirt, I sat in a pool chair gazing at her reclined on a blue canvas chaise longue. Because she was wearing large, dark sunglasses, I couldn't tell if her eyes were open, if she could see that I was, through my own Cool-Shades, staring at the freckles that formed a constellation of four Pleiades upon the firmament of her heavenly belly.

As Eve lay there in silence, I thanked her for the *Prophet,* insisting that I loved it: "That line about love sifting you to free you of your husks, grinding you up, and making bread out of you is really good." I did not know what to say next. By shouting out from the back porch to ask if we wanted anything to eat or drink, Sally May Carter rescued me from an awkward silence. Eve asked for a rum and Dr Pepper.

After going into the main house to get the friendly pepper-upper from Sally, I took Eve into the pool house to add the hard stuff to her soft drink. She sat on the daybed, with its Hawaiian floral print spread, matching bolsters, and throw pillows, as, after mixing our cocktails in authentic Polynesian ceramic Tiki-god goblets from the Don the Beachcomber gift shop, I demonstrated the progress I had made on my mastery of the French inhale.

Hoping to engage and entertain Eve, to charm her and make her laugh, I was, apropos of the pool house decor, telling her an embellished version of the saga of the shrunken head. I was just getting to the good part, where Debbie B. Toyland eats it, when, all of a sudden, Eve set her drink down, lay back in the flower field of pillow and bolster cover, and said, "Kiss me."

The ice in my drink sounded like the chattering teeth of the Tiki god on the cup as I fell as mute as the old woman in *The Tingler.* The Tingler was about to break my backbone. When I moved to the couch, overcoming fear enough to wrap an arm around Eve, the Tingler squirmed down my spine into my stomach. And then, when I dared to demonstrate that my French kiss had improved almost as much as my French inhale, the Tingler slithered from my guts into my groin, where it seemed at home and happy, directing me from there to kiss harder, longer, deeper.

Although Eve showed no signs of timidity, propriety, or modesty, I was afraid of going too quickly, worried that if I dared to reach down the bikini top and touch her nipples with my trembling fingertips as I so ached to do, she might say, "Stop." I never wanted to hear that bitter word out of the sweet mouth that was simultaneously feeding and devouring me with kisses, never wanted my fingers restrained by the soft sure hand that, under my T-shirt, made my shoulder blades feel like vestigial wings. Outside my shirt, her other hand stroked my back just as years before it had stroked the back of the red velvet couch in my room.

As my lips, in their exploration of cheeks, chin, forehead, and hair, settled by her ear, sucking on the wet lobe with passion swelling and love welling, I was losing control. The harder I struggled to contain and restrain it, the more vehemently it defied me. I couldn't hold it back any longer. All of a sudden it burst out of me in three spurts—three syllables: "I love you."

I was embarrassed, afraid she'd consider it a premature exclamation and stop. But, no, she persisted with sigh and heavy breath, muscles flexing and easing, simultaneously daring and promising with succulent and ravenous kisses, more and more fervent, and then, though garbled by the wild play of tongues and passionate press of lips, the three sounds gushed out of her too. Her head fell back. I said the same words to her for the second time, without embarrassment. And then we repeated them, that time at the same time. And again. And again. And then in a sumptuous silence, we lay still, my arm wrapped around her back, my hand relaxed upon the bikini cup over her breast, her head at rest upon my chest, her ear over my heart.

How long afterward it was that Eve came to a slow consciousness that she was smiling happily in my arms, neither of us could tell. All we knew was that, after what seemed a mighty stretch of time, both of us awoke out of a dead stupor of sleep. We shared a cigarette.

After Sally had called out to us from the house to let us know that her mother's driver had arrived, we walked hand in hand across the yard into the main house. Before opening the front door for her to leave, I gave her the copy of *Sonnets from the Portuguese* that I had bought for her and nervously muttered, "Ah, oh, yes. Ah . . . I've got something else for you, if you want it."

While the chauffeur proclaimed impatience by honking his horn with enough fervor to shrink up any Tingler that might have been on the prowl in Beverly Hills that Saturday evening, I took off the ID bracelet that I had retrieved from Candy Canter and presented it to Eve W——. Her mouthwatering smile said everything I wanted to hear: not just "thank you," not only the three words she had uttered in the pool house, but also "I want to melt in you and be like a running brook that sings its melody to you, to know the pain of your tenderness as well as all of its pleasure, to be wounded by your love so that then that love may heal me."

That night on the telephone, I repeated the three words to her and she repeated them back to me, the words which mean everything and nothing, re-re-repeated to punctuate the meandering babble that went on and on just for the sake of the saying and the hearing.

After more than three hours on the telephone, I suddenly realized, by the sound of her breathing and her failure to answer when I asked if she would like to go to Hawaii with me someday, that she had fallen asleep. Nestling the telephone receiver into my pillow, I lay my head down next to it, feeling that, as long as neither of us hung up, we were in bed together. Falling asleep, I spent my first night with Eve.

Going down for breakfast in the morning, I found Sally May Carter sitting at the kitchen table in tears. It was the only time in my life I had ever seen Sally cry, and it was the most tumultuous sobbing I had ever witnessed, an almost operatic cataract of caterwaul. Shorty had delivered the news that her mother had died in Mississippi. Sally claimed that the woman was 113 years old, "born before Mr. Lincoln freed us slaves. Mama picked enough cotton in her time to put a shirt on the back of every white man in America." As Sally packed her bags for the trip back to Mississippi for the funeral, I could hear singing through the closed door to her room:

When Israel was in Egypt's land,
Let my people go!
Oppressed so hard they could not stand,
Let my people go!

"You be a good boy while Mama Sally's gone," Sally May Carter said as she climbed into the Cadillac in which my mother would drive her to the Greyhound bus depot. Despite the tears of grief in her eyes, a smile revealed how brightly the light still sparkled on her gold teeth.

I would, I thought, have liked to have gone with her, to leave Beverly Hills, take the bus and see what I imagined was the real America—to see the cotton fields and shantytowns of Sally's Mississippi and then to set off from there by myself to see the cricks, woods, caves, and the "monstrous big river" of Mark Twain's Missouri, and then Hiawatha's pine-tree forest, lily-blooming prairie, the shores of Gitche Gumee and the falls of Minnehaha. I yearned to see the sprawling farmlands with their amber waves of grain, the wheat and corn, pigs and cattle that, by the time they got to Beverly Hills, had become Cheerios, Fritos, Cocoa Puffs, Oscar Mayer Wieners, and Wilno kosher hot dogs. But I didn't want to see just the bucolic land that American dreams are made of—no, oh no, I was even more eager to explore Allen Ginsberg's America, to "go out whoring through Colorado in myriad stolen night-cars, & lay innumerable girls in empty lots & diner backyards, moviehouses' rickety rows, on mountaintops in caves, or gaunt waitresses in familiar roadside lonely petticoat upliftings & especially secret gas-station solipsisms of johns, & hometown alleys too," and to hitch a ride with Jack Kerouac and Neal Cassady across the sprawling heart of America "into timeless shadows, and wonderment in the bleakness of the mortal realm, hurrying to a plank where all the angels dove off and flew into the holy void of uncreated emptiness."

In reading *On the Road, Howl,* and Gregory Corso's "Poets Hitchhiking on the Highway" in his *Happy Birthday of Death,* I had realized that hitchhiking was not only a significant theme in American poetry and a source of its inspiration, it was also a way of life, a mode of education higher than higher education, a noble defiance of conventional responsibilities, a freedom fight, game of chance, dance with fate, and spree in Serendip. And "Guys who hitchhike," Larry Feinstein had said on the authority of his uncle Mannie, who claimed to have thumbed his way from New York to California at the end of World War II, "get a lot of pussy."

Pretending to be as free as Jack Kerouac, wearing a new black turtleneck sweater and my Cool-Shade sunglasses, a Viceroy hanging from my lips, I went on the road, stepping off the curb on Sunset like an angel off a plank, with my hand extended and thumb up in supplication for a wild ride. How many story-telling strangers would I meet, I wondered (characters for my *Book of Love*), how many crazy adventures (episodes in future installments of the memoir) would I have before ringing the doorbell of Eve's mother's house in Hollywood?

While I didn't expect the Cadillac El Dorados, Lincoln Continentals, or Chrysler Imperials to stop for me, I was a little disappointed that the flatbed truck with Missouri license plates, reminiscent of the first vehicle to pick up Jack Kerouac in Nebraska at the beginning of *On the Road,* sped by. When suddenly I saw a Corvette coming, I jumped back up the curb, dashing to hide behind a hedge just in case it might be Johnny Fox's car.

No sooner was I back in the street, thumb again up, when a Beverly Hills police patrol car, headed west on the other side of the street, made a U-turn to pull over next to me. "Get in," the cop ordered.

"No thanks," I answered. "That's okay."

"Get in," he repeated. "I'm taking you to the station."

"I live just down Maple," I said, "just three houses down. And I need to go home."

Emerging from the car, the cop walked around to open the back door of it: "Are you going to get in by yourself, or do I have to use force and cuff you?"

While waiting for my mother to pick me up at the Beverly Hills Police Department station, I consolingly reminded myself that Gregory Corso had been arrested when he was my age and that was when he had started writing poetry. "Real poets are always renegades," Erato had declared, "and true poetry always breaks laws."

Although hitchhiking wasn't technically illegal, I had nevertheless, I was proud to learn, broken the law: "We could book you on jaywalking for standing off the curb while not at an intersection," the police captain (whom I recognized as the cop who had come to our house years before to investigate the incident of the tall, thin old man in the dirty brown overcoat snooping around in our backyard) informed me: "But we don't want to do that, son. No, we're here to protect you. Yes, we want you to learn from this experience. Standing in the street as you were doing, you could have been run over by a drunk driver. You could have been picked up by a kidnapper spotting you as a Beverly Hills kid whose rich parents would be able to come up with a hefty ransom. Not only that, son, but there are many homosexuals on the road these days. Yes, you could have been picked up by a homosexual. Son, you may think that you can spot a homosexual by his effeminate mannerisms, frilly clothes, limp wrists, and lisping speech, but many homosexuals pretend to be normal. They look just like you and me and seem like regular guys, masculine and virile in every way. Yes, they are out there on the prowl, hunting for prey, and nothing pleases the homosexual more than turning a young boy just like yourself into one of his own kind. Do you know what a pedophile is?"

I guessed: "Someone who is sexually attracted to pedestrians?"

"This is no joking matter, son," the cop reacted with sober purpose. "Sexual perversion is serious business."

While my mother, agreeing with the cops that hitchhiking was dangerous, was upset by the incident, Eve, also mindful of the possible perils of thumbing rides, was impressed. She was flattered that I had risked being run over, kidnapped, molested, and turned into a homosexual in my effort to get to her house. While it might not have been proven that "hitchhikers get a lot of pussy," as Larry Feinstein's uncle Mannie had maintained, at least it was demonstrated that Larry had been right about girls loving "guys who take big risks for their sake and put love above the law." Real lovers, I concluded, no less than real poets, are renegades; and great love, like great poetry, always breaks laws.

On the phone that night, Eve, impassioned by her awareness of what I had gone through for her sake, was especially amorous: "I miss you, darling. I want to see you. I want to kiss you and hold you in my arms. My mom is out with her new boyfriend and I'm alone. I wish you were here in bed with me right now." She repeated the three magic words.

Intoxicated by the nectarous utterances, so freely flowing and more delicious and inebriating than Don the Beachcomber's most potent Zombie, I impulsively promised, "I'll be over in half an hour."

"How will you get here? You can't hitchhike."

"Sally still hasn't come back from Mississippi and my parents went to a dinner party," I explained. "They took the Lincoln. I'll come over in the Cadillac." I imagined that I knew how to drive because, ever since my bar mitzvah, my father had been allowing me to switch the cars around in the driveway for him, and whenever it was just him and me in the car, he would let me sit next to him and do the steering.

Insisting that he was too young to stay home alone and too tired to come along, Robert said that he would tell my parents that I had taken the car, unless, by any chance, I'd be willing to give him my marijuana cigarette. That proposition started a bargaining process that ended with him counting out the eighteen dollars (all I had been able to save up of the forty-seven I owed Cisco) that I, for the sake of being united with my beloved, gave him along with my copy of a *Playboy* magazine I had bought from Larry Feinstein. There were photographs of a naked Jayne Mansfield in it.

After searching through my mother's purses for the keys to the car, I glued my Max Factor moustache to my upper lip just in case a cop, noticing me on the road, might suspect that I was too young to be driving. I dabbed my neck with a hefty dose of my father's Charles Blair de Paris cologne.

Waving good-bye to me from the kitchen door as I backed the Cadillac out of the driveway, Robert advised me to turn on the headlights and, in turn, I reminded him not to stay up too late.

Indifferent to the law against speeding, love pressed my foot to the accelerator. Fear intervened, slamming my foot on the brake just in the nick of time for the first red light on Sunset. Anxiously waiting for that light to change, with both sweating hands clutching the wheel and a foot itching to jump back to the gas pedal, I could picture Eve standing in watchful wait for me at the doorway to her house, clad in a creamy satin robe trimmed with white fur around the collar and cuffs, not so very different, except in size, from the one she had been wearing when I saw her for the very first time. I imagined that she'd take my hand to lead me up the stairs into the darkness of her room and warmth of her bed. As the robe fell to the floor, the bedroom would be illuminated by the splendor of her nakedness—and then the light turned green.

The Max Factor moustache didn't make a difference—it was for speeding, not on a suspicion that I was underage, that the cop pulled me over.

"What's happening to you, Lee?" my mother, her anger tempered by sadness, asked as she drove me home from the police station. "Stealing the car, leaving your brother alone, two trips to the police station in one day, suspended from school, failing English, barely passing French. What's wrong? And there's a smell of cigarette smoke in your room. You're moody all the time, always on the telephone, thinking only of yourself. I don't understand. What's the matter?"

"Love is the matter," I wanted to announce as I removed my moustache. "Love is all that matters. But nothing's wrong. Love is never wrong." But I didn't bother to say a word. She had already admitted it: "I don't understand." Of course she didn't—I was certain that she could never have experienced the intensity of the passion that informed my love for Eve, neither the hellish anguish of separation from her nor the heavenly joy of holding her in my arms. No one understood how I felt, not even Elizabeth Barrett Browning or Kahlil Gibran. Had either of those writers ever been as profoundly and powerfully in love as I they would not have dared to try to put that feeling into words. They would have realized, as I did that night, sitting at my desk by candlelight after my mother had brought me home from the police station and gone to bed, that there were no poetic figures, no similes nor metaphors, no rhyme schemes nor meters, no vocabulary nor grammar capable of doing justice to love. True love takes the words right out of our mouths. Real love cannot be captured. "No," I wrote in my leather-bound notebook, "no, this book cannot be written with words but must be composed with glances and smiles for its prologue, with kisses and embraces for the development of its characters and plot, and, for its climax, the man and woman must *make love.* The *Book of Love* cannot be written on paper with black Skrip ink flowing from a Parker 51 but only with white discharge from an erect penis in the spread-open fascicles of a woman's body." And then, after several big swigs of Italian Swiss Colony wine, I returned my notebook to the red velvet couch, smoked a Viceroy, blew out the Magic Color drip candle, and cried myself to sleep.

It had been over a month since her departure for Mississippi, and Sally May Carter still hadn't returned. There hadn't been a word from her, and my mother couldn't contact her since we didn't have a phone number or an address for Sally or for anyone who might know how to get in touch with her. While, in the ten years during which Sally lived with us and worked for us, she had learned pretty much all there was to know about us, we knew almost nothing about Sally May Carter except that she went to church on Sundays with a man named Shorty, who seemed to love her. We never saw her again.

Coming home on the last day of school before the Christmas vacation, still kind of missing being greeted in the kitchen with the words "Shit, boy, don't go traipsin' any dirt on Mama Sally's clean floor," I went straight up the stairs to my room to telephone Eve. Having been grounded for stealing the car, I hadn't seen her for a few weeks, but I did talk to her every day after school, every night before going to bed, and often every in between. I had dialed no more than the first three digits of her number when I suddenly noticed that the red velvet couch in my room had been replaced by a green satin sofa. Hanging up the phone, I went downstairs to see if my couch was where the green one had always been, only to discover a new beige divan. To no avail, I searched everywhere for my couch, even in the basement that was supposed to be a bomb shelter. It was not until my mother arrived home from Carl's Market that I got the news. Racing downstairs when I heard her unpacking the groceries in the kitchen, I anxiously asked her where the couch was.

"The Salvation Army picked it up today, that and the old Spartan TV, the RCA Victrola, and lots of other old junk," my mother announced as she put the Land O Lakes butter in the icebox. "I wanted to make sure they came for it before New Year's so that we'll get the charity deduction on our taxes for this year. I thought you'd like the green one in your room. It's so much more masculine than that red one was."

A mental inventory of all that had been stored inside the couch in my room was making me queasy: the Trojan rubbers that Larry Feinstein had given me for my bar mitzvah (only two of the three of them since I had transferred one to my wallet in anticipation of an opportunity to consummate my love for Eve, if not my lust for Larry's sister); the lubricated lambskin prophylactic and French tickler that Cisco had recently laid on me, as well as the photograph of the naked Mexican whore that I had procured from him years before; my switchblade knife and brass knuckles from Tijuana and some cherry bombs; a tattered copy of *Titter* magazine, Louis Lapine's *Commie Sex Siren* wrapped in the jacket of the Hardy Boys *Wailing Siren Mystery, The Communist Manifesto,* and, with Connie Feinstein's pubic hair laminated in Scotch tape as its bookmark, the incriminating leather-bound manuscript of my *Book of Love.* There were also a few packs of Viceroys, a nearly empty bottle of Italian Swiss Colony wine, and, last but not least and much to my chagrin, there was a marijuana cigarette. The Tingler tightened its grip on my spine.

When my mother offered to make a Kraft grilled cheese sandwich for me, I thought I was going to vomit. But, standing over the toilet in my bathroom, all I could do was retch. Unable to calm myself down and needing to talk to someone, I turned to my brother: "When the workers at the Salvation Army begin to fix up the couch, they'll turn it over, remove the burlap over the wooden frame, and find my stuff. Naturally they'll conclude that whoever donated the couch was not only a perverted, violent, alcoholic Communist sex fiend, but a drug addict as well. And, because the people who work at the Salvation Army are Christians, they'll think it's their duty to report the illegal switchblade, cherry bombs, and marijuana to the police and to give them Mom's name and address. When the cops show up, they'll ask, 'Who wrote the *Book of Love?*' And I'll have to confess. I'll be sent to reform school or even jail. With this on my record, on top of everything else, my life is ruined."

Robert tried to calm me down with a smile and what he considered a good plan: "Don't worry about a thing. All we've got to do is to find out which Salvation Army store picked up the couch. We'll go there right away, before they have a chance to start fixing it up, and we'll say that we're shopping for a couch. We'll add that we are very fond of red velvet and that we don't care if it's been cleaned or fixed up or anything. And then, when they show us the couch, we'll buy it back from them, get your stuff out of it, take it to the dump, and get rid of it forever. And then your problems will be over. As soon as we can find a pickup truck for you to drive, we can go get the couch." He hesitated, momentarily frowned, and then smiled again: "Okay, I know what you're thinking. You're asking yourself, 'Where am I going to get a pickup truck?' Well, if that's a problem, I've got another idea. We'll go to the Salvation Army late tonight, set fire to the place, and burn it down. You know—destroy the evidence. I saw some guys do it in an episode of *Dragnet.* Jack Webb wouldn't have caught them if they hadn't left fingerprints behind. They were dumb. But we're smart—we'll wear gloves."

"Arson," I muttered on the verge of tears, "is an even bigger crime than possession of narcotics, explosives, pornography, and an illegal weapon."

"Well," Robert sighed, placing a hand affectionately on my shoulder, "I can't think of any other plans. So I guess we'll just have to pray to God that they don't find the pot. But if you do go to jail, I swear to God, I'll visit you every day after school."

Later that night, finally enough in control of myself to complete the call that I had been in the midst of making when I had discovered that my couch was missing, I asked Eve what she would do "if, for some reason—just hypothetically—some day, I were to be sent to jail?" I wanted to know if she would wait for me and be faithful. "Of course," she said. "I love you." I tried both to believe her and to believe that love had the power to make all things better.

The disappearance of my notebook ended work on my chronicle of the sexual life of an American boy in the 1950s. Only now, nearly a half-century later, have I picked up where I left off, trying to reconstruct and rewrite it, to finally finish the manuscript, the first draft of which may well be in the possession, probably unknowingly, of someone, somewhere, who owns an antique red velvet couch.

As Robert and I helped our mother rearrange the furniture and carry the cases of champagne in preparation for the New Year's Eve party, I was feeling happy both because the police had not shown up at our home and because Eve was about to. Because of the sentence of house arrest that I had been serving since stealing the Cadillac, I hadn't seen Eve in over a month. But my mother had invited her mother to the party, and my beloved was coming along.

So eager was I for the reunion that I had begun to wait for her at the front door an hour before the party began. Two hours later, as I was shaking Dr. Isaiah Miller's hand and hearing from him how much I had grown since the last New Year's Eve party, Eve W—— arrived with her mother and her mother's latest boyfriend. She looked more beautiful than any Cinderella ever imagined by any audience for any version of that fairy tale of love.

Throwing all the coats over my shoulder, I asked Eve to come with me to put the garments in the storeroom where Sally May Carter had lived for ten years. And there I kissed her, kissed her again and again, and might never have stopped if Robert hadn't barged in to inform me that my mother wanted me to bring out the silver tray of fried cheese-and-nut balls right away. Following me with a platter of pink boiled shrimp impaled on toothpicks, Eve helped me fulfill my obligations. We toured the room again with bottles of champagne, then the crab dip, then more champagne, and in between each serving we'd duck into the room in which Shorty had formerly spent Saturday nights with Sally for an impassioned kiss, or two, or three, each one an appetizer stimulating hunger and thirst for the richest dishes and most intoxicating wines that might be served at love's most lavish feast.

In the kitchen, when we took swigs from the bottles of champagne before taking them out to the guests, Robert promised he wouldn't tell if I promised to keep quiet about the rum babas he had eaten.

After kissing Robert goodnight and wishing him a happy new year, my mother told me to take him up to bed. Eve came along, and I could sense that my brother had a little crush on her. That accounted for his quick and cheerful obedience when she told him to wash his face and brush his teeth, and for his eagerness to have her tuck him in. He tried to impress her by saying "Now, this is my kind of woman!" as he showed her the pictures of a naked Jayne Mansfield in his *Playboy* magazine.

After turning out the lights, Eve kissed Robert goodnight as I stood in the doorway. "Happy New Year," she whispered. "I don't want to hear a sound out of you." He probably wouldn't have fallen asleep if not for the effect, on top of all the rum babas, of the champagne I had let him drink from the bottle that I had stolen from the kitchen. I invited Eve into my room to finish the champagne with me.

She didn't remember ever having been there. "You slept right over there," I told her, pouring a glass of champagne for us to share, then lighting the Magic Color drip candle on my desk and turning out the wall lights. "There was a red velvet couch there. I had draped a blanket over it to make a cave behind it. You crawled into it with me. And then afterward you went to sleep on the couch and I slept here in the bed."

I was silenced by her open lips as, pulling me with her, she tumbled back onto the bed. Her head was on the very pillow that had long before and again recently often played the part of her in nocturnal reveries. That pillow had also, over the years, taken on the roles of Gretel Woodcutter, Clover Wiener, Donna Young, Beatrice Sugarman, Luana the Hawaiian hula girl, Connie Feinstein, Suzie Krasny, Candy Canter, and once or twice, my former Hebrew teacher, Miss Pinchas. Now it was just a pillow.

When Eve whispered it—"I want you"—I knew this was, at last, probably going to be the real thing.

Wrenching myself out of her embrace, I rose up from the bed to lock the door. "Hurry," the girl urged as she removed the undergarment that threatened to impede me, and, as quickly as I could, I took off my shoes (leaving on my socks) and then my trousers and underpants together (leaving on my buttoned shirt and tie).

"Hurry," Eve urgently reiterated as I, more quickly than I imagined possible given the trembling of my hands, unbuttoned the button on the back pocket of my trousers to retrieve the wallet from which I took the foil packet containing the Trojan rubber prophylactic that Larry Feinstein had given me for my bar mitzvah.

In my arms, beneath the blanket that had been the wall of the cave in which, ten years earlier, she had first enchanted me, Eve repeated the three words that, lying in that bed, in that same room, I had heard the little girl say for the first time long ago, when I was a child, and again I could hear the sound of a party downstairs, the same boisterous chatter, swing music, and popping of champagne corks, the celebratory clink and clatter of glasses and plates, and the rising and falling waves of festive laughter.

"Now," love said. "Yes, yes. Now." I heard the whisper—"I love you"—over the sudden outburst of jubilant shouting from downstairs: "Happy New Year!"

The 1950s had come to an end.

And a new life was about to begin.